NOT ONLY IN STONE

To Pat & Mike

Trust you find this interesting,
which gives insight into the
history of Copper mining in
South Australia.

Love Graeme & Joan

NOT ONLY IN STONE

By

PHYLLIS SOMERVILLE

"The whole earth is the tomb of heroes. Their story is not graven only in the stone over their clay, but abides everywhere with visible symbol, woven into the stuff of other men's lives."
THUCYDIDES.

WAKEFIELD PRESS
ADELAIDE • 1984

© Phyllis Somerville 1942, 1946

First published 1942
by Angus and Robertson Ltd Sydney

Published 1984 and reprinted 1986
by Wakefield Press
282 Richmond Road Netley
South Australia 5037

National Library of Australia
Cataloguing-in-Publication Data
Somerville, Phyllis.
Not Only In Stone.
1. Title.
Previously published: Adelaide: Rigby, 1973.
ISBN 0 949268 15 1 (De Luxe).
ISBN 0 949268 03 8 (Case Bound).
ISBN 0 949268 04 6 (Limp Cover).

A823′.2

Wholly set up and produced in Adelaide, South Australia
Printed by K.B. Printing Services Pty. Ltd.
Bound by Advance Bookbinders Pty. Ltd.

DEDICATED TO

MY FATHER AND MOTHER

ACKNOWLEDGMENTS

IN the writing and compiling of this book my thanks and grateful acknowledgments are due to:

The Commonwealth Literary Board of the Prime Minister's Department, Canberra, who assured the publishing of this work, and to the Advisory Board who recommended it.

Advertiser Newspapers Ltd, Adelaide, for the award of £100 for this novel in 1936.

Mr Pitt of the Archives of South Australia who made available various facts concerning the ship *Lady Milton*, also letters and particulars relating to the early history of Adelaide, Wallaroo Mines and Moonta Mines.

Mr Oswald Pryor of Leabrook, South Australia, for his encouragement and also for data concerning the Wallaroo and Moonta Mining Co.

The staff of the Mines Department of South Australia for information given.

Mr F. M. Maughan of St Georges, South Australia, who gave me valuable information of the early days of Methodism in Adelaide.

Mr James Harris of Strathalbyn, who told me tales of "the old days".

My mother, for her faith and encouragement.

PHYLLIS SOMERVILLE

PROLOGUE

OLD Mrs Polly Thomas lay dying in the front bedroom of her one-eyed little cottage in Archer Street, North Adelaide, on a September morning of the year nineteen hundred and twenty-seven. She was eighty-nine years of age, and had seen Death come in so many guises for others that when he came for her she knew him, and was ready to go.

At that first moment of waking in the early dawn, her old heart had contracted with the knowledge of what the dull, aching pressure on her head and the great, engulfing waves of weakness must mean, and she had given one frightened, whimpering cry that had rumbled queerly in her throat, and then had given herself up to the strange and inevitable business of dying.

When the first tremblings of realization were over and she knew what had come to her she lay quietly in bed, feeling the jerky rhythm of her heart's beating, and patiently enduring the knife-keen pain in her chest as she drew each slow breath. After a time she had strength enough to put out a hand towards her silver-topped, ebony walking-stick which rested beside the head of her bed.

A few taps with the stick on the skirting-board and Polly knew that Miss Humphrey, her nurse-companion, sleeping now in the next bedroom, would scramble from her bed and, gathering her scarlet dressing-gown tightly about her and forgetting to take her top set of false teeth from the glass of water on the chest of drawers, would rush into Polly's room and smile toothlessly and consolingly from the doorway, saying, "Here I am. Now, what is it?"

Polly Thomas moved her old head restlessly on the cold pillow, and her hand relaxed about the knob of the walking-stick.

"Leave 'er be," she murmured to the waiting air. "She

be kind, but she be nothin' but a grinnin' jinny after all. I'll see to me dyin' meself!"

So well did she see to her dying that it was eight o'clock and bright sunshine before Hilda Humphrey opened her eyes and, listening intently and not without a certain degree of terror, heard the noisy rise and fall of the old woman's breathing, the sound of which filled the little house as with a presence.

Polly was lying back on her pillows and quite unconscious when Miss Humphrey ran in to lean over the bed and place cool fingers on the limp wrist lying on the counterpane. Bending forward, the young woman brushed against the ebony stick, and it slid along the white folds of the sheet and dropped with a clatter to the floor.

Miss Humphrey gave a thin little shriek and leapt back from the bed, her hands on her breast.

The old woman on the bed opened her eyes then, and her gnarled old hand moved a little across the counterpane. The dim, grey eyes, already filled with death, looked up at Miss Humphrey standing there in her red dressing-gown, shivering with fright, and the old lips moved.

Miss Humphrey recovered herself and, taking the restless fingers between her own, bent over the dying woman and caught the last, faint words as the soul was breathed from the tired body.

"Why, 'tis me Annie," came the whisper, soft but clear. "Don't 'ee knaw me, dear? 'Tis mother!"

With a slow, compassionate gesture, Hilda Humphrey crossed the hands upon the silent breast of what had been Polly Thomas, and looked long and tenderly at the quiet face from whose forehead, in a moment's space, Death had gently smoothed the lines that Life had taken almost ninety years to draw.

The summer heat and the autumn rains flattened the mound of Polly's grave in the West Terrace cemetery, and one evening, six months after her death, her eldest son Richard called his brother Robert by telephone from Sydney and this was their conversation:

"Hullo, Bob. Richard here."

"Oh, hullo, Rich. How are you? Anything wrong?"

PROLOGUE

"No, we're all right. I'm just ringing to ask about mother's grave. It's time we had a headstone erected, isn't it?"

"Yes. I've been meaning to write to you about it."

"Can you manage to see to it, Bob?"

"Yes, Rich. I'll get Birmingham and Sons to do the job. They're good stone-masons. I've seen some of their work."

"Whom did you say, Bob?"

"Birmingham and Sons. They are stone-masons on West Terrace."

"Well, I hate to upset your plans, Bob, but I know mother would never rest easily if a Birmingham tombstone were above her."

"Why, good Lord, what's wrong with the man?"

Richard laughed softly here. "It's not the man, it's the name! Don't you remember the story of mother losing her hundred pounds? It was a lawyer named Birmingham who did that for her. She could never bear to hear the name after that."

It was now Bob's turn to laugh quietly. "Of course I remember now. Poor mother! Well, she shan't have a Birmingham stone. She deserves a peaceful rest."

A short silence.

"Well, Bob, I'll leave it to you."

"Good, Rich. I'll do what I think best. You may rely on me. . . . You and Euphemia and the boys well?"

"Splendid, Bob. . . . You all well? Eleanor happily married?"

"Yes, Rich . . . all well this end."

"Three minutes is up."

"Well, good-bye, Bob."

"Good-bye, Rich. Love to the boys and the new grandson."

"Good-bye."

"Good-bye, Rich."

MARY ELIZABETH THOMAS

Born St Ives, Cornwall 1838
Died Adelaide 1927
Arrived in Australia by ship
Lady Milton 1865
" 'Tis not the whole of life to live,
Nor all of death to die"

This memorial erected by her sons

The story of Polly Thomas is not graven only in the stone over her clay, but abides with visible symbol, woven into the stuff of other lives. And this is her story:

CHAPTER I

On the twenty-ninth day of November, eighteen hundred and sixty-five, the sailing ship *Lady Milton* came to her anchorage off Port Adelaide in the province of South Australia. She lay in mid-stream in the inlet from the sea called the Port River, and was anchored stem and stern to two buoys beyond McLaren Wharf, for the low tide prevented her being taken to the wharf's side.

The voyage from Plymouth to Australia had taken one hundred and six days, and the passengers consisted of three hundred and fifty-eight immigrants whose passage the government had assisted. They comprised people from all the humbler walks of life and represented a score of trades, but the number of miners exceeded all other separate callings, there being sixty-four miners and their families on board.

The voyage, but for a severe outbreak of measles and the encountering of several patches of bad weather, had been practically uneventful. The married peoples' quarters, although overrun with children, were well-ventilated, clear and comfortable, and the health officers who boarded the ship in the harbour had commented favourably on the whole aspect of the ship and immigrants.

On the deck little groups of boxes and bundles had been set up, and the older people stood guard about their possessions or mounted to the top of these islands of household belongings and sat there like castaways in a heavy sea. Around them surged the children and the younger passengers, whom the long day of waiting to disembark had not yet exhausted. Jostling, shouting, pointing, people rushed to and from the bulwarks, all eager for the arrival of the lighters which would take them ashore and set them upon the soil of the new homeland.

Soon little boats were seen setting out from the wharf,

some with friends of the passengers on board, and from them came the welcoming Australian call—"Coo-ee! Coo-ee!"—over the calm water.

The groups on the deck began to break up. The lighters were arriving, and there was a rush to be among the first to descend into the flat-bottomed boats and be rowed to the wharf. The confusion on board became greater: men and women were pushing through the crowd at the ship's sides, exchanging good-luck messages with their friends of the voyage or shouting farewells to their more fortunate fellow-travellers in the boats. Flustered immigrants, searching frenziedly for mislaid bundles or calling in distracted tones for missing relatives, bumped into strangers from the shore, these valiantly trying to sort their kith and kin from the excited crowd of passengers whose one thought now was to get themselves and their luggage aboard the lighters and to turn their backs upon the *Lady Milton* which, for so many weeks, had been their only home.

Many of the immigrants were content to stay quietly beside their bundles until the confusion had lessened, and here and there a family sat in deep conclave, heads together, talking vociferously, making multitudinous plans for the future and seemingly oblivious to the noise and bustle about them. Gradually the groups broke up, and as the afternoon waned the crowd grew thinner.

Two women, standing by one of the masts, were sobbing in each other's arms. They were widows, each of whom had seen her husband fall sick, die, and be buried at sea during the voyage. Brought together by their common sorrow, they now were fortifying each other with a pitiful courage to face a new life in a strange, lonely land, with no hope in their hearts. A young couple, married by the captain a few days previously, were busily turning over their families' household goods, extracting a frying-pan, a baking-tin, a few plates and a cup or two and packing them away in a valise—the embryo of a little home of their own, to be made later in some remote township.

Of the miners on board the *Lady Milton* the greater number were from Cornwall. News of the copper mines being opened up in South Australia had been the impetus for these men to set out, with their families, on the thirteen-thousand-mile voyage to ply their picks under freer, more hopeful conditions than those existing in Cornwall at this time.

Many of their countrymen were on the wharf when the ship came to anchor, for word had reached Adelaide the day before that the ship had been sighted in St Vincent Gulf. The lighters, returning to the ship for more immigrants, carried loads of these welcoming Cornishmen, who clambered on to the deck, eager to meet and claim their own.

" 'Ow're 'ee doin', boy?" called out a new chum, recognizing a friend.

"Brave, me son, an' glad to see un!" called back a broad-shouldered colonist.

Greetings flew to and fro across the heads of the immigrants and colonists.

"Mother, 'ere's Willum 'Enery. Willum, I've got Mother 'ere!" shrilled a buxom Cornish lass to her brother, who had settled in Australia eighteen months before.

"Mercy me!" called out the mother in greeting. "If 'e adden gone an' got freckles all over 'is face an' eyes! I da 'ardly knaw me own boy. Come 'ere, me tender dear!" And she opened her arms wide to receive him.

"Johnny Daddow!" another voice exclaimed. "Thee 'ere! Well! 'Ere's me come 'undreds an' thousands o' miles, an' first thing I da see when I get 'ere be thee, an' I lived next door to un for thirty year an' never thought to set eyes on un ever agin. What doin' out 'ere in Australia, Johnny?"

"Nothin', Miz Temby."

"Well, that's all 'ee ever did to 'ome, Johnny, so 'ee must feel quite comfor'ble 'ere."

"Yes, Miz Temby, I be aisy."

Then two sisters sighted each other through the bobbing crowds of bonnets, shawls and black hats.

"So you're here at last, Lavinia! Bless you! We've a house all ready for you, my dear. It's built of wattle sticks and mud, and it's been partly washed away twice by floods, but you won't mind it, Lavvy—really you won't. Kiss me again, and oh, my dear, I'm glad to see you!" And they held each other fast.

A young immigrant, twenty-seven years of age, red-faced, brown-bearded, stocky of build and dressed in a neat, black serge suit buttoned high across his chest, was pushing his way back from the railings and searching the deck for his wife. He found her, as he had left her, seated among the heap of their family goods. She was a little creature, full-bosomed, being the mother of a two-weeks-old infant, with blue-grey eyes set in a round, firm-chinned face framed by a cloud of light reddish hair. She was wearing a purple and white striped silk frock, narrow at the waist and billowing out over the hips, with little bows of purple silk trimming the front from neck to hem. A tiny white hat with a purple feather in it was placed far back on her head and secured under her chin by purple silk ribbons. It truly was extravagant attire for a miner's wife, assisted immigrant as she was; but it was her wedding-gown, now two years old and the pride of her heart. The infant in her arms slept, wrapped in a white shawl, with a lace handkerchief completely covering his little face, the frills of his night-gown flowing out about him in yards of soft whiteness.

"Did 'ee see un, Nathan?" she called to her husband as he came towards her.

"Yes, Polly, 'e be comin' now in one o' they boats. I think 'tis 'e, though I 'aven't laid eye to un for six year or more. I knaw the set of un."

"'Ow far off be the boat?" his wife asked.

"'Tis a purty way off yet, but I be certain sure Peter be aboard. If I 'ad cap'n's spy-glass I could pick un out like a shot. But don't fret, me dear. 'Tis Peter all right, an' no mistake."

"I ain't worried, Nathan—just boilin' up inside. I coulden bring meself to sit 'ere so quiet if it wadden for the babby. 'E's so peaceful-like, Nathan, and dussen knaw what be 'appenin' to us." She looked up at her husband, who was sitting on a box beside her, and her eyes were swimming with tears. "We be 'ere at last, me dear," she said softly, "thee an' me an' the babby. We got 'ere safe an' sound, an' I didden die like I thought I would. Don't seem 'ardly true 'tis all over, do it, dear?"

"'Tis all a dream now, Polly. Things be all right now— you safe, the journey over an' Peter comin' to us quick as they can ply oar."

He smiled at her, but his thoughts flew back to that wild night two weeks before when, after days of agonizing pain for Polly, their cramped little cabin had been filled with the frantic cries of the tortured woman torn with the pangs of child-birth. While the ship rolled and shuddered in the troughs of the great waves and the roaring wind beat upon the straining sails the little mother had wrestled with death and terror, and had given birth to her son at the very height of the storm. The night had passed, and when morning had dawned all was well with the ship and mother and child, and the wild sea had lost its power.

A sailor approached them as they sat on the wooden box holding hands, and he spoke to the young woman.

"You're Mrs Thomas, aren't you?" he asked.

"That's me," said Polly.

"Captain Davis wants you in his cabin. You're not to leave until he's seen you. Better come at once."

"Good Law!" said the flustered Polly. "What think 'e da want? Is our papers to rights, Nathan? Didden 'ee say we was all fixed to go ashore?"

"Evrathin' be fixed, Polly. Don't get all of a trimble, now. I'll go with 'ee, and I'll wait outside the door till 'ee come out."

They got to their feet, and Polly looked quickly about amongst the crowd.

"Where's Ellen? She didden ought to 'a' left me like this. Oo'll look after the things till we come back?"

"Things'll be all right, Pol. Come along, get goin'. Us can't keep cap'n waitin'."

But Polly had set her pretty lips firmly together, and her square little chin was stuck out sharply.

"I'm not movin' till I see Ellen. Like as not the 'hole parcel o' things'll be gone afore we come back." She sat down suddenly on the big wooden box and announced calmly: "Cap'n nor no cap'n, I don't move till thee's found our Ellen."

Her husband looked at her face and recognized there such signs as he had grown accustomed to with passing years. Polly meant what she said. She would not move until Ellen was found! Nathan turned about and, walking away, bumped into his young sister-in-law returning from the ship's side. She was a tall, slightly built, black-haired, clear-skinned girl of eighteen, clad in a maroon-coloured woollen dress strained across her young bosom, pinched in very tightly at the waist and very full about her ankles. Black braid patterned the bodice of her dress, and on her head was a little black chip-straw hat, held in place by a cord tucked under her hair, which was braided low on the nape of her neck.

"Coulden come back afore this, Nathan. Be Polly wantin' me?"

"Yes," said Nathan, relieved at having found her so quickly. "Polly 'ave got to go to cap'n's cabin, an' thee 'ave to mind the things."

Polly was already moving off, and called to her sister, "Sit down, Ellen, there's a good girl, an' don't go traipsin' off till we come back. Don't 'ee let that box out o' thy eye. The quilts be in there, an' I woulden get off ship without un."

"I'll sit meself on it, Pol, and ooever takes box'll 'ave to take me," called out Ellen, sitting down on the box and drumming the low heels of her little boots against its sides.

Nathan waited outside the captain's door with his hat in his hand, and Polly went into the cabin with the baby. Nathan watched her purple and white silk skirt trail across the threshold, and his eyes caught the flash of purple binding on the hem as the door closed behind his family. He was left there, holding his hat in his hands, pressing it against the wide lapels of his Sunday suit, and wrinkling up his broad forehead with the effort of wondering what was going on inside the cabin.

Captain Davis, immaculate and shining in the full glory of his well-brushed and burnished uniform, was sitting in a comfortable chair behind a heavy table. He nodded his head in acknowledgment of Polly's curtsy, and spoke hurriedly and tersely as one pausing a moment in a rush of duties—which, indeed, he was.

"Mrs Mary Thomas?" he questioned Polly.

"Mary Elizabeth Thomas. Yes, sir," said Polly, with another little bob of a curtsy.

Captain Davis studied the list before him. "I want," said he, "last minute particulars of the child born to you on the voyage." He glanced at the little figure in Polly's arms, wrapped so closely in such quantities of wool and fine calico. "It lived, I see. Male or female?"

Polly whisked the handkerchief from the face of the sleeping infant, and propped him up in her arms so that the captain might see his red little face.

" 'Tis a boy, sir," said Polly, proudly. "Richard Milton Thomas."

The captain's face relaxed, and he permitted himself a glance at the child. "Named after the ship? Well, that's very appropriate, Mrs Thomas—very much so."

"The 'Richard'," added Polly, "be the nearest we could get to the doctor's name. 'Tis due to 'im me babby an' me be 'ere this minute."

"Dr Rickards is honoured indeed," the captain answered, breaking into a pleasant smile. "Well, that will do, Mrs Thomas. My best wishes for the child's future. Good afternoon." And he picked up his pen and made a mark on the list before him.

Polly, blushing and happy, was not so busy dropping her curtsies that she could not manage to read, upside-down though it was, what was written on the page on the captain's table. She saw that it was the passenger list, with her own name there and Nathan's, and in the quick look she gave while the captain's pen was placing the mark on the list she read the word "confined", scrawled in the margin just above her name.

How could Polly know that nearly sixty years later, when she was an old, old woman, the son whom she now held in her arms would take her into the little church-like building where the archives of South Australia are stored, and would show her this self-same passenger list—with her name and Nathan's, the mark and the word "confined" in the margin— preserved as a concrete memory of those early days when the State was young?

"A purty lot o' water 'ave gone under the bridge since last I seed this 'ere," Polly was to say, sadly, bending her old head near to the blue paper and tracing out the words with a black-gloved finger. She would shake her head slowly. " 'Tis all so long ago an' far away."

Nathan questioned her as they walked along the deck. "What did 'e want, Polly? What did 'e say to 'ee?"

Polly paused for a moment, and then replied proudly, "'E wanted for to see the babby, Nathan." And as she said it she convinced herself it was so.

Nathan stopped still with astonishment, the quick upward movement of his brows almost lifting off his high-crowned hat. His face glowed. "Well, that were a fine-spirited thing to do," he said enthusiastically, looking back over his shoulder. "That were a kind thought."

"I told un we'd named 'im for the ship an' the doctor," said Polly, all smiles.

Nathan turned to her, his forehead crossed with wrinkles of delighted anticipation. "You did, Polly? Well, what did 'e say? What did 'e say to that, eh?"

"'E up an' says, 'Good luck to un'," said Polly, her bosom lifting and her eyes bright. "Leastways, 'e didden say ezacally that, but that were what 'e were meanin' right enough."

Nathan bent his broad back forward and brought his two hands on to his knees with a terrific whack. "Land o' Goshen, thee's copped the babby a mighty good blessin', me dear. Not another woman aboard coulda done it." And he looked back over his shoulder. "That were a mighty kind thought," he said again.

They returned to Ellen, and Nathan left the women together and walked to the ship's side to watch the progress of the boat that was carrying nearer his cousin, son of his mother's sister.

Polly, seated on a bundle of bedding, undid the hooks of her frock and proceeded to nurse her baby, who was now awake and crying. Ellen followed Nathan and stood beside him, watching the approaching boat, but after a while, hearing Polly call, came reluctantly back to her.

"Ellen, dear," said Polly, striving to keep her voice calm, for she was as keen as her sister to be up and ashore. "Do 'ee mind all I've said to 'ee about bein' an 'elp an' a comfort to Nathan an' babby an' me? Thee's been a marvel to me aboard ship, dear, an' no mistake. Will 'ee stick by Nathan an' me, Ellen, an' take 'eed what we tell 'ee?"

"I'll not be a trouble, Pol, don't worrit. I'll do me share

wi' the rest. I'll not be idle nor contrary, don't fret. 'Twas good o' ye to bring me, an' I'm mindful o' that. There would'nt 'ave been much for me to 'ome wi' thee gone, Pol," she added, smoothing out the crumpled calico of the baby's night-dress.

Neither spoke for a time, then Ellen, running her fingers across the soft skin of the baby's little hand, said gently, "Idden 'e a darlin', Polly? 'E's so sweet an' soft, sometimes I want to cry when I looks at un. Look at 'is little ears, like curly pink shells."

Polly did not reply, and Ellen continued speaking.

"Polly, I'll get married some day an' 'ave one o' me own." She let the baby's fingers clutch her thumb. "I wish 'e was mine," she said lovingly.

Polly tucked back the baby's head into the curve of her arm and began to fasten the hooks of her bodice. When she had finished and all the little purple bows were straightened she looked hard at her young sister and then away across the blue water.

"Ellen," she began, " 'twas strange 'ee should say that there. I were just goin' to ask if——" She stopped suddenly.

Ellen was looking at her, now.

"Yes, Pol?"

Polly brought her gaze away from the water with an effort, and looked into Ellen's face.

" 'Tis like this, Ellen——" and her voice faltered.

"Spit un off thy tongue, Polly," Ellen encouraged.

"Well, I will," said Polly firmly. " 'Tis this. Will 'ee promise to look kindly-like on Nathan's cousin Peter, when 'e da come aboard? Nathan da want that 'ee two should like each other."

Ellen gave no sign that she had heard, so Polly had to speak again.

"Well, what think of un?"

Ellen stood up. "I can't say till I've seed un, an' I shan't say then," she answered calmly.

"Sit down, cheeld, and 'ear what else there be to un," said Polly in a strained voice. "I told Nathan I'd tell 'ee afore Peter came aboard. Ellen dear, sit 'ee down, do."

Ellen sat down on the wooden box, her eyes on Polly's hot, flushed face.

" 'Ere, let me take 'im," Ellen said, slipping her hands beneath the baby and transferring him to her own lap. "What 'ave thee an' Nathan been up to about me? I've a mind what 'tis about, too."

"Well, what?" parried Polly.

" 'Ee tell," returned Ellen.

"Well," said Polly, very determined and red in the face. " 'Tis like this 'ere. Peter Tilbrook did write Nathan a long letter two year ago an' told un all about Australia an' what a chance there were for Nathan an' me out 'ere in this country."

"I've 'eared all that afore," put in Ellen.

"Well, 'ear un agin," Polly answered sharply. "So, Nathan wrote 'im back an' said that I an' 'e were comin' when we could save enough, an' glad we'd be to get away an' try our luck."

"Well?" said Ellen patiently.

"Well, Peter wrote back agin an' said 'e were 'appy about us comin' out, and 'e nominated us for our passage an' undertook to be responsible for us when we got 'ere. 'E wrote 'e 'ad work for Nathan when we come an' were buildin' an 'ouse, an' we could put up with 'im when we got to Adelaide. An' tucked away in corner 'e put this. Now listen," said Polly with a sly glance at Ellen, " 'ee ain't 'eared *this*! 'Nathan,' says 'e, 'tell thy good wife I be a lonely man, an' tell 'er that when she da come she'd best bring out a cheery, willin' little body, young an' good-tempered, an' if the lass be 'greeable I will be too!' So Nathan an' me just thought o' thee, an' asked 'ee to come along too."

Polly waited, but Ellen had no questions now.

"Didst 'ear, Ellen, me dear?"

"Yes, I 'eared, Polly."

"Well, can't 'ee speak?"

Ellen could not speak. She burst into tears. Her brave little hat bobbed down, and one of her small, red hands went up over her face, and the tears dropped slowly on to the baby's shawl.

Polly was totally unprepared for this. She put her arms about Ellen and rocked her to and fro with many a "There, there!" and "Now, don't take on, there's a dear, Ellen!"

But Ellen still sobbed on. At last Polly stood up and, thrusting out her little chin, grasped Ellen by the shoulders and gave her a good shaking. This brought the little hat up again and also succeeded in awakening the baby, and when he was hushed they were both calmer.

"What made 'ee go off like that, Ellen?" said Polly at last. "Thee's not the cryin' kind."

"I couldn't 'elp it," Ellen whispered, her lips trembling and showing all signs of "going off" again.

"Stop it, now!" commanded Polly, "There be nothin' to cry over. Thee don't 'ave to like un if 'ee don't want to. Thee've come out 'ere wi' Nathan an' me, an' stay with us 'ee may an' welcome, dear. But," she added matter-of-factly, "'tis terrible aisy to like a man oo've got an 'ouse and 'ome all ready an' a pound or two put by. Wait an' see, Ellen. Nobody'll make 'ee 'ave un if 'ee don't want to, me dear."

"Why didden 'ee tell me all this afore, Pol?" wailed Ellen.

"Well, dear, 'tis like this 'ere," answered Polly slowly, "thee be sich a queer one, Ellen, allus dreamin' of meetin' some nice, fancy man an'——" She tried hard to finish but could not, so Ellen continued for her.

"An' fallin' in love an' all o' that? Yes, I be, Polly, an' I'll meet with 'im some day, and," she added with spirit, "'is name won't be Peter Tilbrook!"

Polly went on as if there had been no interruption, "——So I knawed that if I tellt thee all this afore we set sail thee's 'a' got thyself into sich a state by time we got 'ere we none of us shoulda knawed if we was on 'ead or 'eels."

"Don't think I shoulda given a thought to un," said Ellen, quickly.

"Give a thought to un, Ellen? Why, I knaw thee through an' through, me dear, an' 'ee woulda been madly in love with un afore we left Plymouth, an' never a free minute would Nathan an' me 'ave 'ad all the trip. Besides," Polly said tenderly, shading the baby's face with her hand and looking down at him, "I 'ad other things on me mind!"

This was too much for Ellen, who surrendered the baby and got slowly to her feet.

"Polly, thee's done a nasty thing by me." She was crying again, very quietly. "I shan't forgive 'ee, an' I shan't stay to set eyes on that cousin o' Nathan's. I'll run off, I will. I shan't be married to please thee, nor no one."

Polly stood up and put her arm about Ellen. "Why, dear," she said, "I'm an interferin' old 'umbug, an' I've done more 'arm nor good." She spoke tenderly, then her voice changed and sharpened. "Stop snivellin', do! 'Ere come Nathan an' Peter Tilbrook. For pity's sake!"

Ellen lifted her head and, through a misty veil of tears, she saw him. He was younger than Nathan, tall, with a soft, curling beard and brown eyes set wide apart. He wore a grey cut-away coat and black trousers and carried his hat in his hand. The brown hair waved back from his broad, white forehead, and his whole face wore a calm, serious look.

Nathan drew him towards the group about the wooden box.

"Polly," he called, his face beaming, "this be Cousin Peter."

Polly made a little bob of a curtsy, smiled and held out her left hand.

"Welcome! And how do you do, Cousin Polly?" said Peter in his London voice.

"I'm brave and 'earty, Cousin Peter, an' I 'ope as thee's the same," said Polly, primly.

"An this," said Nathan, his face positively aglow, "well, this be our Ellen."

Peter looked hard at the brim of the brave little hat, which was all he could see of Ellen.

"How do you do, Cousin Ellen?" Peter Tilbrook said quietly, holding out his hand.

She gave him the tips of her fingers, and a brief glance from under the absurd brim of the chip-straw hat, and that was all.

CHAPTER II

It was not until the next day that Polly, Nathan, Ellen and Richard left the *Lady Milton* in a lighter and were rowed from the anchorage to McLaren Wharf and stepped at last upon Australian soil.

A fresh wind springing up late the previous afternoon and Peter's intimation that it would be dark by the time they reached their new home in Adelaide had forced the decision on Polly that, for the baby's sake, it would be safer to spend the night on the ship and to leave early the following morning. Peter, applauding Polly's good sense, decided to return to Port Adelaide, find accommodation for himself there and await their arrival at the wharf next day.

Irked by the necessity for changing plans at this last moment, Polly grudgingly undid the bundles of bedding and made up the bunks for their last night on board the ship. Ellen was permitted to stay with them in the married peoples' quarters 'tween decks. She had previously occupied one of the ill-ventilated compartments with some of the thirty-four other females in the single women's quarters in the foremost division of the ship. Several other families remained on board for various reasons, and nobody slept well that night for all were excited and restless with the anticipation of the morrow and the prospect of acquainting themselves with their new country.

Before the first dawnlight stole in upon them Polly was up and placed the baby beside Ellen as she lay sleeping on shawls and blankets close by. Then she crept up on deck, very carefully so as to waken none of the other women and children who were now resting quietly.

The ship lay listlessly at anchor and the mists were rolling back across the water disclosing Port Adelaide with the tops of tall trees beyond and, away to the south-east, the three tiers of hills that were the Mount Lofty Ranges. At the foot of the hills smoke wreaths were winding, for, out of sight, the city of Adelaide was wakening from sleep.

From the schooner *Daphne* and the barque *Isle of France*, anchored beside the *Lady Milton*, came signs of life, and smaller craft about them in the stream unfurled a grey sail or two, and fragments of talk were tossed to and fro across the space of water.

The early breeze of morning waved the soft ends of Polly's hair as she stood on the deck with a blue shawl about her head. She felt vaguely disappointed that it was like all other breezes she had known and bore no strange, sweet essence from the new land. The scents and the sounds of the sea, to which Polly had been accustomed all her life in St Ives, were here in this new country just as they were at home. The tarry smells, the fishy smells, the husky voices of the sailormen and the cries of sea-birds on the rigging were the same the whole world over, and the grate of rowlocks somewhere below on the smooth water and the rattle of a ship's chain were homely sounds to her. The plop, plop, plop of the sea about the vessel's side sounded like the rise and fall of the water beneath the wooden pier at home; but here, on the water of the "river", she missed the old familiar beat of breakers foaming against clodgy Five Points, and here the morning mists rolled back as greyly as they did on Carbis Bay, but revealed only the sluggish smoothness of a quiet sea—no rugged coastline like the shores of home.

Port Adelaide was not a pretty sight, but looked its best in the gentle light of morning. The river, or rather the inlet from the sea, from whose bed the silt had been lifted to reclaim the earlier swampy wastes about its edges, lay silvering under the lightening sky. Its swampy borders, during latter years, had been built upon, and as each succeeding layer of mud had been laid down the levels of the streets had risen and, at one time, had seemed to form stairs. The constant flooding of the land by high tides had caused some of the earlier colonists to build houses on piles with steps leading up to the doors. Now, all this was changing, and deepening operations in the harbour and the depositing of silt on the shore were reclaiming the swamps and altering the whole contour of Port Adelaide. A town had grown up about the waterfront and beyond McLaren Wharf, which had been opened twenty-five years before, with a gun salute and the benediction of a chaplain's prayer. Now, there were streets of clustering, low stone houses and bare-faced double-storied buildings, with here and there the glimmer of a glass-windowed shop front and the sheen of paint on ugly wooden balconies that stretched their short distances across the upstairs rooms of public houses. Above the rest rose the sharp angles of church roofs, and upon all was that grey drabness which, while having nothing whatever to do with those rolling mists of morning that vanish with the rising of the sun, encompasses, as with a mantle, every shipping port in the old world or the new.

A step behind her caused Polly to turn about. Nathan, walking along the deck towards her, smiled and said, "Well, Pol, what do 'ee think of un?"

"Precious little," Polly replied shortly. " 'Tis not much to see, Nathan, an' we've come a purty long way to see un."

"Close touchin' thirteen thousand mile, me dear," said Nathan, gazing out over Port Adelaide. "Thee was pleased enough 'bout un yesterday, Pol. What's made 'ee change thy tune?"

"Well, 'tis like this 'ere. I were all stirred up inside like anathin', if 'ee will, an' what with all the talkin' an' bustlin' goin' on all 'bout me I never did give a good 'ard look to shore; but now, standin' 'ere by meself an' lookin' towards the promised land, as one might say, I'm cruel disappointed. 'Tis a take-in, an' no mistake."

"Steady, Polly, me dear, be aisy. We idden there yet. This 'ere be only the jumpin'-off place for Adelaide. See," he said, pointing away towards the tiers of hills, "Peter tellt me yesterday that 'way off there at the foot o' they 'ills be the city. 'Thirty year old,' 'e kept sayin' to me. 'Thirty year old!' That da mean, Pol, that 'tis neither just begun nor any way toward finished. 'Tis in the makin'. 'An',' says Peter, ' 'tis 'alf-in-'alf an' not much of either.' So don't be disappointed, Pol, if tissen what we both thought 'twould be. We be lucky to be 'ere with the babby an' all. Me with 'ealth an' strength an' a terrible itch to get me

'ands on a pick agin. The government 'elped to get us out
'ere, Pol, an' they wanted men an' women oo bain't
afeared o' work. We ain't afeared, are us, Pol?"

"Course not," she replied firmly.

"An' we ain't goin' to be disappointed 'bout little things,
are us, Pol?" he said, lifting up her chin with his great
hand.

"Course not, Nat," Polly said, smiling tremblingly. "I be
wantin' milk and 'oney, when all us 'ave been used to be
a bit o' strong tea an' a saffern bun."

After an early meal, the family goods were mounded
into a heap on deck once more, and once more Polly farewelled those friends of the voyage who were still on board.
Mrs Ben Wilson, whose husband rejoiced in the name of
Benaiah, she was especially sad to leave, for it had been
Mrs Wilson who had assisted Dr Rickards at Richard's
birth.

"Never thee mind, me dear," comforted Mrs Wilson,
"us'll meet agin, never fret, Miz Thomas. Me Ben an' me
an' the childern be goin' to Wallaroo Mines as quick as
we may, an' I don't mind sayin' that 'twill be there us
two'll meet agin, for my man be a miner same as yourn,
an', think what 'ee will, 'tis at the mines thee'll finish
same as me."

"I be goin' to Adelaide," said Polly, with spirit.

"But thees'll end where the copper starts," Mrs Wilson
said knowingly.

Polly paused a moment, then nodded her head. "I think
Nathan be wantin' to go there this minute," she said
resignedly.

Peter was standing on the wharf when the lighter brought
them from the ship. A hot north wind was blowing, and
Polly and Ellen stood shakily on the wooden planks of
the wharf with the whole world rising and falling about
them and the wind billowing out their skirts and tipping
Ellen's straw hat over her little nose. Even Nathan who,
being of the sterner sex, was expected to be superior to
such things, could not adjust himself to the fixity of land
after one hundred and six days of successfully maintaining
his balance on the rolling deck of the *Lady Milton*. The
sensations persisted, and it was a comfort at last to secure

a seat on the steam train which would take them to Adelaide.

The train line from Adelaide to Port Adelaide, opened for traffic in 1856, was the first steam-train line in South Australia, and now in 1865 other lines linked Adelaide with Gawler—a distance of twenty-five miles—and one was in slow progress toward its destination on Yorke's Peninsula.

"Did you expect we should have a train for you to ride in, Cousin Ellen?" asked Peter as the train started.

Ellen gulped and blushed. "No, I can't say as I did espect a train," she said, shyly.

"Did you expect a coach?" Peter asked.

"No," said Ellen.

"A horse omnibus?" he persisted.

"No," said Ellen, faintly.

"Well, how did you think you would get to Adelaide?" She reddened to the tips of her ears. "I didden think anathin' at all about un," she breathed.

"Naught worries our Ellen," put in Nathan, good-humouredly. "She didden trouble 'ow 'twas to be done, but she knawed she'd get there all right. Ellen idden one to fret. Polly, 'ere," he said, laying a hand gently on Polly's knee, "da say, an' I knaw 'tis true, that Ellen be the sweetest natured, most trustful, most accommodatin' little woman that ever lived. She'll make a fine wife for some lucky man, no mistake."

From behind the shelter of their bonnets Polly and Ellen exchanged a swift glance. Ellen's eyes were swimming in tears of embarrassment, and Polly's were bright with vexation.

"I'll 'ave to up an' tell Nathan to lay low when we da get to Adelaide," she thought. " 'E'll up an' spoil evrathin' if 'e idden careful."

When the train reached Adelaide Peter left the others on the narrow platform while he went in search of a carrier with whom to entrust the Thomas family's goods, and on his return they all set off for his house in Brown Street.

They walked by common consent. None of them was used to any other means of moving about, never having owned horse or vehicle, and as Polly put it, " 'Twill give us a chance to see what's what."

North Terrace seemed wide and empty, flanked on one side by scattered stone buildings with many vacant lots between. A lone horse cab stood where King William Street, the city's main thoroughfare, bisected North Terrace. Peter turned their faces to the west and they walked on to Trinity Church; then turning left, they were, so Peter told them, in Morphett Street. They came to Hindley Street and, pausing in the centre of it, Peter made them look down the length of Hindley and Rundle Streets, which run from east to west of Adelaide, each more than half a mile in length and making, together, a straight thoroughfare over one mile long. They stood in the dust of Hindley Street and looked about at the scattered low buildings, surrounded by stubbly paddocks, that bordered either side of the road. The nearer the buildings came to King William Street, which divided Hindley from Rundle Street at right angles, the closer they grouped together and the fewer became the empty, sun-baked paddocks.

"There," said Peter, shading his eyes from the hot sun and pointing along the street, "there you will see the business section of Adelaide: shops, a horse bazaar, the auction rooms, public houses, stage-coach stables—and anything else you want."

Polly was amazed. "Shops galore an' public 'ouses aplenty!" she marvelled. "Oo ever woulda thought it?"

"Didn't you think we'd have shops here, Cousin Polly?" Peter, who had begun to walk on with Nathan, called back.

"Never in this world," said Polly. "Public 'ouses I knew thee'd 'ave for sure, but I thought the rest'd be naught but pug 'ouses."

"Pug houses? Why, we've been a colony for nearly thirty years! They did have mud huts here in 'thirty-six. Why, Government House was made of reeds and mud in the early days, and the builder even forgot the viceregal fireplace, and all the cooking had to be done outside. But that time's long ago, Cousin Polly. Even Nathan, here, can't seem to connect the colony with steam trains, stone buildings and a new town hall. We've a fine bridge across the River Torrens now, that cost a good round sum to build, and there's talk of a great post office building to be erected in King William Street, by the squares. My word, you'll all be surprised to see our own new chapel in Franklin Street, too. It has a brick spire that can be seen all over Adelaide. We're very proud of that spire, and when you stand on the front step of our house, Cousin Polly, you'll be able to see it through the trees."

Polly passed her hand across her damp forehead. "Evra-thin' be strange an' new, Peter," she said. "Lord in 'eaven only knaws what 'twas we thought to see, but anyways they wasn't chapel spires an' steam trains, I knaw that."

Nathan could not get the fact of the wide streets out of his head. Streets he had expected, but *broad* streets with two-storied shops, houses and stone buildings ranged along the sides and more buildings in the course of erection standing in naked ugliness near by were beyond him.

"Why, this be wastin' good land! What do they want with streets so wide, Peter? We didden 'ave no use for un 'ome to St Ives."

"But," said Peter, "this is to be a brave, new city, Nat. Don't you understand? We are building here for years to come. Have you forgotten how cramped it was in some parts of St Ives? We want to do better here, Nat."

Nathan paused to rest, and looked about him. Morphett Street had joined Brown Street, and it was pleasing to rest awhile in the shade of the gum-trees there.

"What's good enough for us at 'ome should be good enough for thee out 'ere," he said at last.

The day was hot, and the sun shone steadily from a blue November sky. The light rain that had fallen the previous night had not been sufficient, here in the town, to lay the dust and, as the wagons and horses passed, clouds of fine dust arose from the uneven surface of the road and blew into the faces of Nathan and his family straggling towards the new home in Brown Street.

Peter very proudly pointed it out to them as they came near, and Polly, hot and tired, was glad to see it at last. The house was one-storied and squat and, like others dotted along the street, was built of stone, the two windows and the door in front giving it the appearance of a fat, benevolent face. Built on a level with what would one day be the footpath and standing in a space of dry dusty grass, it was made to the pattern of hundreds of houses springing up about the growing city. There was no veranda or shelter to keep out the intense Australian heat: just a small, bare, three-roomed stone house, with a lean-to of boughs at the back, set on the side of a road.

Nathan liked it and said so many times, and Polly praised Peter for a good job, but Ellen could not be brought to say anything.

There was a pleasant smell of whitewash and new wood inside the cottage and, although there were only earthen floors in all the rooms, it was a haven of unexpected comfort to the immigrants and, as they looked into each little room, Polly and Nathan praised Peter with nearly every breath they drew.

The front door opened into the main living-room where, before the chimney with its open fireplace, Peter would sleep on his canvas bed at nights, and on which camp oven the meals of the household would be cooked. A cedar table was here, and four strong cedar chairs made and polished by Peter himself, for he was a carpenter and cabinet-maker and worked at his trade in the shop of Mr Henry Bonde in Rundle Street.

In the front bedroom, which opened off the living-room and was the room Peter had arranged for Nathan, Polly and the baby to share, were two canvas beds, a carved wooden cradle, and a chest of drawers made of shining cedar. Polly stood before this chest and rubbed her hands across the satin smoothness of the wood.

"Thee's made a beauty 'ere, Peter. 'Twill be just the same in an 'undered year from now."

But it was the cradle with its spindle bars that won Polly's heart. She laid the baby in it and touched the rocker with the toe of her buttoned boot.

" 'Ow did 'ee knaw we'd be needin' un, Peter? Did Nathan tell 'ee?"

"Yes," said Nathan, "I told un that by the time we landed the little babby'd be borned an' 'e'd 'ave one more to greet 'im. I 'ad to tell un, Pol, as 'e wasn't countin' on babbies when 'e asked us all to come."

Polly looked at the child sleeping in the cradle, and her voice trembled as she looked up at Peter. "Bless 'ee," she whispered.

The little room at the back, with the small window set in one of its walls, was for Ellen, and here, among the boxes and bundles of household belongings, she would sleep.

So their life in the new colony began, and their days were filled with hard work for the women and men alike. Peter went to his work each morning with his midday meal in a knotted handkerchief, and came home to a cheery household, an appetizing tea and a quiet rest at night. Nathan worked about the house, turning over the dry hard soil again and again, loosening it and making it arable and ready for when the long-delayed rains should come. Peter, before their arrival, had sought after and had found work for Nathan as a builder's labourer, but the work would not be in hand until after Christmas.

Polly and Ellen bent long hours over the wash-tub in the lean-to at the back of the house—a mere shelter of wattle sticks and boughs, but neatly and strongly made— and they rubbed and scoured the clothes that had been yellowed with weeks of wear and many an ineffective laundering on the ship. At night, while the house slept, the moon shone down on countless intimate articles of the Thomases' clothes-chest, hung out over bushes and boughs to bleach in the evening dews that the new chums hoped might fall. Not one drop of the precious soapy water from the washing was wasted, but was poured lightly over the earthen floors in the house, and by degrees each floor was dried and then stamped down hard and smooth.

Ellen did not sing at her work as did Polly. Polly's wavering soprano was always wobbling up and down the lovely cadences of the hymn "Lyngham"—"O, for a thou-ou-ou-ou-ousand to-ongues to-oo sing"—one of the most exhilarating and tuneful hymns ever written, and the favourite hymn of many a Cornish Methodist. Ellen went about her work quietly and hardly spoke unless she was addressed, and such was both her and Peter's embarrassment that they avoided one another as much as possible, for it was evident that on the walk from the station Nathan had told Peter the reason for Ellen's coming to Australia.

Many a musing look did Polly cast on Ellen, and her singing would fade thinly away as she watched her young sister's unhappy face. She could not bring herself to talk of the matter to Ellen, but, had she guessed how often Ellen cried herself to sleep in the darkness of the back bedroom, she would have been cut to her tender little heart. The strangeness of it all was that Ellen did not know what it was she was really crying about. All she knew was that everything was wrong and that Polly and Nathan and Peter—oh yes, Peter—had cheated her of something, had just spoilt everything for her.

Polly knew quite well what was turning happy, loving-hearted Ellen into a quiet, miserable girl, and in bed at night she railed at herself and kept Nathan awake blaming both herself and him for ruining Ellen's chances and for having fooled Peter.

One evening she decided to "have it out" with Peter and, while Ellen was walking in the summer dusk with the baby in her arms, went to him as he sat at the table, put her hand on his shoulder and looked down at him woefully.

"Us 'ave spoilt things for thee, Peter, boy. Nathan an' me be just dunderin' chuckle'eads. I shouldn't 'ave tellt 'er anathin' about un, an' she'd be lovin' 'ee by this time. I knaw Ellen."

Peter stood up, and his face, where the beard was not, flushed brick red. He looked down at Polly and made as if to speak, then turned about and went towards the back door. She ran in front of him, and her grey eyes, bright as a bird's, shone in the candlelight.

"Can't us do naught?" she pleaded.

"We can't do anything, Cousin Polly. You and Nathan did what you thought was best and I'm sorry Ellen feels toward me as she does, but—don't ask me to say anything, because I couldn't." He spoke slowly, but with finality.

Polly watched him open the door, and then she called to him sharply. "Peter, shut door an' come 'ere!" she said, and there was a ring in her voice that made Peter shut the door reluctantly and come back to her.

"What do 'ee think of our Ellen?" Polly asked bluntly when he was standing by the table again. "Tell me true what 'ee think of 'er."

Peter waited before replying, but, after staring at the candle on the table for a few moments, he looked at Polly across its steady flame and said slowly, "I could be very fond of her if she'd let me."

Polly smiled broadly at that and, taking Peter's hand, held it tightly in her own. "Listen, Peter, I knaw what'll do the trick. Give us thy ear an' I'll tell 'ee."

Peter bent down and Polly whispered into his ear and then, hearing Ellen's step at the door, put her finger to her lips and, running lightly across the room, shut herself in her bedroom.

Ellen came into the living-room with the sleeping baby in her arms and, seeing Peter standing by the table, her cheeks went white, and the bodice of her frock rose and fell quickly at her heart's furious thumping. Neither spoke, and Polly's bedroom door opened.

"Let me 'ave the babby, Ellen dear," she said and, taking the child from Ellen's arms re-entered the bedroom and closed the door.

Ellen was left alone with Peter. She was undecided what to do, and in that moment's hesitation Peter spoke as with an effort. "Cousin Ellen?"

Ellen did not reply, so he had to begin again.

"Cousin Ellen, may I ask you to step outside with me a space?" And he walked to the front door and held it open.

Ellen was shaking like a leaf in a breeze, but she walked outside into the twilight, and Peter closed the door behind them. They walked straight on, and in the centre of the road Ellen turned and waited for whatever dreadful thing was to happen. But nothing dreadful happened at all: merely something astonishing. Peter held out his hand to Ellen, and she found herself slipping hers into it; and then he said in the kindest and most natural manner in the world:

"Can we be friends, Ellen? Can you forget all the blundering things we've done to you between us?"

Ellen stopped trembling, and tears gathered in her eyes and rolled down her cheeks. The true Cornish heart is strong to stand the shocks of circumstance, the poverty and the injustice of the world, but the tender word can immediately shatter its strength and melt it into tears. She gave one look at Peter, then ran back toward the house. When she reached the door she turned her head and called softly to the dark bulk of Peter standing in the shadowy road: "Don't 'ee fret about me, Peter." And she was gone.

Peter knew then that, somehow, everything would be all right and that he and Ellen would be friends.

Later, lying on his bed in the living-room, he thought of Polly's advice to him earlier in the evening: "If thee da want to be friends with our Ellen, take bull by 'orns an' tell 'er so, but, be gentle with 'er, do!" He laughed quietly to himself as he remembered Polly's serious face that had looked so earnestly into his, and then he fell to thinking of Nathan; and Nathan, snoring placidly in the next room, would have been mightily surprised if he could have known Peter's thoughts. Stolid, unimaginative Nathan, who had read so literally a lonely young man's postscript in a letter which had taken months to be received and answered; Nathan, who had fulfilled to the best of his ability what he considered was his duty to that cousin who would give him and his family hospitality in a strange land—he would never know what he had done or how nearly he had blundered.

At sundown on 23 December which, because the following day was Sunday, was designated Christmas Eve, Nathan, Polly and the baby, together with Ellen and Peter, set out walking along Brown Street to Hindley Street to see the sights. The day had been hot, and the air was still warm and oppressive. It was drought weather, and there had been many weeks of this dry clear heat, which had followed an almost rainless winter, before Nathan and his family arrived in South Australia. Apart from the discomfort and inconvenience to the new chums, caused by the dryness and heat, the problem of water for the whole colony was becoming serious, and care had to be exercised in the use of that which came so slowly and tepidly from household taps.

Five years before, on 28 December 1860, water from the Thorndon Park reservoir had been turned on for the first time in the city of Adelaide. The original eighteen-inch cast-iron mains laid from the reservoir to the city had been built so well and strongly that they were to remain in commission for over seventy-five years. A smaller main, traversing the East Parklands to Pulteney Street, branched out in a network of pipes, supplying the households and business places of the young city. This reservoir water was later connected to most of the homes in Brown Street, and the occupants gladly stopped buying from water-carters from the River Torrens who, until then, had made a profitable living from this occupation. Unfortunately, at this time—only five years after the reservoir water had first flowed through the iron pipes to the city—the supply afforded was insufficient, and by 1866, definite schemes were to begin for an extension of the catchment or the erection of some new storage area.

In Brown Street, in the front gardens of each of two of the larger residences, was a fountain; and Ellen and Polly often argued about the merits of each. The fountains were able to play only in the early morning or late evening, when the pressure of water was sufficiently strong; and many a time Ellen and Polly would walk down the street to see the homely sight. Peter, who had seen the great fountains about the Crystal Palace dashing their sparkling water high into the air from among the sloping areas of velvety green turf and the majestic splendour of the oaks, was secretly amused at Ellen's pleasure in these miniature jets of water flung up by the Brown Street fountains; but he said quite sincerely, with his eyes on her face, that he thought it very pretty.

Ellen and Polly now stopped to admire them.

"Dr Mayo's be the best," said Ellen.

"Mr Cawthorne's da shoot the 'ighest," said Polly, decisively.

"Like as not, the water in them be warm," said Nathan, thinking of the tap in the back yard of Peter's house.

"What woulden I give for a drink o' cold spring water!" sighed Polly, wiping her hot, sunburnt face with a dampened pocket handkerchief.

"Many a time," said Nathan, "I've thought o' thee, Peter, when we were to 'ome an' I were stoopin' down to take a fill o' cold water from a well under the old oak-tree. 'Peter Tilbrook out in Australia would give a purty lot to be tastin' o' this 'ere,' I'd say, an' I'd drink to 'ee, boy." And Nathan laughed ruefully at the remembrance. "I'd give a purty lot now meself to be tastin' of it this minute."

"The coldest, sweetest water I ever tasted in the old country," said Peter, "was a drink I had when I was a lad, before father took mother and me to live in London, and it came from a cave on Holywell Beach."

Polly lifted her head quickly. "What do 'ee knaw 'bout 'Olywell Beach, Peter? 'Ast been dipped?"

"Dipped? No!"

"Well," said Polly, "listen 'ere. When I was a babby, like Richard 'ere, me mother took me to 'Olywell Beach—we was livin' in they parts then—an' I were dipped in the waters o' the cave. I'm terrible proud o' that, Peter. Mother says she carried me up the beach into a cave, an' in this cave there was fifty steps cut out o' the rock. Up top was a pool o' cold fresh water, bubblin' from the sides, an' mother took off me clothes an' dipped me in. There's long life to them as 'ave been dipped in 'Olywell."

"Why wasn't I dipped?" struck in Ellen.

"Well, we'd moved to St Ives when you come. An' anyways, preacher told mother 'twas a old 'eathen custom, an' 'e kept on so at mother that she up an' promised never to do it agin. 'E got me baptized up to St Perrans in the old font there—for mother were still belongin' to 'stablished church then—but she were allus doubtful if even that could take away an 'eathen charm. There's a purty lot of 'eathen things us Cornish bodies still do, an', preacher nor no preacher, us can't be changed."

"What a shame we can't take little Richard an' dip 'im in 'Olywell, too," said Ellen, lifting a corner of the handkerchief and peeping in at him. "A sweeter little babby never lived."

"Give 'im 'ere," said Polly brusquely, and then, seeing Ellen's surprised look, added lamely, " 'Tis too 'ot for 'ee to carry 'im far."

Ellen, now growing accustomed to Polly's little spurts of maternal jealousy, handed him over willingly.

The kerosene lamps and flares were already alight and surrounded by myriads of flying ants and little grey moths when they reached Hindley Street, the business hub of Adelaide. Lamps in some of the shop windows shed a cheerful glow over the mixed collection of goods set up to attract the Christmas shoppers. People pressed about the doorways, intent on having their wants supplied early and the rest of the evening left free for pleasure.

A pair of ducks hung by their feet from the doorway of a poulterer's; and in the window, grouped about the light, was an array of appetizing pork pies and pasties, and three fowls, plucked and lying on their backs, lifted their legs into the air in naked abandon.

Polly merely glanced at the pork pies and pasties, and sniffed disdainfully. "Call they there 'pasties'? Law, I coulda baked a better batch wi' both 'ands tied be'ind me."

Nathan hung about the doorway of the ironmonger's store and cast an eye at the array inside. There, on view, was every article that could be made in iron and that might be of any use to the colonists.

Polly looked over Nathan's shoulder and said aloud, "Evrathin' in the world on show—but I can't see no jinny-quicks. I'll warrant they 'aven't got a jinny-quick in the shop, Nathan," she declared at last.

The storekeeper heard her and called out, "Come right in, missus. I've got a jinny-quick here if you want one." And he proceeded to turn over a stock of iron saucepans and kettles in his hunt for it.

"Leave un be," called back Polly from the doorway. "I want un, me son, but I can't buy un."

The shopkeeper held up the curved piece of iron used by women to goffer their laces and frillings, but Polly gave a quick look at it, shook her head and, grabbing Nathan's arm, drew him away from the door.

"I'll use straws same as me mother did afore me. When thee's gotten good work, Nathan, 'ee can buy me one; but till then I'll 'ave to use straws."

Peter and Ellen had walked on, and Ellen was gazing into the window of Walter's drapery shop. The window, on a level with her waist, was filled with women's hats. Little tuscan straw bonnets, with bows of ribbon and birds' wings for trimming, jostled sun-bonnets of strong pink calico, and bobbed to perky little hats of velvet with ostrich tips on the brim and trailing ends of coloured faille to tie under one's hair.

Ellen pressed her face to the window, and Peter watched her. Ever since that evening, two weeks before, when he had taken the bull by the horns, she had changed towards him. Shyly at first, and hardly perceptibly, she had made friendly little advances to him, her eagerness to be friends with him showing no hint of coquetry, but rather a childish desire to give him pleasure. Sometimes, while looking at her round little face set in its frame of black, shining hair, Peter was uncertain whether he was receiving all this service in a spirit of mere cousinly friendship, for in his heart was a strange secret knowledge, which had begun from the first moment of their meeting and which was now becoming plain, that being friends with Ellen was all over for him and being in love was well begun.

Peter was not unconscious of the looks cast on Ellen in her pink cambric dress, with its narrow pointed bodice and full skirt, so very wide about her little ankles and so high about her little, creamy neck. The frills of lace bordering the collar of her dress were no whiter than the soft skin they touched. Peter, standing by her, thought how curious it was that the nape of Ellen's neck where the black braids of hair rested should be so soft and white and so infinitely attractive. He found himself wondering if it would feel cool or warm to his touch, and rammed his hands into the pockets of his tight grey trousers to prevent the possibility of gratifying his curiosity.

When Nathan and Polly joined them the two women entered the shop together and Polly purchased two sun-bonnets, one for herself and one for Ellen, and a large cabbage-tree hat for Nathan.

"What fits me'll fit 'im," said Polly, as she tried on the cabbage-tree hat. " 'E wants one bad. There be three skins burnt off 'is neck already, an' 'e adden 'ad time to grow a new un."

As they were leaving the shop, Ellen caught Polly's arm. "Us 'ave bought our Christmas presents, Pol, but what 'ave 'ee got for Peter? Cussen 'ee see 'e'll be terrible disappointed if we all 'ave 'ats an' 'e 'as nothin'?"

"Well," said Polly, looking into her black bead purse, "shall us get un an 'at like Nathan's? I can manage un."

"No-o. Let me see." And Ellen looked about the shop so crammed with merchandise, and her eyes ran over the lines of garments hung from the ceilings and suspended over the counter. Mostly, they were women's garments, and whatever clothing for men could be seen was far too intimate to be considered even by Polly. Ellen's eyes skipped over the bolts of muslin and foulard, lingered an instant on a length of green, black and blue tartan, completely ignored the rolls of calico and blue denim, and at last came to rest on a piece of shimmering, ruby plush-velvet. She had an idea instantly and, leading Polly to the other side of the shop, whispered in her ear.

Polly's eyes opened wide. She turned to look at the velvet gleaming in the lamplight, and finally said, doubtfully, "Thee'll 'ave to sit up all night to finish un, for to-morrow's Sabbath an' next day's Christmas."

"If thee'll let me buy it, Pol, I'll promise to 'ave it ready by mornin.' Let's 'ave it, dear," she pleaded.

Polly counted out the coins from her purse into Ellen's hand. "Take un an' welcome, me dear." And all the time that she and Ellen were bargaining for a piece of the velvet Polly was secretly smiling.

An eighth of a yard of velvet, a wisp of ruby satin, a threepenny bundle of beads and a piece of stiff buckram comprised the purchase, and Ellen carried it carefully, all of an itch to be home and at work on it.

Before they reached the corner of Hindley and King William Streets they stopped at Polly's exclamation to admire two little English sparrows in a cage, marked "10/- the pair". They were the last of a consignment of sparrows brought from England to Australia by the ship *Orient*.

"I woulden mind a pair o' they little birds," said Polly, making a twittering noise with her lips to attract the sparrows. " 'Twould serve to remind a body o' back 'ome. Poor things, they won't last long in this country. 'Twas a shame to bring un out to furrin parts."

By the time they had crossed over King William Street and had inspected the shops for a distance down Rundle Street they were all tired and ready to set out for home. Nathan had his eyes on the picks in Carlin's ironmongery, and Polly and Ellen were busily contemplating the patterns of baby-clothes in Chappell's window, but Peter walked along to the site of Peter's and Martin's new store.

"When they begin here I may be able to get a job for

you, Nat," he said when Nathan had caught up to him. "I've a chance to get some of the work on the fixtures."

Nathan beamed. "Thee's good to me, Peter, lad, but I won't trouble 'ee long. When there's work to be 'ad I can go to like a good un."

They pushed their way back through the crowds on the footpaths until they reached King William Street, and then walked down past the town hall with its unfinished Albert Tower blotting out the stars, and entered the darkness of the squares. They passed through the white gates of the fence that shut off this tree-shaded area from King William Street, and Nathan walked ahead carrying the sleeping baby, and Polly hung on his arm. Peter gave Ellen his arm, and so they went home through the night.

Presently Polly began to sing, very softly:

> Glory be to God on high,
> And peace on earth descend.

Nathan's soft, sweet tenor took up the strain,

> God comes down, He bows the sky,
> And shows Himself our friend.

It was irresistible. No Cornishman with any sense of tune—and there are very few without it—can withstand the charm of a Christmas carol; and soon Peter, in his deep basso, added his share to the harmony. Ellen too—shyly at first, and then as if gaining courage from the night and the darkness—joined in. Sweetly the old Christmas hymn sounded in the heavy air.

> Stand amazed, ye heavens at this!
> See the Lord of earth and skies
> Humbled to the dust he is,
> And in a manger lies.

When home, Ellen slipped into the little back room, lit her candle and, unbuttoning her boots, tucked herself up on the canvas bed and unwrapped her parcel. Out in the kitchen Polly set the table for the morning meal, then went to bed; but Ellen still sat sewing in the back bedroom, and it was almost morning before the little shoe-shaped, red velvet watch-pocket, encrusted with shiny steel beads (that a gentleman uses to store his watch in at night) was finished and tucked under the pillow beneath her head.

CHAPTER III

THE city of Adelaide, which was surveyed by Colonel Light in 1836, is laid out in the form of a parallelogram. In the plan of the city, three wide thoroughfares run from north to south and from east to west. At their points of intersection open spaces are reserved, called "squares"; but these spaces are not square in shape, and were intended by Colonel Light to be planted with trees and evergreen shrubs. Other streets, narrower but wide enough for traffic, run parallel with the broad thoroughfares, and altogether the mathematical plan of the military colonel is effective and practical. But in the early days of the colony the surveyor was subjected to harsh criticism, and to some extent his plans were altered. King William Street, which was to be divided by the main city square, has in late years bisected it; and a noble thoroughfare, running in an unbroken line north and south, is a definite improvement on Colonel Light's original plan.

Almost twenty-five years elapsed before the colony had expanded sufficiently to warrant one steam-train line, a steamship mail service from England every two months, a town hall which would eventually cost £20,000, a reliable service of stage-coaches, a fine road over the ranges, the Thorndon Park Water Scheme which, six years after completion, was to become inadequate for the city's needs, a city bridge which, when finished in 1856, had cost £22,778, and a residence for the governor of the province costing £5700. In these twenty-five years land values had so increased that, in one instance, £2000 was paid in 1859 for a city block on which to build the new State Savings Bank.

During these years and in those that followed them private enterprise had not been wanting, for a flourishing little city, encircled by wide commons called "parklands", was springing up on the Adelaide plains; the plans of the long-dead colonel for an ideal city were being gradually fulfilled and, by 1865, the success of his scheme was becoming apparent.

At this time Adelaide's skyline was broken by the pointed spires and high-gabled roofs of churches, and Adelaide was beginning to be known as the "City of Churches"—a title she has proudly kept through the years. Trinity Church, St Paul's in Pulteney Street, Pirie Street Wesleyan Methodist, Flinders Street Baptist and Flinders Street Presbyterian, Wakefield Street Unitarian, St Andrew's and Chalmers', both Presbyterian churches, the Roman Catholic cathedral, Franklin Street Methodist New Connexion, and Hindmarsh Square Congregational churches were all imposing edifices playing a splendid part in the early spiritual life of the young city.

It was during the morning service at the Franklin Street New Connexion chapel on the first Sunday after Christmas that Polly and Nathan, sitting in one of the stiff-backed pews near the front of the church, were waiting for the preacher to begin his sermon. Nathan, sweating in his dark cloth suit, folded his arms and, pulling in his chin so that his whiskers encircled his face in a fine brown fringe, looked up at the preacher from under heavy brows, awaiting with pleasurable expectancy the "introduction to the subject". Polly, her head on a level with Nathan's shoulder, sat with hands folded lightly in her lap, her eyes on the preacher, but her thoughts and ears busy with everything and everybody about her. Her hearing was so sensitive that when Toby Paull dropped his hymn-book in the middle of the sermon, she had no need to look back at him as some of her fellow-worshippers did and, although she did not know his name, knew just who it was who had been wriggling. Nobody could sneeze without Polly's knowing from whose nose it had come, and no cough broke the Sabbath stillness that she could not recognize. She was conscious of everything about her, yet her eyes never left the preacher's face.

The first Sunday on which she had attended worship in this church she had been aware of a rustling and a whispering as Nathan and she had taken their places in one of the pews and, while bending her head in silent prayer, had heard a whisper behind her.

"Oo's she?"

"Well, it's like this 'ere—Willum John Tretheway's wife's mother knawed 'er mother 'ome to St Ives, 'at's oo she be."

And in a young girl's voice, "Look at her bonnet! Isn't it the prettiest thing? Who is she?"

Polly's cheeks had been red when she had finished praying, but she had not even cocked an eye at the whisperers. It was quite a few minutes before the flush of pleasure had faded from her face, but that chance word had filled her with a determination always to have the prettiest bonnet in chapel. Back at home, in St Ives, she had been apprenticed to a milliner, and had worked at this trade for five years before her marriage and, given a remnant of lace, a plait of straw and a handful of trimmings, she could evolve a little hat that would fill any woman with envy.

This was her trade and she loved it, and was never so happy as when she was unpicking her little bonnets and retrimming them; and so it happened that each Sunday she had what appeared to be a new and charming creation on her head. Nathan, manlike, professed an aversion to Polly's harmless vanity, but in his heart he was very proud of his wife and of the work she could do with her clever fingers.

At the morning service on Christmas Day, while standing talking with new acquaintances outside the chapel, she had chanced to hear Mrs Tamplin—who drove to church in a landau and who had two maidservants at home preparing her Christmas dinner and was reputed to have "a pack o' money"—say to the wife of one of the stewards, "I call it decidedly bad taste of that new young woman to air her gaudy millinery in the chapel. As a labourer's wife she dresses far above her station." And Polly had watched Mrs Tamplin seat herself in her landau, open her parasol, nod her Sunday bonnet at the steward's wife and whirl away in a cloud of dust.

Everybody watched Mrs Tamplin's departure from church. It was considered very gratifying that such a person should attend chapel, and in a landau. It was not that famous landau, first in the colony, which had belonged in 1840 to the rich heiress Mrs James, and whose appearances in the unmade streets of the town had caused the wags to call, "What's moving?"—"Mrs James's carriage!" But it was built to the same pattern and was quite as sensational to the New Connexion chapel-goers.

And here was Polly, on this first Sunday after Christmas, sitting immediately behind rich Mrs Tamplin, and—oh perfidy!—the little vixen had copied Mrs Tamplin's Sunday bonnet. There they sat, Mrs Tamplin all unconscious of Polly's treachery, and Polly with her grey eyes fixed so steadily on the preacher's face; and on each of their heads was a bonnet of grey straw with two little curled ostrich tips and a sprig of dyed ornamental grass, a ruching of grey silk under the brim and two long ends of grey ribbon tied beneath.

It was a sensation. The worshippers in the seats behind Polly were in such a state of nervous excitement that Louisa James went off into a fit of the giggles and was led from chapel in confusion. The preacher, whose wife was not present at the morning's service, never knew what had made his congregation so restless, and nobody dared to tell him.

When Nathan, Polly and Peter returned to their house in Brown Street Ellen had dinner all ready for them: a meat pie, cooked on the previous day, now reheated and oozing luscious brown gravy.

Nathan attacked his share with vim, but paused after the first mouthful to say to Polly, "Polly, didst see the woman ahead of us in chapel? She 'ad an 'at ezacally the same as yourn on 'er 'ead."

"Yes, I seed un," said Polly, and was in the act of raising her fork to her lips when she encountered Peter's eyes. He was looking steadily at her, and his lips were firmly pressed together. Polly's fork returned to her plate, and she lost all interest in her dinner.

Just before Peter left in the afternoon for Sabbath-school she spoke to him alone. "I be mortal sorry, Peter. I won't do it agin. I've made 'ee cross an' I knaw it, but I'll never do sich thing agin."

Peter, very dignified in his long black coat and high-topped hat, merely said, "It wasn't kind of you, Polly—and in God's house, too."

Polly was crushed, but not for long. She dashed into her bedroom and, laying hold of the grey straw bonnet, pushed it, feathers and all, into the fire, and put the kettle on top.

"I be a vain, wicked creature, but I'll 'ave a change of 'eart, Peter. I will for sure." And the straw-bonnet incident was forgotten—except, that is, in Mrs Tamplin's heart and in the hearts of the chapel-goers; but while, in future, Mrs Tamplin treated Polly with contumely, the chapel-goers showed her a strange respect.

On 31 January 1866 Peter, as a local preacher of the Franklin Street Methodist New Connexion chapel, with the minister, the Reverend Mr James Maughan, and all the officers of the church, attended the quarterly meeting in the lecture-room at the rear of the church building. The Reverend Mr Clement Linley of Melbourne was present and, after the usual items of the quarterly business were discharged, several brethren, awaiting their appointment as local or "rounding" preachers, gave trial addresses. Peter, solemnly listening to their earnest though halting orations, was reminded of the occasion when he too had stood before his minister and the officers of the circuit and, for the first time, had proved his ability to speak for God and His church. This method of receiving and encouraging suitable members of a congregation to undertake the duties of assistant preachers is one of the corner-stones of Methodism. Anglicanism would not suffer a great deal if its laymen were dispensed with, but Methodism could not continue without its laity.

Since Charles Wesley's day there had been a number of changes in the membership of the Methodist church, and several groups had formed, each calling themselves Methodists but modifying or enlarging upon the principles of faith laid down by Charles Wesley in the foundation of Methodism. There were in the main, four distinct groups: the Wesleyan Methodists, the Primitive Methodists, the Methodist New Connexion and the Bible Christians. The principles of worship of the two former were practically the same, but the Bible Christian and New Connexion movements differed slightly from the others in origin and procedure.

The Bible Christian branch of Methodism was begun as an Evangelical Movement at Lake Farm, Shebbear, in Devonshire in 1815, by William O'Bryan who, having been rejected by a Methodist circuit, began his ministry among the people in that part of England. Later, members of this movement, who became known as "Bryanites" were to be found in all parts of Cornwall and Devon.

The Methodist New Connexion had its origin in the north of England, and its influence spread slowly to the south.

The Reverend Mr James Maughan was the first minister of this section of Methodism in the province of South Australia, and Peter Tilbrook was one of its first members, he having worshipped with them in 1862, in a room in Hindley Street. Land being secured later in Franklin Street, a cathedral-like church was erected which, with the land, cost £4750, and was opened for worship on 12 December 1864.

On Sunday 4 February 1866 the Rev. Mr Clement Linley preached at the New Connexion church in Franklin Street in the morning and evening, and the Rev. Mr W. Taylor of California delivered an address in the afternoon. The temperature rose to a hundred and ten degrees in the shade, and at each service the church was crammed with hot, perspiring, eager worshippers.

After the evening service the women stood about in groups, fanning themselves with handkerchief or hymn-book and talking of the big tea meeting which was to be held in the lecture-room on the following night.

"My Law! if 'tis as 'ot as this 'ere come to-morrow, I shan't be able to come along. Mary Jane Addicoat or somebody'll 'ave to look after my end o' table. I'll be laid up, like as not," said Mrs Henry Wallis to one of the groups about the church gate.

"Be thee jokin', Miz Wallis, or be thee done in for sure?" asked one.

"I can't stand no more, Miz Rogers. If cool change idden 'ere to-morrow, some other body'll 'ave to do my share at tea meeting."

And that was why on the morrow, when the thermometer registered over a hundred degrees—such heat as Polly had never endured at home—a message had come to Polly from one of the stewards' wives, and she and Ellen had to set to and bake for the public tea meeting.

The little camp oven was nearly red hot, and the two women were flushed and tired out by the time the cooking was finished. Nathan, coming home from work for his lunch at midday, had been given a piece of potato cake and a plate of scones and told to keep out of the kitchen.

"What's all this to do for?" he said, with his mouth full of potato cake. "Why don't 'ee just give un all a pasty? There'd be more sense to un than fillin' men up with all that there mullock."

"Mullock?" cried Polly with wrath, gazing at the table full of cakes and buns. "Wait an' see, Nathan Thomas. There won't be a better tray nor mine there. If 'ee don't like what 'ee see when 'ee get there, well go 'ome, me lad."

"Well, I woulden do that, Polly. I can eat buns wi' the best o' them, but I like to get me teeth on solid vittles, tea meetin' or no."

At a quarter to six that evening Polly and Ellen, with their white-covered baskets of eatables, arrived at the lecture-room. Mrs Rogers saw them and beckoned them in. Polly by this time knew most of the women belonging to the church, and was just beginning to feel at home among them.

"That's your end of the table," said Mrs Rogers, pointing towards one of the trestles which were ranged in lines down the room; and Ellen spread their white cloth across the table top and Polly unpacked the basket.

Little meat pasties she had, and jam turnovers, and two plates of scones that had no equal for lightness in the room, some saffron cake and seedy cake and curranty buns.

Polly gave a cursory glance at the other tables and whispered to Ellen, "Us 'aven't got cold duck like they've got over there on Miz Trotter's table, but wait an' see. When they start on ours there won't be a skerrick left."

By six-thirty the tables were filled with people—men mostly, whose wives were waiting on the tables or super-intending the copper of boiling tea at the back door. And after "Be Present" had been sung slowly and dolefully to the tune of "The Old Hundredth", those seated at the tables fell to. Women were kept busy running to and fro with tea and dirty dishes. A continuous clatter of knives and forks arose, every one talked and ate, some simultaneously.

"Well, Miz Thomas," said one red-faced diner at Polly's table who had been eating stolidly for half an hour, "that were good." He pushed back his plate and looked rumin-atingly around at his friends. "Funny thing about me," he said, "I've got three stummicks, one for workin' an' two for eatin'!"

Everybody knowing him for the laziest man in the colony, the laugh that went up was instantaneous.

When all had finished and many had gone out into the evening air Polly looked at her end of the table with pride for, except for a crumb or two, nothing remained on any of the plates.

At eight o'clock the public meeting began. The women, white aprons tucked away in their baskets, sat with their men folk and children on forms placed across the room; and how they sang, and how they prayed! The heat and the earlier festivity were forgotten. A spirit of thanksgiving and praise was upon them, and the crudities of speech and behaviour were put away from them like the white aprons of the women, and they gave their whole hearts to the joyous business of praising God.

Their spirit of thanksgiving was genuine and sincere. Nearly every one present had known either actual poverty or unhappy living conditions in their homes in England, and those among them who had been born in the colony had been raised with the words of their parents' gratitude in their ears—gratitude for the freedom and the oppor-tunities of this new country, and the chances it offered for all who were brave enough to take them.

For Polly, Ellen and Peter the church was the one great interest outside their home and their daily work. They attended every Sunday service and every meeting during the week. Their life was so bound up in the life and the affairs of their church that even the days of the week, when they named them, had reference to what was happening at the church or in its lecture-room. Nathan alone refused to let his life be chronicled and dated by church doings. His evenings he spent for the most part in the big living-room, seated at the table reading; and the book he read on nearly every occasion was the Bible.

"I like to read un, Pol," he would mildly protest when Polly would urge him to put the book away and come with her to mid-week service—which meant it was Wednesday evening. "Leave me be, an' go to chapel an' enjoy thyself. I'm not doin' no 'arm to no person, an' I like to read un."

"It da 'ardly seem natural, Nathan, that 'ee da want to sit an' read Bible an' not want to come chapel. What's wrong with 'ee? If 'ee like the Lord's Book thee should want to come to Lord's 'Ouse. Shoulden 'e, Peter?"

"I don't know, Polly. Let Nathan be his own judge," said Peter slowly, while Nathan shut the Bible and gave Peter a grateful look.

"Well," said Nathan, getting up reluctantly and pushing back his thick hair, "I'll come to chapel with 'ee if 'twill please thee, Polly, but cussen 'ee see I'm 'appy to 'ome? I'm not comfor'ble at chapel, I don't mind tellin' 'ee. Me rheumatics plays up soon as I sit still, an' anyways I'm not a chapel body like thee an' Peter."

"But 'ee be a Christian, Nathan," put in Polly.

"No," said Nathan slowly and with emphasis, "not what thees da mean by a Christian, me dear."

"But 'ee read the Book, Nathan. 'Ee da *believe*."

"I believe, Polly, but——" And he paused before adding shamefacedly, "I read the Book because I like un. There! I like to roll the grand words on me tongue an' learn them off. I like to do it, Pol. An' even if I idden what preacher calls a chapel-goin' Christian, I like to do it—an' that's all there is to un."

"That's a fine thing to own up to, anyway, Nat," said Peter sincerely, and he gave a funny lop-sided smile. "I call myself a Christian, yet sometimes, when I stop to look into my own heart, I wonder if, when I preach, I do it because I like to hear my own voice and to feel the power I have over the flock in the pews below. They must listen to me and do as I say, though more than half of them would as soon get up and walk out. And," he went on, as if he really did question his own heart, "when I lead in prayer, do I do it because I think I can pray better than any one else in chapel? And do I sit up in the singing seats because I've got a good bass voice and like to use it? Or am I filled with grace, and do I honestly speak for the Lord?" He raised his eyes to Nathan's quickly. "I wouldn't like to be as candid as you, Nat. I really wouldn't dare!"

"Now then, Peter, lad," said Nathan hastily, "don't listen to a clumsy body like me. Thee's 'seen the light' an' 'felt the Spirit'. Thee's got no need to question thy 'eart, boy."

"Well, don't 'ee question it for 'im, Nathan," interjected Polly, who did not like the trend of the conversation at all. "Don't 'ee sit on judgment on we oo—oo——" Her lip began to quiver, and she looked appealingly at Nathan who was agitatedly rubbing his rheumaticky knees with his hands and whose forehead was criss-crossed with little wrinkles of dismay. "Oh, Nathan, dear, why must 'ee make me ask meself if I be goin' to chapel meetin' for love o' God or Polly Thomas?"

The great revival meetings were held during the winter of 1866, and the whole church community was in a furore of religious fervour. There were meetings set aside on each night of one week for the rejuvenescence of the faith of professing Christians and the conversion of sinners.

The church was crammed for each service, which opened with singing and prayers and proceeded to the great denouement when every one present was exhorted to look to Jesus, to turn to Him, to love Him and to give their lives to Him.

Beginning with solemnity and dignity, the service gathered from the songs a freedom and a sense of joy. The prayers were earnest and full of ardent appeal. In the silence that followed one of the hymns the oppressive still-ness that came over the standing people was so real and awful that, one by one, the worshippers dropped to their knees. Those who did not feel the awe-inspiring compulsion to prayer stood still; but they too, from example or desire, gradually knelt, until of all that congregation only Nathan Thomas remained standing. The preacher's voice, solemn and compelling, echoed through the quiet church; but still Nathan stood his ground. Polly, her head bowed on the back of the pew in front, tugged him by the coat; and at last, with a despairing look at the bent heads about him, he too sank, very slowly, to his knees.

> There is life for a look at the Crucified One,
> There is life at this moment for thee.

sang the choir, and the congregation joined in, many rising from their knees with a look of happiness on their faces and singing with their whole hearts.

More songs—a verse of a favourite hymn, begun each time by one whose heart was moved or who secretly liked the tune—were taken up by the whole assembly.

> Sinner, whosoe'er thou art,
> At the Cross there's room,

and the rousing harmony of

> Whosoever heareth! Shout, shout the sound!
> Send the blessed tidings all the world around!
> Spread the joyful news wherever man is found:
> Whosoever will, may come!

Polly was on her feet now, and in a twinkling she had begun her favourite hymn:

> O! for a thousand tongues to sing
> My great Redeemer's praise.

The lovely tune was taken up and wafted towards heaven in a rush of sound.

Almost every one was on his feet by now, singing with whatever power the Lord had vouchsafed to him or her; but some remained on their knees, praying earnestly, with many a sob and groan, "God be merciful to me, a sinner!"

The last to remain kneeling was Nathan Thomas and he, from sheer physical incapacity, was unable to stand. His knees, stiff with rheumatism—that miners' heritage—which had troubled him all his working years, were held in an iron grip. It was as if the Lord Himself had laid His hand on Nathan—not upon his head, but upon his straining, trembling knees. The sweat poured from him, and he clasped his head in his hands in an agony of pain and terrible embarrassment. All about him shouts of "Praise the Lord!" "Hallelujah!" "Bless His Holy Name!" came from the throats of those whose hearts were moved by the power of the moment, the beauty of the hymns or the ardour of the prayers.

"God 'elp me!" moaned Nathan, struggling on his knees, and he groaned aloud.

A man in the pew in front stopped singing and turned about, "God will help you, brother. Give yourself to Him and He will deliver you. God be praised, another brand plucked from the burning! Hallelujah!"

It is quite reasonable to suppose that Nathan would have remained on his knees until he collapsed from pain and mortification had not Polly, who possibly had known about it all the time, dragged him to his feet. It was not given to any one present to know what anguish of spirit Nathan had suffered during his Gethsemane on the floor of the church or in the months that followed it. Sufficient it is to say that he never went to chapel again as long as he lived.

CHAPTER IV

"I, Peter Tilbrook, take thee, Ellen Jane Menadue, to be my lawful wedded wife."

Peter's voice did not tremble at all. Ellen, with her head bent over the bunch of pink and white geraniums in her shaking fingers, wondered how he could be so calm while she had choked and trembled, and had managed her responses only in a funny little whisper.

By means of much trying she raised her eyes to the white collar of the preacher, and there they remained as if mesmerized. She could not look into his kindly, bearded face; and even when Peter put the ring on her finger her eyes fell only to the second buttonhole of the preacher's long black coat. She seemed too frightened and too happy to move. Only when it was all over, and the preacher's hand rested on hers and Peter's and she heard the familiar words of blessing, did she feel that she could as much as blink her eyelids. Then Peter's arm was about her and his kiss on her cheek, and she drew a long, deep, deep breath and looked into her husband's face.

Polly, who had been following the service with such careful sisterly-motherly attention, now took a deep breath too. It was over, and Peter and Ellen were really man and wife. Polly had had a great fear that marriage in a house could not be quite the same as marriage in a church, but by hard listening she had failed to find any alteration in the service. The words and blessing were the same. It was as the preacher had told her, a true marriage before God.

It had all been very awkward about Nathan. After Peter and Ellen had begun walking out and after they had been tokened the matter of the marriage had arisen, and Nathan calmly and obstinately had stated that if it were to take place in chapel he would not be present. Polly had urged and wept, cajoled and threatened, but all to no purpose. Nathan would give the bride away, but not in church. So it had had to be the living-room of Peter's house in Brown Street, and Ellen and Peter were secretly very happy about it. The whole service would cast a blessing and a sanctity upon their home. Peter had said as much to Nathan, and set his heart at rest about the matter; but Nathan, curiously, said nothing of this to Polly.

Polly embraced her sister, deftly twitching the white ribbons on the bride's bodice into place as she did so, and then, taking her white apron from a drawer in the new chiffonier—Peter's wedding gift to Ellen—she attired herself for the homely and necessary duty of feeding the guests.

The table, all set and ready and hidden under a large white cloth during the ceremony, was now pushed from the side and brought back to its usual place in the centre of the room, undraped and its glory exposed. Nathan, his face beaming above the wreck of his frilled shirt front, rounded up the guests and allotted them to their places.

"Peter an' Ellen up top, an' parson next," he called out cheerily. "All the rest sitty down where they may, an' welcome. Mother an' me'll sitty down where we can."

Everybody rustled or squeezed into their seats, which Polly had borrowed from the neighbours, and amid smiles and a little laughter the wedding-breakfast began.

Polly could not sit still a moment. What with jumping up to make the tea when the big kettle boiled on the fire, and carving the fowl and passing the cakes and seeing that everybody was really eating, she could not find a moment to be still in. And then Richard, now a year old and able to sit on a high chair at a corner of the table, fell off to sleep with his head on his plate and, awaking as suddenly and screaming lustily, had to be carried off and hushed to sleep in the bedroom.

Old Mrs Phillips, who had come out with them in the *Lady Milton* and who now sat at the table in a black silk dress and a white pleated cap, waxed anecdotal, and would have succeeded in making everybody homesick and miserable had not fiddler Jim Barlow, who had brought his violin, thought it time for a tune.

Then Mrs Martin Potter, the steward's wife who had

brought her little girl and who, having been uninvited and there being no chair for her, had had to stand on a hassock all the time, was persuaded to recite. Mrs Potter recited on any provocation on any occasion, and now rose from the table with a little simper of feigned embarrassment.

"Not a *real* recitation piece, Mrs Thomas," she purred to Polly. "Just a fragment of advice to the—" she glanced a trifle archly towards Peter and Ellen, "—the bride and groom. A little homily, if I may say so."

She stepped to a corner of the crowded room and began:

> A paver complained as his living he gained,
> And he wept and wailed full sore,
> "Here I work all day, get little pay,
> I swear I'll do it no more."
> As he stood at the gate and railed at his fate,
> A good little boy passed that way,
> Who, pitying his state, looked him
> Full in the face and said,
> "Pray, work no longer to-day!"
> "Work no longer, me lad? Do you think I'm mad?
> Not work and have nothing to carve?
> I complained, it is true, but between me and you,
> 'Tis better to work than to starve!"

The energy Mrs Potter managed to put into the disillusioned paver's reply was astonishing. The scorn and the sarcasm were only the more effective coming, as they did, before the sad philosophy of the closing lines. The reception of this piece was so gratifying that she was, with a great show of reluctance, about to be persuaded to repeat it when a knock sounded on the door, and the voice of the preacher's servant was heard outside calling, "The 'orse phaeton be 'ere, master. All's ready, an' she's a-rearin' to go."

Ellen had to rush to the bedroom then, to put on her silk dolman, and Polly threw open the front door and every one streamed out into the street much to the alarm of the servant, who rushed to the horse's head and hung on to the bridle. But the horse was showing not the slightest evidence of being "a-rearin' to go", and the preacher, after shaking hands all round, got up into his seat, held the reins and waited for the bride and groom.

Peter and Ellen were taking their wedding-trip with the

preacher in his phaeton. He had church business to see to in Hope Valley where a new Methodist Church had just been built, and had kindly asked Peter and Ellen to accompany him for a day's journey through the hills. Such good fortune as this could not come every day and so, for a wedding-trip, Peter and Ellen would go driving with the preacher.

Peter lifted Ellen over the wheel, and himself got up beside her. The preacher waved his whip, spoke to the horse, and they moved sedately off down Brown Street toward South Terrace and on toward the distant hills.

Peter turned about and smiled and waved his high-crowned hat. He had never looked so handsome nor so happy. Ellen, all smiles, waved her handkerchief, wildly at first, then slowly and then not at all. The watchers saw Peter bend his head towards her, and all felt a little catch in their throats. Behind them, in the little house, Polly was crying into the lace window-curtains.

So, by November of 1866, Peter and Ellen were married, and Nathan, Polly and the baby, now toddling about in his little skirts, had moved to a house in Wyatt Street and were living with an old shipboard acquaintance and his wife. But by January of the new year Nathan had made up his mind to go to Wallaroo Mines on Yorke's Peninsula and to try to get work at his old calling and to make a house for Polly in which to begin their real home life in the new land. It was a big decision to make, but it had been in their minds ever since word had come home to Cornwall in 1861 of the great finds of copper in South Australia. They had wanted to come to Australia, and the discovery of copper and the opening up of the mines had given them heart for their venture; but it had always been a secret hope of Polly's that Nathan might be contented in the city.

Nathan had been in continuous work since two months after his arrival in the colony and that, considering the drought and the young country's consequent financial distress, was very heartening; but Nathan felt that he was only marking time. He was a miner by birth, upbringing and inclination, and he wanted to be about his business.

When Polly knew what Nathan had known for some

time—that they must eventually set out for Yorke's Peninsula—she was strangely settled about it in her mind. It was what Nathan had always meant to do sooner or later and, though the parting with Ellen and Peter and the breaking of all the ties she had made since her arrival in the colony would be hard to bear, yet she knew in her heart that every wife must go where her man's work is. She had married a miner, so to the mines she too must go.

Nathan left in January 1867 by the mail-coach, which would take him to Kadina, the town nearest to Wallaroo Mines; and Polly and Richard went back to live with Peter and Ellen until Nathan should send word that he was ready for them.

Polly, who was never one to sit quietly by when anything was afoot, was in a fever of excitement, and was packed and ready to be off a week after Nathan had left. She laboriously wrote letter after letter to Nathan, full of injunctions and directions: advice on what to do if his rheumatism were to seize him at the change of the weather, and sundry orders about the construction of the cottage. "Be shure to dig down a bit afor ee start, then walls dont ave to be so hi and keep cool," and "Keep a spase for a garden to front an a big chimbly." She wrote this and more so often that, unless Nathan did not read her letters or did not heed what he read, she might expect her new house to be built somewhat to her liking.

Nathan had left a small sum of money for her needs and, as she told him, what had she to worry about? " 'Aven't I got Peter to see to me, Nathan? Don't 'ee fear. Peter won't see me want for naught. An'," she continued, her eyes bright, " 'aven't I got the *note*!"

Nathan had nodded many times, well pleased.

This note was a bank-note for one hundred pounds—a Bank of England note, tucked away in a little chamois bag and sewn to Polly's stay-bodice. It consisted of practically every penny they had in the world, saved from the results of their joint labours in the old country and supplemented by a gift of twenty pounds from Polly's brother Robert, who had left St Ives in his youth and had gone to work in a warehouse in London. This was the Robert Menadue who had saved his money, riding in neither omnibus nor phaeton, steam train nor coach, having sworn to walk on his own legs until he was rich enough to drive behind his own horses through London streets. Generous-hearted Robert, slaving and saving all day in the warehouse, had managed to add his share to Nathan's and Polly's nest-egg and had brought their savings to the grand total of one hundred pounds, put all in one note and tucked away in the chamois bag now sewn to Polly's stay-bodice.

What to do with this fortune had puzzled and worried both Polly and her husband. It had given them anxiety at first, but now was only a cause for hope and speculation. What could be done in a new country with one hundred pounds? What could *not* be done, indeed?

But after Nathan's departure for Wallaroo Mines Polly began once more to worry about the precious note. Peter suggested putting in into the bank.

"What! Put all that in the bank? 'Ow would I knaw 'twas still there if I should ever go for un? No, Peter, banks be all right for them as don't 'ave to fret where their money goes, but I want mine where I can lay 'and to un any time I want to."

"But Polly, it's not safe to carry so much about with you all the time. I certainly don't think it's right for you to take it with you on the coach when you go. I don't mean to frighten you, Polly, but coaches are not the place for women carrying all that money with them."

"Do 'ee think we might get 'eld up, Peter?" asked Polly, round-eyed.

"It could happen, Polly, though I don't think it would. Still, I'd be much easier if you put it in some safe place in Adelaide until you needed it."

Polly did not say anything further about the money until, by dint of much questioning among her friends out-side the home, she chanced upon the knowledge of the hold-up of the Mount Gambier mail-coach by a masked bandit four years previously. That decided her, and one evening, hardly waiting for Peter to finish asking the blessing at table, she spoke to him, all smiles.

"I've a surprise for 'ee, Peter, lad. I've stopped worritin' 'bout the note, an' I've put un away in a safe place, like 'ee tellt me to."

"Wherever did you put it, Polly? Banked it, I hope."

"Oh no, somewhere much easier than that, an' no trouble at all," Polly answered.

Peter was instantly alarmed. "Out with it, Polly," he commanded. "Whatever have you done with your money?"

"Don't be so 'arsh, Peter. Listen, do."

But Peter would not listen. "Polly, what have you done with it? Ellen, make her tell us. Make her talk sense."

Peter talking in this way was enough of itself to upset Polly, but also a vague little feeling of alarm was making itself noticed in her mind. Nevertheless she stuck to her guns. "Don't make sich fuss, Peter, an' I'll tell 'ee. See 'ere. I took un to Lawyer Birmin'am in King William Street, an' 'e put it in 'is safe, an' I signed papers aplenty. I'll get 'em for 'ee." She saw Peter's amazed face. "That's all right, idden it, Peter?" she asked quietly after a moment's silence.

"Bring me the papers and let me see," was all Peter said, but it was enough for Polly. She sensed his doubt, and felt it in her own heart too.

"They look all fair and square," he said, after he had read them through several times. "He promises you good interest, and it sounds safe enough. But whatever made you go to him?"

"Oh, that's where 'tis to. Don't 'ee knaw 'im, Peter? 'E da sit two up from us in chapel. 'E da wear broadcloth every day an' an 'igh topper. Thee da knaw 'im, Peter. Think!"

"Now, I do remember him. Nice singing voice he has, too. Yes, I do know him."

"Then 'tis all right? 'E goes chapel 'long a we. That makes it all right, don't it, Peter?" Polly cried hopefully.

"Well," said Peter, with a laugh, "that makes it better, perhaps, but not 'all right', Polly. Will you let me come with you to see him, to-morrow?"

Polly was delighted. "Now," she beamed, "thee'll see for thyself I said right."

But later, when she was undressing in the back room that had been Ellen's, she felt grave doubts as to the good sense of her impulsiveness. She saw the place on her stay-bodice where the little chamois bag had been for so long, and for the first time she let herself think what might happen if the hundred pounds were really not safe.

Mr Birmingham received Polly and Peter very kindly in his office in King William Street. He ushered them to a seat, and Polly, red and anxious, sat on the extreme edge of her chair.

"Now, what is it?" said Mr Birmingham with a smile, settling back in the chair behind his table and fingering the gold seals, of which he had several, on his watch-chain. "Not regretting your little piece of business already, Mrs Thomas?"

Polly, grateful for this opportunity, began, "Oh, yes sir, I be. I be indeed, sir. Will 'ee——"

Peter silenced her with a look, and began his request to know more about the matter. Mr Birmingham was delighted to oblige, and told the story of Polly's approaching him after an evening service at the church and of her having asked his help in the matter of investing one hundred pounds. Polly nodded her head at this and settled back in her chair, watching Mr Birmingham delicately caress his gold seals and letting his nicely modulated voice soothe her anxious fears.

Peter and Mr Birmingham talked together for some time, and then the lawyer rose and, turning to Polly, said smilingly, "So you have decided that you want your money back, Mrs Thomas? You have some other use for it, perhaps?"

"Oh, no, no, sir," said Polly, sitting up with a start. "I just want it back, sir."

"Oh, so that's it," said Mr Birmingham, with the smallest possible nod of his head. "So that's it, Mrs Thomas?"

"Yes, sir, that's all 'tis."

"Very well, my dear lady," said Mr Birmingham, and he moved towards a large safe in the wall by his side. "You shall have it. 'Wilful woman must have her way,' as they say, Mr Tilbrook." He smiled at Peter and let the tail-end of his smile light on Polly before he bent to fumble with his key in the lock.

Polly strained forward in her chair, her eyes on the solid door opening outwards.

"Your brother-in-law has agreed to settle any little

charges arising from the breaking of our contracts, Mrs Thomas, and the other minor details. And here, my dear madam," said he, turning from the safe, "here is the hundred-pound note you gave me. See, actually the same note."

"Why, so 'tis!" said Polly, a great weight lifted from her. " 'Tis the very same one."

"Well," said Peter, who knew quite well that the lawyer was guessing who had put the doubts of its security in Polly's head. "Take it, Polly. You wanted it back, and now you have it—the self-same note!"

He should not have said that perhaps, for the fact of its being her own hundred-pound note had already made a great impression on Polly. She also knew that, if she took it now, all the worry of finding a safe place for her fortune would have to begin again. The sight of the solid-looking safe in Lawyer Birmingham's office and the solidity of Lawyer Birmingham himself, alone seemed security enough, but in spite of this she reached out her hand to take the note. She paused, and her eyes fell on the prosperous-looking, rich, golden seals again in the lawyer's fingers, and suddenly her mind was made up.

"Put un back, Mr Birmin'am, sir. I've changed me mind. I want 'ee to keep un in that there safe till I need un agin. I trust 'ee for certain. It wasn't me as——" She glanced up at Peter and, seeing his confusion, finished lamely, "Well, I just wanted to see if 'twere still in the safe, an' now I knaw it be all right."

Then Peter, squaring his shoulders, talked with the lawyer about means of investing the note, and made an appointment to see him next day and discuss it; but Polly heeded nothing. She was quite happy.

They were ushered from the office with quiet dignity, and Polly smiled to herself as she thought of the worrying bank-note now locked away in that solid safe in the lawyer's office: just lying there awaiting the day when she and Nathan would really need it. She smiled happily to herself through the years that followed when, several times a year, the tiny sum of interest came to her from Lawyer Birmingham himself. Everything she did from that time was flavoured with the thought that she and Nathan could afford this little thing or that, and that they were well-to-do folks—or nearly so. They had a hundred pounds "put by"!

It has been told already that Polly lost her hundred pounds, and, although she did not know it, Lawyer Birmingham spared a thought for her, years later, as he scrambled together his papers for that rush to Melbourne when Adelaide had grown too uncomfortable to please him. He saw her name, and smiled a little to himself. "Poor trusting little devil," he thought as he tore the papers into tiny strips.

It was in April that Polly had a letter from Nathan saying that the house he had been building for them was almost completed.

Nathan was being employed by the Wallaroo Mining Company, and told Polly that he was confident that his work there would be permanent. There was copper in plenty; not such rich ore as at the mines some few miles off at Moonta, but good. The mine captains were Cornishmen and knew what they were about.

Nathan had himself built his house between shifts at the mines, but a carpenter had made the inside fittings, the doors and the windows, and the house was now habitable and ready for them.

Back in Adelaide, however, there was now a reason why Polly would willingly have stayed. In October Ellen would be expecting her child, and Polly, with a motherly affection for her younger sister, woud have loved to remain with her during all the months of waiting. Ellen was so tiny, so young and sweet to have to go through pain and fear alone.

"Shall I go or shall I bide, Ellen?" asked Polly, torn between love of her sister and the call of her home.

"Go to Nathan, dear. I'll be all right. I'm feared, I knaw, when I think on what 'ee went through comin' out on board ship, an' I don't knaw 'owsumever I'll stand it without thee to be near."

But Peter solved it all for them. "Polly must go to Nathan now, and get herself settled in her new home; and then, if all is well there and she can be spared, I shall send the money for her trip to Adelaide, and she'll be here by October and in plenty of time."

So it was decided that Polly should go to Wallaroo Mines, and that upon receipt of Peter's letter in October she should come to Ellen.

The day came, in the last week of April, when Polly and Richard set out at six in the morning for Yorke's Peninsula. Except for their personal luggage they took very little with them, as Nathan had told Polly that anything they needed for the new home would be obtainable in Kadina, the township adjacent to the Wallaroo Mines.

Stowed away in a corner of the coach, she was weary but contented. Richard slept in her arms, and all his immediate needs were in the carpet-bag by her side. In the box at her feet were little flower-pots with cuttings of geranium, rosemary and fuchsia, taken from the bushes that Ellen had grown in the same way from little cuttings brought from the barren back garden of the old home in St Ives.

Polly leant back against the hard sides of the swaying coach, and for the first time in many days felt happy with the consciousness that she was going to her new home. Her bundles of linen and clothes were packed away in the wooden box which was now lashed atop, her child was in her arms, and she was riding away into goodness only knew where.

Twice before drawing up at the inn at Port Wakefield the coach had stopped for change of horses. Now, Polly was tired and aching, her head reeling from the unaccustomed jolting and the strain of holding Richard in that stuffy crowded vehicle.

Then, after a meal and another change of horses, they set off again across the arid stretch at the head of St Vincent Gulf, and then began to ascend the long hill, or "hummock" as it is called, to the west of Port Wakefield. Half-way up, to ease the horses, every one had to dismount— every one, that is, except Polly and Richard, who sat inside among the bundles belonging to the other occupants; and Polly pretended that the coach was her carriage and, like Robert in London who believed that wishes *were* horses if one worked hard enough, she thought what a grand thing it must be to be rich enough to be able to ride in state always.

At the top of the hill another great hummock rose on their right, capped by dark trees whose feathery foliage made Polly think of nothing so much as the hair on a woman's underarm, but of which she thought better than to make mention when every one else was in raptures over the charming effect of the dark trees against the creamy yellow of the autumn grass.

The axle of the coach became red hot descending the hill on the other side, and every one dismounted again and sat by the roadside while the driver attempted to do some good by throwing a can of cream over the wheel.

Polly, standing up in the dust of the track, could see the flat, wooded plains stretching interminably on and on. Strange birds called in the stunted mallee and tea-trees beside the road, and a flock of galahs, like birds in a dream, wheeled in a pink and grey cloud across the sun.

On they went all through the remainder of the day, with a change of horses at Green's Plains. The journey had been a long and trying one to Polly, and she thought sympathetically of what it must have seemed to Nathan in January at the height of summer.

Nathan was awaiting them at the Exchange Hotel corner at the end of their ninety-mile journey, and Polly rushed into his arms.

" 'Ere we be, me dear," she said. " 'Ave 'ee got our place ready for us? Are 'ee all right, me dear?"

Nathan gave her a hug and kissed her soundly. Richard he took into his arms, and he cradled the tired child as he had done when Richard was but a tiny baby.

"An' see oo's 'ere!" said Nathan to Polly, and Polly found herself encircled in Mrs Ben Wilson's strong arms.

"Welcome, Miz Thomas. Welcome 'ome," said Polly's friend, while Nathan nudged Ben Wilson forward.

"See 'ere, Polly. Dost remember Ben Wilson, me dear? We be on forenoon shift together. 'E come along to 'elp bring 'ome the bundles."

Ben Wilson, short and stout, with a cheery red face and one of the true, spade-shaped Cornish beards, smiled broadly and saluted Polly. "Glad to see 'ee again, missus," he said, and Polly gave a little bob.

" 'Ow be 'ee Mr Wilson?" she said with a tired smile,

Mr Wilson lifted the box on to his broad shoulders, Nathan carried Richard, Polly and Mrs Wilson managed the rest of the luggage, and they began their long walk, with many a rest, to Wallaroo Mines.

"Why," said Polly, in astonishment, when they had gone some distance down the road, " 'ave 'ee got a steam train 'ere, Nathan? Do tell!"

"No, Pol, that be 'orse-tram rails you be seein'. We've got a fine new tram that runs through Wallaroo Mines to Wallaroo, an'll go to Moonta soon. Ore trucks run on them lines to the smelters at Wallaroo, too. Thee's got lot to learn, Pol, for sure."

They passed the township crossing and approached the first mines crossing.

"We're close touchin' now, Miz Thomas," said Ben Wilson, chuckling, "but 'ee coulden pick yourn out from the rest. They be all alike. 'Tis a purty 'ard job findin' where a body lives, comin' off shift in the dark. 'Ee can't tell t'other from which, can 'ee, Nat?"

Away ahead, the poppet-heads of the mines reared themselves into the dusk, and the tall bulks of the stone engine-houses, housing the Cornish engines, showed dark against the sunset. Then Polly looked at the miners' cottages, grouped on the flat wooded land about the mines. It was as Ben had said, one couldn't tell t'other from which.

The cottages were low, and each was made of wattle and daub—a mud and lime mixture poured between and around supports of wood, often wattle saplings or mallee—with two rooms across the front and a skillion-room at the back. At one side a wide, squat chimney, made from limestone rocks, buttressed out from the wall and ended in an iron chimney-pot. Two small windows and a low door were let into the face of the front wall, and the roof above had a ridge running the full length of the two front rooms, and wooden palings, cut from forests in Van Diemen's Land—now, since 1856, Tasmania—were nailed closely together and formed the roof. A guttering ran across the front face of the house, and a gutter-pipe from this ran into a square iron tank at the side of the house. Very little rain water was collected in this way from the wooden roofs, and an underground tank to catch the surface water in winter was usually constructed in the back yard of each cottage. On completion the cottage was given several coats of white-wash inside and out, and the property was surrounded by a fence of wattle saplings.

Thus, rent free, the miners lived in little cottages which they themselves had built upon crown land leased by their employers, the Wallaroo Mining Company. The cottages were the property of the miners to live in, or to sell, if desired, with the company's permission. As a miner's family increased he merely added another two rooms across the front or back, with another ridged roof exactly similar to the previous one and with a leaking gutter between—and there 'ee were!

"Which be ourn?" breathed Polly.

"Thee be walkin' in at the gate," laughed Nathan, and pushed open the sapling gate of the first cottage on the right-hand side just over the first mines crossing, and Polly was at home.

Polly did not say anything, but just looked about at the fresh whitewashed walls, while Nathan stood waiting for a word of praise. Polly gulped, and looked at him, stricken.

The light faded from Nathan's eyes. "Well, Pol, what's wrong with un?" he asked tersely.

Polly was careful not to break down in front of Ben Wilson, and when she could master her voice she turned to Nathan. "It be purty as a picsher, Nat, me dear, but oh, I wanted a bit o' room to the front for me little garden. Don't 'ee remember I asked un to leave a space for un?"

Nathan looked at the arm's length that remained between the front door and the sapling gate. "Land o' Goshen," he groaned, "I knawed there was summat I 'ad to remember."

"Well, 'tis too late now, me boy," said Ben Wilson cheerfully, leading them in at the door.

CHAPTER V

So Polly went to Wallaroo Mines in April 1867 and felt quite at home there. Most of the miners and their wives were Cornish. Hard-working, honest, religious, often extravagant and often intemperate—all these qualities in every one of them, and good miners every man jack of them.

"Cousin Jacks" they were called, for some unaccountable reason. Unlike the later colloquialism "pommy", used in reference to the pink-cheeked English immigrants, which might easily be a shortening of "pomegranate" and a commentary on their complexions, the "Cousin Jack" had a kindlier sound and, like the earlier term for the immigrants, "new chums", had a welcoming, friendly note; but its inference is vague. Possibly it has reference to the extraordinary capacity the Cornish have for ferreting out a relationship.

It is almost impossible for a person of Cornish extraction to meet and converse with a true Cornishman without Cousin Jack managing in a short time, by downright inquisitiveness, to learn all the other's most private and personal business. The ramifications of whole families are known to him, and whether he be right or wrong in his knowledge of a fellow countryman's family tree hardly matters, for to him that man is of the brotherhood of Cornishmen. " 'Ow are 'ee, me son!"

Benaiah Wilson, Nathan and Harry Pearce were working a stope between them at this time and made a splendid trio. They all three had been miners in Cornwall, but Nathan had had the widest experience. He had worked for years in the Botallock copper mine near Cape Cornwall, a few miles north of Land's End. In those workings, which descended from the edge of the cliff to four hundred and eighty feet beyond low-water mark, the thunder of the stormy waters above him had formed a constant accompaniment to his work and added a deep undertone to the sharp notes of the miners' picks as they struck the ore. A nerve-racking job for a man, working by candlelight in a dark tunnel under the sea! But to Nathan it was good work and fairly profitable.

Here in South Australia at the Wallaroo Mines good conditions existed for those miners who were experienced and not afraid of work. Cornish mine captains, whose word was law and to whom a great respect was given, knew the type of men under them and how to manage them, and these mine captains and a general manager had charge of the mining operations of the company.

Although the copper was neither as abundant nor as easily accessible as that in the mines at Moonta, a few miles distant on the edge of Spencer Gulf, the Wallaroo Mining Company carried on operations successfully for almost thirty years and, after amalgamating with the Moonta Mining Company in 1889, continued to do so for many more years before the slump in the price of copper.

Polly, not many days after her arrival, had solved the matter of the fence's proximity to the house by moving it outward, sapling by sapling, and redriving each post firmly into the ground, thus increasing the space for her garden between house and fence. Nobody questioned her right to do this, but many stopped to remark upon it in a neighbourly fashion.

Ted Polderrick, lounging at his open doorway in his shirt-sleeves early one morning, saw the little woman in the faded pink sun-bonnet and large white apron moving the sapling fence, and he knocked the ashes out of his clay pipe on the heel of his boot and called out to his wife inside their cottage. "Ay, mother, see 'ere, quick."

"What's to do, Ted?" called back Mrs Polderrick. "Well, well," she exclaimed, as she stood in the doorway, with her hands spread on her hips, "if it idden that little Miz Thomas makin' of a new fence! Go on over an' lend an 'and, Ted."

"Not me," said Ted, who was waiting for his breakfast.

Mrs Polderrick went to her own front gate and leant her arms on the sharp points of the wattle saplings. "Mornin', Miz Thomas. Thee's up betimes."

"Mornin', Miz Polderrick," Polly answered, straightening her back and looking across the track.

" 'Ow're 'ee doin'?"

"Fine, I thank 'ee."

"Movin' fence?"

"Yes, movin' fence," replied Polly, and calmly went on with her work.

Joe Penworthy, coming off shift, stopped beside her a few minutes later, put down his crib-bag and began relighting his pipe. "Movin' fence, Miz Thomas?" he said, when the pipe was well alight.

"Yes, movin' fence, Mr Penworthy," said Polly, and waited for him to speak again.

He picked up his crib-bag and started off towards the crossing. "Well, thee's got a nice day for un," he said, with a look at the pale blue autumn sky.

When Nathan came off shift he walked in at the gate and took two steps towards the door, then stopped, looked about and opened his blue eyes wide. "Polly," he called, as he opened the door, "Polly, where 'ee to?"

"Well," said Polly, coming forward, "what now, Nat?"

"Thees 'ave shifted the fence?"

"I 'ave!" This with a hint of pride.

"Land o' Goshen, oo gave un leave?"

"Nobody gave un, so I just took un."

"What'll cap'n say?" said Nathan, in a hushed voice.

"If cap'n da say aught I'll up an' tell un I 'ad to 'ave me garden an' 'twere easier to move fence than 'ouse, any day."

Nathan rubbed a calloused hand across his chin and looked at Polly, and there was awe as well as admiration in his eyes.

The house they were furnishing piece by piece from the shop of a cabinet-maker in Taylor Street, Kadina. Polly yearned for cedar furniture like Ellen's, and a sofa with horse-hair upholstery, but, because she was determined not to use any of the precious hundred pounds in the lawyer's safe in Adelaide, she decided on plain deal chairs and tables and narrow canvas beds. When her lovely old knitted quilts were placed on the beds and the rag rugs she had made in St Ives were put on the kitchen floor, she cheered up and told Nathan she would not change with any other woman in Kadina.

Nathan bought a little goat for her, and there was milk for them all. Almost every family on the mines owned a goat, cows being too rare and too expensive. Goats were smelly, but the milk was pure and rich, and Polly vowed that goat's milk was more nourishing than cow's. She would point to Richard, toddling about the house in his little tartan skirts with braid on the hem, and would feel his sturdy limbs and kiss his firm cheeks.

"Don't tell me goat's milk idden best for childern. I knaw 'tis!" It was a belief she held until her death.

As there was a Bible Christian chapel in Wallaroo Mines Polly attended there, and took up her work in the church as if it had never been interrupted by change of scene, and she was gladly welcomed as a member of the Methodist New Connexion.

There were three Methodist churches in Wallaroo Mines at this time, all in a straight row and only a short distance apart; in fact the Wesleyan and Bible Christian Churches stood almost side by side. A mile away, in the township of Kadina, there were also three chapels for these branches of Methodism: the Wesleyans, the Primitives and the Bible Christians.

Polly was very happy in her cottage and, sitting in the rocking-chair that Nathan and she had bought so carefully and holding Richard in her arms, she would often lie back and let the warm autumn sun, with its last hint of summer, beat down upon her as she sat rocking with closed eyes and thinking of her old home in St Ives by the sea.

She heard every month or so from her youngest sister, Ruth. Her mother, who could neither read nor write, would sometimes draw a little scene in an uncertain, childish fashion and enclose it in the letter to her daughters in Australia. Once she had drawn a picture that Polly could recognize as being meant for their old home: a narrow, quaint house with four windows, two upstairs and two down, and a door between the two lower ones. The scrawly marks by the door were for the fuchsia bush she knew. She recognized the water-butt, more from its relation to the house than its shape; but what puzzled her most was the upstairs window, the one on the left. It had been the room that Polly, Ellen and Hester, a young sister who had died in adolescence, had always shared. Polly's mother had darkened in this window until it was just a black square, while the other windows, though also square in shape, were not filled in with markings. Polly puzzled long over this dark window, and cried very bitterly when she at last understood her mother's meaning. A great wave of homesickness swept over her, and she longed for the sound of her mother's voice and the sight of that old house that had been her home, and in a moment her new whitewashed cottage, the homely quilts and rugs, the new kitchen clock with the painted glass front, and even Nathan and Richard themselves had faded away, and Polly was just a lonely child crying for the mother she would never see again.

Ellen wrote once a week, her letters short, but full of the happy excitement of being a married woman with a home and husband and a baby coming soon. Ellen was well; her state of health was not worrying her at all. The ailments of other women in her condition seemed to pass her by; and after a while, as each weekly letter brought only happy messages and reassurances, Polly ceased to worry about her.

Polly herself dug the ground for the garden plots and planted the precious slips and cuttings that she had brought with her from Adelaide. She bordered the paths with empty bottles which she buried, neck down, in the grey sandy soil, allowing only the rounded end of each to show above the level of the garden bed. It had been a slow and laborious business gathering bottles enough to border her garden, but by means of constant soliciting among her new friends and hastily finishing off everything in bottles that comprised her own kitchen stores, she managed at last to complete the artistic design to her utmost satisfaction.

Nathan was frankly amazed at the collection of bottles Polly had got together. He admired the finished effect—who wouldn't?—but he scratched his head in perplexity and asked, " 'Ow did 'ee manage un, Polly? Neighbours'll think I be an 'eavy soaker or summat. Parson'll 'ave a word to say to 'ee about that. Thee da knaw I never touched drop nor never shall, but all that pack o' gin bottles'll take a power o' explainin'. 'Ow ever many castor-oil ones did 'ee get?"

"Twenty, if there be one," said Polly proudly. "Look 'ere, Nat." And she pointed to some of the upturned bottle ends. "See them there ones? Well, they two be soothin' syrup, that one be toothache balm, this 'ere row be Roger's Royal Liniment ones from old Miz Clampett's and five more liniment ones o' yourn, Nat. But see 'ere, this one be what I calls the bobby o' the lot." She pointed to the end of a small, blue, triangular based bottle which had pride of place at one corner of the garden bed. "Come close an' I'll tell 'ee," she said. "That be the bottle that Father Ryan brought the 'oly water in to Miz Flinn's babby. I didden knaw 'er but I knawed they was Irishers, an' when I 'eared tell that their babby were sick I up an' took down a basin o' gruel. They be terrible poor, Nat. The poor little babby were near dead when I got there, an' priest were just goin' off. 'Wait there, missus,' says she to me, 'I dunno oo 'ee be, but no one sets foot in 'ere till I sweeps out after 'im!' An' she made the dirt fly off the path with 'er broom. Then she rushes in agin an' comes out wi' this bottle, an' she throws un after priest an' it smashes agin fence, an' she come on out to me an' puts 'er arms on me shoulders. 'Come in, me dear,' says she, 'an' give me an 'elpin' 'and, for I'm Cornish borned though I be wedded to Mike Flinn. I be 'alf crazed an' don't knaw what I be doin'; an' oh, missus, me little babby's dyin', an' they say as 'e'll go to 'ell for I won't 'ave un sprinkled an' mumbo-jumboed over. No, no, I never will!' So when I seed 'er dear mite so peaked an' thin I bade un warm up the gruel, an' I fed un, an' we kept lavin' im with plain cold water from the tank, an' afore night come the tender dear were sleepin' an' all the fever gone from un. Come evenin'-time I 'ad to go 'ome meself an', goin' out the gate, I just bobbed down an' picked up the 'oly-water bottle. Its neck were broken, but that didden make no diff'ence to me, an' I like un now, best o' the lot!"

From Polly's front door she looked out towards **Kadina**. This little township, nourished by the mines, was flinging out its bounds and extending itself into streets of houses and short rows of shops. In front of Polly the Matta flat, surrounding the Matta-Matta mine, stretched out towards the thick mallee scrub beyond. To the right of her were the Wallaroo Mines themselves. From the tall, stone engine-houses which stood by the mouth of each shaft and held the Cornish engines a continuous noise arose. The stone chimneys leading from the cylindrical metal furnaces at the side of each engine-house belched smoke continuously, and the rattle of the skips bringing the ore to the surface hardly ceased by day or night.

Never before had Polly known the life of a miner's wife for, shortly after their marriage in Cornwall and before they had settled down, the Pentoll mine, where Nathan had been working at this time, closed down, and he and Polly had returned to St Ives, Polly to take up her work in the millinery shop again and Nathan to work as builder's labourer when such work was to be had. Nathan was very contented now at Wallaroo Mines and, after a short period of working "tribute" with Ben Wilson and Harry Pearce, he gradually reverted to contract work and was receiving at that time two pounds per week in wages, paid to him monthly. Polly was as well pleased as anybody in all Kadina and Wallaroo Mines together, and as happy as any other miner's wife, whose life, like her man's, is run in shifts, and who, like he, must oftentimes turn night into day and day into night, nor worry about that other night, always so close at hand in the dark shafts and the treacherous tunnels of the mines.

When the summons to come to Ellen arrived from Peter, Polly had known for three months that she herself was with child, and the prospect of the coach journey to Adelaide filled her with apprehension. "But," she thought, "if I can set out from the old country wi' Richard in me an' can bear un at sea in rain an' storm, nothin' can 'appen to me on dry land that'll cap that!"

Richard she left with Ben Wilson's wife, who had a neat little cottage over by the Primitive Methodist Church, and Nathan was left to do for himself.

It was towards the end of October, and the coach was full. People who had business in Adelaide had left it until this time of the year, for the Queen's son, His Royal Highness the Duke of Edinburgh, was expected to arrive in South Australia towards the end of October or the beginning of November. Already several false reports of His Highness's arrival had reached the Peninsula towns, and the fact that these reports were soon proved to be premature only seemed to create more excitement, and all who could afford the journey and were sure of accommodation when they arrived made the trip to Adelaide to see the duke.

When the train, with which the mail-coach had linked up, arrived in Adelaide Polly alighted tired and with a dizzy headache. She longed for nothing more than a rest in a clean white bed in a quiet room, and a cup of strong hot tea. She looked about for Peter but could not see him, so she sat down on one of the station seats, put her feet on her carpet-bag and wished she could just fall asleep where she was.

Suddenly she saw Mrs Lillywhite, whom she had known in the Methodist chapel in Franklin Street, and Polly called to her.

"Miz Lillywhite, 'ow are 'ee?"

The woman turned about, and ran to Polly with a relieved look on her face. She did not seem surprised to see her, and Polly thought suddenly that Mrs Lillywhite must be there to meet her. As that thought came to her another followed it, and Polly sprang to her feet, her face white.

"Summat 'ave gone wrong!" she said, her eyes searching Mrs Lillywhite's face. "Be there aught the matter with our Ellen?" But she knew before the words had left her mouth that there was something very much wrong with Ellen.

Mrs Lillywhite led Polly back to the seat and, with an arm about her, told her what to expect. The two women cried openly for a few moments, then Polly rose and, clutching the carpet-bag, said to Mrs Lillywhite in a strong, firm voice:

"Don't be afeared, ma'am. If Ellen be still livin' when

I da see 'er I'll keep 'er 'ere." She hit her bosom with her fist and repeated several times, "She'll live! Ellen 'ave got to live!"

There was a cab to be hired on North Terrace, and Polly and Mrs Lillywhite climbed aboard, and while the cabman, urged by Polly, drove at a fast pace through the streets Mrs Lillywhite told her for what she must be prepared in the home in Brown Street.

"It came on suddenly, my dear, yesterday, and Mr Til-brook put your sister to bed and sent a neighbour for the doctor and a midwife, and he also sent for me. My dear, the baby was born—a little girl—but the doctor had had to fight so for her life and the life of Mrs Tilbrook that in the finish one of them had to live and one to die. So it was the mother that was saved, but now, in spite of that and in spite of all that doctors or nurse or any of us can do, it seems the mother may go too."

"Oh, oh!" sobbed Polly. "Me tender dear, me little Ellen!"

"You see," said Mrs Lillywhite in a broken voice, "she bleeds so. Nothing can stop it, and if it goes on nobody on earth can save her."

"She allus were a bleeder," cried Polly. "If she'd 'a' cut a finger 'twould bleed hour 'pon hour."

"Did she think to tell her doctor that?" asked Mrs Lillywhite.

"Doctor? Rubbish! 'Twere I goin' to be doctor to 'er. That's what I be 'ere for. Oh, if only I 'ad come afore! This woulden 'ave 'appened then, I knaw."

"My dear," soothed Mrs Lillywhite, "don't think you should have come sooner or even that things would have been different if you had been here, for the doctor told me to-day that your sister could never have had this child alive. She was too small-boned. I can't remember his words, but he made it plain to me at the time. Don't cry, my dear! There is a lot for you to do, and you must be brave."

Polly stepped from the cab and walked towards the door of Peter's house as in a dream. How long ago it seemed since they had first seen this cottage—how long ago, and how far away that time! She hesitated at the step as if she were dazed, and Mrs Lillywhite reached across her and gently opened the door.

The living-room was the same. The sunlight played on the warm wood of the cedar chiffonier; the same kettle bubbled on the same stove as that before which Ellen and Peter had been married. Mrs Lillywhite untied the bows of Polly's little straw hat and placed it on the table, then, turning Polly about gently by the shoulders, led her to the door of Ellen's bedroom and softly opened it.

Ellen, as white as the sheets that covered her, lay on the big new cedar bedstead, which was raised at the foot and tilted back; the bed Peter had made for their marriage-bed. And, holding Ellen's blue-veined hand, he now sat beside her in the cool dimness of the room.

"Polly, Polly!" called Ellen, so softly that it wrung Polly's heart to hear.

"Ellen, me dear, me little dear!" Polly cried, as softly, and ran lightly to the bed and kissed Ellen's white fore-head and smoothed back her fine, black hair.

Peter stood up and, putting his arm about Polly, looked deep into her eyes. "It *will* be all right now, Polly, won't it? Won't it Polly?" he insisted.

And as Polly nodded and said very gently, " 'Ush, 'ush! Ellen's all right now I be 'ere, Peter," she saw the strained, white look in his face and a frightened, lost look in his eyes, and in her nostrils was that sickly sweet, terrifying smell of blood—so much blood.

In spite of all the doctor could do, the continuous cold compresses, the raising of the foot of the bed and the encouraging presence of Polly, Ellen died that night, and Polly and Peter spoke very tenderly and very pitifully with her at the end, but, strange as it may seem, they parted from her without tears.

She lay as if she slept, and Peter, rising from his knees beside her bed in the early chill of morning, said to Polly in a strange, hard voice, "She lies as if she's still asleep. Stay with her Polly. Don't leave her. I'm going to work."

Polly ran to him. "Peter, art mad? Ellen dead, an' 'ee to be talkin' o' goin' to work! What ails 'ee?"

"Nothing but a broken heart," he answered coldly, and opened the front door. "If any one should want me they'll find me at the shop in Rundle Street, making my wife's coffin." He shook Polly off when she would have detained him, and walked away down the street.

Left behind in the house, Polly gave way to terrible weeping, and was so exhausted that Mrs Lillywhite put her to bed in the little back room where Ellen's baby lay in the wooden cradle under a white towel; and Polly slept and, for one short hour, forgot her sorrow. All the rest of the day she sat in the room with her dead sister, just as she had promised Peter she would do; but it was not until eight o'clock that night that Peter came home, and with him his employer, riding in a mourning-carriage with Ellen's coffin between them.

Even then, when Ellen and her child—whom she had said was to be called Mary Ellen, after herself and Polly—had been laid in the wooden casket that Peter had made for them, Peter would not set the hour for the funeral. It seemed to Polly that, though he knew Ellen to be dead, he would not believe it in his heart. Even the minister could not prevail upon Peter to name a time.

"It must be to-morrow," they said kindly. But Peter turned his back, and his features writhed in a pitiful manner.

"Peter, me dear, do 'ee think she mayn't be gone?" said Polly at last in a choking whisper to him.

He answered her calmly, but in a low voice. "I know her life must be gone, Polly. I know that must be so. But I wonder about her spirit. I can't help thinking her spirit is still there. She was so young, Polly. Everything can't be all over and done with for her. I can't believe that the something that made her laugh and speak and live is really gone. Don't you understand, any of you, that I want to wait until—until I'm sure!"

"Thees da want to wait to be sure she be—really dead?"

"Yes."

"Oh!" said Polly, aghast.

"Are you afraid too, Polly?" he said, turning quickly upon her, his whole body trembling. "Are you afraid to see the proof of the spirit's going and the body's end?"

"Not afeared for meself," said Polly, quietly, "but afeared

for thee, Peter. If I stay by Ellen, will 'ee trust me to tell 'ee when I be sure the time be come?"

"Do you mean it, Polly? God knows I'm afraid—afraid of what I might see. Oh, Ellen, my little Ellen, what's to become of me without you?" And he leant his forehead against the wall of the living-room, but his eyes were dry and hard.

So Polly stayed in the death-chamber until the morning of the next day when, with a firm hand, she turned down the white sheet above the face of what had once been Ellen and, in spite of what she saw there, had love enough and courage enough to say, "Good-bye, me purty dear," and, putting back the sheet, went out to tell Peter.

Ellen and her baby were buried at West Terrace on 31 October 1867, in the cemetery that lies beside Holdfast Bay Road, which runs to the seaside town of Glenelg.

The little funeral cortège had reached the junction of South and West Terraces and the Holdfast Bay Road when suddenly a guard of the Volunteer Cavalry, one hundred and twenty strong, led by Colonel Matthews and heralded by a fanfare of bugles, announced the passing-by of His Royal Highness the Duke of Edinburgh on his way from Glenelg to Adelaide.

The horses of the funeral carriage tossed their black-plumed heads as the cheers arose from the crowd of people who had gathered there to see the duke ride by. Some stood on the steps of the mourning-coach and some on the hubs of its wheels, the better to see the gay procession and to glimpse the figure of the Queen's son on this the first visit of royalty to South Australia.

"God bless the Queen!" they shouted, and the duke, hearing, raised his white-bandaged hand in salute, and again the people cheered.

CHAPTER VI

In the week that followed Ellen's death Polly, while she stayed in Adelaide with Peter, suffered very greatly. Her tender heart was torn with the sudden shock of parting, and no one could dissuade her from the thought that, had she come before, this tragedy could not have happened.

The doctor had tried to make Polly see reason on two occasions, but had received little thanks from her for his pains. When he had come on the day after Ellen's death to give his certificate and Polly had again bewailed the fact that if she had been there things would have been different, he lost his customary calm and, raising his voice a little in the darkened house, had said succinctly:

"Madam, I respect your grief, but you may keep your opinions. Because God saw fit to let you bear and be delivered of a child in safety gives you no divine right to think yourself an oracle on child-birth. When you contradict me, madam, and deny my ability as an accoucheur you pit your personal experience against the knowledge of the whole College of Physicians, of which I am a member. When I say nothing could have saved that young woman I mean nothing—neither God nor man!"

"Thee's reckonin' without a lovin' sister, sir," said Polly, unabashed, her voice trembling but her head high.

"Pshaw!" said the doctor contemptuously; and then, as if recollecting himself and determining to be a little pleasanter, he added, "Your courage, my dear, outweighs your common sense. Not all the sisterly love in the world can widen pelvic bones nor stop persistent haemorrhage."

Polly did not understand that, but if she had she still would have said he lied.

For a week she stayed with Peter, caring for him and his home and seeing to that unhappy business of sorting and packing Ellen's clothes. They were to go home with Polly. Peter wished it, and Polly was too careful to want to give them away and too tender-hearted to think of destroying them. Peter, dazed and unhappy, wandered aimlessly about the house, and Polly, looking up from her work, would sometimes see his quiet figure leaning against his bedroom door, looking sadly into the empty room.

The church people rallied round them in their sorrow, and prayers for the lightening of their burden of sadness were offered up in chapel. Peter and his minister talked long and earnestly in the little study of the new manse in Whitmore Square, and a little of the icy hardness of Peter's bereaved heart began to melt away.

Two days before Polly had arranged to leave for Wallaroo Mines he came to her and, seated at the table, they talked about what was to become of him. It was late, and Peter had just returned from a long walk, in company with the minister, to Norwood, a pretty little village several miles to the east of Adelaide. There, beside the flowing waters of the creek, in the dappled shadow of a group of white-trunked gum-trees, the minister—himself a sick man and already marked with the signs of an approaching and an early end to his labours—had spoken from experience, and with a strange prophetic knowledge of life and death and the mercy of God.

"Polly," said Peter that night, across the width of the table, "I've made up my mind to leave Australia and go back home."

"What," said Polly, "leave all this?" And she gave a comprehensive gesture with her hands as if to include the house and everything in it, the little workshop in Rundle Street and the new-made grave in the West Terrace cemetery.

"Yes, leave it all and go back to England." He spoke with finality.

"Oh, Peter, lad, think 'ard on't afore 'ee does anathin'," said Polly, genuinely distressed. "Cussen 'ee see 'twill be as 'ard for 'ee to bear if 'ee goes or stays?" she added, understandingly. But, after Peter had begun to tell what was in his mind, she became quieter and listened till the end.

When Peter accompanied Polly to the train two days later she put her arms about his neck and kissed him twice.

"One from me an' one from Ellen," she said. "I'll never see 'ee more, Peter, but me 'eart's full with rememberin' what 'ee've done for we as love thee. Oo woulda thought that all the joy would end so soon? . . . What a pity Peter, what a pity!"

Polly's second child, a son, was born at Wallaroo Mines on 22 April 1868, and Polly, drowsy with relief from the past hours of agony, caught a glimpse of the damp streaks of dark hair on the top of his head and saw the shape of his little brow.

"Call un Allen," she whispered to the midwife, Mrs Nankervis, "for 'e's the spittin' image o' me brother Allen what went to sea when I were a bit of a cheeld. 'E 'ad 'air as black as a iron pot."

"This one's 'air's black as two pots!" laughed fat Mrs Nankervis, slapping the baby's buttocks with the flat of her hand as she held him aloft by his little heels, "an' 'e 'ave got a cry on un like a dyin' winnard. Canst 'ear un, missus?"

"I be glad 'e be alive," said Polly wistfully, remembering.

Mrs Nankervis swaddled the crying child into a little red-faced flannel bundle, then laid him in the cradle which had once held Richard, now a little lad of two years and a half, and which had also held the dead child of Ellen and Peter.

Polly, months ago, had secretly envied Ellen her fine carved bedstead and her houseful of hand-made cedar furniture, but now she had no need to envy, for Ellen had the only cedar bed she would ever need, and Peter had sent to Polly at Wallaroo Mines all the furniture that had been in his house in Brown Street.

Peter was already aboard the ship *Great Britain* and on his way back to England where, at Shebbear College in Devonshire, he hoped to begin his training for the work which he felt his God had prepared for him: missionary work among the heathen in China. Already missionaries had been sent to the East from this Methodist Evangelical

College, and news of the progress of their work had reached even the far limits of the colonies.

"Poor lad," Polly had said, when Nathan had read Peter's last letter to them, realizing that the plans he had spoken of in his living-room in Brown Street were really decided upon, "do 'e think in 'is 'eart 'e can do more good savin' a Chinaman for the Lord than savin' a Cornishman—or even an Irisher, for a matter o' that?" Polly lifted up her hand. " 'Ark!" she said, and she and Nathan listened to the loud shouts and singing of a group of drunken miners walking home along the tram line from the Kadina Hotel and making an uncouth noise in the dark. "There be 'arvests 'ere aplenty, ready for any man's reapin'. A body dussen 'ave to go to China to start bringin' in the sheaves for the Lord."

" 'Go ye unto all the nations an' preach the Gospel'," Nathan said.

But Polly only smiled sadly and answered very gently, " 'E be runnin' away from 'is own thoughts, Nat, an' China seemed a tidy way off to run to. . . . Better fit 'e'd stayed," she added after a while.

Richard celebrated his third birthday by coming out in a mass of red spots all over his fat little body. It was measles. Many other children on the mines were in a similar condition, and Polly was very concerned for the safety of her seven-months-old Allen. She was unlike most of the miners' wives, who encouraged their unaffected children to mix with those affected and "make 'aste an' catch un an' get un over", for she carried Allen to Mrs Ben Wilson and asked her to care for him until Richard was well again. Mrs Wilson's two children, Cora and Emily, had both had measles in a preceding epidemic, and as a result Cora had been very deaf ever since. So Mrs Wilson commended Polly's good sense, took Allen to her ample bosom, made him a cradle from two upturned chairs and hung a little rag bag filled with damp bread and sugar to one of the chair legs. This Allen sucked and was perfectly content. He was partly weaned, but Polly, reluctant to forgo entirely the sweet pleasure of nursing him, would hurry down to the Wilson's in the late afternoon while Richard slept, and would feed and cosset her baby for a short half hour.

It was on one of these hurried trips, her pink sun-bonnet on her head and her grey print dress covered by her voluminous white calico apron with its little bib and capacious pocket, that she noticed a stir about the mouth of one of the big shafts where several men were bending over a figure on the ground. Two men ran from the engine-house and joined the group as she came abreast of them, and the significance of this caused her to clutch her heart and run toward them. She remembered with a great surge of relief that Nathan was at home asleep in the big bed; but this did not slacken her feet, and she breathlessly pushed through the cluster of men before they could stop her.

"What is it?" she panted. "Oose man?"

They tried to push her aside, but she had seen the crushed and blood-soaked form at their feet, and her face became as white as her apron. The head of the dead man was flattened grotesquely, and one side of his face was an indescribable and bloody mass.

"Oh! Oh! Oh!" shuddered Polly, and fell back a pace, then, snatching off her apron before those about her knew what she was doing, she threw it over the horrible sight.

"Get along with 'ee," said one man brusquely. "This idden no place for women."

But Polly stood firm and, looking up into his grimy, sweat-stained face, her eyes wide, asked, "Oo is 'e?"

"Joe Brodribb," said the miner. "'At's oo 'e *were*!"

Men from underground came hurrying from the shaft in twos and threes and crowded about the prostrate figure.

"What's happened?" shouted the mine manager, joining the men. He knelt and looked at the man under the red-stained apron. "Oh, my God!" he cried, thickly, as he stood up. Then he looked at the miners. "Quick, how did it happen?"

"Well, cap'n, sir, it were like this 'ere," began one of the men.

Another interrupted. "Joe were workin' stope wi' me, an' things was goin' 'long fine, when——" he gulped and shivered, "when, sudden-like, a great piece o' rock came——"

"Cap'n, cap'n," put in Polly, breaking across the man's agitated speech, "bettn't I go tell 'is missus?"

Nobody had thought of this, and all turned towards Polly.

"I'll run all the way, an' thees can come on be'ind. I'll do me best," she added over her shoulder, then slipped away through the crowd.

With relief the men watched her go, and no one called after her, for no man present wanted the task of being the first to break to Joe Brodribb's missus the news of what had happened to her man. That was a woman's job, anyway.

Away Polly ran. She jumped across the narrow, timbered-up drain which carried away the water from the mines, skirted the treacherous open costeen-pits which had been sunk to find the direction of the lode, and ran on across the Matta Flat towards a small group of miners' white-washed cottages clustered like mushrooms in a clearing of the mallee. Joe Brodribb's house and Dick Turbill's stood apart from the main group, sheltered by a patch of wattles. Dick lived there alone now, since his wife had been taken down to the North Terrace lunatic asylum two months previously.

Polly had her eye on Joe Brodribb's chimney top, and she ran across the flat holding her print skirt high and showing her long white calico drawers and grey flannel petticoat. She picked her way across the slippery patches of mud and among the greenish stones which sometimes stuck through her little boots, and only slackened her pace when she was within a few yards of Joe's home.

It came over her then that she must use all the kindliness and woman's understanding she possessed in this unhappy task before her. She remembered suddenly what people said Lydia Brodribb was and what she, Polly, at the moment when she first had set eyes upon this woman, had known her to be.

She was a tall woman of thirty years, the same age as Polly herself; but there was a mystery about her as old as the grave and, to Polly, as terrible. Lydia's skin was creamy white—like Ellen's, Polly had once thought—and her hair was black and thick, and her black brows met above her eyes in a long, faintly curved line. Her eyes were large and dark, and in them was a secret for women to guess at and men to fathom. Passing her in the street the women looked away, but the men looked at and furtively after her.

In her inmost, vulgar little heart, Polly had a name for this woman—"She-dog! Bitch!" And she used the term in its literal sense and attributed to Lydia a primitive attraction, an animal fascination for men.

There were women on the mines who believed that Lydia Brodribb did not spend the night alone when her husband was underground on night shift, and Polly had heard these rumours over cups of tea in neighbours' kitchens.

Polly opened the sapling gate and ran around the house to the back door, spurred on by the thought of the dead man's companions who soon would be following with fuller details of the tragedy.

"By this time," thought Polly, " 'e be taken to the dry, an' cap'n'll be sendin' Joe's mates to tell 'is missus. I must keep me wits 'bout me an' break it to 'er gentle."

Gone were all the thoughts of Lydia Brodribb's strange fascination. Polly thought of her only as a woman who was about to be told that she was widowed.

As Polly lifted her hand to knock on the closed door at the back of the house she heard a woman's voice within. At the sound of Lydia's voice Polly's heart gave a frightened bound as she thought of the news she was bearing, and she began to tremble with a nervous dread of the ordeal before her but, remembering the need for haste, she gathered her strength and, calling out in a panic, "Miz Brodribb, be 'ee there?" pushed at the door with both hands and almost fell headlong into the kitchen.

There were two people in the kitchen—Lydia Brodribb and a man. Neither had known of Polly's presence until she had called out and burst so suddenly into the room, and for a half-minute's space all three stared at one another across the kitchen; then the man, turning away quickly with the merest glance at Lydia, hurried into the next room, and in another moment they heard the sound of a door's opening and closing.

Lydia's great black eyes narrowed as she looked at Polly and, very calmly, her eyes still on Polly, she began to button up the bodice of her dress. Polly seemed rooted to the floor.

She could neither move nor speak, and it was not until Lydia had finished with the buttons and had begun to talk that Polly could as much as stir, and then, at the first sound of Lydia's voice, she turned to run from the kitchen.

Lydia, as quick as a swallow, darted across the room and, grabbing Polly by the arm, wrenched her inside and closed the door behind her.

"Well," said Lydia again, "what do you want here?"

Polly twisted her hands in her grey print dress, but was too upset and too indignantly and virtuously shocked to say anything.

"I know you, Polly Thomas," Lydia went on, "and it wasn't your man who was here, so what right had you to come ramping into my——"

"Me man!" gasped Polly. "Me man be 'ere? Thee's a varmint! Thee knaw me man Nathan never set foot near 'ere." She raised her hands in a passion of righteous wrath, ready to tear the smiling-faced harlot's hair from her head or scratch the smooth white skin of her neck, but her arms suddenly dropped to her sides and she leant back against the door. With hands on her wildly beating heart she watched, as if fascinated, the woman before her.

"Well," said Lydia, one arm on the door and looking down on Polly. "What are you going to do now?"

Polly's eyes never left the other's face, but tears came into them and her lips began to quiver.

"Frightened of me?" Lydia laughed down. Then her voice suddenly changed. "My God, I'll frighten you," she said in a low, tense voice, "if ever you say a word about what you saw a minute ago. Remember! You know Dick Turbill when you see him, and that was him. His wife's away, and there's going to be no trouble. . . . See?"

Polly continued to stare at her and Lydia, growing uncomfortable under this quiet scrutiny, took her arm away from the door, but kept the toe of her boot against it as a hint to Polly that she was not yet at liberty to go.

"What is the matter with you, missus? What are you staring and staring at me like that for?" she demanded. She drew a deep breath, and the tightly buttoned bodice of her pink frock strained across her full bosom. She lifted back her head proudly and, putting one hand on her hip and with the other hand making a slow sinuous movement from shoulder to waist, narrowed her great eyes and smiled slowly at Polly.

Polly caught her lower lip between her teeth, and a pulse deep in her body throbbed, and the tears dried in her eyes.

Lydia walked to the table and, thrusting her hands behind her, leaned her weight against it. "You are frightened, aren't you, Mrs Thomas? You've never seen a good-looking woman like me, have you? Look hard. Go on!" She thrust out a foot, clad in a buttoned black boot. "There's an ankle for you. See, I can span it with a finger and thumb. And my fingers? Look, not short and knotted like yours, and red and broken-nailed. Why can't you other women look after yourselves and learn a trick or two? Then your men wouldn't come creeping here to me to watch mine."

"Me man never come within a mile o' this door," said Polly, gaining her voice in a hurry, "an' thee da knaw it."

"Well," laughed Lydia, who had enjoyed baiting Polly, "what are *you* doing here, then?"

She watched Polly's face for a moment. Then, as with some women's intuition, she stiffened and stood still, and at that moment there came a dull, heavy knocking upon the door of the other room.

Lydia was at Polly's side in a flash, her face close to hers and ashen pale. "What is it? You did come to tell me something. You did, didn't you?" Her voice rose to a scream. "What *is* the matter with you, woman? Can't you speak?"

Polly shuddered and tried to say something, and in the stillness the knock, insistent and not to be denied, came again.

"Go 'long an' answer it," said Polly at last. "Don't 'ee knaw what 'tis? Thee be miner's missus. Can't 'ee guess?"

The other woman's eyes widened with horror. "Joe!"

"Yes," said Polly, brutally. " 'E's dead, an' they be bringin' the news 'ome to 'ee. Answer door thyself, for I must be off. I've a sick cheeld to 'ome." And she opened the back door and, seeing a gap in the sapling fence, slipped through and ran stumblingly home across the flat.

Nathan did not go underground that evening, nor did any of the other miners; and after Polly had told him all that had happened he comforted her, and tucked her into bed himself, and brought in a basin of bread and milk, and sat beside the bed while she ate it.

"There's naught so good as milk-sop with a bit o' salt on un to make a body feel comfor'ble," said Nathan, taking great pleasure in seeing Polly eat the bread and milk.

" 'Tis the first bit I've tasted for many a long year that I never cooked meself," said Polly, licking the last little piece of bread from the edge of the bowl with her tongue. "I've eat the lot," she added, putting back the spoon, "an' I don't feel bad no more, so I better get up agin."

"No," said Nathan. "Bide there an' I'll read to 'ee."

He brought his favourite book, and they sat for an hour, she in the big bed and he in the rocking-chair; and Richard, now fed and quiet in the back room, heard Nathan's sonorous voice sounding through the cottage, and fell asleep to the rhythm of the Psalms.

Suddenly there was a tapping at the window, and a voice that Nathan recognized called from outside, "Nathan Thomas, if thee's 'ome, come out. We've summat to say to 'ee."

Polly was out of bed almost before he had finished speaking, and was scrambling into her clothes.

" 'E didden call you, Pol," said Nathan, getting up from his chair.

"Sh!" said Polly, wrestling with her stay-bodice. "What would 'is missus say if she thought I were in bed this hour o' day, an' not sick? She'd think I be sluggard."

"Thee da just want to knaw what's goin' on," Nathan called back, with rare insight, as he opened the door and went outside.

Polly heard the men talking for some time as they stood by the front gate in the dusk. She heard the different tones of their voices and knew there were three men, and by and by Nathan opened the door and came into the living-room. Polly peered over his shoulder at the two men standing by the gate and saw they were Newman Hobbs and a Charlie Pearce, both of whom she knew by sight.

"Well," she said, "what be it?"

Nathan's brow was criss-crossed, and he rubbed up his hair with a heavy hand.

"Well?" said Polly, waiting.

"Polly, 'tis like this 'ere. There's trouble up to Brodribb's, an' nobody can't do nothin' wi' Miz Brodribb. She've been carryin' on summat awful since they brought Joe's body to 'ome."

"She've got plenty to carry on 'bout," said Polly, calmly. "What's it to do with we?"

"Well, she won't listen to no person, Pol, an' she've shut the door on poor Joe an' won't let no one in to 'im, an' she's screechin' mad."

"What's she screechin' for?" put in Polly.

Nathan rubbed his chin hard. "She's screechin' for thee, Pol," he said at last.

Polly drew herself up, and Nathan went on hastily, "Now, look 'ere, me dear, thee dussen 'ave to go if 'ee don't want to, but Charlie Pearce 'e says to me 'tis summat cruel to 'ear 'er goin' on like that wi' poor Joe dead in the next room."

"Well, she can screech till doomsday for aught I care," said Polly, loudly.

Charlie Pearce put his head in at the door. "Come on, Miz Thomas, do! Joe were a friend o' mine, an' though I didden 'ave no time for 'is missus—an' I won't say she liked me for that—I can't stand for 'im to be lyin' in there wi' nothin' bein' done for 'im an' 'is woman yellin' out for you, Miz Thomas, at the top of 'er voice. 'Get Polly Thomas,' she says to me. 'Tell 'er I want 'er. Tell 'er I must see 'er. Nobody goes in to Joe till I've seen Miz Polly Thomas.' That's what she said, so put on thy bonnet an' come, do!"

So, leaving Nathan with Richard, Polly went with the two men across the flat, wondering what Lydia had to say to her of such import that it held up all the ritual of death.

When she entered the Brodribb kitchen, she hardly recognized the dishevelled woman standing by the table. The room was half filled with men and their wives—all neighbours or workmates of Joe Brodribb—who had come from either curiosity, kindliness or sense of duty to see what use they might be in this house where death was. The women were feeling an unaccustomed superiority over the harassed woman at the table: there was no arrogance about her now, and very little beauty. The men were standing a little behind their wives, curious and a little sheepish, and wishing mightily they had not come at all.

Lydia ran to Polly, and her face resumed some of its old disdain. She turned to those already in the kitchen. "Let me talk to Polly Thomas alone. Go along with you, every one. I want to speak to her, and I want nobody in my home while I do it. I know you meant kindly by coming, and some of you," she glanced at the women, "who wouldn't care to talk to me a while back are glad to be here to watch me now I'm widowed. But I won't talk about that now, though I know it's true right enough. If any of you men want to go in to Joe, you can do it when Polly Thomas and I have finished what we've got to say."

When the room was empty of all except Lydia and herself Polly, very self-possessed, seated herself at the table and stuck her firm little chin into the air. Lydia came to her side and, smoothing back her own untidy hair, began to speak.

"I sent for you to ask you to lie low about what you saw here this afternoon. Give me a chance, Mrs Thomas—and give Joe, there, a chance," she pleaded. "He was decent to me, and I was a dog to him." She wandered restlessly about the room. "I'm bad all through, but nobody found me out till now. Joe wouldn't have believed it if you'd told him what you saw, and now he's in there dead. And soon all the mines will be talking about me and laughing at him—laughing at Joe, and calling him a cuckoo and saying he was a fool." She turned to Polly, and her face was twisted with a sudden pang of remembrance. "Joe was mad about me, and swelled up with pride when the men admired me. Poor little fool! See? I know he was a fool, Mrs Thomas, and so does everybody; but they've never known for sure just how big a fool I'd made him! Don't say anything, Polly. Don't say anything, for God's sake—for Joe's sake, not for mine."

Polly looked long at Lydia, and then she spoke gently. "Lydia Brodribb, I can't promise not to tell a soul, for I've told me good man already. But don't worrit, me Nathan'd never let fall a word, me dear, for I never 'eared un say a unkind thing in all me days."

"And you?" said Lydia, coming closer, "you'll promise not to tell? You'll give me your solemn word, won't you?"

"There be work to be done," said Polly firmly, rising and going to the stove where the kettle was gently boiling, "an' when that's finished I'll give 'ee me gospel word never to lay tongue to what I seed in this 'ouse to-day."

Lydia bent her head quickly and hid her face in her sleeve, and Polly, looking at her, would have liked to put an arm about her shoulders, but she could not bring herself to do it, and instead began pouring the hot water into a bowl which stood on the table.

"Come 'long now, Lydia," said Polly, briskly. "There be work for 'ee that'll break thy 'eart if thee's a scrap of love in it. 'Twill be a penance for 'ee, too. Bring clean cloths, for we're goin' in to wash thy good man—an' oh, me dear, 'tis a terrible sight to see!"

CHAPTER VII

It was in the afternoon of the twenty-fourth day of June 1871 that Polly's and Nathan's third son was born.

His first lusty cry in the quiet house—quiet now that Polly had ceased to moan—came to Nathan's ears as he sat in the kitchen.

"A boy!" said Nathan to himself.

Mrs Jabez John Nankervis, poking her smiling, wrinkled face around the bedroom door a few moments later, confirmed it with a terse "Another o' the same!" and shut herself inside again, leaving Nathan to write his new son's name, Robert Menadue Thomas, in the centre page of the family Bible.

Dusk came early on this wintry day, and with it came hurrying figures from the miners' cottages: men and women well wrapped in greatcoats or shawls, all chattering and laughing like magpies in the scrub at nightfall.

Nathan opened the front door of the cottage, leading from the kitchen-living-room.

"They be lightin' un!" he called to Polly as she lay in bed in the candlelit bedroom. " 'Tis cracklin' fine. Up go the flames, like billy-o!"

"Wish I was there," Polly called back. "I da dearly love bonfire night."

"They got empty tar barrels too, mother. She be flamin' up fine."

"Get a tatty from the box in the back room and roast un for me. There's a dear, Nat. Bring un back all black outside an' white as flour atween."

Nathan pulled his coat about his chest and, wrapping Polly's shawl about three-year-old Allen and lifting him in his arms, called to Richard who was leaning over the sapling gate yelling with excitement.

"Go in an' get thy coat, Rich, me boy, an' bring three big tatties from the box. We be goin' to see the bonfire, so make 'aste."

In Cornwall on 24 June it has been the custom, since pagan times, to light bonfires, celebrating Midsummer Day with flames and rejoicing. The fires, which burn on that day in towns and on headlands, stony moors and smooth hillsides, commemorate the rites of the ancient barbarians who once inhabited this part of England. Elsewhere also in the British Isles bonfires burn on that night, but in no county does the custom flourish so strongly as in Cornwall.

In heathen times this was the day set apart for the frightening of evil spirits from the land, and the flaming beacons and the screaming abandon of the fire-dancers were to placate the powers of darkness and to drive away the devils. From ancient days this rite has descended through invasion, civilization and Christianity. The Church, unable to quell the pagan celebration, compromised by giving it a Christian significance and dedicated the Midsummer-Day festival to John the Baptist, christening the day St John's Day. The Cornish immigrants brought the custom to Australia and, although 24 June is mid-winter in the Southern hemisphere, the fête-day is celebrated here in much the same way as in Cornwall.

Great preparations had been made that the bonfire at Wallaroo Mines might be a success. Tar barrels, straw, pitch, huge piles of dry wood and anything inflammable were piled into a heap on the flat, and as twilight fell the mass was lit, and soon the fire was burning with a great volume of smoke and ruby tongues of flame. A circle of wood impregnated with copper salts ringed the blaze about and burned with an eerie greenish flame. Childish screams of pleasure were heard from all sides, and children darted everywhere among the watchers. The more venturesome, shielding their faces from the fierce heat, advanced as near as possible and dropped a potato or two among the glowing coals on the edge of the fire.

"Come 'ere, 'ee little varmint!" cried a burly Cornish woman, with head swathed in a woollen shawl, grabbing her son by the ear and pulling him to her side.

"Leave go, mother! Cussen 'ee see I've lost me tatty now an' don't knaw where I put un in?" he bellowed.

His mother gave him a smack on the side of the head and pushed him from her. "Don't be sich a aggravitin' ijit!" she said good-naturedly, getting her hand ready to give his other ear a slap. "Get along with 'ee! A body'd think us 'ad tatties an' to spare. Be off with 'ee!"

The lad ducked away from her descending hand and, with a whoop, began to search about for the spot in the fire where he had put his precious potato.

Many a potato burned away to a cinder, leaving nothing but a faint smell of charcoal; but the process of its cooking had released a pleasant odour into the night: an incense as of burnt offering.

Richard, muffled to the ears in a huge white wool comforter of Nathan's, wandered among the crowd like a little, lonely ghost. Nathan had lost sight of him from the moment they arrived at the fire and, after a frenzied search, found him standing three feet from the blaze, his white comforter taking a blood-red hue from the flames; and his eyes, wide and staring in his hot, red face, were gazing into the heart of the fire.

His father grabbed him back and scolded him gently. "Rich, me son, don't make off agin. Mother'd never forgive me if aught 'appened to 'ee."

Richard was unmoved, and said stolidly, "I saw a green lady in the fire, father. She had long green hair, and she waved her hands at me and went up with the smoke."

Nathan was at a loss. "That were make-believe, Richard. Time for 'ee to be in bed."

They roasted their potatoes in the coals, and Nathan and Allen shared one, burnt black as a coal on the outside but like white snow when broken. Richard, his eyes on the fire, set his strong little teeth into the hot, floury centre of the potato and chewed without apparent emotion or enjoyment.

Nathan shook him by the arm. "Rouse up an' come to 'ome!"

Richard turned reluctantly from the dying fire and followed his father through the crowd.

Polly's daughter, Annie, was born on 10 June 1873, and at the first sight of the little red-faced girl-child Polly heaved a tired sigh. "I've got what I wanted. God be praised, a little maid!"

The first Sunday that Polly was up after this confinement she sat in the rocking-chair by the kitchen fire with her family all about her. She was wearing a dark blue merino frock—her Sunday one—with a little knotted-fringe collar about the throat; and on her head was a white cap—a matron's cap, for Polly was thirty-five now. It was not the first occasion that she had worn this adornment of feminine maturity. She had made it to wear on her birthday the previous January. But the effect of the new cap, combined with the unshapeliness of her maternity dress with its wide yoke from which fell the multitudinous folds of stifling linsey-woolsey cloth, had made her look so unfamiliar and incongruous that Robert, eighteen months old and impressionable, had screamed himself black in the face at the sight, and she had had to take it off to restore him.

Nathan, too, was thirty-five. His hair was streaked with grey, but the beard upon his chin was as dark as ever it had been. He was sitting on the other side of the hearth and, with one leg of his Sunday serge pants rolled back, was tying a poultice of hot salt about his rheumaticky knee. As he turned to set the kettle back a little on the stove Polly saw the bend in his broad back, and a strange little fear shot through her. It seemed that the week in bed, away from them all and the familiar pleasantness of old Mrs Nankervis's services, had, like a long visit away from home, rested and changed her; and now, returning amongst them, she saw her family as after a long separation. With a keenness of sight which the years of close contact with them all had previously denied her, she saw them as with a stranger's eye—Nathan's bent back, his greying hair, his knotted fingers and the swollen joints of his knees. She remembered, with a curious detachment, his nights of sleeplessness, when he could get little relief from the pain in his joints until she had lit the candle and had warmed the salt-bag in the oven and placed it where the pain was worst. Polly had done all this for him with wifely pity;

but now, with a pang, she realized all that he had suffered and so quietly had borne.

She stretched a hand to him, and her eyes were wet. "Love 'ee, Nat," she said softly.

Nathan looked up from clumsily tying the salt-bag to his knee and, seeing the look on her face, nodded three times, slowly and understandingly. He glanced at his children in the room and back again at Polly whose eyes, bright with tears, had not left his face. He smiled and nodded again. "We be lucky ones, we be, me dear."

Richard lay flat on his stomach under the cedar table threading quandong stones on a piece of string. Every now and then he would spit upon one of the pitted stones, rub it furiously on his serge blouse and admire it at great length before threading it. Polly saw his brown hair, from which the curls had been cut but two years ago—a tiny ringlet of which lay in a little packet in Polly's bedroom—and his thin little neck, and the lankiness of his limbs no longer babyishly fat and dimpled. Richard, at seven and a half, was a serious, imaginative boy, showing a remarkable apti-tude for his lessons at Mr Sullivan's school and having a passionate love for his mother.

Allen, five years of age at this time, was a sturdy, grey-eyed little lad with straight, light brown hair and a winning smile. He was affectionate but not demonstrative, and was so willing and eager to help that for his own good it was often wise to restrain him. He put his whole heart into his work, whether it was playing with mud and water in a corner of the yard or digging the potato patch or raking the skimpings on the garden paths.

" 'E be a worker," thought Polly with pride. "Menadue through an' through."

Robert, a few days short of two years old, was sitting with Richard under the table, legs tucked beneath him and eyes on Richard's hands as he threaded the quandong stones.

"Pitty?" he would say, when Richard paused to admire a stone that he had dyed in the schoolmaster's green ink. "Pitty?" said Robert again, stretching out his hand.

"Get out of it!" said Richard sharply. "These are my peachies."

Robert pulled back his hand an inch or two, but otherwise took no notice of Richard's churlishness. Richard could do no wrong in Robert's eyes. "Pitty?" he said once more, tentatively.

Annie Ellen slept in the old cradle at Polly's feet. A rung or two had gone, and the railing was well worn by the application of three sets of infantile teeth. The rockers were dented and the mattress sagged, but it still rocked fairly silently with the motion of Polly's foot—to and fro, to and fro. Little Annie, with her mouth like a rosebud and a wisp of chestnut hair that Polly knew would curl, was rocked into baby dreams in the bosom of the family that had received her so boisterously a short week ago.

Looking at them all from the isolation of her convalescence, Polly vowed in her heart that she would be kinder, more loving, more steadfast and more truly understanding to them all. She shaded her face from the heat of the stove and, in the shelter of her hand, her lips moved.

"Dear God," she prayed, "give me the time to see me dear ones as they really be. Give me the time, dear Lord, to be a mother to un, ev'ry one."

Nathan had widened the lean-to room at the rear of the house and had added a window to it in place of the four castor-oil bottles, with necks and base removed, which had formerly been built into the walls to provide ventilation.

Richard had wept stormily when the oil bottles had been taken out, and his tears had affected Robert almost to the point of convulsions before harassed Polly could quieten them or get a sensible reason out of Richard for the tears. Between great sobs he told Polly that the chief delight of his young life had been to lie in bed with Allen and to watch the reflections cast on the walls by the blue glass bottles.

"I could see the whole world on our walls, mother, when the sun shone in. All the men carrying their crib-bags and going off shift—we could see them going away as far as the crossing. And the green pepper-tree! Oh, mother, the green pepper-tree was the prettiest of all."

"What about the tram? What about the tram?" put in Allen with great excitement. "We could see the tram coming this way on the line, mother, and we'd rush inside to see it go by. Four trams on the walls, all blue and wobbly and little as little!"

"Thees 'ave never said nothin' o' this afore," said Polly.

"It was a secret 'tween Rich and me," Allen said woefully. "And now there's no secret left."

"But thees'll be able to look through the window now, chuckle'eads. Thees'll be able to see tram proper, not all wobbly an' 'indsy-forsy," argued Polly.

"But there's no fun in it now!" Richard said dejectedly.

Towards the end of the year 1873 Nathan built another room on the back of the house and added a ridged roof like that above the two main rooms. Thus the house now contained four apartments: Nathan's and Polly's bedroom, a dining-room (formerly the kitchen), the boys' room, a new kitchen with a wide stone fireplace and, at the back, a lean-to of wattle boughs for a wash-house.

Polly was very happy. She was always busy and had hardly a moment in which to rest during the day. Clothes to be made in thick navy serge for Nathan and her two elder boys, Allen's braided in black with a row of big black buttons down the front, and little Robert's dresses of wincey with pantalettes of white embroidery showing below the hem cost Polly many a headache from eyestrain as she worked on the soft material by candlelight. All the hundred and one family cares and pleasures were hers at this time.

The first cloud that darkened the Thomas horizon came in the form of a letter from St Ives. In this letter, from her sister Ruth, Polly read what she had always feared to know. Ruth, now a married woman and addressing Polly with an aloofness that eight years of separation had engendered, wrote:

By the time ee get this, me dear sister, mother will be dead an laid to rest. She ave been sick with cramps in the stummick for a week past, an Doctor Bonnythorne do say as she as but a day or two to live. So by time as ee get this she will be in churchyard an all over. She do ask for thee, an tell me to write an say she loves thee dearly an good-bye.

Polly read no farther, but sank in a faint by the side of the kitchen table. Such a thing had never happened to her before, and Allen and Robert screamed aloud from fright and Richard, who was home from school at the time, ran for Mrs Trevennick next door, shrieking that his mother was dead.

When Polly had recovered and had had a good cry she got up from her bed with a passion for "doing something". She put on her best dress and, leaving Richard in charge of the children, took some money from the cup on the dresser and walked into Kadina to buy crape for the whole family.

Nathan, under great pressure, was made to wear a narrow black band on his sleeve to the mines next day, and Polly unpicked every scrap of white trimming from her black dress and, attiring herself in this, sat in the front room to await calls of condolence from the neighbours. While waiting she stitched away at black crape bows and streamers for the children's hats and dresses, and at the same time gave way to genuine sorrow for her mother.

The news of her bereavement sped swiftly, and the minister and church members called to sympathize and to eat saffron cake in the dining-room.

On Sunday Polly sallied forth to church with her melancholy procession of mourners, she herself in heavy black, with a bonnet from which every vestige of flower and fruit had been removed. Richard, with a crape bow under his collar and long black ends to his flat straw hat, sulkily walked behind. She held Allen, also decorated with black crape, by the hand, and Robert sucked the little black bow under his chin with great satisfaction.

Nathan gave his opinion as he watched them setting out. "Thee da knaw best, Pol, but don't 'ee think the childern be got up like little black judies, me dear?"

To Polly's great surprise, two months later she received another letter from Ruth in which one sentence on the second page read: "Mother an me be goin to Helston for Furry Dance. She ave a mind to go." So it became obvious, though only after much rereading, that mother was not dead at all, and the crape had been nothing but a waste of money and temper.

Polly ironed all the black yards of it very smoothly and put it away in the cedar chest, happy in a way to know her mother was still alive, but very much worried about what to tell the neighbours. She could not bring herself to tell them anything and when, in Ruth's next letter, she heard that mother was really dead of a chill caught while dancing with the crowds in the Helston streets on Flora Day, she felt she had done the right thing; but she did not take out the crape again. It had served its purpose, even if somewhat prematurely.

Three more happy years followed, with continued work in the mines for Nathan, his pay of approximately eight pounds a month coming to him regularly.

Nathan and his friend, Ben Wilson, were now employed underground by the contract system—or "tutwork", as the Cornish miners called it. By this system the miners are paid by measure, at so much per fathom, irrespective of whether they obtain good ore or not; and the bulk of the miners at Wallaroo Mines worked tutwork.

Previously, Nathan, Ben and Harry Pearce had done "tribute" work, on one occasion profitably; but on each of the other two they had had the misfortune to strike a bad pitch and, the lode being unproductive, they had surrendered. Unlike tutwork, in the case of tribute both the quality and quantity of the ore obtained is equally important, for the miners, by previous price agreement with the mining company, receive a certain percentage of the actual value of the ore raised, paid by the company at the rate of so many shillings in the pound of that ore's value. The time given to work a certain pitch by tribute is two months, and if before that time the vein of ore peters out the miners may, if they wish, cease work, and fresh tenders may be called for the pitch. In Cornwall, at this time, a fine of twenty shillings was imposed on miners who surrendered before the expiration of the two months.

After Nathan's two unfortunate experiences he, ever cautious, had decided to do tutwork for a set wage; but Polly still secretly hankered after those luxuries that were coming to the cottages of astute tributers who had made a good bargain with the company or who had been successful in working a productive pitch and having a good sturt.

"Us'll never 'ave a 'armonyum at this rate," Polly mourned.

"Well," soothed Nathan, "what'd be the use? Nobody in the 'ouse could play un if we 'ad un."

By November of that year, 1876, they had been in the colony eleven years.

Richard, Allen, Robert and little Annie were eleven, eight, five and three years old respectively.

Richard, a tall thin lad, was "Rich" to everybody, and still at Mr Sullivan's school—at an age when most miners' sons were at work in Kadina or at the mines, working at the picking-tables, sorting ore.

Allen, still the same serious-faced youngster with the infectious smile, was in the third class at school. He was not brilliant like his brother Richard, but was a "plodder"— Polly's own word—with a passion for drawing ships, and possessing a wander-lust that took him on every possible occasion and in every available conveyance to Wallaroo, to stand on the jetty there and watch the tall-masted ships in the bay.

Robert, now "Bob", still as passionately attached to Rich and still as assiduously snubbed as ever, was a fat, roly-poly, bright-eyed boy with a remarkable aptitude for bartering. On the evening of his fifth birthday he was discovered with a varied collection of rubbish under his bed, and irate Polly later found out that these were the results of certain exchanges of birthday presents. Chief among them was a large cow-bell, cracked but still clamorous, exchanged for his new boots, and a box of odorous cockle shells that had been considered fair value for his shiny tin whistle.

Annie was the sweetest little creature that ever played on a skimp-path at Wallaroo Mines. She had hair like molten copper, and it curled about her head in a bright halo. Her eyes were blue as periwinkle flowers, and her face too was like a blossom. Polly loved her with all the ardour of a demonstratively affectionate nature, and Nathan never ceased to wonder that such beauty was his own flesh and blood.

On the afternoon of Richard's birthday, in November, Rich and Allen were playing in a little wurley they had built under a pepper-tree in the back yard. Polly had consented to their having the afternoon away from school, for birthdays in the Thomas household were events worthy of a holiday. Nathan, his crib-bag containing a Cornish pasty in his hand, stood watching the boys before going to the mines to begin his afternoon shift.

Suddenly, running steps were heard on the skimpings, and Lenny Trevennick from the next-door cottage dashed around the corner of the house. He was a lad of eight, and to-day his face was deathly white and his eyes were like saucers. He saw Nathan leaning against the door-jamb, and ran right into his arms.

"Oh, Mr Thomas, Mr Thomas, come quick!" he gasped. "Mother's thrown herself into the tank. Mother's drownding herself, like she always said she would. Oh, Mr Thomas, come quick!" And he grabbed Nathan's arm and tried to pull him towards the front gate.

"Wait a minute, wait a minute," said Nathan, releasing himself and putting his crib-bag on the ground. He took off his hat too, with its butt of candle stuck in the front, and laid it carefully on top of the bag before taking the boy's hand and running with him towards the front of the house and out of the gate.

Richard and Allen, who had been listening open-mouthed, crept from under the lacy pepper leaves and stood looking after their father, their eyes round with excitement.

"Did you hear what Lenny Trevennick said?" asked Allen, wondering if his ears had deceived him.

"Yes!" said Rich incredulously, still disbelieving this piece of good fortune. "He said his mother was in the tank!"

"Dad's going to fish her out. Come on!" said Allen, eager to be off. "Hurry!"

"We ought to tell mother," Rich said, hesitating; but Allen was already running towards the gate and, after a second's indecision, Rich was after him, like a shot from a gun.

Nathan and Lenny were entering Trevennick's front gate when, looking back, Nathan saw the boys following. They were still some yards away, for, although the two houses were adjacent, a wide space separated them.

Nathan waved the boys back. "Go for 'elp!" he yelled to them. "Find Ben Wilson an' tell 'im to bring a thick rope. Go 'long!" And he disappeared around the corner of the house on his way to the underground tank, which he knew would be almost full of water after the spring rains.

Outside the house, the two lads stopped short and looked at one another.

"Well," said Allen at last, "you go, Rich. You're the biggest."

"No you don't! You go! I'm going to watch father."

"Oh," said Allen, white with disappointment, "I wanted to see Lenny's mother swimming in the tank!"

"She won't be swimming for long," Rich said, giving his brother a push on his way. "She'll be drowned dead by the time you get back if you don't hurry and go for Mr Wilson."

Allen turned his face in the direction of the mines and ran off down the road, fear of missing the excitement lending wings to his feet.

When Richard entered the back yard of the Trevennick home he rushed to the familiar underground tank by the back door. The lid was off, and sounds of splashing and faint calls for help came from the dark interior of the tank.

"Rip off a board or two!" called Nathan, frenziedly wrestling with the rope clothes-line that hung between the two mallee posts in the yard.

Rich pulled and tugged at the wooden top of the tank, conscious of the lessening of splashes in the darkness beneath him, and of the gurgling gasps that were growing fainter and fainter.

His heart was sick with dread. "Father, father!" he called, as at last he wrenched back a board. "She's nearly gone. Oh, dad, she's stopped splashing. What are we going to do?"

Nathan was at his side then, peering into the water.

"I be goin' down, Rich. Thee an' Lenny tie the blankets o' the beds into good 'ard knots an' throw un down to me. The clothes-line's rotten an' broke in me 'and. I'll 'old 'er up. Make 'aste!"

He stepped on the edge of the tank and lowered himself into the cobwebby space between the wooden top and the water, and Rich heard him drop into the tank with a heavy splash.

Lenny and Rich dashed into the cottage and, turning up the beds, dragged the sheets and blankets from them and, with hands that shook, tied them fast together. Running into the back bedroom for more blankets, Rich was horrified to see Mr Trevennick, Lenny's father, lying on one of the beds. He was breathing stertorously, and the air was filled with his tainted breath.

"He's dead drunk," said Lenny, behind him. "Mother said time and time again she'd throw herself into the tank if he didn't stop, and now she's been and done it." He spoke dispassionately, but his voice was hard and his eyes, as they fell on his drunken father, were filled with hate. "I'll kill him for this, if mother's drownded," he said, and he clenched his hands with a fierce upward movement.

Gathering the knotted blankets, they ran to the tank and threw them in, keeping one end fast.

"Good lads," called Nathan, splashing to catch the woollen rope.

Almost five feet below them the boys could see Nathan in the dark water, holding Mrs Trevennick in his arms. She was unconscious and Nathan, holding her head above the water and placing the blankets under her arms, managed with great difficulty to knot the blankets across her breasts. By standing with the tips of his boot soles on the slimy bottom of the tank Nathan was able to lift the senseless woman in his arms and keep both their heads above water.

"Pull up," he called to the boys. "Slowly—slowly!"

The boys pulled, and eased the weight of the woman from Nathan's arms, but they could not draw her up beyond the level of the water.

"Isn't Allen back yet?" Nathan asked, his teeth chattering. " 'Avven any men come by this?"

"Not yet," panted Rich, straining on the woollen rope.

Allen, with singleness of purpose, had fixed his mind on Richard's injunction to find Ben Wilson, and as he raced along the road he passed several miners carrying their crib-bags and making for the shaft heads. So conscientiously did Allen fulfil his instructions that he arrived at Taylor's shaft almost exhausted and completely out of breath. As he sagged there, holding on to the ironwork for support, several miners spoke to him as they entered the gig preparatory to being taken underground.

"What's up, sonny?" called Joe Penton, but the platman's lusty voice drowned Allen's reply. "Any more for eighty level? Any more for eighty?" called the platman.

The gig had begun to descend with its load of miners when Allen found his breath.

"I want Mr Wilson," he gasped. "I want Ben Wilson. My father's in Trevennick's tank, and he says for Ben Wilson to bring a rope, quick!"

Questions and explanations followed, and men shouted at each other, and several grabbed a length of rope that was lying near by and ran back along the road toward Trevennick's cottage. Allen sped back after them, and Ben Wilson, having heard the news which had spread quickly underground, came up in the next gig and ran belatedly after the group with the rope.

More than ten minutes had passed since Allen ran for help, and another five elapsed before the miners arrived on the scene and began the task of raising Mrs Trevennick to the surface where many willing hands soon commenced the work of restoring her to life and her troubles.

Nathan presented a difficulty. It was easier for him to get into the tank than to be got out of it; but at last after two attempts, in one of which the rope had broken and he had fallen back into the cold water, they brought him up to the top of the tank.

Polly was there awaiting him. The news had spread, and, having paused only to lock Bob and Annie in the dining-room and to grasp an armful of bedding, she had rushed, sobbing, to the tank. Nathan's rheumatics! It was her only thought. " 'E'll die for sure, or catch a fever!"

Two hours later when Dr Fisher had left Mrs Trevennick's cottage and pronounced her out of danger, and had called at Polly's cottage and examined Nathan, he told Polly that what she had feared might indeed take place.

"He has taken a severe chill," said the doctor. "I cannot say how it will go with him. There is no danger of his life, but there is every chance that he will be very ill. Already he has a temperature and is in pain."

Polly, now that Nathan was safe in bed, gave vent to her anxiety and relief in a burst of scolding. She slapped Allen for making a noise and slapped him again for crying. She put Annie to bed forgetting to kiss her and, seeing the boys waiting quietly in a group in the kitchen, crossly told them to set to work and do something. Set the tea, chop the wood, anything—anything, as long as they were doing something.

"That ever I should live to see the day!" she moaned as she mixed Nathan's gruel on the fire. "As if there wassen a pack o' able-bodied men on the mines oo coulda jumped in after Mary Ann Trevennick without me Nathan 'avin' to do it! Standin' in cold water up to 'is nuddick, an' 'im with 'is rheumatics! 'Twill be 'is death."

She rubbed Nathan's back with Royal Liniment till he was almost raw and groaned for her to cease. She gave him a double dose of his Chelsea Pensioner Medicine, a recipe that he had great faith in and which had often given him relief, all the time keeping up a furious tirade about his quixotry. He did not utter a word, only a groan or two as he moved in the bed so that she could rub some other part of his aching body and, his silence exasperating her the more, Polly finally burst into tears and went out into the kitchen.

Rich had made bread and milk for them all and was washing up their plates in the tin dish on the kitchen table. His hand, where the boards of the tank had cut it, was sore and stinging from the hot, soapy water.

"Leave that be," said Polly sharply, "an' go to bed!"

Allen spoke up then. "Can't we go to practice, mother? 'Tis Anniversary practice at the chapel, and I have to sing a piece."

This was the last straw for Polly. Why couldn't the boys go quietly to bed and let her bide in peace to cry her bad temper away and get back her peace of mind?

She hustled Bob off to bed, and superintended the other boys' washing and dressing with many complainings. As they stood before her, ready to leave for chapel, she spoke in a harsh voice, very near to tears.

"Go on off, all of 'ee. Leave mother to 'ome with a sick father an' go off to chapel if 'ee must. Like as not thees'll find *me* in the tank when 'ee da get 'ome." And, turning away, she sat down at the table with her head on her arms.

Rich and Allen set out into the darkness. They did not speak for a while, and Rich sucked his aching hand and wished that his mother had not been so angry and upset and that he could have asked her to bandage it for him.

"Do you think she meant that?" asked Allen as they came in sight of the lighted church.

"I dunno," said Rich, doubtfully.

They sat next to each other on the wooden platform made to hold the Sunday-school scholars of the Bible Christian chapel and erected in preparation for the Anniversary services to be held on the coming Sunday.

Rich and Allen did not join in the preliminary giggling and talking as they usually did. They sat still and, when the other boys would have kept up a long conversation about the event of the afternoon, they answered in monosyllables.

When the conductor tapped with his baton on the top of his music-stand and the talking ceased and the singing practice began, they were glad. Now it would soon be over and they could race home.

"Like as not thees'll find *me* in the tank!"

Rich shut his eyes, and in his mind he saw his dear mother in the cold water as he had seen Mrs Trevennick that afternoon. He shuddered, and held the hymn-sheet in front of his face so that the other boys might think he was singing; but his throat was dry and hard, and the pain in his hand was growing worse.

It was towards the end of the practice that Allen's turn to sing arrived. He stood up bravely and gave a glance at Rich, but his brother had his head bent, so he got no courage from that source.

The stringed instruments began the opening bars of "Pilgrims of the Night". The music of this hymn was new to Wallaroo Mines, and the band of musicians who always accompanied the special singing services at the chapel gave a pleasing lilt to the seesaw four-two rhythm of the tune.

Allen began to sing. He faltered and missed the beat,

and the conductor tapped on the music-stand and Allen began again. His thin, sweet soprano wavered, tears rushed into his eyes and he glanced down at Rich. Rich was staring up at him, and Allen gave him one despairing look, then grasped his hand and whispered in desperate entreaty, "Rich, let's go home!"

Their hands clung. At once Rich was on his feet and they were pushing and scrambling down from the platform. They did not hear the conductor's voice calling after them, but rushed out into the open air and away down the road.

As they neared the cottage their pace slackened, for they were afraid to go home. Suddenly they stopped. From their house sparks were flying upwards: great spots of light mounting into the darkness from their kitchen chimney. They were off like the wind. "What's mother done now? She's not in the tank, *but what's the matter at our house?*" was the thought in both their minds.

They dashed around to the back of the house, each of them giving a thankful look at the closed lid of the tank. They burst into the kitchen, their faces masks of fright. Polly was standing in a clean white apron by the roaring stove, and turned as they stood trembling in the doorway, and held out her arms to them.

"Oh, me dears," she said, "come 'ere to mother! Father's easier an' 'e've gone to sleep, an' I've been makin' 'ot scones for 'ee 'gainst 'ee come 'ome!"

They ran to her, their hearts singing with love and relief. She put her arms about them and kissed them, and Rich, placing the palm of his aching hand against the cold whiteness of his mother's apron, imagined that it did not hurt at all now.

CHAPTER VIII

"An' 'ow's thy man, Miz Thomas? 'Ow's 'e doin'?"

"A mite better, Miz Roberts. 'E be up to-day for first time in five weeks."

"Don't I knaw it, thee poor dear! Thee's been a tower o' strength to 'im in 'is sickness," sympathized Mrs Roberts.

"Don't think o' me, think of 'im. A able-bodied man crippled up in bed for hour 'pon hour all that time, an' all of a mind to be up an' doin' summat," said Polly, giving her skirt a hitch and digging up a spadeful of earth from the garden at the back of her cottage.

Mrs Uriah Roberts, a stout matron in a shiny black dress with a large black apron tied round her waist, sat down heavily on a seat that Polly herself had made from a barrel and put in the garden in the shade of the dolichos creeper. Mrs Roberts fitted into the barrel seat like a sword into its sheath and, smoothing out her apron, settled back for a talk. She had expected to be asked inside the house, but Polly, who had seen her entering the front gate, had hastily grabbed a spade and, advancing to meet her with this in her hand, had led her into the back garden before Mrs Roberts could know what was happening. Polly wanted Nathan to have a spell by himself on this his first day out of bed, for his sickness had sadly changed him and she did not want him to see the sympathy in a visitor's eye. He looked ten years older, his hair was greyer and his back very bent. Polly sensed the tragedy he formed—a crippled miner—and she wanted to shield him from the pity of his fellows a little longer, until he should be able to walk again and be strong enough to bear Cornish sympathy.

"Let us sitty down 'ere in the cool," she said, resting her spade against the pepper-tree bole and, pulling a box from

under the tree, sat beside Mrs Roberts in the shade cast by
the dolichos vine.

It was a grey day. A light rain had fallen in the night,
after a week's hot weather, and now it was a little cooler.
A grey day in early summer or autumn in Australia is a
lovely thing. All the drying grass and dusty roads take on
a milder tone, and to-day the green of the pepper-trees—
the only trees besides the native mallee and American
tobacco-bush that flourished at Wallaroo Mines—looked
soft and feathery in the mellow light. The occasional bursts
of sunlight that made the shadows run away across the
ground were gentle and golden, unlike the blazing sunshine
of true summer.

"Parson says thy man 'ave been terrible bad," said
Mrs Roberts when Polly was settled beside her.

" 'E've been as bad as mortal man can be, Miz Roberts,
an' still go on bein' mortal. 'E've suffered, me Nat 'ave.
'E've suffered cruel."

"I knawed a man back 'ome oo never walked agin after
rheumatic fever," said Mrs Roberts conversationally. " 'E
were a cripple all 'is days."

"An' I knawed a man oo 'ad it an' 'e's up an' 'bout like
anabody else," Polly put in quickly. "Me Nathan's own
brother 'ad it when 'e were a little lad, an' 'e's journeyman
carpenter now, an' walks on 'is own legs all over Cornwall."

"Ah," said Mrs Roberts slowly, "then 'tis in the family?
That's terrible bad."

Polly stiffened. "Don't go on, Miz Roberts. Don't! I knaw
'tis terrible bad, an' I knaw Nathan's mother, poor soul,
were on 'er back for fourteen year afore she died, but
'twill be diff'ent wi' my Nat. 'E's up on 'is feet aready, an'
the sun'll fix 'im."

"Well, I only 'opes as thee's right, me dear. I only 'opes
'ee are," said Mrs Roberts complacently, "but I knawed a
man once——!" And she stopped significantly, and the talk
ebbed.

"Be the childern goin' to the Sunday-school picnic come
Saturday?" she went on after a long pause.

"They be goin' with Ben Wilson's missus," said Polly,
"an' I wish I be goin' too. I dearly love a picnic, an' this
year 'tis to be out Alford way."

" 'Tis late in the year, I be thinkin'," said Mrs Roberts. "Snakes be about now, an' lizards. Parson didden oughter 'a' left it so late. September's the time for picnics in the scrub, when the daisies be out."

"There'll still be daisies, p'raps," said Polly wistfully. "I allus wanted to go pickinin' agin out Alford way in daisy-time. We've only been there once, when Bob were a babby. Allen were only a little tacker at the time, an' 'e got lost an' went to sleep with daisies all about un. Nathan an' me found 'im, an' 'e were the purtiest sight we ever did see. We sat 'longside an' let 'im just wake up by 'isself. I'll never forget un to me dyin' day."

"Yes, 'tis purty in the scrub when the wildflowers be out," said Mrs Roberts. "But parson 'ave missed the boat this time."

Polly called Annie to her and, bidding her talk to Mrs Roberts while she prepared a cup of tea, went towards the house.

"Don't 'ee trouble, Miz Thomas. I'll come on in with 'ee," said Mrs Roberts, struggling to rise from the barrel seat. But she was stuck fast, and the agile Polly was inside her kitchen in a trice and already had the teapot down from the dresser.

"Be 'ee all right, me dear?" she called to Nat, who was sitting in the rocking-chair in the dining-room. "I be gettin' rid of 'er fast as I can."

Mrs Roberts and Polly had a cup of tea and a curranty bun in the back yard, and deferred the problem of Mrs Roberts's rising from the barrel until their afternoon tea was finished.

"Now," said Polly, "if 'ee be goin', we'll 'ave to set to an' get 'ee out o' that there."

"Well, I s'pose I'd better be off—leastways, if I ever get meself out o' this contraption. I dunno what possessed me to sit meself down on this crazy thing," panted Mrs Roberts, struggling to get on her feet.

She stood up, and brought the barrel chair with her.

"Lawks, can't 'ee pull un off?" she said to Polly heatedly.

"There be a nail . . . !" said Polly slowly, after a wrestle with the barrel.

" 'Twill be tearin' me best alpaca!" groaned Mrs Roberts.

"Best sit down agin, an' I'll get the little axe an' chop it off 'ee," said Polly.

Mrs Roberts and the barrel sat down again. " 'Urry up, for Lord's sake!" gasped Mrs Roberts, wiping the perspiration off her face.

Polly got the axe from the lean-to wash-house and, pushing Mrs Roberts's head forward, attacked the back-rest of the seat with great energy.

Mrs Roberts shuddered with every crash of the axe, and buried her face in her hands. "Don't go through to me back," she moaned.

"Well, I'll try not to," said Polly viciously. "But I knawed a man back 'ome once . . . !" And she gave the barrel a terrific whack, and Mrs Roberts shivered with fright.

At last the barrel fell in pieces, and Mrs Roberts fell among them.

"Oh, me sakes alive!" she gasped, as Polly hauled her to her feet. The alpaca dress was dusty but still intact, and she smoothed her apron and shook out her skirt, then, leaning on Polly's arm, tottered towards the front of the house.

Polly shut the sapling gate behind her and spoke consolingly. "Well, I be mortal sorry about un, Miz Roberts, but next time I'll make 'ee come inside, no matter what 'ee say."

Mrs Roberts was too bewildered by her recent experience to reply. She merely waved her hand in farewell and walked away towards Kadina.

Polly watched her go, then went back to view the ruin of the barrel seat. She picked up the pieces and put them on the wood pile, then kicked them suddenly and with great energy.

"Thee knawed a man oo were cripple all 'is life?" she said in a voice that trembled. "Thee knawed a man oo coulden use 'is legs after fever, did 'ee?" Then her voice took on a fierce note. "Well, thee were lucky to get off so light when I 'ad the axe in me 'ands, that's all!" And, at the memory of Mrs Roberts shaking in the barrel, she began to laugh, and Annie, too, joined in because Polly laughed, and Polly picked her up in her arms and carried her towards the house.

"Come in to father, me purty pet. 'E'll want cheerin' up, poor dear."

Saturday dawned clear and bright with the promise of heat to come, and Polly was up and about very early giving the boys their breakfast and getting them ready for the picnic.

Rich had finished his Saturday morning tasks before the meal was ready. The wood-box was full, two buckets of water had been drawn from the tank, and the family boots, cleaned well with Day and Martin's, stood in a row awaiting their owners. Allen had been busy plaiting a lash for a whip to be used on the horses if permission could be obtained from the owner of the picnic drag, and Bob's pockets were filled with string and a tin to put wattle gum in, and he carefully wrapped up a gimlet of Nathan's and stowed it away in his jacket, all ready to bore holes in quandong peachies if he were lucky enough to find a quandong-tree.

They were waiting at the crossing a full hour before the drags were due to start, and at nine o'clock, when the full complement of Sunday-school scholars and their parents from the Bible Christian church had been settled into seats on the drag and in the spring carts, the drivers cracked their whips and, amid shouts from the children and much giggling from the young ladies' class, they moved off towards Kadina.

Polly, leaning over the fence, could see Rich on the front seat with the driver, Bob with Mrs Wilson on the second seat, and Allen on the back seat with his legs hanging over the wheel. By frenziedly shouting and waving Polly managed to make him understand that he must pull his legs up and sit down properly, and she had the satisfaction of seeing him dragged back to safety by a member of the choir and given a cuff over the ear for his venturesomeness.

Polly sighed thankfully. "Allen be the worst o' the lot. E's a young limb, an' da give me more trouble than the rest put together, but I think 'e'll beat the other lads 'ollow. Thomases be all right, but us Menadues be allus full o' go. Rich and Bob be real Thomases if ever there were, but Allen's ezacally like me."

She told Nathan of this incident when she went back into the house and he smiled.

"Allen's so unexpected," said Nathan. "I never knew lad so full o' surprises. Seems to me 'e dussen even think like ordinary folks. 'E's allus opposite, allus 'agin the govern- ment', as parson says."

" 'E've got a mind of 'is own," said Polly with pride. " 'E's diff'ent from others 'is age."

"All same, 'e da look at things from a contrary angle, Pol. Dost mind years ago when I were readin' the story o' Abra'am an' Isaac on the top o' Mount Moriah? 'Tis a story I can't abide meself, for it da allus seem so unneces- sary an' unnatural, but anyways we'd got up to it, so it 'ad to be read. Well, after I'd finished un an' were feelin' sore meself at 'avin' to 'arrow a cheeld wi' sich a tale, that Allen burst out cryin' an' I weren't surprised. ' 'Tis a sad story, Allen,' says I, 'but don't fear. God woulden 'ave let Abra'am kill Isaac, 'is little boy!' 'No-o,' says Allen, 'but 'E let un kill the ram. I weren't cryin' for Isaac, but I don't think God shoulda let Abra'am kill a sheep. That were a cruel thing to do!' "

"Dost mind 'ow 'e carried on last week over the story o' Christ stillin' the storm?" put in Polly. "I won't never forget that."

"Nor me, Pol. Allen showed me that day God's aboundin' care for even the least of us, 'Is childern. An' God showed me summat too, that day—thee knaw what, Pol."

" 'Ee mean about Rich?"

"Yes, an' I thank 'Im for it. 'E showed me that me eldest son 'ad summat in 'im I'da yearned to 'ave. 'E 'ad the grace o' learnin', an' the power to use un too. Dost mind 'ow Allen took on when I were readin' about the tempest? 'E were real upset when I got to that lovely bit, 'An' there were with 'Im at the time, *other* little ships!' 'E didden 'ave no interest in what 'appened to the Lord's boat. 'Tell me,' says 'e, 'what 'appened to the *other* little ships.' Then," said Nathan, continuing in a proud voice, "then Rich, oo 'ad been listenin' to us, went out into the kitchen an' wrote a poem, didden 'e, mother? 'Im, just eleven year old, an' could feel to write a poem! 'E brought un back to me, didden 'e, Pol? An' I were struck all of an 'eap. Listen Polly:

> "On far off Galilee,
> When Jesus calmed the sea,
> Shared that serenity
> Other little ships.

That's 'ow it da go, an' nobody da knaw what that meant to me. God's mercy be 'bout all 'Is works! 'Tis like a stone dropped in a pool, the ripples da touch evrathin' on the pool, an' so da the calm that follows on."

That portion of the country between Kadina and Alford, where the picnic was to be held, was a lovely part and typical of the mallee scrub all over the northern part of Yorke's Peninsula. There, in spring, the everlasting daisies bloomed in a vast carpet of rustling whiteness, and the white-flowered clematis looped the mallee-trees with stars.

In September the golden wattle would have been filling the scrub with its heavy scent and tea-trees would have been blossoming, and that tiny insignificant flower that children love and call "man's hands" would have been blooming by the bush tracks, and billy-buttons and the yellow ever-lastings would have added their gold to the sweet-scented scrub. But now, in December, the wattle blossom and the tender flowers of spring were gone, although some ever-lasting daisies were still blooming; and in many places the clematis flowers had fallen, and the fluffy down about their seeds shone like white silk and was as soft and feathery as thistledown. "Old man's beard" the children called this, and broke off long trails of it to wreathe about their hats.

Rich leapt down from his seat beside the driver as soon as the drag was at a standstill and, remembering Bob and Mrs Wilson in the seat behind him, held up his arms to help them down.

"Where's thy brother Allen?" said Mrs Wilson, smoothing out the crushed fullness of her cambric frock and pushing back her straw bonnet from her flushed and heated face. " 'E were in back wi' the choir. Go round t'other side an' see if 'e jumped off that way, Rich."

She untied her bonnet and turned to her friend, Mrs Pentoll, who, just as red in the face as Mrs Wilson, was wiping her forehead vigorously and switching viciously at the flies with a twig of tea-tree.

"Look at me," said Mrs Wilson. "I'm so 'ot the sweat's runnin' off me like water!"

Just then Rich returned. "He wasn't on board," he said. "Andrew Jolly said he got down off the drag while we were waiting for the parcels outside the baker's in Kadina, and said he was going to ride out to the picnic in one of the carts."

Mrs Wilson rushed around to the other vehicles which had just drawn up beside the drag.

Allen, however, was not to be seen, and in the wagonette there were only the picnic baskets and parcels of cake that had been obtained from the local baker, a great iron copper for boiling water and a tea-urn, trestle-tables and two cans of milk.

" 'Ave 'ee seen Allen Thomas?" asked Mrs Wilson, agitatedly, of the driver.

The driver shook his head. "Can't say as I 'ave, missus. What's 'e like?"

" 'E 'ave got a plain-lookin' face wi' freckles across the nose of un. 'E be—let's see—'e be 'bout eight year old, an' 'e were wearin'——" She floundered. "I dunno what 'e were wearin'. 'Ere, Rich!" she called. "Come over!"

As soon as the driver saw Rich he said, "Course! Now I knaw oo thee da mean. Nat Thomas's boy." He scratched his head. "Wait a minute till I cast back. Yes—I reckon 'e did come 'angin' round the wagonette whilst we was in Kadina. I shooed 'im off agin, an' I thought 'e went back to the drag. Why, 'ave 'ee lost 'im?"

Mrs Wilson blanched a little under her sunburn. "Call parson," she said to Rich firmly.

After hearing Mrs Wilson's story the minister took the big brass bell from the rear of the wagonette and rang it vigorously. Nothing but the brass bell, with its message of buns and apples, could have brought the children together once they had been let loose among the trees. They came running from all directions. Already the little girls had begun rooting up the paper daisies and dragging down the clematis trails, and the boys, even at this early stage of the picnic, were sticky with wattle gum or snoddy-gobble vine. On being questioned, one of the stickiest came forward, wriggling with confusion.

"Please, sir, Jimmie Harris an' me saw Allen Thomas getting up in Joe Lampin's cart while we was waiting, back in Kadina."

"Didn't you ask him what he was doing up there?" said the minister.

"No, sir, we didn't, sir."

"You knew he was supposed to be coming to the picnic, didn't you?"

"Yes, sir."

"Well, why didn't you call out to him? What do you think he was getting up in Joe Lampin's cart for? Didn't you think that was strange?"

"No, sir."

"Well, what *did* you think?" the reverend gentleman demanded exasperatedly.

"Just thought he wasn't coming to the picnic, that's all," said the lad doggedly, forgetting his mother's injunctions always to "sir" the parson.

Nobody else had seen Allen, and already the children were making off into the scrub again, disappointed at the prospect of no buns, so the minister turned to Mrs Wilson.

"It can't be helped, Mrs Wilson. He evidently stayed behind. Perhaps he rode back home with the fisherman. Well, I must get on with the business in hand." And he turned to help with the setting up of the copper.

"If Allen got in Joe Lampin's cart, then he'll go with him back to Wallaroo. Allen would give up any picnic to go fishing with Joe. But mother will give him a lamming when he gets home. I know that," said Rich, with some satisfaction.

A steely gleam came into Mrs Wilson's eye, and she looked steadily at Rich and Bob. "Now look 'ere, you two, if there be any monkey-tricks with 'ee while I be s'posed to be lookin' after 'ee to-day, well thees'll catch it, good an' 'ard. Now mind what I'm tellin' 'ee. An' if I could lay 'ands on that Allen . . . !"

At this moment Allen was sitting beside Joe Lampin the fisherman in his cart, and jolting down the road towards Wallaroo. Joe was a jovial, bearded, disreputable figure in a flannel shirt, and his dungaree trousers were tied with string below the knees. His feet were bare, and he wore a battered cabbage-tree hat on his head. His whole person and his rickety cart were redolent of the flavour of fish. With the wind behind him, it was said he had no need to shout "Fisho-o, fisho-o, fisho-o!" as he went about Kadina, for the very winds carried the message of his presence.

Allen, holding the reins, sat beside him on the board at the front of the cart. He had taken off his straw hat and had placed it inside the cart, anchored with a bundle of corks and a fish-knife. He had rolled up his sleeves to the elbow, and flapped the reins up and down on the mare's rump with a feeling of almost perfect pleasure. He sniffed the aroma of the whole conveyance, and whistled a tune between his strong, white teeth.

"By gosh, I'm glad I didn't go to their old picnic," he said, as they jogged along. "See this whip, Joe? I put a new lash on it this morning, but I wouldn't have been let to use it. They get the horses for the drag from the mines stables, and Mr Grey won't let any of us boys touch them."

"Thee'd rather be 'ere with old Joe, now, woulden 'ee? Old Joe don't mind 'ee usin' thy whip on 'is 'orse. Look 'ow Topsy goes for thee. She don't go at this trot for me."

"Doesn't she, Joe?" said Allen. "Do you think I really do know how to drive?"

"Thee'll be a reg'lar coachman afore thee's done—or a fisherman. 'Ow'd 'ee like to be a fisherman, little un?"

"Not much," said Allen. "I don't mind fishing," he explained. "It's not that, Joe. Being a fish-o is as good as anything else—anyways, better than being a miner. But I want to go on a sailing-ship when I get bigger. I want to be a sailor."

They were in sight of Wallaroo with its tall chimney, built in 1861, rising from the stone buildings of the smelters. Here the ore from the Wallaroo and Moonta mines was smelted and shipped away. At one time some of the ore was shipped and taken to the subsidiary works erected at Hunter River, New South Wales, the vessels that carried coal from Newcastle to Wallaroo taking back the poor-quality ore to be smelted where fuel was plentiful and cheap. In the early days of the Moonta Mines, the rich ore was taken direct to Swansea in England, to be smelted there.

Through the murky haze of smoke Allen saw the masts of two three-masted ships at anchor by the jetty.

"I won't come fishing with you, to-day, Joe. I'm off down the jetty to see the sailing-ships. Can I have a line and a hook and some cockles? Then I can sit by one of the piles and fish from the jetty if they won't let me go on board and have a look around."

Joe took the reins from Allen as they drew near the head of the jetty. "Well, look out for thyself, little un. Don't go fallin' in. The bay's full o' sharks when there's a ship in. If I get enough fish I'll be waitin' 'ere for 'ee at five o'clock, but if I don't, well, thee'll 'ave to get 'ome best way 'ee can. 'Ere's a line. 'Ee give it back when I sees 'ee agin. Good luck, little un!" And he drove off, out past the great slag heaps towards the sandy beach where his little boat lay, high up on the sands near the blackfellows' wurlies, by the fresh-water spring at the foot of the sandhills.

Allen took off his heavy black boots and, knotting their laces, hung them over his left shoulder. His stockings he rolled into a ball and stuffed into his pocket. He had forgotten his hat, which still reposed among the fishing tackle in the back of Joe's cart.

The day was hot, but the salt breeze from the gulf was cool and fresh. As the day advanced, the breeze would lessen and then cease altogether, springing up again at about four in the afternoon.

Allen sat down on the jetty and, leaning against a pile, gave himself up to the pleasurable survey of the ships. The sea below him lap-lapped with an even, rhythmic rise and fall; the white gulls flew about him; the sailors called a greeting to him and, away beneath him in the cool translucent depths, the little fish darted about, nosing his cockle bait, turning away with a lightning flip of tail and fin and making off into the cool shadows under the jetty. What bliss!

Dinner-time came, and still he sat by the pile. He had caught four small whiting and was feeling very hungry. The noise of the winches at the ships' sides and the rattle of the trucks upon the rails of the jetty had ceased, and here and there men were sitting with their legs dangling down towards the green water, eating their crib before going home for the week-end, and dropping a crust or two down to the darting fish below them.

Suddenly Allen noticed a figure leaning over the rail of the three-masted *Flying Gull*—a swarthy figure, wrinkled and brown. The sailor beckoned with his hand, and Allen came over to the ship's side with alacrity.

"You got no dinner?" called down the sailor in a low voice.

Allen shook his head, and the sailor beckoned him again and pointed to the gangway. "Come up," he said, invitingly.

Allen went back and tied his line to the pile, then ran towards the ship and up the gangway.

"Hey!" called a man on the jetty, pointing at him with the butt of a pasty, but Allen did not turn back and at last stood on the deck.

"You hungry?" said the sailor, in the manner of a man unused to much talking.

Allen smiled his wide smile, and the man's face broke into a hundred new wrinkles. "Come below," he said, "and eat."

Allen's heart pumped like an engine, and he followed the man below. They went into the galley at last, and there the sailor said to the cook—a fat man in a greasy greyish apron, "Can you give him something?"

The cook grinned, and his open lips disclosed a gap in his blackened teeth. Allen thrilled queerly and smiled back.

"There's a bit o' skilly left. Will that do you, you young squirt?"

"Yes, mister," said Allen with enthusiasm. And when the bowl of something that was not skilly was put into his hands he ate it eagerly, savouring every mouthful of sailor's fare.

"Come, I'll show you over the ship," said the sailor. "But look slippy and keep your eyes skinned. We don't want little jokers like you running into the captain or falling down the hold."

For an hour Allen, in his bare feet, padded after the sailor all over the ship and, under the radiance of this boy's smile, the old fellow blossomed into a raconteur. He told the most hair-raising tales of ships, gales, sailors' fights, the lure of foreign ports and the menace of foreign seas. He felt the lad's interest and keenness to know more and, under the compelling power of his own loquaciousness, carried them both far away from Wallaroo and the calm waters of Spencer Gulf. But at last the torrent of his speech slackened and he became once more the wizened old sailor who had little use for speech.

Now it was Allen's turn. He asked the names of the sails, pointing as he did so to the lines of rigging above his head. His brain became a whirl of exciting sounds: flying jib, martingale, royal yard, bowsprit, fore-topmast stay sail, spanker, topsail, signal halyards and a dozen more, to be sorted out days after in the solitude of night before sleep and dreams claimed him.

He was shown the sailor's way of tying a knot that would not budge, and tied one himself a minute later for the old sailor's approval. He heard a smattering of sea jargon and knew it for a familiar language.

"I'm going to sea when I'm a bit older," he confided to his new friend as they stood together by the gangway and Allen was preparing to descend. "P'raps 'twill be on the *Flying Gull*."

"Ah," said the sailor, "the old sail-ships will be done for soon, now that steam boats can do the trips in half the time. Wind or no wind makes no difference to steam boats, and soon, my lad, we sailing ships will be in the doldrums in more ways than one."

Allen had been waiting nearly an hour at the head of the jetty, then at last put on his stockings and boots, and had just begun to think of walking the six miles home to Wallaroo Mines when Joe Lampin and his horse and cart appeared around a bend in the road.

"Still there?" roared Joe. "I thought 'ee woulda been gone by now. I be late, but I've got a good 'aul. Jump up."

It was almost six o'clock, and Allen was in a fever to be home. "Make haste," he said to Joe. "The drag'll be back by half past six. I want to get home when Rich and Bob do. Mother mightn't ask questions if we all get in together. She'll think we all went to the picnic. I won't let on till bed-time, and if I show her the fish she won't mind so much."

Joe whipped up Topsy and they did the distance in fine style.

"We'll be home in time," said Allen, looking back towards the sun which was low on the horizon. "Go it, Topsy!"

Arriving at the crossing, Allen saw no sign of the drags, but glimpsed Mr Grey leading back his fat bay horses to the stables and knew that all was lost. He put the four whiting, limp from lying in the afternoon heat, inside his tunic and walked slowly toward his gate. He went around to the back and saw Rich sitting on the tank, eating a slice of bread and dripping in the dusk.

Rich saw him at once, and cautiously walked to the corner of the house, and whispered in a voice choked with excitement and bread, "You're going to get it! Mother's ramping mad. We had n'awful lot of fun at the picnic. You should've been there. Dickie Treloar brought a branch of wild tobacco with him and put it in the copper and they had to chuck away all the tea, and Lizzie Innes fell out of a tree and broke her arm, and somebody set fire to the scrub and we spent all the afternoon beating it out. You should've been there, Allen! We had good fun!" He chewed for a minute. "Where have you been, anyway?"

"Sh! I've been to Wallaroo all day with Joe Lampin."

"Where's your hat?"

Allen looked about him as if he might find it somewhere on the ground. "I dunno. Must've left it in Joe's cart," he said at last in a weak voice.

"My word, you're going to catch it!" said Rich slowly.

Allen walked with lagging steps towards the tank and left his offering of fish on its wooden top. "Don't touch them," he said to Rich. "They're for mother."

Polly opened the door, and the anxious look on her face gave way to relief as she saw the drooping figure of her son; then her face changed, and Allen advanced slowly to meet his mother's wrath.

They all went into the lighted kitchen. Nathan was sitting at the table, with pillows piled behind him and the patchwork quilt about his knees. He looked at Polly's angry face. "Don't, Pol," was all he said, and Polly turned away, and Allen was left standing before his father.

"Well, me son?" said Nathan.

"Don't scold me, father," said Allen, going to him. "I shouldn't have done it. I know I ought to have gone to the picnic, but I wanted to go to Wallaroo more." And other words came tumbling out of his mouth like water from a fountain.

Nathan listened to him in silence and heard his story of the sailor of the *Flying Gull*, and at last he spoke.

"Well, Allen," he said, "I can't knock the sea out of 'ee, me son, for thy mother's people, an' mine too for a matter o' that, were sailors and fisherfolk, an' the sea do come out in a lad, an' us can't do naught about un. But," and his voice grew stern, "us can do summat for a boy what disobeys 'is elders an' da worrit 'is mother. Polly," he said, "take Allen out into the wash-'ouse an' give un a thrashin'. I woulden ask 'ee to do it, mother, if I wassen sick an' bad meself."

Nathan had not meant this last to wound Allen, but the boy, of a sudden, felt the pathos of this part of Nathan's rebuke and burst into tears. Polly led him out into the wash-house and, taking up a stick kept in a crack in the rough wall for such a purpose as this, let down Allen's trousers with many an angry word.

"*This*," she said, giving him three sharp cuts on his buttocks with the switch, "be for runnin' away from the picnic. *This* be for messin' up thy good trousers wi' sea water an' comin' 'ome stinkin' o' dead fish. *This* be for losin' thy new 'at, an' *this*," she finished, grabbing him by the arm and giving him a good shaking, "be for worritin' thy poor father. Now go off to bed without any tea, an' if ever I 'ear tell of 'ee goin' off to Wallaroo agin with a crazy old fisherman, an' goin' on strange boats with a pack o' cutthroat sailors, I'll—I'll——" she was at a loss. "Go on to bed!" she finished, lamely.

Later that night when the house was still and the regular breathing of Rich and Bob, tired out from the rigours of the day, came to him in the hot stillness of the back bedroom, Allen crept painfully from bed and, opening the back door, walked out softly into the moonlight. For one instant he thought of the *Flying Gull* lying at anchor under the stars, the next his eyes alighted on the bodies of the four small fish glistening dully in the light of the moon.

With one stride he was at the tank and had the fish in his hands. He thought of the scene in the wash-house; he thought of his mother sleeping in the front room of the cottage and, with one free sweeping movement, flung the fish far out into the night and went back to bed.

CHAPTER IX

THUMP, thump, thump!

The sound of the big drum in the yard of the school by the Kadina mill reverberated throughout Wallaroo Mines on this March morning in 1877 and beat with intensified volume in Polly Thomas's brain. Thump, thump, thump!

Nathan was walking in the back yard of the cottage, both hands leaning on a heavy stick. He walked slowly and painfully, his whole body bending forward. Before him ran Annie who, discouraged by his slow progress, would grasp, now and then, at a corner of his coat and tug him on towards the pepper-tree.

Under the low, hanging branches of this shady tree Polly had placed a seat for Nathan, and he would lower himself thankfully into its cushioned softness and stretch out his legs a little for Annie to clamber up to his lap. Here they would sit by the hour, and Annie's prattling talk would charm away the thoughts of his helplessness, for, contrary to the doctor's opinion and Polly's hopes, the heat of summer had not cured Nathan. Certainly he could now walk slowly about the house and garden, but the swelling of his joints had not subsided and any thought of his going to the mines was not to be considered. It would be many months before the effects of Nathan's immersion in the tank and of his consequent illness would leave him. Polly, looking at his swollen fingers, would wonder sometimes with a strange frightening dread, if those fingers would ever hold a miner's pick again; but she said nothing of this to Nathan, and both of them strengthened each other according to the nature of each.

"Bless the Lord, O my soul!—Oo 'ealeth all thy diseases," prayed Nathan with the sustaining comfort of his simple faith.

"Faith without works be dead," supplemented Polly. "Turn over, Nat, an' let me give the other side a good rubbin'. That'll fetch it out of 'ee."

Looking out at him from the vantage point of the little kitchen window as he sat under the tree on this hot March morning, Polly twisted and retwisted her white apron with shaking fingers. She had, a few moments before, dragged the wooden box—companion of all their travels—from under Nathan's bed and, searching round under the heap of winter garments it contained, had drawn out a tin box in which they kept every penny, except the hundred pounds, that they owned in the world. It contained nine pounds, seventeen shillings and fourpence.

For five months now Polly had had to dip into this savings-box for living expenses. She had not extracted a great sum, it is true, for the mine captain had kept a fatherly eye upon them in the early days of Nathan's sickness and for three months Nathan's sick-pay had come to him every Saturday morning by the hand of the paymaster himself. But the mines' sick fund had had many calls of late and was almost exhausted, and pay from this source would soon be discontinued.

Neighbours too, with practical Cornish sympathy, had baked for Polly, and many a gift of fish, fowl and eggs had come to the Thomas household in the earlier part of Nathan's illness; but now it was becoming different. There were fewer visits from kindly inquirers bearing baskets of good things and, with the exception of a large load of fire-wood and a side of bacon at Christmas-time and a supply of candles sent to the house, help from the mines had ceased.

"This be the time," thought Polly, twisting her apron at the kitchen window, "this be the time to use the 'undered pounds! I allus knawed 'twould come a time when us'd need un bad, an' this be it. Summat allus kept me back from writin' to Lawyer Birmin'am to ask for un. Summat allus tellt me there were worse to come, an' the worstest thing were this—Nathan crippled up. What's to come of us! What's to come of us!"

From a drawer in the cedar chiffonier in the dining-room she drew out two sheets of writing-paper, and from the kitchen dresser she took a penny bottle of black ink and a pen and, sitting down at the kitchen table, gave herself to the exacting task of letter-writing; this time a letter to Lawyer Birmingham asking for her money.

She filled the two pages with her stiff handwriting. Many words were ill spelt and a line here and there was scored out heavily, but she used every inch of space on both sides of the pages and, by constant reiteration, felt that she had at least made it clear that she was in trouble and wanted her hundred pounds.

This business of the hundred pounds did not prove the blessing that Polly had hoped it would. When she left the note with Lawyer Birmingham in the fastness of his solid-looking safe she had had a hazy idea that there it would remain, and the interest she would receive quarterly was to be Lawyer Birmingham's contribution for the pleasure of keeping the note in his safe. Such ideas had been promptly knocked out of her head by Peter two days after they had made their visit to the lawyer's office.

"Now look, Polly," Peter had said on that occasion, "I think I've done right in letting you leave your money with this man. He is a respected member of our chapel, and I have no business as a Christian to question any man's motives; but, as your cousin-by-marriage and, in your husband's absence, the one responsible to him for your conduct, I have the right to find out all I can about this lawyer and his business. From what I know of him he is an honest man, and your money will be as safe with him as with any other man in the colony. He has promised to find an investment for you. You have a receipt for the money placed in his care, and that covers you. In the matter of the nature of the investment I can give you no advice, but I do say this: if it is something in city property—and he has hinted it will be—then you and Nathan would be well advised to take it. There will be fortunes made in this way, Polly, and you and Nat may be the lucky ones. Besides, it will be safer for you to have your money invested in this way than to carry it about with you as you have been doing. A good investment means something put by and interest always accruing for you and your children. It would not be wise for you to have the spending of so large a sum,

Polly. It is too great a responsibility. Now that Nathan has employment at Wallaroo Mines and has health and strength to work, it is far better that your money should be earning more for you. There may come a time when you will be in need, and then you can realize on your investment, and if you are fortunate it will return you more than you put into it and will also have paid you interest over a period of years."

Peter, with his explanation and advice, had helped Polly as nobody else had ever done during her life. Polly herself was a saving woman and would never spend for spending's sake, but she had no business head—few women in 1867 had—and knew absolutely nothing of the business side of money-making or investments. Married to Nathan, she was handicapped: linked to a kindly, devout, hard-working partner who, unaided, had rarely made a decision of his own in all his life and knew even less than Polly of the ways of the world. Spurred on by Polly's hopes of advancement, better living conditions and constant employment in the new country, Nathan had willingly fallen in with her idea to emigrate to Australia, and never afterwards did he regret the decision that Polly had helped him to make.

Three months after they had settled at Wallaroo Mines a letter had come from Lawyer Birmingham saying that, with Polly's permission, he proposed buying for a hundred pounds—minus ten pounds for his fee—a two-roomed house in Norman Street, Adelaide, built of stone and now tenanted. The rent, eight shillings, received each week, minus Lawyer Birmingham's commission of half a crown on each week's rent collected, would be sent to Polly in a lump sum every quarter-day. In this way, after deducting for rates and taxes, Polly and Nathan had a fraction over thirteen pounds a year from their investment.

After much calculating Polly had announced, "Looks to me as if us'll get thirteen pounds a year out of un an' still 'ave the 'ouse to sell or do what us want with un. Nat, we be landowners. Back 'ome we could 'ave pew in chapel!"

Nathan had slapped his knees, delighted. "Sign the papers, Pol, an' send un back to Lawyer Birmin'am," he said with unaccustomed haste. "Thee's got an 'ead on thy shoulders, me dear," he added with great pride.

Polly had added her signatures to the documents that the lawyer had send and posted them next day, then for months went about her work with suppressed excitement, not really believing her good fortune until the quarter's money was actually in her hands. Each quarter-day the full amount was put into the tin in the clothes-box, and was extracted only for necessities that Nathan's pay could not cover. On occasions, when from illness Nathan had been unable to work, the contents of the little tin had kept them until he was able to go underground again.

For eight years this welcome addition to their resources had put in a regular appearance and then, nearly two years ago, the payments had ceased; but a polite note from Lawyer Birmingham, accompanied by a long list of repairs done to the house, informed them that urgent renovation had been necessary. On each of the following quarter-days other notes had been received by Polly with more items of repairs for explanation.

"Lawks," said Polly, as she read the list, "they must be rebuildin' the 'ole place: new fence, new front door, an' another roof to the wash-'ouse an' board floors in both rooms. 'Ow long be this 'ere goin' on?"

Last quarter-day there had been neither letter nor money from the lawyer and Polly, deep in her troubles, had forgotten to expect them; but by the time Nathan had begun to walk about again the urgency of funds grew more and more obvious to her. This, surely, was the time that Peter had said might come to them! The house in Norman Street must be sold!

She walked into Kadina next day to post her letter. As yet she had said nothing of this matter to Nathan.

"Evrathin' be in my name," she reasoned with herself, "an' I can fix un all up. I'll tell Nat when I 'ave the money, then 'e won't feel so bad about not workin' an' all. There's no sense nor reason in lettin' 'im knaw we be in want."

That night, after the letter had been posted, the family sat down to tea in the kitchen and were about to begin when Nathan, looking up at the clock with the painted glass front, asked, "Where's Allen?"

"That I'd like to knaw!" said Polly, cutting thick slices from the bread. " 'Tis light now till close on seven o'clock,

an' 'e'll be playin' round till dark. Nothin' I can do can
teach un to be 'ome at set times. 'Tis no good talkin'. 'E
don't take a scrap o' notice."

"He was out on the flat when I came in to tea. I called
out to him, but he wouldn't come," said Rich.

"Go on out an' 'ustle un up," said Polly. "If 'e idden in
in ten minutes 'e shan't 'ave no tea."

The rest of the household went on eating the brawn
that Polly had made the night before from a shin of beef
and some scraps of bacon, and Rich's calls rang pleasantly
through the house as he stood at the open front door calling
into the twilight.

"He's nowhere in sight!" he called out to his mother.
"Shall I walk up the road a bit and see if I can find him?"

"No, come on in," said Polly, exasperatedly. "We don't
want the 'ole 'ouse traipsin' about at this hour. If 'e come
'ome in ten minutes, well an' good. If 'e don't 'e goes
without. Come on an' finish thy tea."

The tea was finished and the table cleared. The clock
stood at seven, and Allen had not returned.

Rich and Bob were washing up the dishes in the kitchen,
and Polly had lain Annie in her little night-gown on top
of the sheets on her bed in the front room, where she lay
singing to herself, kicking her toes against the whitewashed
wall of the bedroom and watching her mother expertly
undressing Nathan, clothing him in his frilled night-shirt
and deftly lifting him up on to the big bed.

Annie never tired of watching father being put to bed.
First Polly took off his coat and shirt, changed his flannels
and, quickly popping his night-shirt over his head, buttoned
him into it, and then gently sat him on the edge of the bed
while she wriggled his other clothes from under the
enveloping folds of his night-shirt. Invariably she forgot to
remove his boots before beginning to undress him and
would have to sit on the floor and try to get them off his
feet, encumbered as these were with the folds of his trousers,
which had slipped about his ankles.

"Drat it!" Polly would say, rising at last with the boots
in her hand, and her face red and hot with exertion.
"Cussen 'ee 'elp me to remember thee's got feet? I allus
forget the pesky things."

Then she would take off Nathan's trousers and socks and, adjusting his knitted knee-bands, would grasp his ankles and swing his legs up and on to the bed. How Nathan would groan! Annie waited for this moment.

"Aw!" groaned Nathan, slowly lowering himself down into the bed. "A-a-w!"

"Never mind, faver," Annie would say, repeating what she had heard Polly say quite often in Nathan's illness. "Good job to-day's over."

"Thank God for bed!" Nathan would invariably reply, earnestly and thankfully. Now the rubbing-time began. Annie would lie on her stomach with her feet in the air and watch mother rubbing the liniment on father's back and knees. The long time that father took to turn in bed was inexplicable to Annie. She could turn three times round, and often did so, to father's turning half-way. And now father, too, lay on his stomach, with his night-shirt rolled up into a fold between his shoulders, and the pungent odour of Royal Liniment floated out into the night. As Polly rubbed she sang, and Annie, feeling sleepy now, would drop her head on to her pillow and, still lying on her stomach, would abandon herself to the pleasing sensations of Royal Liniment, the swish of mother's hand on father's big back and the rhythm of mother's song.

> Ring the bells in the old steeple,
> Ring the bells in the old steeple.

Polly sang on and on, up and down, always the same song about the bells in the old steeple, ending at the fourth line with "Father's gone to town". Then it all began again.

> Ring the bells . . .

"This be the nicest part o' the 'ole day," thought Annie drowsily, on the borderland of sleep. "Dear mother."

The candle in the front bedroom was out, and Polly was leaving the room. She turned at the door and called back softly, "Good night to 'ee, me dear," and Nathan sleepily replied, "God bless 'ee Polly," in a faint soothed voice. Polly would not have missed that for the world.

She went to the kitchen. Rich had his history book on

the table and was reading in the candlelight. Bob was setting up the draught-board and pieces that his father had made for Rich on his ninth birthday.

"Where's Allen?" said Polly, looking about.

"He hasn't come in yet," said Rich, not raising his eyes from his book.

Polly glanced at the clock and, opening the back door looked out into the dark, moonless night. The air was warm and still and the sky, overcast with clouds now and without a single star, seemed to be pressing down towards the earth. Seeing a flash of sheet lightning in the west, Polly said, "There's thunder in the air to-night. 'Appen there'll be rain by mornin'."

Slight sounds from far away came to her above the familiar noise from the mines: the trampling of horses in an adjacent stable, the bark of a dog out Newtown way, a neighbour's laugh, and the faint sound of singing from the Wesleyan Church.

"What's Allen up to? Where's 'e to?" questioned Polly.

"I dunno," said Bob joining her at the open door. "Are you going to give him what for when he comes home, mother?"

Polly was noncommittal. "I'll see what 'e 'as to say first," she answered.

She went back into the kitchen, but could settle to nothing. Nine o'clock came, and time for the boys to be in bed. They had finished the game of draughts, and, as the last stroke of nine sounded in the room, Polly got up and said to them in a firm voice, "Put all they chattels away, an' the pair of 'ee start at Johnnie Flint's an' go to ev'ry 'ouse on the mines where there be young lads, an' ask if they've seen aught o' Allen."

The boys were dismayed.

"It's dark as pitch," said Bob.

"Everybody'll be in bed," protested Rich, "and we can't go walking about in the dark, stumbling over things and getting lost and falling down the costeen-pits."

Polly's hands flew to her heart, and her face was the colour of her white apron. "Allen!" was all she said. Quickly turning to Rich and Bob, she spoke in an agitated voice. "Thees two stay 'ere. Don't breathe a word to father.

If 'e wakes up tell un 'tis only nine o'clock an' I've slipped over to Miz Polderrick's to borrow a cup o' flour. Don't let father be worrited. An' Bob, thee go to bed. Thee should've been in bed a full hour agone. Make 'im go, Rich, there's a good lad." And she was out and running off into the night before the boys could move.

Bob began to cry, wiping the tears away with the back of his hand. "I don't want to go to bed. I want to wait up for Allen," he sobbed. "He's got my alley-tor. I swapped it with him for a piece of candle, and now I want it back."

"Shut your noise," said Rich tersely, "and come on to bed."

Bob was put to bed, and lay in the boys' bedroom with the door ajar so that he might watch Rich in the kitchen. For a while he kept up a one-sided conversation with his brother, and finally went to sleep.

Rich, in the kitchen, put his elbows on the table, rested his head on his hands and gave himself up to imagining all the horrible things that could happen to anybody who lost his way at night among the terrors of the open shafts and pits. Why hadn't he gone instead of mother? Why had he been so cowardly and afraid of the dark? He went to the door now and looked out into the blackness, broken here and there by a cottage light, and something of the still heaviness of the night that had so oppressed Polly weighed upon him, too. Mother! Allen! What was the menace of this quiet night?

His eyes would hardly keep open, and the muscular twitches of his tired limbs were making him irritable and unstrung when, at something past eleven, Polly pushed open the door and walked into the kitchen. Her hair was dishevelled, her apron torn and dirty. She saw at a glance that Allen was not there, and sank into a chair with a heavy sigh.

"Nobody's seen un," she said at last. " 'E played wi' Ted Walsh till dark set in, up by Taylor's shaft; then 'e come away 'ome." She lay her cheek on the cold table top. "Oh, Allen, Allen, where 'ee to, me dear? What 'ave 'ee been doin' of, lad?" She raised her head. "I even went to see that old man up Kadina, in the lane at the back o' Birks's the chemist. 'E were workin' late on some jim-crack machine 'e were inventin'. Allen were allus 'angin' 'bout there watchin' all they there contraptions. But 'e adden seen me boy. . . . Oh, Allen, where 'ee to?"

A short while after, a knock was heard on the kitchen door, timid and questioning, and Polly rushed to lift the latch. Johnnie Flint, a rough-looking miner of Nathan's age, stood there with a lantern in his hand.

"What news?" asked Polly, breathlessly.

"No news at all," answered Johnnie, coming into the kitchen. "It beats me, Miz Thomas, where a little lad coulda got to atween school an' 'ome, but 'e could333 come to no 'arm, that's certain."

"Not atween school an' 'ere," said Polly. "But me Allen were a wanderer. 'E were allus goin' off somewhere. Like as not 'e've gone off on summat or other an' 'ave forgot to come 'ome."

"Well, I only 'ope as thee's right, Miz Thomas, but I must say 'tis a dark night to be wanderin' 'bout in. 'Tis workin' up for rain."

"Thees da knaw, same as I do," said Polly, after an awkward pause, "there be many a place for a rovin' boy to fall into on the mines. I can see thee's fearful too, Mr Flint."

Johnnie Flint shifted from one leg to the other. "Well, 'tis like this 'ere," he said at last. "If 'e be comin' 'ome 'e woulda been 'ere by now, an' 'e ain't 'ere, so us 'ave to think 'e can't do it for some good reason or t'other. There 'tis, Miz Thomas, an' can't be no tisscr."

Polly nodded her head slowly.

"Well, ma'am, mother be comin' over to sit with 'ee till we gets back. Bob Walsh an' me be goin' out to look for the little lad."

"Let me go too," put in Rich, springing up. "I'm not afraid of the dark or anything."

Polly grasped his sleeve tightly. "Stay 'ere!" she commanded. "I coulden abide two sons out on the mines to-night."

All through the night Polly and Mrs Flint and Mrs Wilson sat in the kitchen, and Mrs Flint comforted Polly with rough sympathy that she could understand when, in the hours after midnight, she broke into pitiful sobbing.

Out on Matta Flat and in and out of the engine-houses, the stables, the offices and about the gaping costeen-pits bobbed the yellow lights from the lanterns, and the faint halloahs sounded in the clear, rain-washed air. "Coo-ee! Coo-ee! Coo-ee!" a dozen voices called.

About three o'clock in the morning Nathan awoke and, although the bedroom and kitchen doors were closed, he heard through the thin walls the low tone of voices. He felt the empty space beside him in the bed, and called to Polly. She came in immediately with a candle, and Nathan saw at once the disordered state of her dress and hair.

"What's amiss, Polly?" he questioned, his face filled with alarm.

Polly knelt beside the bed and pressed her face into the warmth of Nathan's breast. "Thank God 'ee be awake, Nat. I need 'ee terrible bad. 'Tis three in the mornin', an' Allen be still out, an' oh, Nat, there be a feelin' 'ere," and she placed her hand on her heart and looked into Nathan's face, "that tells me summat 'ave 'appened to un. Speak to God for me, Nat. Pray for me, for I can't do it meself. God bless me little boy an' bring un 'ome!"

The first faint tinge of dawn was showing in the east when Polly, with her shawl about her head, pulled the kitchen door to behind her, leaving Mrs Flint, Mrs Wilson and Nathan by the fire inside the cottage.

It was five o'clock, and there remained two hours before the men coming from night shift would be about and the miners who had been searching for Allen would be returning to their homes to snatch a hasty breakfast before setting forth again with the first morning light.

Polly ran through the cool greyness like a ghost and, coming at last to Bob Walsh's cottage behind the Wesleyan Church and seeing a light in the kitchen window, she went to the back door and knocked loudly.

Bob Walsh opened the door. He started when he saw Polly. "Have you brought news, Mrs Thomas?" he asked. But, as Polly walked into the lighted kitchen and he saw her face, he knew she had no tidings.

"Oh, my dear," said fat little Mrs Walsh, coming forward from the fire where she was cooking some bacon, "I'm so sorry." And she put her arms about Polly and kissed her on the cheek and led her to a chair. They were not very friendly as a rule, for Mrs Walsh had been a lady's maid in London, and it was reported on the mines that she was stuck up, and that, to a Cornish mind, is a cardinal sin. But there is no caste in trouble; all men at some time are sorrow's sons.

"Tell me what our Allen were playin' at when 'e an' thy young Ted were on the flat last night," said Polly when she had refused a cup of tea that Mrs Walsh had poured out for her. " 'Ave 'e told 'ee?"

"We've asked him many times, but he only says that he and your Allen were playing on the flat—just racing and jumping, he says. And when he came home to tea Allen stayed behind. When Ted was nearly home he turned around to whistle to Allen, but couldn't see him. What he did or where he went in that short time Ted doesn't know."

"Is he asleep?" said Polly, after a pause.

"Yes, he's asleep now. But if there's anything you want to ask him, then I'll wake him up and bring him out. It was a good while before he dropped off again after Bob and Mr Flint had finished questioning him. I had the work of the world to get him back to bed at all."

After a short absence in the next room, during which time Polly drank a little of the tea that she had previously refused, Mrs Walsh returned with Ted, her only son, aged nine. He had a brass-buttoned coat over his night-shirt, and hung back in the doorway when he saw Polly. His mother pushed him forward, and he stood blinking in the light.

"Come 'ere to me, Ted," said Polly. "Thee were the last to see me boy Allen. What were 'ee and 'im doin' out there on the flat last night?"

Ted blinked his eyes and swallowed hard. "We were playing touchy and having jumps."

"What were Allen doin' when thee come on 'ome to tea?"

"He went on playing round and having jumps by himself," said Ted, rubbing one bare foot over the other and looking down at his toes.

"What were 'ee two boys jumpin' over?" asked Polly at last, slowly.

Ted lifted his head and looked at her, and then his gaze

shifted to his father and mother and back again to Polly. He remained silent and his father was about to speak, but Polly held up her hand and quietly spoke again to Ted.

"What be 'ee afeared of, Ted?" she said, going to him. "Tell me. What were thee an' Allen jumpin' over?"

The boy's chest heaved. "Dad'll lick me if I tell. He said he would if I did it again."

"Then I know what it is," said Bob Walsh, his face bright with relief. "They must have been jumping over the drain, Mrs Thomas. I told Ted I should whip him if ever he did it again. Last time he played by the drain he fell in and was covered from top to toe in black mud. His mother, there, couldn't get the stuff off his clothes for days." He got up from his chair. "Now, don't think that Allen could have come to any harm there. You know your-self a cat couldn't get drowned in that bit of water. And anyway, Mrs Thomas, I was all over that part of the flat, and if Allen had fallen in and couldn't get up again any of us chaps would have heard him. No, I'm afraid he wandered farther afield, and we can only wait till morning."

Polly had her hand on the latch of the door. "Good-bye, all," she said as she opened the door, "an' thank 'ee."

Out in the road again, she gathered up her skirts and ran off in the direction of the mine drain.

This drain, about five feet deep, with roughly timbered sides, carried the water away from the mines, ran through Wallaroo Mines and out along the back road for two miles towards Kadina Cemetery, and finished in an open paddock where the water eventually soaked away. There was always a small quantity of water in this drain, perhaps a foot deep; and under the stagnant water was a layer of sand and thick black mud. The drain itself varied in width from two feet to about three feet six, and a favourite pastime of the youngsters was straddling it and walking so until, owing to its gradual increase of width, they had either to fall in or go back. This required too great a stretch of leg for the smaller lads, who had to be content with jumping from side to side.

"Poor Allen!" said Polly, as she ran. " 'E 'ave fallen in for sure, an' were too scared to come 'ome an' show 'isself."

She peered over the edge of the drain and walked quickly

along beside it across the flat. She could see nothing but the dull gleam of the water below, and the sheen on the leaves of the slimy water-weed that grew there. Suddenly ahead of her she saw a shape: a figure in the water. She stumbled forward and, looking down, saw Allen lying on his face in the drain with water-weed tangled in his hair. She grasped the strong mallee posts timbering the sides of the drain and lowered herself into the water, which did not reach her knees. She knelt in the cold water and mud beside her child and, with an anguished cry, took him in her arms and turned his face to the morning light.

She had the strength to behold him, with only one sharp cry for expression, and, cradling his cold, stiff body in her lap, tenderly wiped the mud from his dead face. On his brow was a great bruise, darker than the mud itself; and the purplish hue of his face she could not entirely wipe away.

Bob Walsh found her there a while later, and until his death could not erase from his memory the sight of Polly in the narrow confines of the drain, soiled with the black mud and stagnant water and holding in her arms the dead body of her son who had wanted to be a sailor, to ride the seven seas, and who, by the irony of fate, had died a sailor's death.

CHAPTER X

Two weeks after Allen's death Polly put her sorrow behind her and, with Bob, journeyed to Adelaide to interview Lawyer Birmingham.

As the train drew into the Adelaide railway station Polly remembered her journey of ten years back, and shuddered when she saw the seat whereon she had sat then, listening as Mrs Lillywhite had told her of Ellen's approaching death. Try as she might she could not help a backward glance at it as she hustled Bob from the train, and the sight set her lips a-trembling.

"Allen and Ellen! Allen and Ellen!" Tears rolled down her cheeks, but she ignored them and, thrusting out her chin, said to herself, "Tears be for the weak uns, an' from now on I 'ave to be the strength o' them all."

An hour later Polly and Bob stood at Mrs Lillywhite's front door in Brown Street, and Polly rapped upon it with a steady hand. The door opened and Mrs Lillywhite, in a black silk dress and shiny black apron, was framed in the opening.

"For goodness' sake!" she said at last, after a long look at Polly. "It's Mrs Thomas! Why, whatever brings you here, my dear? Come inside, do."

Polly and Bob entered.

"I've come to Adelaide to do business," said Polly.

"Good gracious!" replied Mrs Lillywhite, not without admiration. Then, "You staying long, Mrs Thomas?"

"Can't 'ardly say, me dear," said Polly, sitting down and settling her carpet-bag beside her.

"Who're you staying with, Mrs Thomas?" said Mrs Lillywhite, whose natural curiosity was not yet appeased.

"Wi' thee, Miz Lillywhite," Polly answered calmly, and began to remove her Sunday bonnet.

With this matter satisfactorily disposed of, Polly and

Mrs Lillywhite settled down for a long talk. All the sad tale of Nathan's illness and Allen's death had to be gone over and wept over, and after a while Bob edged towards the door, and sidled out into the room beyond and then into the open air of the Lillywhite back yard.

In this yard was a fowl-house and, looking pensively over its wire and board enclosure, was a young boy of Bob's age or a little older. Bob stood still by the back door; and the lad by the fowl-house, turning about in the course of his survey and seeing a strange boy standing in his back yard and almost in the doorway of his house, stiffened his back and, taking his foot from the railing of the fowl-house, stared at Bob. Bob stared back at him, uncertainly.

The two boys eyed each other like two dogs across the space of the yard; then the elder boy came towards Bob, negligently kicking a stone or two in his progress, during which Bob edged away towards the corner of the house. At last they were a yard or so apart, and something had to be said, although, until then, each had endeavoured to keep up a grand show of indifference.

"What's your name?" said Bunty Lillywhite in a husky voice.

"Bob Thomas," replied Bob, jerkily.

Bunty digested this while he examined Bob carefully. "Where do you come from?"

"Wallaroo Mines."

"What you doing here?"

"Mother and me've come to stay with your mother," said Bob, rubbing his spine on the sharp angle of the house wall.

Bunty was interested, but not impressed. "How old're you?" he said at last.

"Going on for six. . . . My brother Allen got drownded week before last. They put him in a big hole up at our cemetery."

Bunty was impressed this time and regarded Bob with a kindlier eye, then volunteered his part of the introduction. "I'm seven. My birthday's on Christmas Day, and I get my birthday and Christmas presents all in one."

"Do you?" said Bob, casually but not discouragingly.

Conversation languished until Bunty put his hand into

his pants pocket and drew out a marble-bag of striped galatea. "Can you play marbles?"

Bob nodded.

Bunty knelt down on the ground. "Come on, I'll give you a game."

But Bob pressed his back harder into the angle of the wall, and looked away into the middle distance.

"Come on," said Bunty in an almost friendly tone.

"Can't," said Bob in a strangled voice.

"I'll lend you some," said Bunty magnanimously. "Come on."

Bob didn't move.

"What's the matter with you?" said Bunty in a hostile tone, putting his marble-bag back into his pocket.

Bob swallowed. "I got me best pants on," he said at last. "I'll get 'em dirty."

Bunty brightened. "You can kneel on me marble-bag," said he, dragging it out again.

Bob crimsoned to the roots of his hair and, bending over, directed Bunty's attention to the knees of his Sunday pants.

Bunty stared hard at Bob's pants, and more particularly at the spot in the centre of each knee where Polly, determined to prevent any such possibilities as this, had sewn, very firmly, a round black button, set about with a swirl of braid.

Bob's embarrassed eyes reverted to mid-distance, and Bunty stowed the marble-bag away in good earnest. Then quite suddenly he spoke. "Ay, have you ever seen a fowl lay an egg? Have you, Bob?"

"No. We haven't got any fowls now," said Bob, his eyes on the fowl-house. "We've eat ours!"

"Well, come down here," said Bunty. "If we watch out we might see one do it. Come on."

Bunty made off across the yard, Bob following on his heels, and a friendship began that was to endure for fifty years.

That same evening, when the tea dishes had been wiped and put away on the dresser and the boys were lying on their beds in the back room talking in husky whispers, Jabez Lillywhite took his pipe from the shelf above the fireplace and sat down beside his wife and Polly, who had drawn their chairs up to the warm crackling blaze.

"And now," said Jabez, when his pipe was drawing and when he had partially concealed himself behind a barrage of smoke, "mother, there, and I have got a piece of bad news to tell you, Mrs Thomas. When she knew why you'd come to Adelaide, mother wouldn't hear of you going straight off to Lawyer Birmingham's office to-morrow without having a word with me first."

"That's true," put in Mrs Lillywhite. "I had to tell father. He's a man and knows how to go about these things. I couldn't have told you the bad news for the life of me, Mrs Thomas."

"News? Bad news? What're thees two talkin' of?" interrupted Polly, who had begun to realize that something was amiss.

The two Lillywhites exchanged a glance through the smoke.

"Spit un off your tongue, quick!" said Polly. "What is't?"

"Well, Mrs Thomas, ma'am," said Jabez, heartily disliking his task, "it's hard to tell you, but I s'pose I must, though it may be worrying you without cause—" he spat into the fire, "and I'm sure I hope it is—but they do say in chapel that Lawyer Birmingham has cleared out, done a bunk!"

He *had* "done a bunk"—safe, gold seals, black broadcloth and all. And it took two visits to the new Bible Christian minister and two to a reliable lawyer of the minister's recommendation to convince Polly that the house in Norman Street did not belong to her, had never belonged to her and was lost to her for ever.

"Me papers? Me deeds? Me titles? Never 'ad any!" said Polly emphatically, in reply to her lawyer's questionings.

"Didn't you sign anything? Didn't you receive any copies of your deed of ownership of the house?"

"Papers 'e did send," put in Polly, "an' I signed un all an' sent un back to un."

"You sent them back to Mr Birmingham?" said the lawyer incredulously. "And never made any attempt to get them again?"

"No. Why should I of?" said Polly, flustered.

"For the simple reason, my dear lady," said the lawyer, placing the tips of his fingers together, "that they were the only proofs of ownership you had, besides the registration of sale in the lands titles office. This registration was made, but not in your name. We can find the record of the sale of the house in Norman Street to Alfred Cummings Egerton Birmingham, and there is nothing more to be concluded than that he relied on your implicit trust in him and your ignorance of South Australian laws and entered the sale and deed of ownership of your home in his own name."

"But 'e've been sendin' us the rent all these years," said Polly, unconvinced. "Surely that da show 'e knawed 'twere our 'ouse?"

"In court of law that possibly could make a case against him, unless he were clever enough to find a satisfactory explanation, which I doubt. But meanwhile, this Mr Birmingham is reported to have left the State, and rumour has it that he has gone to America. He was seen on the wharf at Sydney, and there has been no further trace of him. You see, you are not the only person he victimized. Unfortunately, Mrs Thomas, others too have suffered from his duplicity. It seems he made rather a habit of this kind of thing among the immigrants."

"An' I sought un out!" said Polly. "More fool me! I liked the look of un," she added bitterly.

The lawyer nodded his head sympathetically. "You have a good case against him, Mrs Thomas. If he is caught you stand a chance of getting your house back, and getting him a good stiff sentence as well. But in the meantime. . . ."

"Yes?" said Polly.

The lawyer appealed to the Bible Christian minister who accompanied Polly. "Well," he said, with genuine feeling, "there is nothing to be done."

"But the 'ouse in Norman Street? I bought that wi' Nathan's an' my good money!" said Polly, her voice quivering.

"Unfortunately, Alfred Birmingham sold it a week before he left Adelaide, and the present occupiers are the registered owners of the house," continued the lawyer. "They bought it from him for one hundred and twenty pounds, and already are adding two stone rooms at the back. This, of course," he added, turning to the minister, "further complicates matters. These people bought from Birmingham in good faith and, until I interviewed them at your request, they had never heard Mrs Thomas's name."

Polly buried her face in her hands. "One 'undered an' twenty pound!" she said, again and again.

The day following this interview dawned frosty and clear and Polly, rising early, dressed herself in her heavy black merino with the black lace filet at the neck and, lifting up the heavy fullness of her skirt, she knelt on the cold floor of the Lillywhite bedroom and made her petition to the Almighty.

Since Allen's death and Nathan's collapse upon hearing the tragic news on that fateful March morning, Polly's heart had been closed to everything but the enormity of her sorrow and the futility of expecting any divine help or comfort. Her soul was numb with the shock of bereavement and the loss of her child and when Nathan shivered under the blow and his heart, weakened by the strain of illness, almost died in his breast, Polly rallied to this new disaster and, in spite of her bitter grief and except for the short hour she spent by Allen's graveside, she never left Nathan for three whole days and nights, until his heart had strengthened and the great weakness that had engulfed him had passed away.

Nathan, secure in his love of God, could see the divine hand even in this, the death of his son.

"God 'ave taken 'im 'ome, Polly," he said, with a quiet assurance. "Oo be we to question the will of our 'Eavenly Father? Allen were 'Is child too, Polly. Can't 'ee leave 'im wi' God, 'is Father? Nothin' can separate us from the love o' God, me dear. Think of 'Im as the Good Shepherd. Why, Polly, 'E calleth the sheep by name. 'E 'oldeth the lambs in 'Is bosom. 'E've but called our Allen 'ome."

"Words! Words!" Polly had cried passionately. "Let 'Im give back me cheeld to me an' I'll believe there be a God o' love—a tender Shepherd an' an 'eavenly Father. All the words in the world can't give me back me boy, an' neither can Bible-talk, nor God 'Imself."

But here in Adelaide, following the night of her last visit to the lawyer, Polly had lain awake in bed, her mind seething with thoughts of all that lay behind her and before. The consciousness of its having been her fault that so much trust had been placed in a scoundrel did not ease matters, and ever and about her was the certainty that Nathan would never work again, and that that which had meant a home and safety for them all was lost to them. Her eldest boy was too young to take his father's place, and Polly, with a sickening terror at her heart, faced the truth that she alone, by the skill of her hands and the strength of her spirit, must support and sustain her family. She had clasped her hands together on her bosom and stared up into the darkness of the cold bedroom.

"God!" she had whispered, straining her hands together and trying to pierce the night's blackness with her wide, wet eyes. She had called again into the stillness, "God!" No answer came, and her whispered cry for help had sighed upwards: "Be 'ee there, God? 'Elp me to do me best. 'Elp me for Jesus' sake. Amen."

Then, in the chill of the early morning, she had risen, dressing herself in her black merino, and once more had knelt by the bed, and prayed long and fervently with many a quaint phrase and Cornish twist in her petitions; and Bob, coming quietly to the door of his mother's room and opening it, was surprised and frightened at the sight of his mother's face. Polly saw him, and after a moment got to her feet and, brushing down her dress and smoothing back her hair, came towards him.

"What were you doing that for?" asked Bob from the doorway.

"Doin' what?" said Polly, with a hint of colour in her cheeks. "Prayin'?"

"No," said Bob, innocently enough, "rolling your eyes up to the roof and grabbing your dress front."

Polly gasped, and the red flooded into her face. Her most sacred moment to have been spied upon and ridiculed! She looked hard at Bob, but his eyes were wide and clear of guile. She faltered, then said with an attempt at sternness, "I were prayin' for 'elp to look after 'ee childern. That's what I were doin'."

"Yes, and you were going so hard I could see the steam rising out of your head," said Bob, and Polly leaned her hand on the door-post and laughed and laughed and, Bob pointing to the mist of her breath, they laughed again.

"Get along with 'ee," said Polly at last. "Can't I 'ave a minute to meself?"

Eleven o'clock found them both in Hindley Street. Already Polly had a scheme in her mind: to return to Wallaroo Mines, to sell the house there and to rent a shop in Kadina, where she would make and sell bonnets.

"'The Bonnet Shop' I shall call un," said Polly aloud. "An' I'll make the purtiest hats an' bonnets that anabody ever laid eyes on. They'll be waitin' 'pon doorstep to buy un off me, an' I'll make un pay a purty penny for un into the bargain."

Walking boldly into a milliner's shop in Hindley Street— that same shop in whose window Ellen had looked so longingly years before, but now replete with gaslight for illumination and a great quantity of mirror for reflection— Polly rapped on one of the small tables, and looked about her at tall, thin iron stands and into wide cupboards with sliding glass doors. In fixtures on one side of the shop was a collection of narrow boxes covered with shiny green paper bearing a variety of names: "Ostrich tips", "Sprays", "Mourning Flowers", "Ornamental Grasses", "Hatpins". Polly had not been able to spell them all before the proprietress, a tall black-haired woman in a smart toilette of mastic and puce, entered from the curtained recess at the rear of the shop.

Polly gaped with amazement at this vision of fashion, and ran her eyes over the other woman's draped, short-trained skirt of puce wool broche with a princess tunic garnished with mastic faille. The turned-back edges of the tunic and its *revers* were trimmed with puce silk, and a band of fringe in mastic and puce bob-bobbed against the full skirt as the tall woman came forward into the shop.

The curtains of the draped doorway marked "Show-room" fell into place behind Mrs O'Shaughnessy, and she swept onward with a burst of smiles. She eyed the stout little woman in the black dress, and the cape with its jet trimmings, and the bonnet with the wisp of black crape and bunch of black shivery grass for trimming, and nodded **very affably.**

"Yes, madam, a hat for yourself?" she asked brightly, deftly whisking her train past a hatstand.

Polly was dumbfounded. "Be 'ee sellin'?" she asked, eyeing the puce and mastic confection. "I thought 'ee must be buyin'!"

Mrs O'Shaughnessy paused for a moment and then, realizing a compliment was intended, airily waved a hand and said, "Now, what is it you are wanting?"

Polly looked about for a chair and, seeing a low walnut one with a nicely padded back, sat down in it and, resting her hands in the basket she carried, said carefully, "Well, 'tis like this 'ere. I be wantin' for to start in business in the 'at way on me own account, but I don't knaw nothin' 't all about the shop part, though nobody can't tell me nothin' 'bout the makin' part, an' I can trim a bonnet with any one. But the shop part flummoxes me, an' I thought I'd just come in an' get a notion or two an' get 'ee to tell me 'ow to go about un."

Mrs O'Shaughnessy clutched the cameo on her bosom and doubted the evidence of her ears. "Starting in the hat way?" she repeated, curling her top lip in grand contempt. "Well, I do declare!" she continued, in a good imitation of her most well-to-do customer. "And why do you come to me, pray? To what do I owe the pleasure of this visit?" she continued bitingly.

"Didden 'ee 'ear me last time?" said Polly. "I want 'ee to up an' tell me 'ow to get a start in the millinery."

Mrs O'Shaughnessy reverted to type. "Sure, I heard you the first time and I've heard you the last time, and never a word do you get out of me. And the cheek of you's beyond telling. I'll be pleased if you'll take yourselves outside. It's not you as'll be getting anything out of me. Be off with you, the pair of you!"

Polly was on her feet in two seconds, her face ablaze. "You—you dressed-up Judy, you!" she said fiercely. "Swishin' 'bout thy fine shop wi' lady ways an' carryin's-on, an' never a civil word for a woman oo's up agin more than thees'll ever knaw. 'Ere's me, wantin' a word of 'elp from a mortal creature, an' naught do I get but a pack of abuse, an' then ordered out o' shop like I was a dog!" She looked up into the angry face of the shopowner. "Do 'ee think I be goin' to set up 'ere an' put 'ee out o' business? Never fear!" she added, before the other woman could speak. "I were goin' to set up shop an 'undered mile from 'ere, down Kadina way. I got a sick 'usband an' four childern to feed." She put her hand to her head. "No—no, only three little uns," she said, all the bluster gone from her voice.

Here Bob put in a word for himself. "My brother Allen got drownded two weeks ago, my brother Allen did." It had been the greatest and most mystifying incident in his young life, and he always made the most of it.

"Make 'aste out of 'ere," said Polly, pushing him before her towards the door.

But under the puce and mastic gilet and under the heaviness of the cameo brooch was Mrs O'Shaughnessy's heart: a staunch, a fiery and a sentimental one.

"Come on back!" she called to Polly. "Come into the showroom and be telling me your troubles. I've had a dose of my own, and not a few of 'em were due to being in the millinery. I'd have been glad of a word myself when I started out, I would and all."

Polly came back a step or two, then stood firm. "I've 'alf a mind not to," she said. "Thees were purty rude to me."

Mrs O'Shaughnessy's black brows rose up a full inch.

"But I got back a few on 'ee," Polly continued good-naturedly.

So, turning to Bob, she gave him directions to walk along Hindley Street as far as the shop with the gold sheep hanging outside and then to walk slowly back and, with a smile at Mrs O'Shaughnessy, she followed her into the cerise-draped recesses of the showroom.

The shopwoman was regretting her generosity almost before the curtain fell behind them, but Polly, resting her basket on a chair, flew to a stand on which was displayed a little rose-coloured hat.

"Oh!" she cried. "Oh, what a beauty! My, but 'ee be 'andy wi' thy needle, missus. An' what a plume! Didst curl un thyself? I curled aplenty in the old country—three rows deep an' every curl the same. But this da beat all I ever set 'and to."

"Come out into the workroom," said Mrs O'Shaughnessy,

completely won over, "and I'll be showing you what can be done there. I've got two girls working for me, and I taught them everything I know."

"An' now they don't knaw nothin'!" smiled Polly. "Yes, I knaw what girls be—all fingers an' thumbs, an' more bother than they's worth."

Mrs O'Shaughnessy could not think up a reply soon enough, for already Polly was full of praise for the lovely trifles that were being fashioned in the back workroom and soon, rather against her will, Mrs O'Shaughnessy began pulling down some of the green-papered boxes to let Polly look in at the bewildering collection of trimmings there.

Polly sniffed the stuffy, gluey, camphory odours of the interior of the boxes, and breathed them deep into her lungs. "I loves even the smells of un," she said, fingering the soft swirl of an ostrich-plume with the tip of her broad forefinger.

She stayed an hour in this shop of *modes de Paris*, and Mrs O'Shaughnessy farewelled her from the door with the good-natured smile of an Irishwoman who has done a good turn and is pleased about it.

"Good luck to you, Mrs Thomas," she said to Polly. "Plumes *or* flowers, mind you. Never plumes *and* flowers. And give the women what they want, but make them pay hard for having ideas of their own!" She pointed south-east. "Now go along with you, and turn where I told you of, and when you get to the warehouse go right up and say you come from Mrs Mary O'Shaughnessy in Hindley Street, and they'll listen to you and give you a helping hand. Good day to you."

Polly and Bob walked arm-in-arm to King William Street and, following Mrs O'Shaughnessy's directions, soon found themselves before the brass-bound doors of the warehouse that Mrs O'Shaughnessy had mentioned. This firm, beginning in 1853 in a modest way from a corner retail store, had expanded and developed until now in 1877, despite severe losses of stock by fire a few years previously, it had an annual turnover of £300,000, and merchandise was indented by it from all over the world.

So vast did the building appear to Polly when she and Bob were inside, and so full of goods that it seemed to be packed from floor to ceiling with clothing of every description, neatly folded, and laid with meticulous care on tables and fixtures. Behind a small counter on Polly's right were several elegant young men with bergamot on their hair and a languid droop to their moustaches, stowing garments away on shelves. Polly hesitated before addressing these superior beings, and suddenly became aware of a gentleman beside her: a man of about fifty, even-featured, with a well-shaped head already showing signs of baldness and a bearded face of ruddy complexion. He was dressed in black broadcloth, a grey stock at his throat, and gloves and silver-topped stick in the hand which also held his beaver hat. Polly was impressed by these signs—that her station in life had taught her to recognize—of prosperity and authority, and ventured to speak to him as he passed her.

"Sir?" she called. Putting out a hand to restrain him, her eyes fell on the gold seals which hung from his watch-chain, and she drew back her hand quickly and shut her lips tightly. "Never agin," thought she, "will I be led away by baubles. Once bit. . . ."

But the gentleman had heard her voice and, turning about, faced her in the aisle formed by the racks of clothing. Polly, looking into his keen blue eyes and being warmed by the pleasant smile that hovered on his lips, forgot her hatred of broadcloth and gold watch-chains and asked, very politely, to be shown the way to the "head man". The gentleman directed her to follow him and Polly, adjuring Bob to sit still on one of the tall, round-seated bent-wood chairs by the counter and to wait for her, followed the distinguished broadcloth back of the gentleman with the kindly smile and the Scotch twist to his speech. She went before him into the office that he indicated and, to her surprise, he followed her in and, giving his stick, gloves and hat to the small, red-faced lad who came in from the warehouse and departed again after putting the gentleman's things in a cupboard, sat down behind the wide mahogany table and, with a quiet smile and a rising inflexion in his voice, said "Yes?" to Polly.

Polly could not conceal her surprise and pleasure at the discovery that she was addressing the man she had come to seek and, after a few rambling sentences, began the story

of her life in Australia: her first years as a miner's wife at
Wallaroo Mines, the illness of her husband, the death of
her son and the crowning disaster, the treachery of Lawyer
Birmingham. She told him, too, of the years spent working
at her trade in a millinery shop in St Ives, and she told
him her plan to take up the same work again and her
hopes of earning enough to keep her family and to give
her boys a start in life.

"And where does this firm come in? What is your reason
in coming to us?" said the gentleman at the desk.

So Polly had to tell the tale of her visit to Mary
O'Shaughnessy's shop. " 'They'll give 'ee an 'elpin' 'and,'
says she to me," said Polly, "an' I believe 'er!"

"What can you do at your trade?" he asked.

Polly took a long breath. "I can plait straw, clean Italian
hats, reshape an' make un like new, trim a best bonnet
from a ha'puth o' scraps an' make a wire shape to fit any
'ead from the good Queen's down." She paused, and added
with quiet confidence, "I can do anathin' I set me 'and to."

"And what is it you would like us to do for you? Set you
up in business?"

"Aw, no. I shudden espect 'ee to do that for a stranger,
sir. What I da want be this 'ere. When I be settled in me
little shop at Kadina or Wallaroo, wherever 'tis to be, I
want 'ee to let me 'ave a few pound worth o' goods to start
off with. I'll pay when I can, but thees'll 'ave to trust me."

The gentleman at the desk did not hesitate an instant.
"Certainly, Mrs Thomas. You may rest assured that when
you let us know you are about to commence business we
shall have trust in you to the extent of stocking your shop
to the value of twenty-five pounds. I know quite well it will
take a good many bonnets to pay off twenty-five pounds,
but, looking at you, Mrs Thomas, I know you'll do it." He
stood up. "Come in to see me this afternoon at three
o'clock, and I shall give you our agreement in writing."
He held the door open for her, and her face was pink with
smiles.

"I'll pay it back, sir, ev'ry farthin'. I'll work till I drop."

He patted her lightly on the shoulder, and she turned
and gave him a curtsy, low and submissive. He looked at
the stout little woman, almost forty, with lined, pink

cheeks, her greying hair framing her face under the black bonnet, and thought her slightly ridiculous but said kindly, "You're a brave wee body."

Polly's heart was singing in her breast as she turned to look for Bob, and once more the gentleman spoke to her in a quiet, low voice.

"How old, Mrs Thomas, did you say your laddie was—the one that died, I mean?"

The light left Polly's eyes. " 'E were eight and an 'alf, sir—goin' on nine."

"Oh," said the gentleman in what might even have been a casual tone. "I had but one laddie myself, and he died when he was nearly five. You are fortunate, Mrs Thomas, in having two more sons to take your laddie's place. . . . I wish you good morning."

CHAPTER XI

POLLY could hardly wait to get home to Wallaroo Mines to see her family, to do for them and tell them the results of her visit to Adelaide. She had been absent for a week, but to her it seemed a year. In that short time she had lived through so many uncertainties and disappointments and had made so many resolutions and decisions that she was frantic to be with her family again, shut in behind her flimsy front door, at peace in her cottage home. Her throat ached with homesickness for Nathan, and she fretted with impatience to be on her way back to him.

She had not written to advise Nathan of her return, for as soon as she had become settled in her mind about their future had packed her carpet-bag and, with Bob, had caught the early morning coach and returned to Wallaroo Mines late in the early twilight of Friday evening.

As they walked over the mines crossing and set their faces towards home, Polly was astonished to see how small the cottage looked, and how white and clean. A wreath of blue smoke spiralled upward from the kitchen chimney.

"Mary Ann Blackett 'ave got the fire goin', so there'll be a cup o' tea for me in two-twos, praise be!" she said to Bob.

Suddenly the front door was wrenched open, and Annie and Rich ran down the short path and through the sapling gate, their faces aglow.

"Mumma, mumma!" called Annie, running with arms spread out towards Polly. "Rich an' me woulden 'ardly look, case 'ee didden come." And Polly, setting down her carpet-bag in the middle of the road, flung wide her own arms, and Annie ran into them like a bird.

Rich, after his first wild dash from the house, held back and walked quietly towards his mother and Bob.

"Hullo," said Bob. "What's the matter with your face?"

Rich put his hand to his swollen cheek, which was swathed with red flannel, and rubbed it tenderly.

"Got the toothache?" persisted Bob.

Polly, by this time, had put Annie back on the ground and was looking at Richard standing beside her with the red flannel around his head.

"What 'ee got that on thyself for?" asked Polly, speaking abruptly, for she was disappointed that Richard should have welcomed her so soberly.

"I've had the toothache nearly all the time you've been away," said Rich in a low voice, his eyes welling with tears of self-pity and his heart full of love for his mother.

Polly bent only a little towards him, for he was almost as tall as she. "Poor lamb!" she said in a tender voice. "Come to 'is mother!"

Rich looked up at her through a mist of tears, and felt his mother's kiss upon his swollen cheek. He put his arm about her then and, when they were behind the comparative safety of the sapling fence, he hid his face in the black folds of her cape and sobbed as if his heart would break. Polly ignored Mary Ann Blackett standing smiling in the doorway and led Rich to the side of the house. There she spoke to him, smoothing his bent shoulders with a comforting hand.

"Does it 'urt 'ee awful bad, me son? Tell mother."

And Rich answered in a muffled voice, "It's not the toothache. That doesn't hurt any more. It's something else."

Polly's hand stopped moving, then resumed its soothing rhythm, but in that second's pause Polly had a flash of intuition. "Did 'ee miss me, dear?" she said.

Rich nodded.

" 'Ave 'ee been missin' Allen?" she said, as steadily.

Rich buried his head closer into the hollow of her arm and nodded twice; and not even Polly, with her motherly insight, could guess what tales of lonely, terror-haunted nights since Allen's death lay hidden in those two nods of Richard's head.

"An' 'ave 'ee been worried what's to become of us now father's sick an' can't work no more?"

Rich nodded his head again, then lifted it, and wiped

his nose on the back of his hand and his eyes with the edges of the red flannel bandage. Now that Polly had plumbed the depths of his heart, his fears and sorrows had risen to the surface—and had vanished away.

"Evrathin' be all right now mother's to 'ome," said Polly, straightening his serge blouse and pushing back the hair from about his flushed face. "I've got plans aplenty. Come along inside to father."

Walking on towards the back door with her hands on Richard's shoulder, Polly, looking at the height and the breadth of him and ignoring the ludicrousness of the red flannel, said wonderingly to herself, " 'E've growed up in a week. Not twelve year old yet, but I be thinkin' p'raps 'e be old enough to take 'is father's place!"

From that day Richard ceased to go to school, and his play-days were finished forever.

After tea that night, while they were still seated about the table and when Mary Ann Blackett had stuffed the seven shillings Polly had given her into a purse and pushed it between the gaping buttons of her dress front and had gone her ways out of the gate, Polly began the story of what had happened to her in Adelaide.

"Land o' Goshen, what thieves there be in the world!" cried Nathan from his couch in the chimney-corner, upon hearing the story of Lawyer Birmingham. "What thieves an' robbers!" He clenched his swollen hands, then let them fall listlessly into his lap. His heart-beats thundered in his ears. "Oh, Polly, Polly, look at the broken 'ulk o' me, an' not able to lift an 'and in defence o' me 'ome or family. 'Here I sit like a sick babby while evrathin' be taken from me—cheeld, our bit o' property an' me 'ealth an' strength. Evrathin' gone, gone!"

"Don't take on," said Polly, practically. " 'Earken 'ere while I tell 'ee the rest." And, having told of her plans for the bonnet shop and of the help she might expect from the warehouse in Adelaide, "So," she ended triumphantly, " 'tis all settled. First thing come Monday I'll be up an' off to Kadina to find a little shop with a couple o' rooms to it, an' us'll move in soon as can be. Our money's gone, so us'll 'ave to be smart 'bout it. Cheer up, Nat, me dear!" And Polly's eyes shone in the candlelight. "Things is goin' to be all right. Don't 'ee fret!"

Then Richard said quietly, "Mother?"

"Yes, me son?" said Polly.

"Mother, the schoolmaster says he knows the editor of the paper at Moonta, and he's spoken to him about me. He says, that when I'm thirteen they'll take me into the printing office there, if I want to go."

"Well?" said Polly, as he paused.

"If we move to Kadina, could I still go into the printing office at Moonta next year, when I'm thirteen? I don't see how I could, do you?"

" 'Ee could not!" said Polly, decisively.

The light died out of his eyes. "Schoolmaster says there's no work to be had at the *Wallaroo Mining Journal Office*," he said, dolefully.

"Well then, there's nothin' for un but for us to move to Moonta. From now on us'll 'ave to ferret for work, an' must go where it da offer. There be as many women wantin' 'ats in Moonta as elsewhere, I be thinkin', an' it don't matter where we be so long as we be kept workin'. While thee's waitin' for the printin' job, Rich, me boy, 'twill 'ave be the picky-tables at Moonta Mines for 'ee." She stretched a hand to him across the table. "Us ain't afeared o' work, eh, Rich?" she said, smiling at him. "Not even 'ard work!"

Two weeks later a new-chum miner, a Devon man, Francis Herrick by name, bought the cottage from them. He had a wife and five children, and was more than satisfied with his bargain in buying the neat, four-roomed, whitewashed wattle and daub house, set in the trim garden. He paid Polly thirty pounds for the house and Polly, who had asked thirty-five, was satisfied too; and there had been no difficulty with the mining company in obtaining consent for the sale of the cottage.

"Thees can 'ave evrathin' in the garden," she said to Herrick, as they stood in the rain by the back door of the cottage. "I don't want anathin' but they cabbages there, an' a slip or two o' fuchsia an' a sprig o' rosemary."

"But," said Herrick, "I bought the garden 'long wi' the 'ouse, an' they cabbages be in the garden."

"Was they mentioned in writin'?" asked Polly cunningly, suddenly grown property-wise.

"Well no, naught was said 'bout cabbages nor any other growin' thing, as I remember. But I maintains they're mine, mention nor no mention," said Herrick, sticking up for what was his due.

"Well," Polly reluctantly added, "I s'pose I'd best give in, but I 'ad a leanin' towards they cabbages, Mr 'Errick. 'Twould 'a' been a comfortin' thought for me to knaw there was a cabbage or two of our'n growin' for dinner, whenever things got short down Moonta way an' when I weren't sure if there were goin' to be a dinner or no. It da frighten me summat to think as I've got to earn 'nough to fill all our mouths. Ev'ry mite we eat I'll 'ave to work 'ard for, an' sometimes I wonders if we won't be 'ungry off an' on."

Who could refuse Polly her cabbages after that? Not Francis Herrick, although by doing so he deprived his own children of two dozen vegetable dinners and afforded his wife a subject for perpetual and voluble reproach.

Polly had found an untenanted shop in Robert Street, Moonta, close to the new and beautiful Wesleyan Methodist Church. The shop, although removed from the business part of the town was well suited to Polly's trade.

"Near the chapel!" said Polly with satisfaction. "The women'll geek in on their way to service. I'll 'ave me purtiest bonnet in the window Saturday nights, an' many a look the women'll sneak at un as they goes by on Sunday."

The window could accommodate three hats on stands and three on the floor and still have room for a drape of curtain at the back. The shop itself was small, being only ten feet six inches by twelve feet, but there was a tiny room off the shop with a skylight in the roof. "The show-room!" said Polly, with visions of *modes de Paris* and Mrs O'Shaughnessy and, without looking farther, decided that the shop would do. At the rear of the shop was the dwelling part of the building, consisting of two rooms divided by a short passage and a long narrow kitchen; and at the farthest end of the back yard was a stone shed and a small stone outhouse. This comprised the whole property, and Polly could rent it for twelve and sixpence a week. Now, twelve and sixpence was reckoned by Polly to be a fair price for a hat, excluding plumes or ribbons. "So," she said to herself, "one 'at must be sold each week to keep the roof over our 'eads, an' whatever else I sell goes into our bellies or on our backs—if we be lucky!"

The kitchen was the best room of all. Here, the heat of the stove would dry any moisture that came through after a heavy rain, and the chimney jutted into the room, leaving space on either side which was filled with cupboards and shelves. There was a small window on the back wall by the door, and on the wall opposite the fireplace end was another window, with a sill wide enough to stand a pot-plant on and with an iron hook to fasten open the glass on pleasant days.

Polly saw all this at a glance, and also saw the dark rain stains in the two bedrooms and felt the floorboards give beneath her feet.

"There be damp rot on the walls, master," she said to the owner, "an' dry rot in the floors. But beggars can't be choosers, an' if 'tis 'greeable we moves in come Tuesday."

The congregation of the Wallaroo Mines Bible Christian chapel honoured the Thomas family with a special mention in the prayer on Sunday night and in a speech of farewell at the prayer meeting on the Monday evening before their departure for Moonta, and on that occasion reduced Polly to tears by the presentation of a flower-painted biscuit-barrel with a plaited reed handle, as a "love gift".

At twelve o'clock precisely on Tuesday morning Roger's spring dray was at the gate of the cottage and, by a curious mischance, the Herrick family and their goods arrived at the same moment. No sooner would one article of the Thomas household be carried out to the dray than a corresponding piece of the Herrick furniture would be hauled in to take its place.

"Can't 'ee let us get ourselves out in peace?" protested Polly, struggling with a bundle of bedding and running into Mrs Herrick, tall and lean-faced, similarly laden.

" 'Ee've 'ad all the mornin' to do it in," retorted Mrs

Herrick, dumping her blankets inside the door where everybody would be sure to fall over them. "Hey!" she called
to one of Polly's carriers who was helping to lift the
chiffonier towards the door. "Be careful, there! This place
belongs to me, now. Don't go makin' skegs in the wall wi'
that there. Watch out!" And she followed them outside
with many more instructions.

Polly was seething. It was bad enough to have to leave
a home where one had lived, loved, been happy and known
death and sorrow, without being hustled out of it like an
interloper or an unwanted guest.

The confusion in the little house was becoming greater
every minute, the five Herrick children, who ran yelling
in and out of the rooms, adding their share to the disorder.
Suddenly Mrs Herrick gave a shriek.

"Where's our little gate-leg table gone to?" she yelled.
"Where's our gate-leg table? It were 'ere just now." She
came out to Polly in the kitchen. "I want our gate-leg
table," she announced belligerently.

"Lawks!" said Polly, stopping to wipe the perspiration
out of her eyes. "What sort of a contraption's that? Never
'eard of un."

"Perhaps 'ee've not," said Mrs Herrick with asperity.
" 'Ee don't knaw evrathin'."

"Thee's right there!" said Polly heatedly, eying Mrs
Herrick across the untidy room. "I didden knaw thy sort
till to-day, thank the Lord."

"Polly, Polly!" called Nathan soothingly from his chair,
but Polly disregarded him.

"Don't 'ee bully-rag me!" continued Polly in a cold voice,
to the cross-faced woman opposite her.

"Well, where's me gate-leg table, then?" said Mrs Herrick.
"I brought that table all way from Devon, an' I brought it
right into this 'ouse. Now, where's it gone?"

"Go an' look for un," said Polly, picking up a bundle
from a corner and turning towards the door. "I ain't seed
un, an' what's more I woulden knaw sich a thing if I did."

" 'Ere, what you got there?" Mrs Herrick called out,
going to Polly and pointing to the bundle of clothes in
her arms. "Them's mine. Put 'em down."

Just then Willie Herrick, a ruddy-faced seven-year-old in

a dirty navy greatcoat garnished with tarnished gilt buttons, rushed into the kitchen.

"Ma, ma," he shouted, "Thomases 'a' got our best table loaded on their cart, an' a man's takin' our organ out o' the front room."

Mrs Herrick stiffened, and looked malevolently at Polly. "What's all this?" she demanded, and made for the front room. Her progress was blocked by the American organ which had been brought in by her carriers and was now being taken out by Polly's. "Put that back!" she screamed, and pushed and tugged with them until it was back in position again.

Just as this was finished she was confronted by Willie with the wreck of the gate-leg table in his arms.

"Look, ma," he said, holding up a splintered table leg. "Look what they done to it!"

" 'Ere, you limb o' Satan!" bellowed one of Polly's carriers, coming from the cart and blocking up the front door with his broad body. " 'E jumped up on our cart, missus," he said to Polly, "an' yanked that table off, an' it smashed on the ground."

"Oo's to pay for this?" cried Mrs Herrick, snatching the table from Willie and waving the splintered leg in the air. "Oo's goin' to pay for this?" she screamed. "What's goin' to be done 'bout it?"

Before Polly could reply the big-chested man from the doorway said dryly, "Well, *I* knaw what's goin' to be done 'bout it. Somebody's goin' to get a damn good punch on the chump if we can't get on with our job." And he glowered at Mrs Herrick.

"Oh, oh!" she cried, looking about wildly. "Why isn't my man 'ere? If 'e was 'ere instead of on shift underground you'd 'ear about this."

The big man laughed a throaty laugh and said to the two men by the organ, "I bet sometimes 'e wishes 'e was underground for good an' all, with a marble cross stickin' up on top of 'im!" He threw back his head and roared with laughter, and Mrs Herrick, red with rage and mortification, dropped the ruined table to the floor with a crash and swept out into the kitchen and into the back yard without a word, and the moving went forward with hearty good cheer.

A little later Polly, armed with a garden fork, went out to the cabbage patch and, while Mrs Herrick, standing beside the dolichos creeper and savagely stripping leaves from one of its tender sprays, watched her every movement with silent hatred, Polly stuck the fork firmly into the damp soil, then looked up at her.

"Thy 'usband promised I could 'ave the cabbages any time," she said sweetly, disregarding Mrs Herrick's speech-less anger. "But after what's 'appened to-day, I think I'll take un while me luck's in." And she tenderly dug up each cabbage plant and carefuly placed it in a page of the *Yorke's Peninsula Advertiser*. When not a cabbage remained in the plot she turned again to Mrs Herrick and said, with-out any trace of unfriendliness, "Good-bye, Miz 'Errick. We be all ready to go now. I 'ope as thees'll be 'appy 'ere. . . . Good-bye."

But Mrs Herrick regarded her stonily, and only unlocked her lips to state icily, "I 'ave nothink to say."

As it was a blue-skied May day, with no cold wind at this midday hour, Polly felt no anxiety about Nathan.

"The sun'll do 'ee good, me dear," she said, and watched with tender care while Nathan was lifted in his chair to the wagonette which was to take the family to Moonta. With his legs supported by a soft mattress and his back and head made comfortable with pillows, Nathan was enveloped in quilts and blankets, and Polly, Richard and Bob climbed aboard the wagonette, and Annie was lifted up to them. The cavalcade, constituting the wagonload of the Thomas furniture and the wagonette containing the Thomas family with Nathan sitting enthroned on his chair and Lily the goat beside him, caused quite a sensation as it passed through Wallaroo Mines, and was remembered by the miners' wives as an outstanding incident, and kept recurring in their memories despite the subsequent exciting occasion when someone shot at the teacher of the Wallaroo Mines Model School, and left a bullet in the class-room lintel the mark of which remained there for fifty years.

The road from the mines linked up with the backroad

to Moonta, and the wagon and wagonette jolted slowly over the uneven, sandy surface.

About them was the scrub, and the mallee and tea-tree came to the road's edge, bordering and shadowing it and overhanging it with green. The odour of damp undergrowth and rotting leaves and the wild, sweet scents of the scrub enfolded them all, and the blue of the sky above and the clear warmth of the autumn sun, with the sharp coolness of the shaded patches for contrast, went to the boys' heads like wine.

"Let's get out and walk, mother," pleaded Bob.

"We'll keep close beside the cart," put in Richard. "Go on, mother, let's."

"Jump off, then," said Polly good-humouredly, holding back the driver's arm until the boys were safely on the road. " 'Ave a care, now!"

They chased each other in and out of the wattles, slipping sometimes on the wet smoothness of the rotting leaves. Then they picked up fallen twigs and small boughs, bending and cracking them in their hands with pleasant rending sounds, and with sharp, stinging sensations on their palms. They raced to the cart, jamming the firewood into the back and making Lily the goat bleat for her freedom.

Several times the cart was stopped while Polly rearranged the pillows about Nathan's back and uncramped his legs; and once, seeing the whiteness of his cheeks against the brown of his beard, she gave him a dose of ammonia which she carried, already mixed and tightly corked, in a bottle in her carpet-bag.

Polly had persuaded the drivers to take a back road into Moonta so that Nathan might see the Moonta Mines, so they jolted on past Cross Roads and Yelta and soon the poppet-heads and engine-houses of the mines came into view. How eagerly they strained forward, inhaling the smoke from the furnace chimneys and listening to the familiar workaday sounds of a big mine in ceaseless, noisy activity! They approached and passed the stables, offices, miners' cottages and manager's house, and the driver, answering their many questions, considerately stopped and, pointing with his whip, explained the whole lay-out of the mines to them.

The three towns, Kadina, Wallaroo and Moonta, form a triangle whose three sides measure as follows: Kadina to Wallaroo six miles, Wallaroo to Moonta ten and a half miles, and Moonta to Kadina twelve miles. The area contained in this triangle, including the Wallaroo Mines, was to yield some of the richest copper ore in the world, the accessibility and great quantity of this making two of the townships famous as mining centres and the other, Wallaroo, a busy port for the transhipment of copper that had been smelted there.

The discovery of copper at Wallaroo Mines came about in a strange manner. In 1860 the northern part of Yorke's Peninsula was occupied by Mr Watson-Hughes, and over its mallee-covered plains were pastured many flocks of sheep. Often had the shepherd's remarked upon the green stones on the beach at Wallaroo and, as they boiled their billies, had regarded superstitiously the baleful green flame of the wood found at certain spots. But it was James Boor who, while out with a flock of sheep about five and a half miles inland from Wallaroo, caught his foot in a wombat's burrow and later, while trying to dig out the wombat, found the burrow full of small stones of copper ore. He took these home when he returned with the sheep and gave them to the manager of the head station, Mr Duncan, who enthusiastically showed the samples to Mr Watson-Hughes.

The Wallaroo Mining Company was straightway formed, and Mr Hughes, aided by financial support from Messrs Elder, Stirling & Company, battled hard in a valiant effort to carry the company through its early struggles.

Copper at Moonta was discovered a few months after that at Wallaroo, and Patrick Ryan was responsible for the finding of rich ore at what was to be the Moonta Mines. Ryan was a shepherd working for Mr Hughes, and was reputed to be a drunkard. He carried news of his find to Adelaide, but was too vague and illiterate to lodge a proper claim, and friends urged him to return to Moonta and obtain more information.

During Ryan's absence Mr Hughes, having gleaned a hint of what was afoot, lodged a claim in the name of a dummy, which was accepted by the lands office; but this claim, too, lacked specific data. Mr Hughes rushed a surveyor to Moonta, and Ryan and his syndicate, who had arrived there from Adelaide, realized that they would have to complete the survey of their claim and make a dash back to Adelaide before their rivals.

Mr Hughes's surveyor had his plans ready by the following morning, and they were given to Horn,* a young jackaroo who, mounted on a bay mare, faced the arduous journey to Adelaide spurred on by the knowledge that the syndicate was seventeen hours ahead of him.

A station hand accompanied him part of the way, and they foundered several horses in the wildest ride the colony had ever known. Horn, his last horse gone, finished the journey on foot, and twenty-two hours after he had set out from the peninsula he reached Adelaide.

Mr Hughes's agent ran with him to the lands office, and encountered the chief clerk about to enter the offices. He was late on this morning, and the agent, recognizing him, pressed the plans into his hand. A few feet from them stood representatives of the rival syndicate, who had been waiting on the steps of the building for two hours. The agent's application was accepted, and in the space of that moment a fortune was lost and won.

From their inception great success attended the Moonta Mines. No capital was needed to finance the venture, for the valuable lodes discovered supplied all the necessary funds. Lode after lode of great richness was struck, and by 1875 the Moonta copper mine was second to none in the world. From October 1862—when the first dividend was paid—to the year 1872 the mine had paid over £680,000, and by 1875 dividends amounting to the enormous sum of over £1,000,000 sterling had been returned to investors.

The Hamley Mine, adjacent to the Moonta Mine and called, in its earliest days, the Karkarilla, was at first a failure, and changed hands for a little over £1000. A new company, under Captain John Warren who also managed the Wheal James and Parramatta mines, forged ahead, and the mine almost rivalled its neighbour for the richness and quantity of its ore.

Under Captain Cowling's management the Yelta and North Yelta mines, situated north of the Moonta lease,

* See Horn's letter, Archives of South Australia.

paid large dividends, but the same success did not attend the working of the Poona mine.

Previous to their amalgamation with the Wallaroo Mining Company in 1889, the Moonta Mines were to yield £5,396,146 worth of bar copper and to distribute amongst their shareholders £1,168,000.*

To Nathan this journey to Moonta was a great event. The fame of the Moonta Mines had rung in his ears, as it had done in most miners' ears, ever since he had arrived in the colony and, but for the fact that Ben Wilson, who had come out with them from Cornwall on the *Lady Milton*, had secured employment with the Wallaroo Mining Company and had written to Nathan of the Wallaroo Mines, it was almost certain that the Thomas family would, at the outset, have gravitated to Moonta from Adelaide.

Several times, while passing through Moonta Mines, the driver of the wagonette pulled in his horses so that Nathan might gather an idea of the field.

"They say a million pound worth o' cold cash 'ave come from Moonta Mine," said the driver, waving his whip towards its engine-house and poppet-heads. "That's a power o' money to come out of an 'ole in the ground."

" 'Tis famous the world over," said Nathan, shading his eyes with his hand. "An' I 'ear said 'tis as famous for Cap'n 'Ancock's jigs as for anathin' else. 'E used un 'ere at Moonta for the first time. We 'ad un to the Wallaroo Mines too, an' they da take up less space, don't cost so much to run an' use a purty sight less power an' show a bigger percentage o' copper, 'tis said."

"That's where Cap'n 'Ancock lives," said the driver, obligingly pointing the whip handle in the direction of the captain's dwelling.

"Where 'e to?" asked Polly, peering toward the house.

"Oh, 'e ain't to be seed now," said the driver, " 'e's somewheres on the mines. But look!" And he put his head on one side and motioned them all to look beyond the house. "See over there by that clump o' trees?"

"Yes," cut in Bob and Rich, straining forward.

"Summat movin'. Can 'ee see it?"

* See "Geological Survey of South Australia" by R. L. Jack, B.E., F.G.G., *Bulletin No. 6*, page 13, paragraph 7.

"Yes," they chorused.

"Well that," said the driver, leaning back and lowering his whip, "that be Cap'n 'Ancock's white cow!"

They drew abreast of the new model school, an imposing structure and one of the largest school buildings in South Australia.

"Land sakes!" said Polly. "It'd take a power o' childern to fill that there."

"Well, there's plenty 'ere'bouts," said the driver, nodding towards the scores of miners' whitewashed cottages, all so similar in structure and design to the house the Thomases had left in Wallaroo Mines that Polly felt a queer ache in her throat, and every one became suddenly silent.

The horse tram that ran from Moonta to the mines raised no comment, for the boys were familiar with its counterpart.

They entered the township of Moonta and occasioned only mild interest from passers-by as they drove along Robert Street, finally stopping at the shop near the Wesleyan Church, which was a fine new edifice containing a pulpit of Bath stone ten feet high and with a thirty-foot window set in the front face of the building. The church had cost £4000 to erect and was one of thirteen of various denominations, including the five churches at the mines, which stood at that time within a one-mile radius of this spot.

The great bed was lifted down from the wagon first of all, and Polly, rushing after it with bedding and blankets, made it up as soon as it had been erected, and ran out again for the hot salt-bags and two hot stones wrapped in an old flannel petticoat that had warmed Nathan during the journey down and, directing the men to lift Nathan "careful-like", she followed after into the bedroom. There, while the carriers wrestled with the furniture and tramped to and fro across the shaking floorboards, Polly got Nathan into his night-shirt and lifted him into the warm softness of the big bed where he lay very still, his face to the window, looking out at the blue sky with pain-filled eyes.

It was a week later that Polly was advised by letter from the warehouse in Adelaide that, following her intimation that she was about to start in business in Robert Street,

Moonta, a first consignment of millinery goods and a miscellaneous collection of haberdashery, together with three wooden head-shapes, were being forwarded. Twelve pounds' value in all was being sent to Polly and might be expected to arrive in Moonta Bay on the Friday night of that same week.

Polly and Richard mixed limewash and whitened the ceilings and walls of the shop and showroom, and Polly scrubbed the uneven boards of the shop floor until they looked, if not white, at least pale yellow. The doorstep was blackened with stove black, the window was cleaned, and the counter at the back of the shop was painted brown with material left over from last year's house-painting at Wallaroo Mines. In front of the counter, which was merely a plank of wood on two wooden supports, Polly hung what had been in the other home the bedroom curtains. The shiny chintz with the rosebuds and gaudy birds brightened the interior of the little shop, and when the faithful rag rugs, beaten and shaken into something of their youthful brightness, were placed end to end before the draped counter, Polly beamed with pleasure.

"Bring the best chair," she cried to Richard, "an' place 'ere. There!" she said with satisfaction, when the cedar chair was stood beside the rose-flowered chintz. "That's fine."

When the packing-case arrived and was unpacked and the contents were spread about, Polly was deliriously happy to touch and smooth and admire the finery, but it was Bob who, with a masterly sense of the fitness of things, found places for all the shiny green boxes and busied himself in arranging everything upon the lower of the two shelves that formed the shop's fixtures.

At the bottom of the packing-case was a parcel addressed to Polly "with the firm's compliments". Richard drew it to the surface, and Polly had the wrapping off in a trice. Inside were a dozen cards of bright brass buttons as large as halfpennies, a bolt of sea-green gauzy tulle, three cards of narrow coloured silk cord, a dozen plaits of straw in various shades, several odd lengths of faille ribbon, a book of silk patterns, a page from a ladies' magazine showing a group of matrons in fashionable hats and bonnets, and a box of assorted sewing silks.

"An 'elpin' 'and put in that there parcel," said Polly, spreading the trifles about her.

Polly's first customer walked into the shop at ten o'clock on the Saturday following the Monday when Polly had begun her millinery business: a stout, middle-aged woman in a maroon woollen frock with striped satin revers on the basqued bodice. On her head was a large, Italian, hand-plaited straw hat, and in the basket on her arm was a velvet bonnet that evidently was intended for wear with the maroon woollen dress.

Polly, in a fever of excitement, hearing the bell from out in the kitchen, whipped off her white apron and wiped her face hurriedly with a little bag of rice flour that she kept in the pocket of her underskirt; then, with a smile and a nod at Nathan who was in his room, tense with expectancy, she opened the door leading into the show-room and walked into the shop and behind the counter.

"Good mornin', ma'am," she said, with a hint of a curtsy.

"Good morning," said Mrs Hanover. "I see by the notice in your window you clean hats."

"Yes, ma'am," said Polly, "cleans, bleaches, presses and trims them." She spoke slowly, trying to make the best of her manners and to be careful of her speech.

Mrs Hanover took the hat from her head and laid it on the counter. "That hat," said she, "has seen me through seven seasons. I want it cleaned and made shipshape, if you can."

Polly looked at the stained yellow hat, lifting up a torn and drooping pink rose with her knotted forefinger and viewing the unfaded straw beneath.

"I can do it," said Polly, "an' trim un, too."

Mrs Hanover hesitated. "Oh, I don't think it——"

"Wait," said Polly, and went across to the fixtures and brought down a green box. She opened it and held it out to Mrs Hanover. "Leave me put they grapes on it," she pleaded, putting a bunch of deep purple grapes on the brim of the yellowed hat and deftly twisting a piece of purple and rose shot ribbon across the crown. "There, leave me trim it, do. An' if 'ee don't like un, I'll take un off agin like a shot."

"They're pretty," said Mrs Hanover, yielding a little.

"Thees'll never see their like in Moonta," said Polly, and clinched the bargain.

Mrs Hanover put on the maroon velvet creation from her basket and went out, leaving Polly jubilantly snipping the faded flowers from the Italian straw hat.

One of the branches of the millinery trade that Polly had learned and practised in St Ives was the cleaning of straw hats. This was done firstly with warm suds and a fine brush. Then, when the hat was dry, it was put in an air-tight box with a crucible of live coals on which sulphur had been generously sprinkled. The fumes from the sulphur bleached the hat to its former pale gold, and the pressing with hot irons on a specially made wooden hat-shape completed the metamorphosis.

Polly scrubbed the soiled hat and dried it in the oven. Then, putting a tin of coals in the wooden box that had once brought Nathan's and her clothes from England and had accompanied them ever since, she tenderly placed the hat inside, and sat on the lid while she pondered which hat-shape would best suit the publican's wife's middle-aged features. Later that night she pressed the hat with her heavy iron, rolling up the brim at the back and bending it down in front, and sat up until midnight trimming it with the purple grapes and the gleaming faille ribbon. On Monday morning she herself took it to Mrs Hanover, who was delighted with it.

"I wanted it renovated to send to my sister who is in a low state of health down in Adelaide. Her husband's a waster, and they've got nothing in the world between them but five children. But——" she said, looking at her profile in the smoke-dimmed mirror of the hotel parlour, "I think I'll keep the hat for myself, and send her a pair of Ted's old trousers to cut down for the boys instead. This suits me," she added finally, "and I shall want you to make me a bonnet in the spring."

So Polly knew then that The Bonnet Shop had begun to do business.

CHAPTER XII

"COME day, go day, God send Saturday!"

On Saturday afternoons and Sundays Richard could be a boy again. On every other day of the week he worked at the picking-tables at Moonta Mines where, with dozens of other young lads, he sorted the ore at long wooden tables for five shillings and sixpence a week. Wages were paid monthly, and it was a proud day for Richard when he brought to Polly his first month's pay.

He had a mile to walk to and from the mines each day, and no boy hated his work more than Richard and no boy complained less. His back and arms ached continuously, and his finger-nails were torn to the quicks with the ceaseless rapid sorting of the good ore from the "attle" as it was brought in skips from the mines and wheeled on to the picking-tables.

The "picky-boss", a tall, big-boned man who habitually wore a calf-skin waistcoat over his grey flannel shirt, gave the new boys, upon arrival a few minutes' information about their work. He would pick up a lump of ore and, pointing at it here and there with a dirty, scarred forefinger, would throw it back on to the table and, with a quick survey of the table and a rapid movement or two, would discard the attle and retain the ore; and this comprised the complete five-minute course of instruction necessary for a "picky-boy". But Richard found there was more to be learnt than the boss had shown him. He had to learn to disregard his cut and stinging hands and to bear the pain of aching muscles, to forget the dank smell of the ore that penetrated his clothes and lungs and tainted his food. He tried to concentrate upon the knowledge that he was playing a waiting game—waiting for the job in the Moonta printing office—and, after the first unhappy weeks at the tables, he was content to work and wait in patience.

During the mile walk to the mines in the early morning he studied—recited or learned by heart from the books he carried in his coat pocket—and on three nights of the week, after he had eaten his tea, went for two hours to the house of a Mr Bourne Martin, a clerk at the mine offices who lived in the township and coached scholars in his spare evenings. Nathan had insisted upon Richard's continuing his studies. It was, perhaps, the only occasion on which he had overridden Polly in the management of the house and the upbringing of the children and, despite all her arguments, in this case he was adamant. Polly had gone to interview Mr Martin soon after their arrival at Moonta, for he had been recommended to her as a clever man, and it was with great satisfaction that Polly returned to Nathan with the news that all was successfully arranged and that, the fee being very low, Richard would be able to start lessons with Mr Martin on the following Tuesday evening. In the arrangements with Mr Martin who was, as Polly had previously found out, newly married to a pretty young wife, a curious matter of ladies' smart hats had arisen; but this was not repeated to Nathan or Richard, and only Polly in the Thomas family knew that part, at least, of Rich's book-learning was paid for by his mother's nimble fingers and her ability to make a bargain.

Saturday afternoon and Sunday were the highlights in Richard's life at this time. On these days all the dirt and drudgery of the picking-tables was forgotten, and he could return to the childhood which had been filched from him.

On one Saturday afternoon during their first September at Moonta, Richard and Bob were down in the shed at the back of the yard. It had been raining in sharp, drenching showers throughout the day, and the boys had given up their plans of going fishing from the jetty at Moonta Bay. Richard was making a flat-bottomed toy boat from a piece of Tasmanian hardwood brought home from the mines, and he sat with the hull between his knees, carefully shaping it with a chisel. Bob was sitting straddle-legged on his father's upturned Cornish wheelbarrow. He had tied an end of a long piece of rope to one of the spokes and was busy turning the wheel round and round, winding the rope about the axle. When the rope was wound up he grabbed one end tightly and, with a yell of "Look out, here she comes!" pulled hard with a hand-over-hand action, and the rope unwound and the wheel revolved at a good rate with a great deal of noise. This went on for some time; then, growing tired he righted the barrow and sat curled up in it, watching Richard.

"When'll you have her finished?" he asked.

"By next Saturday," said Rich, not looking up.

"Can I come with you when you try her out?"

"Oh, I dunno. I mightn't have her finished, anyway."

"Well, can I come when you do get her finished and when you do try her out?" pleaded Bob.

"Aw, you always go out too deep an' get your pants wet, and then I get blamed."

"I won't this next time, Rich. Cross me heart."

"You can come if you want to, I s'pose," said Rich disinterestedly, after a close study of the boat's bow.

Bob beamed, but thought it best to remain silently appreciative.

Just then, heralded by a sniff, Toby Watts walked into the shed. He was a freckle-faced lad with red hair, and was dressed in a long coat two sizes too large for him and the worse for wear, and he was continually trying to roll up the sleeves which were much too long for him.

"Hullo, yous," he addressed both boys.

"Good day," said Bob.

"What d'you want?" said Richard.

"Say, Rich," said Toby, "Skinny Soper wants you to come down to his place. He's got something to show you."

"What's he got?" said Richard, chiselling off a shaving of wood from his boat.

Toby looked at Bob standing stiffly at attention beside the wheelbarrow. "Come on outside and I'll tell you," he said to Rich.

Bob shuffled his feet and looked away.

"He won't listen," said Rich. "Whisper it."

Toby came closer and, putting his hand up to his mouth, whispered behind it into Richard's ear. Richard's eyes opened wider at each sentence. When Toby had finished Richard nodded his head and, laying his boat and chisel on the box beside him, got up on to his feet.

"Wait there, Toby. I'll go and ask mother. I'll tell her we're going for a walk."

"I'm coming, too," said Bob.

"No you're not," said Toby and Rich together.

"Yes I am. I heard what you said, Toby. You said Skinny had nicked some dynamite and you were going out into the scrub to blow up some trees. I heard you."

The two elder boys were nonplussed.

"You little sticky beak," said Toby.

"He can hear anything, that kid can," said Richard disgustedly.

"Well, you've got to let me come, else I'll go in an' tell mother," said Bob stoutly.

"What are we going to do?" Richard appealed to Toby.

"Well, he's your brother, not mine," said Toby carelessly. "Shake it up, anyway. I'm off back to Skinny's. Don't waste all day."

"Can I come, Rich?" asked Bob in a small voice.

"Right-o," Richard said grudgingly. "Cut on in and ask mother if we can go for a walk. The rain's stopped."

A few minutes later the three boys, each eating a piece of bread and jam that Polly had given them, walked into the back of Skinny Soper's home. Skinny's father kept a shop. "Hardware Store" the board on the veranda informed one, but inside was gathered together a miscellaneous collection of almost everything under the sun that could neither be worn nor eaten. Anything and everything in iron and tin—fishing tackle, an anchor, a walnut suite, cooking utensils, bird cages, a brand new American organ covered with dust, boot scrapers, tin tubs, guns, tools, chains, butter churns, kettles, candle snuffers, cow yokes, a mahogany table on huge castors, a dilapidated baby cart, a keg of nails—all grouped together on shelves and fixtures and on the floor of the shop. The boys loved Soper's shop and all that it contained, and young Skinny Soper was the most popular boy in the town. To be the son of the owner of this treasure trove was no mean lift in a boy's world, where popularity is measured by the foot-rule of possessions: the more interesting the possessions the more interesting the possessor.

Skinny was waiting for them in the stable. He looked

hard at Bob as the boys came towards him. "What did you have to bring him for?" he asked truculently.

Toby took a deep breath, preparatory to reciting the incident of Bob's inclusion in the party, when Richard spoke up for him.

"Let him stay, Skinny. He's all right. Now show us what you've got."

Skinny took them to the chaff-bin and, leaning over and scratching about there, presently drew to light two plugs of dynamite—a new invention lately introduced to Moonta Mines—also a length of fuse, a paper packet of powder and shot, and an old gun.

The group, eyeing the new-fangled explosives, was thrilled into silence. At last Skinny spoke.

"Now you've seen, you've got to spit your deaths you'll never tell."

The boys spat quickly and expeditiously.

"Cross me heart," they all said, making the sign on the front of their coats.

"Do you know how they work?" asked Bob, tentatively touching the soft candle-shaped plug.

"My dad took me along when him and Mr Pearson were trying some out last Sat'day, down on Poison Flat," said Skinny. "This sort of stuff's going to be used underground at the mines instead of blasting powder, but me dad says the miners won't take easy to it."

"Why for?" asked Toby.

"Oh, I dunno. Just 'cause it's something new, I s'pose. Anyway," said Skinny, "come on out to McGinnes's paddock. I'll take the plugs." He stowed away the dynamite in his large serge blouse, and the other boys gingerly picked up the gun and the rest of the ammunition and followed him out of the yard.

It was almost four o'clock when they reached McGinnes's paddock, a partly cleared area just off the Wallaroo Road. They climbed through the fence and went in among the patch of mallee-trees.

"What are we going to blow up?" asked Toby, dragging out the fuse from his pocket.

"We'll send up one of those trees," said Skinny, pointing

to another group of mallee beyond. "Let's have some shots with the gun first!"

They loaded the gun with powder and shot, and blazed away at a magpie who, with commendable singleness of purpose, had been pulling a long worm from the ground, overlooking the boys in the anxiety of family cares. The magpie flew away squawking, and frightened a half-wild tortoise-shell cat from a low patch of scrub. The boys loaded and were after it, but could not get a shot at it and were reduced to setting up, as target, a bough a good way off and blazing away at that. They each had a turn and nobody shot the bough, but Richard, finger on trigger and eye on the target, turned suddenly to speak to Skinny, wriggled his finger and shot Bob in the leg.

Bob lay on the ground, his leg covered with blood. He had given one screech and then was quiet. Skinny ran to him and wiped away the blood. Bob, surprisingly, was not killed or badly wounded, they found; merely, the fleshy part of his leg showed four small dark holes where the shot had entered. He stood up at last, and the boys drew long, deep, thankful breaths. He could even walk slowly, and made very little complaint about the pain.

"You've got pluck!" said Skinny admiringly. And Bob forgot the stinging shot holes in his leg, and beamed.

When they found that Bob could walk the boys looked about for something else to do. Unanimously it was decided to abandon the gun practice.

"Let's blow up the tree and go home," said Richard, just now recovering from his fright.

They emerged from the mallee and walked across the cleared space to the farther group of trees. Suddenly, Skinny stopped.

"Look," he said, pointing a hundred yards westward. "See that? That's Shepherd Joe's hut. He used to look after McGinnes's sheep. He's gone to Port Hughes now, and the hut's caved in."

The boys looked at the ruin of the limestone hut, then with one accord looked at each other.

"Hokey," said Toby. "Shall we?"

Skinny hesitated.

"Ain't you game?" said Toby tauntingly, rolling back his sleeves.

"I'm game all right, but what if McGinnes finds out?"

"Well, it's half broken down now. Won't hurt to finish it off," said Toby.

"I'm off home," put in Richard decisively.

Bob held on to Rich's hand. "My leg's hurting me. I want to go back."

"Wait on," said Skinny. "Let's do this one, then we'll all go back home." And he held up one of the dynamite plugs while Toby fixed the fuse and set the cap.

Rich and Bob backed away. "I'm off," said Richard, edging slowly towards the mallee and the road.

Skinny and Toby ran forward quickly, placed the plug by the wall of the tumbledown hut and lit the fuse, then ran for their lives back to the shelter of the damp scrub. The four boys scrambled through the bushes. Then, as a deafening roar split the air and shook the ground, they stood still as if turned to stone.

"She went up all right," said Toby. "Come on back."

When they returned to the edge of the mallee scrub and looked about, there was not much of the old hut to be seen. The dust was settling about the heap of stones that remained, and the boys crept quietly forward and gazed with beating hearts at the jumbled mass. Then, as they gained courage, they jumped up and down on the fallen stones and kicked them this way and that.

"Come here," called Richard, and the boys pressed about him. "What's that?" he said, pointing with the toe of his boot to something in the ruin.

There was a silence, then Toby said in a queer voice. "It's a bit off a bed. Look, there's the pillow under that stone."

"Here's a piece of rug and a bit o' canvas," put in Richard.

"Somebody must have been living in it!" exclaimed Skinny, surveying the heap of stones. "Somebody must have had a bed there!"

"We've blown up somebody's house!" Toby said, aghast.

"What if they was inside?" said Skinny in a hushed voice.

The boys looked quickly at the heap of stones, the broken bed and the torn pillow.

"Come on, let's get!" said Toby and, with white, frightened faces, they all ran off into the scrub, Bob limping after them; and close behind followed the tortoise-shell cat, calling like a lost soul.

They kept among the bushes and walked parallel to the road, stopping only now and then to swear vows of secrecy or to discuss the dire possibilities of their act.

"If any one splits, the rest of us'll blame it all on to him," said Skinny, stooping down for a handful of stones with which to pelt the cat. And the boys all spat their deaths and crossed their hearts very fervently, and vowed to say nothing.

In the Thomas boys' bedroom that night, silence reigned after Polly had blown out their candle and said good night. Silence still reigned when Polly, in the other room, having finished massaging Nathan's back, had got into bed beside him. But under the bed-clothes, curled into a heap, Bob was sobbing, his leg and his conscience paining him. After some time he came up for air, and sent a sorrowful sniff into the darkness.

"You awake?" whispered Richard from the bed by the door.

Bob lay down quickly and, bursting into tears, retired again under the bed-clothes.

"What's up?" called Richard softly.

There being no answer from the bed by the window, Rich got out of his and crossed the cold floor.

"Don't do that, Bob," he said, uncovering Bob's face. "Is—is your leg hurting?"

Bob raised his head. "It's burning like fire," he whimpered. "I'm frightened. . . . I want mother."

"Lie there and I'll creep out and get some hot water and bathe it for you," said Rich, and he made his way quietly from the room and out into the kitchen where, by the light of the embers in the stove, he found a bowl, a clean cloth and some warm water and, returning to the bedroom and closing the door, bathed Bob's leg until most of the pain and stiffness had gone from it. The pellets of shot could easily be felt under the skin, but the boys could

not extract them, so left them there in the firm, young
flesh.

"You're certain sure I won't die?" whimpered Bob, when
he was in bed again.

"It'd take a cartload of that sort of shot to kill anybody,"
Rich assured him, and Bob fell asleep very soon after that
and left Richard alone with *his* particular conscience.

The boys lived in fear and dread throughout Sunday
and Monday, but when Richard returned from the mines
on Tuesday night his step was light and free, and he said
quite casually at tea-time. "The boys at the mines told
me to-day that somebody blew up an old stone hut of
McGinnes's on Saturday."

Bob dropped his knife and fork with a clatter, and sat
transfixed.

"Shepherd Joe's brother's been camping there for a
week," continued Richard, "using Joe's things; and they do
say Mr McGinnes says he's glad the old place was blown
up, and it seemed to him a pity that Joe's brother was in
the township at the time boozing at the hotel all Saturday
afternoon, 'cause he's nothing but a drunken loafer and
nobody'd miss him. Mr McGinnes says it's a good job the
hut's gone 'cause now he's rid of Joe's brother for good,
and anyway the place was so full of fleas, nobody but a
nuisance like Joe's brother would ever sleep there. Mr
McGinnes says he's going to cart away the stones to mend
his stable with."

"But 'ow come the place to be blawed up?" asked
Nathan, puzzled.

"P'raps all they fleas inside jumped to once!" said Polly.
And in the laugh that followed, Bob and Rich exchanged
a long wink.

The following Saturday afternoon was also wet and, as
the clouds had not lifted by three o'clock, Rich and Bob
reluctantly gave up all ideas of sailing the boat that Rich
had been finishing each evening in the kitchen.

"Get the wood ready for thy bath," Polly called out,
coming to the back door, her arms white with soapsuds
from scrubbing the kitchen floor. "Put the water in the
boiler an' get the fire goin' right 'way. If 'ee can't find
naught to do 'ee can fill in time gettin' thyselves clean.

Carry the tub into the bedroom. An' if there's any muck made, thees'll 'ear o' it. Wash thy hair, an' when I've changed me dress I'll cut un for 'ee."

The boys set about getting the chips and bark ready for the fire. Richard found the tomahawk in the shed and began to cut the mallee sticks into short lengths.

"Shake it up," he said to Bob, who was at the other end of the shed. "Throw us over a few more bits to chop."

Bob came across with an armful and dropped it by the chopping-block in the shed doorway, then squatted on his heels and watched Rich cut the thin, dry mallee sticks and add them to the heap on the ground. He watched in silence for a while, then said: "Give us a turn with the axe, Rich?"

"You're not allowed to touch it."

"I know I'm not, but give us a turn. Go on!"

"No," said Richard cleaving a knobbly stick in two pieces with one stroke.

Bob resorted to abuse. "You think you can cut wood, don't you?"

"I don't think, I *know*," Rich answered.

Bob waited for a while. "You think you're clever, don't you?" he said at last.

"Well, I wouldn't have to know much to beat you."

The axe slipped and stuck into the chopping-block.

Bob laughed derisively. "Look what you did. You can't cut wood."

"You shut up!" said Rich, annoyed at last. "I can cut anything."

"Bet you couldn't. Bet you couldn't cut this whole shed down."

"Bet I could!"

"You'd be too frightened to."

"Huh! I'm not too frightened to cut down anything."

"Let's see you then!" taunted Bob.

"All right," said Richard, sitting back on his heels. "What'll I cut?" He waved the axe up and down in a determined manner.

"Bet you're frightened to cut *that*!" said Bob, and laid his right forefinger on the chopping-block.

"Bet I'm not," said Rich, waving the axe closer and

bringing it down towards the block. The axe struck the wood and stayed poised there, but Bob's forefinger was neatly cut in two and the top joint lay on the chopping-block, and blood was pouring from his hand and dropping on to the floor of the shed.

Two seconds passed in deathly silence while the boys looked with staring eyes at what had happened. Bob was first on his feet, and scream after scream echoed through the shed. Richard staggered to the door-post, and stood there white and faint. Then Bob, blood running down his arm and holding his hand high, ran towards the house, yelling for his mother. Polly came to the kitchen door in her petticoat bodice, and Bob threw himself on her bosom, staining it red.

"What's to do? What's to do?" she cried, alarmed at Bob's screams and so much blood.

"Richard's cut me finger off. He's cut off me finger. Oh! Oh! Oh!"

Polly looked at Bob's forefinger with its top joint and nail missing. "Lawks!" she cried, feeling sick in her stomach. Then she screamed to Rich. "Bring me the top of 'is finger, 'ee young Turk! Bring it 'ere, an' I'll clap it on agin."

But Richard leaned his head against the shed door-post and, without more ado, began to vomit.

"Stay there," said Polly to Bob, who stood in the kitchen doorway holding up his hand and bellowing with pain and fright, and she ran towards the shed.

"I'll settle wi' thee, later," she said viciously to Richard as she pushed past him.

She ran to the chopping-block, but Gray's rooster from next door was there before her and, reaching up his neck and cocking his glossy black head on one side, pecked up the top of Bob's finger just as Polly bent to retrieve it. Polly, her hand poised over the block, saw the bulge in the rooster's throat descend into his feather-covered crop, and she sent up a wailing cry. She turned to Richard, leaning weakly against the shed.

"Thees'll answer to God for this, me son," she said tensely. "Make no mistake about it. Thees'll answer to God!" and she sped back to the house.

"I never meant to—I never meant to—the axe slipped out of my hand—I never meant to, mother," Richard called out in an anguished voice. But Polly took no notice, and pushed Bob before her into the kitchen.

Nathan, nearly frantic at the sound of Bob's screams of pain, sat helplessly in the bedroom where Polly had led him when she had begun to clean the kitchen floor. He held Annie tightly, although she struggled to get away and investigate the trouble in the yard—held her in the crook of his arm hushing her, and straining every nerve to guess at the reason for the rending cries and for Polly's horror-stricken shout. He had heard Polly tell the boys to prepare the boiler, and at once thought of fire! Fire! Nathan shivered with dread, and stretched his nostrils wide to catch a whiff of smoke or burning. It was his greatest fear that he would be helpless to do anything in such a crisis, and ever-present with him was this foreboding of fire.

He heard Polly and Bob come stumbling into the kitchen.

"What's wrong, mother?" he called hoarsely.

"Rich 'ave nearly killed Bob wi' the axe," said Polly shortly, rushing to the dresser for pepper to sprinkle on the stump of Bob's forefinger.

"Land o' Goshen," groaned Nathan, "what did 'e do to un?"

But Polly was too busy to reply. She was winding a sooty cobweb from the chimney about Bob's finger, liberally dusting it all with black pepper. Then, taking a strip of clean, washed calico from the chintz bag that always hung on the back of her chair, she bound it firmly about Bob's finger, and also made a sling for him in which to rest his bandaged hand, then led him in to Nathan. While Polly was lifting Bob up on to the bed she told Nathan what had happened.

"There," she finished, "that's what da go on while me back's turned. Chasin' each other with axes! 'Ere's Bob with 'is finger cut off. 'Ow'll 'e ever learn a trade? What will 'e turn an 'and to, 'im a finger short?"

Bob began to cry again, and Nathan said in a low voice to Polly, "Call Rich."

Polly called Richard from the kitchen doorway. "Come in to father!" she said sharply.

Richard came to the bedroom door and hung back in the shadows of the passage. His face was drawn, and his eyes were fixed in dumb entreaty on his father.

"Come 'ere, me son," said Nathan, moved at the sight of his boy's misery. "Tell mother an' me 'ow come this to 'appen."

The telling did not take long, and after Richard had finished Nathan drew his son towards him and said:

"Rich, thee's been punished for this, me dear, and the knowledge o' what thee's done to thy brother'll allus bide with 'ee." Here Bob gave a whimper. "An', Bob, thee's done thyself a sad turn too, this day, wi' thy tauntin' tongue." And Nathan, in his quiet voice, drew a band of words about the brothers. He told them of their duty each to the other, of the cord of love and kinship that should bind a family together. He paid honour, too, to Richard as the man of the family. " 'E oo earns the bread earns the right to man'ood," he said to his eldest son. "God bless 'ee for a good son, Rich, an' to 'ee both I say this 'ere: never question the responsibilities 'ee bear each t'other. Brothers must back each other up. Remember oo 'twas complained, 'Am I me brother's keeper?' Cain 'twas oo said that there, an' Cain 'twas oo took 'is brother's life."

And something of Nathan's meaning was interpreted by each boy's heart. And Bob's blood, like Abel's, cried from the ground, though not of kinship violated but of brotherhood bought at a price.

CHAPTER XIII

TRAGEDIES like the cutting off of Bob's forefinger loomed large on the horizon of the Thomas family during those early years in Moonta. Struggling as they were, every set-back took on huge proportions when viewed in the cold light of getting on in the world, and every hindrance to their chances of making a living and having enough to eat and drink became a calamity.

It was a tragic Saturday when Richard, handing over his pay to Polly, had let a silver florin slip between his fingers and on to the floor, where it had rolled away and disappeared between a crack in the boards.

"There!" said Polly, on her knees by the spot where the florin had vanished. "That's what da come of 'avin' board floors! Now that da mean short commons for us. That were a week's meat went rollin' 'way under that there."

Then there was that time when Polly had lost a customer. She was a miner's buxom wife from Moonta Mines, with very definite views about what she wanted in the shape of a winter's bonnet.

"Thee can stick all the plumes thee's got about un," Polly's fat customer had said. "I got money galore. Me Tim 'ave just finished his sturt, an' we be goin' to 'ave a splash."

Polly had taken a little measuring tape from the square pocket of her dress and approached the miner's wife, who had laid aside her old straw bonnet and was waiting for Polly to measure her for the new one. Polly, with every intention of being pleasant and no thought of anything except the work in hand, had run her tape about her customer's large, untidy head.

"Lawks," said Polly affably, as she read the figures on her tape, "thee's not got an 'ead. That's an 'ead an' an 'alf!"

Whereupon the miner's wife had seemed to swell up and burst and, after the explosion of words, had slammed her straw bonnet sideways on her head and marched from the shop. At the doorway she had turned and shaken a red fist at the astonished Polly.

" 'Ee can't insult Tim Bennett's missus, I'll 'ave 'ee knaw. Fat I may be, but I'll 'ave nobody tell me so. Keep thy bonnets. I'll go elsewhere!"

That had been a bitter pill to Polly. "I never meant no 'arm," she moaned to Nathan later that same night. "I were just talkin'. She shoulden 'ave took me up so. Anaways, she did 'ave an 'ead an' an 'alf. She were as fat as a girt pig."

"Well, Pol," said Nathan, "open thy eyes to it, but shut thy mouth!"

Her impulsiveness of speech lost her another customer, but this time Polly did not realize it, and always wondered why she was never again summoned to Mrs Noah Temby's to make and fit another lace house-cap for that old lady.

"Well, what 'arm were there in that?" Polly would have questioned angrily if told that, on the occasion of her first visit to the immaculate Temby home, she had broken off her conversation in the middle to run an inquiring finger across the glass surface of the portrait of the late Mr Noah Temby, posed for in the Crown Studios in Adelaide and now hanging in a prominent position in his widow's parlour. Polly's damp forefinger had squeaked across the glass.

"Sorry," she had said to the indignant old lady. " 'Tis only a crack, I thought it were a cobweb!"

Then there was the loss of the cabbages—those healthy green cabbages that Polly had transplanted from the cottage in Wallaroo Mines. Two wandering billy-goats, passing along Robert Street one night and hearing Lily's tender love calls, had together butted down a paling from the Thomas back yard and had rushed in to Lily and the cabbages. Polly had wept hot, scalding tears the next morning on beholding the wreck of the vegetable patch.

"There go our dinners, walkin' round the township in a billy-goat's belly," said said crudely, with a world of feeling in her voice.

To Polly, struggling to find time to do all the work in her house, to care for three children and an invalid, to attend to the little millinery shop and to make, trim and clean the hats that must be sold in order that her family might live, every moment was golden and every hindrance an exasperating waste of precious time.

Polly did not dare to stop and wonder how all the work of each day was to be fitted into her waking hours or how one pair of hands could contrive to do everything. Scarcely surprising is it that her temper suffered and her tongue sharpened. Many, many times she worked far into the night doing household tasks while the rest of the family slept. Tasks that other housewives did lightly and carelessly in the hours before midday Polly sweated over at night. Washing clothes by candlelight, scrubbing floors, blacking stoves, and baking saffron cake and leek-and-tatty pasties in the eerie quietness of night: trying to catch up on one day's duties by taking an hour or two from the next!

Sometimes, shutting the passage door, she banged and jostled the baking-tins in the kitchen cupboard and abandoned herself to the unsatisfying and dangerous luxury of self-pity. Tears of tiredness and exasperation would run down her cheeks on these occasions, and she would sweep back the ends of hair from about her face with savage hand jerks. Worn out, she would often sit at the kitchen table and cry away her misery, and once on a cold August night she had fallen asleep so, and Richard had found her there in the morning with her head on the table and her hands splayed out before her like a swimmer in a heavy sea.

Yet, had any one asked Polly at this time if she were unhappy she would have given a vigorous and an honest denial. She neglected nothing and managed, with her clever, stubby fingers, to make a livelihood and keep a home together; and there is happiness in that and satisfaction, even if little rest.

On one damp day in September, provoked to distraction by the drip, drip, drip of the water leaking through the roof and dropping into a tub in the boys' room, Polly waited for the rain to cease; then, when the spring sunshine showed through, she slopped across the muddy yard to the shed, to find something with which to mend the hole in the roof. She would not trust Bob up on the roof alone, and Richard had so little time that it was evident that, if the leak were to be stopped, Polly must do it herself. She scrambled up the slippery iron with a paint pot in one hand and a square of coarse canvas in the other and, from the vantage point of the roof ridge, looked about her. She cried out with surprise and pleasure, feeling like Satan himself, with the kingdoms of this world spread out below her.

From this unconventional position she could look beyond the pointed roof of the new Wesleyan Church. The silver sunlight lightened the grey waters of Moonta Bay, and out in the gulf itself a white-sailed boat scudded before the wind. Polly breathed in the salty scents from the sea and the heavy perfume from the wattle-trees showing yellow in the scrub about the township. The mines themselves were hung about with smoke, and Polly could see the horse tram moving out toward the mines from the town. She looked down, too, into her neighbours' back yards.

"Miz Gray be washin' 'er back bedroom curtains," said Polly to herself. "Must be goin' to 'ave in a new boarder. . . . Mulligans must 'ave bugs in their beds. Else why they got their best bed out in the back yard for?"

Polly dried the rusty spot on the iron roof above the boys' bedroom and proceeded to paint it over with thick brown paint; then, pressing the square of canvas over all, she gave this a covering of paint too, and considered it a job well done. She reluctantly took a last, long look about her over sea, scrub, mines and town; then, looking down, saw two passers-by in Robert Street watching her as she sat on the ridge of the roof. She slid along out of their sight, and then began the troublesome descent to the gutterings and, via the ladder, to the ground. It had been fairly easy in Polly's slippered feet to climb up the face of the roof and now, clinging with both hands to the ridge, she let her body lie flat on the roof with her toes a foot from the guttering.

" 'Ere goes," she said, gingerly releasing her grasp of the ridge. She had expected the guttering to hold her while she got into a stooping position, then to support her while she felt with one foot for the ladder; but the guttering was rusty and insecure and, when Polly's weight dropped on it, gave way with a crash and fell to the ground. Polly fell with it, but the hem of her black skirt, catching on a cleat, held her suspended in mid-air.

There she dangled. Her slippers dropped from her wriggling feet, and her black-stockinged legs tied round below the knees with white tape, and her white drawers with the hand-eyeletted embroidered frill, and her red flannel petticoat, and her grey flannel underskirt with the scalloped hem all hung aloft in a most indecorous and revealing fashion.

Mrs Gray, going to feed her fowls five minutes later and chancing to look Thomas-wards, saw her and, dropping the fowls' food, rushed in, grabbed Polly's waving legs, propped the ladder beneath them and succeeded, after a great deal of straining and tearing, to release the skirt and help her to the ground.

Polly sat down on the doorstep and rested her head on her trembling knees.

"Lawsey me, Miz Thomas, 'ow come 'ee to get strung up there, me dear?" asked Mrs Gray solicitously. "What was thee doin' on roof?"

"Just tearin' me best workin' skirt to pieces and makin' a monkey-show of meself!" Polly said in a weak voice.

"No, but 'ow come 'ee to be up on roof a 'tall?" insisted Mrs Gray, " 'Tain't fitten."

Polly lifted her head quickly. " 'Ow come I to be on roof, Miz Gray? I'll tell 'ee. 'Cause I be a hard-workin' fool of a woman as must go round findin' summat to do in most awkward places. As if me 'ands wassen full 'nough on ground as 'tis. But no, I must go up top mendin' roof, an' come tumblin' down like the fool I be. A purty penny it'll cost now to put me to rights!"

Another expense that had to be considered in the weekly budgeting was Bob's school money. He attended at a dame's school, and for sixpence a week and the cost of his books and slates Bob was well grounded in the elementary subjects of education. For this small sum the children of the township were taught to read and spell, to recite "Meddlesome Mattie" and "The Caged Bird" alternately with the Apostles' Creed and the multiplication table, to associate Nijninovgorod with annual fairs and never dissociate them all their lives, to write a thin sloping handwriting with an abundance of curlicues, and to do a vast amount of addition of laces and cottons on smudgy slates with squeaky slate-pencils.

Upon Nathan this removal to Moonta had had a deeper effect than upon the other members of the family. Transported bodily and dumped into the cedar bed in the house in Robert Street as he had been, it took many weeks to accustom himself to his new surroundings. Ever since the heart attack that he had suffered after Allen's death he had been conscious of an uneasy tremor in his limbs, and he had an almost childish fear of a repetition of the weakness that had possessed him at that time. Pain he had in plenty and he bore it bravely, but the thought of the strained heart that he carried in his breast and the memory of its anguish stayed in his mind and troubled him greatly. "A rheumatic heart", good old Dr Fisher had called it, for want of a better term, and Nathan had felt since then that he carried within him a sleeping lion which some day would wake to stretch and devour.

Polly would dress him each morning, for his twisted fingers could only fumble with the loops and buttons of his clothing and his knees were so stiff that it was often difficult for him to bend them, and then she would help him to his seat by the fire or in a warm sheltered spot in the yard. Here he would stay until meal-times or until Bob came home from school or the minister called. Many of the miners who lived near by came in for a yarn and a smoke before going on shift, and everybody who passed and saw Nathan in his chair wrapped about with the patchwork quilt had a "Good day" for him. It can be said for certain that, except for the pain in his limbs and the tremor of his heart, Nathan enjoyed his invalidism exceedingly. For the first time in his life he had books galore—obtained by Rich from the mine's library—and all day to read them in. He could find a man for every hour of the day who, between shifts or after shop, would welcome a game of draughts with him or an argument about things in general or just the opportunity to talk to a fellow-man who had time to talk back.

Polly would sometimes place a spare chair beside Nathan

as he sat on the footpath by the shop window in the sunshine.

"Thee be sich a nice-lookin' dear," she said, smoothing back his greying hair, which she kept so well clipped and combed, "that the women see thee 'way off an' can't 'elp comin' closer to 'ave a word with 'ee."

"An' that brings 'em to the shop window, eh, Pol?" chuckled Nathan. "Thees ought to put a bonnet on me, an' I'd show un off for 'ee good an' proper, 'ere in the street."

The extra chair was for the minister or any new friend of Nathan's who might stop to talk with him, but if Polly saw any nondescripts or loafers sitting in it she was outside in a twinkling, hustling Nathan to his feet.

"Too cold (or too 'ot) for 'ee 'ere, Nat. Come in to once!" And she brought him inside the house and the chairs after him, and very soon Nathan learned to differentiate for himself and kept his books on the extra chair if any undesirable acquaintances appeared. He did this without questioning himself as to whether or not it were a Christian thing to do—the yard-stick by which he measured his own and all men's actions—and for Polly's sake kept the shop "respectable".

On Wednesday nights after mid-week service at the Wesleyan Church many of the church members assembled in Polly's kitchen for an impromptu prayer meeting and song service, for Polly now attended the church of her girlhood—the Wesleyan Methodist—and Nathan and the children came naturally into its circle of influence. Two meetings in one evening were not considered too many for these ardent church members, and there was never yet a Cornishman who was too tired to sing a hymn tune.

Polly, standing at the kitchen door, would hear young Jim Nicholas playing the last "Amen" in the church near by, and she would bustle about putting finishing touches to the kitchen. The boys were allowed to stay up, but as it was nine o'clock Annie was in bed and asleep, although she would waken later to be brought into the kitchen, dewy-eyed and very serious. Nathan shut his book, and Polly straightened the narrow black tie about his throat and whisked back his coat lapel so that his silver watch-

chain glimmered opulently in the firelight. The lamp stood
in the window as a polite sign that the Thomas family
was at home and prepared for visitors.

The minister came first, lean-faced and kindly in his
black suit. The two chapel stewards followed in their
black, Wesleyan, long-tailed coats with a handkerchief
negligently hanging down behind. White shirt collars and
black ties were worn by every man, and each carried a high-
crowned hat which was left with its fellows in a neat pile
on the chair by the door.

Joshua Tuckett, whom Nathan had known at Wallaroo
Mines, came next, and Andrew Joel Pearce, and William
Henry Polglone of the rich bass voice, and the choirmaster
with his book of anthems and large-sized hymn-book under
his arm, Job Nankivell of Port Hughes who sang soprano
like a woman, and Hoppy-Dick Trevivers who had one leg
shorter than the other and possessed a fine tenor voice and,
last of all, Thomas Thomas, rubbing his hands and smiling
to all in the room with the easiest grace imaginable. He
was dressed in his working coat, his coarse trousers tied
below the knees with stout cord, his grey flannel shirt
buttoned up to the chin, and his round hat with the stump
of candle in it under one arm and a bulging crib-bag under
the other.

"Don't mind me, Miz Thomas, please," he said to Polly,
smiling widely. "I be workin' last cor' be night, but I
coulden 'elp comin' in on me way to 'ave a word o' prayer
wi' Brother Thomas 'ere, an' an 'ymn toon afore I da go."

After greetings were over, the short calm was broken by
the voice of the minister.

"Now, friends," he said in his pleasant high voice,
"Brother Thomas will lead us in prayer." He looked
towards the miner, who instantly fell to his knees and
bowed his stubbly head over the chair seat.

Nathan's heart had contracted, then beaten furiously,
when the minister had said "Brother Thomas". It was
always so when Nathan thought anything was expected of
him, and it was with great relief that he heard Thomas
Thomas's voice filling the kitchen.

"Lord, Lord," prayed Thomas Thomas with sincerity

and evident pleasure, " 'ear us from Thy mercy-seat an'
bring peace to our 'earts!"

"Amen! Amen!" came from the men's throats.

"Amen!" cried Nathan, listening to the surge of blood
dying away in his ears.

Then Job Nankivell prayed, and the sweat stood out
on his brow as if he were rowing his fishing-boat out in
the gulf under a summer sun. Very earnest he was and very
eloquent. It was his third public petition that evening,
and he was considered a good pray-er.

After Job's prayer the company resumed their seats and,
while Polly poured the hot water into the big teapot and
the aroma of strong tea filled the kitchen, the choirmaster
adjusted his spectacles and the men arranged themselves
about Nathan's chair.

"Mmmm!" sang the choirmaster. "Mmmmmm!"

"Mmmm!" sang the men—soprano, tenor and bass—with
young Richard supplying the alto.

"We'll have 'Great God of Wonders'," said the choirmaster, lifting his hand. "One, two. . . ."

Away they went, to the lovely tune "Sovereignty".
Richard had his chance here, when he and Job Nankivell
had eight bars as a duet. Even Polly, who had her mind
more on supper than hymn tunes, paused and marvelled
at the mingling and merging of the two voices. Then the
four parts resumed the strain, the choirmaster, with one
lift of his eyebrows and a swirl of his hand, safely con-
ducting them over the ticklish change of tempo. Three-
four time now, with William Henry thundering out the
bass. Then they sang it through again, *sotto voce* for the
two-two time and full volume for the three-four.

"That's grand!" said Thomas Thomas, after the choirmaster had cut off the sound with one sharp stroke of his
hand.

"Let's 'ave a go at 'Lydia'!" cried Hoppy-Dick Trevivers,
when all had recovered breath.

"Common metre," said the choirmaster. "Try it to
Wesley's 'Try us, O God, and search the ground. . . .'"

"That's a lovely tune," said the minister, "one of the
best."

They stumbled a little in fitting Wesley's words to the

tune, so they sang it to "Ah!" and the rise and fall of the harmony made an effect of sheer beauty.

"It da take a Cornishman to write a toon like that there," said Nathan.

"Give us 'Lyngham'," said Polly, and added her voice to "O for a thousand tongues to sing . . ."

They sang three verses, knowing every word.

"Let's 'ave 'Irish', master," said Thomas Thomas, "then I must be off. Like as not I'll be singin' all the mile to the mines."

"You could do worse, my man," said the minister good-humouredly.

" 'God moves in a mysterious way'." The choirmaster announced Cowper's words to the old hymn tune with bright eyes. "This be a grand old hymn," he said feelingly, and every one nodded, and not one eye sought the hymn-book as they sang the six verses through. Richard knew every word, and Polly too sang it faultlessly to the end.

Long after the hot strong tea was finished and the seedy cake eaten to the last crumb and the singers gone away home and the house quiet and every one in it in bed, Nathan, his eye on a single star that looked in at his unshaded window, turning in his mind many things and remembering many things, came at last to think of his sickness and his crippled state.

"I must believe," he said to himself, "I must believe that this is all part o' God's plan. 'God is 'Is own interpreter, an' 'E will make it plain.' Amen." And soon afterwards he fell asleep.

CHAPTER XIV

On 9 October 1878 the Thomas family was astir at daybreak. It was the occasion of the opening of the railway line at Kadina and the running of the first "through" train from Adelaide to Yorke's Peninsula, and the Governor of South Australia, Sir William Jervois, was to perform the ceremony. The annual Agricultural Show was also to be held on this date, in the showgrounds at Julia Terrace, Kadina.

Everybody from the townships adjacent and from all over the peninsula who could manage to be present had arranged some means of conveyance. Polly and the children were to go in one of the coaches of the Kadina-Wallaroo Railway and Pier Company, who were running a service between Moonta and Kadina at the rate of three shillings and sixpence for adults and half price for children.

"It be a power o' money," Polly kept saying for more than a week before, "but go I will."

"I'd go if it cost a million pounds!" said Bob, gritting his teeth with excitement.

The day dawned grey and showery. A dozen times Bob walked into the back yard and lifted his face to the rain, and "It's getting lighter. It's nearly gone now," he cried hopefully each time, while Polly scolded him for wetting his Sunday suit, and the rain still drummed on the roof.

Polly, too, was seething with excitement. Except for a Sunday-school picnic she had had no outing for years, and now, between rushing to and fro getting breakfast, overlooking the dressing of the children and washing Nathan and fixing him comfortably in bed, she listened to the rain.

"Drat it!" she said vehemently, looking through the bedroom window at the wetness outside. "Drat it!"

Nathan knew better than either to sympathize or cheer. One word out of place now might turn Polly's annoyance at the weather to annoyance with her family, or tears, or sharp words, or something else which would mar this long-anticipated holiday for them. Polly, working herself up into a nervous tension, would be quite capable of determining, suddenly, to stay at home—or at least of threatening to do so, keeping the family on tenterhooks until a short ten minutes before the coach was due to leave, then bustling them out of doors, uncertain if they were really going or not. So Nathan lay quiet in his bed.

Johnnie Boots was to keep Nathan company for the day, and his wife, who was too far gone with child to contemplate the rough ride to Kadina, offered to see to Nathan's meals.

"Let my man stay with yourn if 'e want to, Miz Thomas," Mrs Boots had said good-naturedly. "All 'e da live for be to play draffs an' talk politics an' 'bout the Russians, an' 'is brownkitis be too bad to go out this bitter weather. Let un stay, an' 'ee go off an' see the fun. I'll stay by."

The sky had lightened by eight o'clock, and Polly, serene now and dressed in a grey stuff gown with a bustle behind and a black corded silk dolman atop which covered her dress bodice and its lace fichu, calmly tied her black bonnet with moire strings under her plump chin and marshalled the children about Nathan's bed.

"Take a look at us," she said, proudly. "Will us do?"

Nathan smiled all over his face, and leaned back on his pillow hugely pleased. Annie primped herself, shaking out the stiff folds of her dark blue dress and cape under which her white drawers showed, and lifted up a little red buttoned boot for Nathan to see.

"Look 'ee, father, look 'ee! Don't 'ee wish 'ee 'ad a pair o' red shoes to come to Kadina in? Seven buttings to each one."

Annie was the only child of Nathan and Polly who spoke as they did. All the children used, on occasion, Cornish phrases and idioms, but the boys, escaping early from their parents' sides, had sought a wider field from which to compile their vocabulary and, entering school at five years of age, had come in contact with teachers and scholars who were not all of them Cornish or of Cornish extraction. The clear, open air of Australia and the free life the children led until working age must have played some part, at least, in changing the timbre of their voices and rounding their vowel sounds.

Every country and oftentimes each section of a country has its own enunciation, and there is something more than inherited phrases and turns of speech that goes to make the variations in a language. A theory has been brought forward, although it has yet to be proved, that besides national character one of the main influences contributing to the tonal quality of racial speech is the nature of the air in a country or part of a country—its density and composition. The American nasal twang, the Australian drawl, the English clipped utterance and the New Zealand clarity of tone could, perhaps, be accounted for in this way, demonstrating varieties of tone and pronunciation in the same language.

Annie, her father's constant companion, gave the lie to the foregoing supposition, for she spoke as broadly as if she had been born and raised in Cornwall itself.

"Father, don't 'ee grieve whilst we be gone, will 'ee dear?" she asked, serious-eyed.

"No, bless 'ee," said Nathan, kissing her sweet face and pushing a finger up a spiral of her bright hair. "Look after mother, an' be a good girl an' tell me all 'bout it come mornin'-time."

"Good-bye, father," said Richard who, having been employed as printer's devil in the printing office in Ellen Street for three weeks—although as yet not quite thirteen years of age—already felt that he had put away childish things and, from now on, must show the demeanour of a man of letters.

Nathan looked long at this, his eldest son, sturdy but with a newly developing leanness of feature and the still sensitive mouth.

"I suppose thees'll be watchin' out for summat for the paper to-day, Rich. 'Twill be a proud day for me when I da see me boy's work in the newspaper."

"Aw, go on, father. I won't be allowed to have anything in for years and years and years and years, but Mr Richards told me that if I saw anything that was really *news*, I could tell him and he'd write it up."

"That's called 'reportin' '," said Nathan. "That's bein'

a reporter, Rich. My! That be grand. Go to, me son!" And he gave Rich a proud look.

But Richard, anxious to be fair, had a request to make about that. "Don't say anything like that to anybody, father. I'm not reporting, only watching out. People would laugh and think I was stuck up, and anyway, Mr Richards wouldn't like anything said that wasn't true. Every one at the printing office says I'm too young to be working there at all, but he says I'm all right and I'll do."

"An' what editor says be right," said Nathan with finality.

Polly carried a carpet-bag of provisions, and also a bundle of white geraniums and a cluster of rosemary wrapped in newspaper to take to Allen's grave in the Kadina cemetery.

"Thee da knaw I shoulden go if 'twasn't a chance to go to Allen too, don't 'ee Nat?" she said anxiously, then added hesitantly, "I don't want to leave 'ee now."

"Get along, all of 'ee, an' 'ave a right royal time!" ordered Nathan.

"I can see the coach," cried Bob from the shop doorway, and Polly, grabbing up a cloak to protect her new silk dolman, kissed Nathan on the forehead and followed the children into the rain-wet street.

At Kadina much preparation had been made for the great occasion. Flags flew from poles above the local shops, and strings of coloured bunting criss-crossed Taylor and Grave Streets, but the stormy weather had wrought havoc with some of the decorations, and torn strips of what had once been gay streamers waved wetly in the wind or wrapped themselves untidily about veranda-posts.

At the spot where Sir William Jervois would stand to declare the railway open, a canopy of pine boughs was erected above a temporary platform, looped about with red, white and blue art muslin. The rain had made the royal colours run together, but when the weather cleared the wind dried the muslin into something of its original freshness and, but for the fact that the same wind would later shake the moisture from the pine boughs on to the heads and necks of the vice-royalty and official dignity below, everybody was highly gratified with the decorations and the display.

When the train bearing the visiting dignitaries arrived

from Port Wakefield amid much handkerchief waving and lusty cheering, Polly and her three children edged up closer to the dais. The ground about the platform was a mass of sticky mud, so the four Thomases planted their feet on the new train rails and stood thus until Annie, whimpering with tiredness, was hoisted up between Polly and Richard, which brought her little head on a line with everybody's shoulders. Peering between the hats of the people in the crowd, her eyes sought, under the urgency of compelling attraction, the fearsome shape of the railway engine, still puffing as if exhausted from its first journey to Yorke's Peninsula.

The engine driver, his hand ready to release the steam which would blow the engine whistle when the Governor's speech was ended and the line declared open, glimpsed Annie's little face turned towards him, and he winked his eyelid and wriggled a finger at her through the window of the cab. Annie turned away her head, and as quickly turned it back again. The funny man inside the puffing engine nodded this time, and Annie's little lips curled upward in a smile. Then the engine driver had his turn at smiling, and Annie, intrigued, nodded her head till her curls bobbed up and down. On the platform, unnoticed by Annie or the man in the engine, Sir William Jervois was rising to his feet in a slow, dignified and impressive manner.

The Hon. R. D. Ross the State Treasurer, and Mr Furner member for the district, formed a background for the military figure of the State Governor. In crisp tones Sir William began:

"Ladies and gentlemen, I have great pleasure in declaring the line from Kadina to Adelaide open. I can say, having just travelled along it, that it is an admirable line——" His voice was lost in a sudden sound of cracking wood and, with a crash, the whole ingenious contraption of pine boughs, bunting, platform, and all its dignified human freight sank from sight as the wooden supports bent and broke.

For one short moment nothing stirred; then a head, rising through the screen of pine boughs, broke the strain, and the fireman, grabbing the whistle release, sent a piercing blast shrilling across the heads of the open-mouthed crowd. It broke the spell: a great laugh, good-humoured and spontaneous, echoed the whistle's blast and only ceased as a tall, military figure, thrusting aside the fallen pine branches, stepped up on a safe corner of the wrecked platform and, without the slightest apparent sign of change in voice or manner, continued his oration.

"However," finished Sir William, "I assure you I hope and trust that the future railway platform will be more successful than this." He gestured eloquently, and the crowd cheered. The speech had been a great success. The Cornishmen, who comprised three-quarters of the audience, appreciated the Governor's wit and presence of mind as much as they had enjoyed the uncomfortable episode eliciting it.

"That were the funniest thing I ever clapped eye on," said Polly, when all was over. "Sich a thing to 'appen! Folks as never seed un'll never believe when we tell un."

"I wish our paper came out every day instead of only on Tuesdays and Fridays," said Richard. "I'd rush off back to Moonta with the story like a shot."

"What! Miss all the show an' evrathin' to tear 'ome to Moonta wi' that there?"

"That was *news*!" said Richard, emphatically. "I know that much."

Later the four of them, seated on a pile of wooden sleepers that lay in the shelter of a tree by the railway line, ate their lunch from the carpet-bag. Polly had spread out her cloak, and all of them crowded together munching the meat-and-tatty pasties that she had made the day before.

"Now, soon as I finish I'll be off to cemetery. Thee, Rich, take care o' Bob an' Annie. 'Ere's money to take 'ee all into the showgrounds, an' don't walk Annie off 'er legs. She'll want to go sleep come mid-afternoon, an' thees'll 'ave to take turns a-nursing of 'er. I got a mile an' an 'alf there an' back to walk, an' I may 'ave to seek shelter by the way if it da rain agin, but see that 'ee be waitin' for me at 'alf past three or summat to four, inside the big gate. If I idden there, thees must wait about till I da come." And Polly kissed them all three and, folding her cloak neatly, put it into her carpet-bag the easier to carry and, picking up her bunch of flowers and rosemary, set off to walk to the Kadina cemetery.

The children watched her as she walked along, parting the groups of people who were passing her in the opposite direction on their way to the showgrounds in Julia Terrace.

After watching Polly's grey and black figure bobbing into the distance the children took hands and, joining in with one of the groups of hurrying people, at last found themselves before the big gate in the stone wall that surrounded the showgrounds. While Rich searched for and found the three threepenny pieces that would admit them they listened to the variety of noises from behind the wall: music, the banging of a showman's drum, the crowing of roosters, the sound of human voices and the bellowing of imprisoned cattle. The children were filled with wild excitement, and all the zest and love for those annual shows which form highlights in the lives of country people was born to them in that minute of anticipation. From so deep a source did this pleasure spring that never afterwards would the boys smell trampled grass and hear the noises of the fair without a memory of these Kadina show-days.

The gateman refused any admission money from Annie. "Little tackers as pretty as that one get let in free," he said to Richard and Bob.

In half an hour they had glanced at everything that comprised the show, and began again another and more intensive round of inspection.

The striped tents with the painting of The Two-Headed Calf and The Floating Mermaid from the Aegean Sea were a source of great speculation, and Bob persuaded Rich to let him have Annie's entrance threepence to spend on seeing the calf.

In due time he emerged from the tent loudly protesting, "I wish I had me threepence back. It's only a stuffed calf with another head stuck on the side."

Several prospective viewers of the calf turned away at Bob's disgusted comments and walked over towards the floating mermaid's tent.

The calf's proprietor gave Bob a word of advice. "Clear away from here," he said under his breath, "or I'll have you run in."

Bob, still indignant at what he considered a foul decep-
tion—having anticipated seeing a double-headed calf crop-
ping grass with two mouths and bellowing a simultaneous
duet from its double throat—still vented his grievance.

"You ought to be run in yourself for not saying the old
calf was dead as a door-nail and stuffed with sawdust.
You're only a take-in, you are!" gibed Bob, holding his
ground.

The showman lifted his tall hat, striped in red and white,
from his head, disclosing a florid face, a bald shiny crown,
freckled forehead and a fringe of sandy hair that hung
below his collar at the back and had given false evidence
of luxuriant growth when under the striped hat. He wiped
his face, forehead and the top of his head with a brilliant
handkerchief, polished the inside of his hat and replaced
it on his head, then walked towards Bob and spoke to him
in a low, throaty voice.

"Is a shilling piece any good to you, young un?" And,
drawing his thumb from his floral waistcoat pocket, he
negligently dropped a coin in the grass at his feet. "If it is,
pick it up and clear off, and if you show your ugly face
here again I'll knock it off your bloody shoulders."

This was said through smiling lips and between advice
delivered in a hoarse voice to the collecting townsfolk to
"R-r-r-roll up, r-roll up and see the wonder of the universe—
Nature's gr-reat mistake—the double-headed calf!" But Bob
caught the steely glint in the showman's eye and, hardly
believing his luck, grabbed the shilling piece and rejoined
Annie and Rich.

"I just made a bob," he said casually.

It was at this show in 1878 that the first three-furrow
plough ever exhibited on the peninsula was shown, and
Richard, with a stub of a pencil, drew a picture of it in
his notebook to take home to Nathan.

At this time at Boor's Plains, a few miles from Kadina,
a few acres were already under cultivation for wheat
growing, but this was rather in the nature of an experiment.
The peninsula towns were almost wholly dependent on the
mines at Wallaroo and Moonta, and little or no thought
had been given to any other industry. The mallee scrub,
which thickly covered the whole countryside, was considered

too great a problem for agriculture to be taken seriously. The trees could be easily cut and burnt, but the countless knuckly, obstinate mallee roots left in the ground were proving an expensive hindrance, and the sturdy pioneering farmers who set themselves the task of clearing the mallee scrub were regarded as eccentric optimists with more muscle than good sense. The day, not far distant, was to come when, with the aid of lever-grubber ploughs and stump-jumpers, thousands of acres of the best wheat-growing land in Australia was to be cleared and made arable in this part of Yorke's Peninsula, where farming was destined to be the chief industry and copper mining a dead thing of the past.

Bob, Annie and Richard pushed through the crowd about the working exhibit of Dobbie's famous seed-sower, mounted on wheels, drawn by a horse and being a contrivance with an elevated hopper through which the wheat seeds descended on to a revolving wheel which flung them out in a wide circle. Every little while the machine was stopped while a tall gentleman with a lined, clever face related the seed-sower's merits to the crowd; then, touching a lever, he would set the machine in motion again, scattering the grain over the ground. It was reported months later that a fine crop of wheat had sprung up on this spot of land in the showgrounds, and it was a great subject of interest in Kadina when later the miniature crop was harvested and piled into two stooks. It is probable that this practical demonstration sold more Dobbie seed-sowers than all the sales talk of the tall gentleman with the lined, clever face.

Richard could not draw the seed-sower, but he made notes of it for his father, and also wrote a description of the prize-winning oil painting of Gum-Tree Lagoon which was drawing a curious crowd in the building that housed the show exhibits. But he might have saved himself the trouble, for he and the rest of the show visitors were to stare at Miss O'Mangen's strange, blue, prize-winning trees for many years. Success in the country dies hard.

Polly, out at the Kadina cemetery, was clearing the grass from Allen's grave and weeping quietly to herself.

"Little boy Allen," she said over and over, and the wood

pigeons in the mallee scrub that bordered the cemetery answered with a melancholy "Never more!"

When Polly had cleared the little mound she planted the white geraniums, and set the slips of rosemary to form a cross.

"When they da grow," she whispered, "thees'll 'ave a green cross o' thy own, Allen, boy. Better nor marble nor stone, for rosemary be for remembrance, an' mother'll never forget 'ee." And she sobbed into her hands, and the tears ran down and dissolved into the ground. "Sich a little fellow," she wept, rocking to and fro. "Sich a little chap to be out 'ere alone."

After a while she rose to her feet and, wiping her eyes, began to shake the earth from her skirt, then, with a last look at the grave, picked up her carpet-bag and turned about. Walking away she saw a fine marble monument erected to one whom she did not know and who had died a few years previously, and Polly crossed and read the inscription:

> Sufferings sore, longtime I bore,
> Physicians were in vain,
> But God did please to give me ease,
> And release me from my pain.

"Poor dear," said Polly. "That da tell its own story, but 'tis a sad libel on the sick woman's doctors."

There was a funeral service taking place in the far corner of the cemetery, and Polly joined the group about the grave-side, hoping later to be able to secure a ride back to the township with the mourners. Before many minutes had passed she was singing the funeral hymn and joining in the prayer and being as deeply stirred by the solemnity of the occasion as any of the deceased's relatives. After the service she was successful in finding a seat beside the weeping widow in the cab which took them even to the main gate of the showgrounds.

"Oh, thee shoulden 'ave troubled," protested Polly, genuinely moved by this kindness. "Thee should 'ave dropped me 'way back on the road. Thee didden ought to 'ave taken me this far out o' thy way."

"Oh, that's all right, ma'am," said the widow, now dry-eyed and a good deal brighter. "We're comin' to the show too!"

Inside the showgrounds by the gate there was no sign of the boys, but, seated under a piece of canvas tied to the back wheels of a stationary wagonette, was Mrs Ben Wilson, nursing Annie who was fast asleep. With what joy did Polly fall to her knees beside her friend, and how they kissed and clung to each other, laughing a little and very happy at meeting again after a year's separation!

"I 'ad a mind 'ee'd be 'ere," said Mrs Wilson, adjusting her bonnet which had been knocked off in the greetings. "I said to Ben last week, 'I'll keep an eye out for the Thomases, come Saturday. I've a mind some o' them'll turn up to see the railway opened and all the goin's-on.' And bless me, I'd 'ardly put foot inside the place afore I seed the boys. Annie were all of an 'eap wi' tired, an' cryin' fit to break 'er little heart. So I told the boys to run off an' I'd nurse 'er till 'ee come along."

"Well, that were kind," said Polly, smoothing back Annie's hair from her flushed face. "Now, tell us all 'ee can 'bout what's 'appened down to the mines."

For an hour the two women talked of all that had happened to them since Polly had gone to Moonta. Then, getting to their feet at last and rousing Annie, they began a thorough inspection of everything in the showgrounds, from cabbages to cattle and from pigs to fat hens, paying special attention to the sideshows which they did not enter, the embroidery exhibits, the machinery, and the refreshment marquee.

At a quarter to six o'clock Polly and Annie, waiting beside the coach that was to take them home, saw the two boys dawdling along, muddy and dishevelled.

"Well!" said Polly. "Well, I do declare! Thees two waddlin' 'long as if 'ee 'ad all day to waste. Coach da go in two minutes, an' 'ere's me been waitin' this 'alf-hour or more. Get aboard, an' don't answer back."

The boys, tired out, scrambled inside, Bob sitting down very swiftly to hide the great three-cornered rent in his overcoat from Polly's eyes.

Nathan was very glad to see them when they returned, and received his fairing which Polly had been at great pains not to forget. It was a pink glass cup, and Polly had stood by the stall while the cup had been engraved with the word "Father" in letters half an inch high. He had a surprise for them too, and waved at Polly a letter bearing a London postmark.

"Must be from brother Robert," he said, excited as ever at seeing a letter from England.

After the children were in bed Polly, having shown the most annoying patience, opened the letter and gave it to Nathan to read.

From the folds of writing-paper fell a ten-pound note, which Polly twirled about and inspected but did not remark on.

The letter read:

> "The Towers",
> Massington Road,
> Fulham.

MY DEAR SISTER MARY ELIZABETH,

Once again, after a six months' lapse, I write to inquire after your and your good husband's and family's health. We are all, including Caroline—who has but lately recovered from a low fever, during the course of which illness she was in a very weak state, though never dangerously so—in tolerable spirits.

Since hearing from you last and noting your change of fortune and realizing all you have to overcome, I have decided after a great deal of thought, sister, to offer to take, care for and assist your eldest son. I am in a position to offer him, I may say, many worldly advantages besides that of residence in London which, with all due respect to our colonies, is still considered the place of greatest opportunities.

You say he has definite leanings towards a literary career. Well, my dear Mary Elizabeth, I can undertake to round off such schooling as he already may have acquired and be the means, later, of obtaining for him a position in a Fleet Street publishing house.

My house will be his home during this time and for as long as he cares to make it so.

This offer, my dear Mary Elizabeth, is made after careful consideration and prayerful thought. Caroline, too, wishes you to know that we shall do our utmost in the boy's interest.

Use the money I have enclosed as you think fit. If you decide to send Richard to us—which is, I think, a remarkable opportunity for the lad—I shall remit sufficient for his travelling requirements and passage, on receipt of your letter.

Do not think I shall find it a burden, sister. I have a comfortable income, and the wants of Caroline and my daughter are supplied adequately enough and, in offering to relieve you of the care of one of your children, I do so in the hope that his companionship, good behaviour, upright character and desire for advancement in his career will be sufficient reward for my wishing to receive him as I would my own son—if God had so far blessed me.

Think well on this, Mary Elizabeth, and be assured of my brotherly affection at all times.

My kindest regards to my brother-in-law Nathan and to my nephews and niece, and to you, my dear sister, my prayers for your continued health and that of your household.

Ever your affec. bro.,

ROBERT MENADUE

Silence in the bedroom, then Nathan whacked the quilt with his hand. "Dang me, but that were a gentlemanly offer, Pol."

"Yes," said Polly, slanting her eyes at him, "but thee woulden want me to say aye, would 'ee, Nat?"

"Why not?" said Nathan, amazed. " 'Tis not ev'ry day well-to-do uncles da ask their nevvies to come 'ome to be eddicated an' brought up like gentlemen wi' good work a-waitin' at the end o' it, Pol."

"Oh, oh, oh!" cried Polly, bursting into tears. " 'Ere we be, just gettin' over Allen's goin' an' all so 'appy now in Moonta, an' this must come an' bust un all to bits. Why can't us stay all together as we be an' take pot luck what da come to the boys? Rich 'ave got a job. Let's be content! I'll work meself to death to keep us all together, Nat. . . . Robert should get a son 'isself, an' not come sneakin' one o' mine."

"Steady, Pol, steady! 'Twas meant kind, an' as sich shall be took. Let Rich decide, me dear. An' anaways, there be more years than this one. If Robert did mean what 'e wrote, 'twill still be open for Rich next year or the one after that. Let's be thankful that one of our boys be provided for in this world, me dear."

"This partin' be a bitter thing to 'ang over a mother's 'ead," said Polly in a sad voice.

"Mother," called Annie from her bed by the window, where she had been lying awake for some time. "Bring me a drink, mother. I can't go to sleep. Me swalla da 'urt me."

Polly felt Annie's forehead. It was hot and damp.

"Lie still, me precious. Mother'll get 'ee a drink of 'oney an' water for thy throat. Thee's 'ad too big a day to-day."

Polly brought the warm honey and water, and Annie sipped it slowly.

"It da 'urt goin' down, mother," she said, and two tears ran down her flushed cheeks.

Tucked up in her bed again, and kissed and sung to, Annie dropped off into a heavy sleep. But just after midnight Polly was awakened by a sharp cry, and found Annie sitting up in bed, red-cheeked and wild-eyed. Polly soothed her as best she could, but the child clung to her, whimpering and frightened, clasping her hands about Polly's neck and saying in a strained, hoarse voice, "Oh mother, save me! The big puffer-train be goin' to ride over me. Take me off'n the rails, mother, quick! Oh! Oh!"

Polly was thoroughly alarmed, and whispered across the candlelit bedroom to Nathan, tense in his bed, "She be sickenin' for summat."

When morning's grey light filled the room Polly knew for sure that her child was very ill and, calling Richard, sent him for the doctor.

The doctor, coming an hour later, listened to Annie's breathing and her metallic, croupy cough. He put the handle of a teaspoon on her tongue and looked at the back of her throat.

"You did well to call me, Mrs Thomas," he said at last. "You have a sick child there."

For four days and nights Polly watched over Annie as she lay in her bed, which had been lifted into the boys' bedroom to be apart from the rest of the household.

"Inflammation o' the throat! . . . Grey throat!" said Polly, in a stricken voice, to the neighbours who came to inquire and to help.

"Membraneous croup," said the doctor to Nathan, and shook his head slowly.

On the evening of the fourth day, while Polly was resting on a couch in Annie's room and listening to her every movement and to the rasping of her breath, the child of a sudden reared herself in bed, clutching at the air with both hands. Polly rushed to her, holding down the writhing limbs, and then, listening for the heavy sound of Annie's breathing, was terrified when it did not come.

"Help! For God's sake!" she called loudly, and in a moment Mrs Gray, who had been asleep by the kitchen fire, hurried into the room, holding her grey shawl about her thin shoulders.

She ran to Polly who was lifting to the window the now choking, gasping bundle that was Annie.

"Open window, quick!" panted Polly, and held up Annie's body in her arms so that the cold night air played on the child's congested face.

Richard stumbled into the room.

"Doctor!" was all Polly could say, and Richard was running down the passage and out through the shop before any more messages could be given.

Back in the bedroom, Polly and Mrs Gray fought for Annie's life—that life which was merely breath. They were still compressing her little chest, alternately raising and lowering her little arms and rubbing her body with swift, tireless strokes when the doctor, whom Richard had hastily brought to the house, hurried to the bedside.

Polly did not pause a fraction in her rubbing, but looked at him with dumb, animal eyes as he examined the child on the bed. The examination was perfunctory, for the doctor had known from his first glance that Annie was dead; and when he gently placed his two soft hands on Polly's swiftly moving ones, she ceased her rubbing and looked into his eyes, and she knew too.

On the morning of the day Annie died, Polly had brought in to her a little egg from the bantam hen Biddy, but Annie had turned away her head, and that had broken Polly's heart. "If she can't eat a egg from Biddy, she must be terrible bad."

That same afternoon, tearing herself away for five minutes, she had sped to the fancy shop of Mrs Trussler and had bought a fine wax dolly in a white bride's dress, with blue eyes that opened and closed and real yellow hair. But Annie had shaken her head very slowly, and Polly had known then, as mothers can, that Annie was through with life, and so, in a way, was prepared—if ever a mother can be prepared—for what was to happen.

That night, when the doctor's palms were pressed so kindly on Polly's work-worn hands and she read the truth in his eyes, something died within her breast, and never again as long as she lived did she know real happiness.

CHAPTER XV

In the years following Annie's death Polly's little millinery business progressed slowly but steadily. Besides Becky Trelawny, who was kept busy in the workroom, Polly was employing another young girl, Grace Treneer, who minded the shop and ran messages for Polly and Becky.

The debt to the warehouse in Adelaide had been paid by degrees, and Polly ordered her requirements from its travellers who came from the city to call on country clients, bringing with them samples of the millinery that was being worn in Adelaide. The little hat shop seemed to be, in Polly's mind, all that mattered now, and gradually her ceaseless activity there formed an outlet for her troubled spirit. By and by she found herself once more taking a new interest in choosing, matching, debating over, purchasing and, later, trimming her hats; and some of her enthusiasm for her stock-in-trade spread to her customers. From as far afield as Port Broughton orders came to Polly for millinery, and it became a recognized thing for Moonta women, and many Kadina women also, to go to Polly first in their search for a new season's hat; and once they were inside the four walls of the shop it was not to be expected that Polly would let them escape empty-handed.

Before long Polly found she was making a little more than a living, and began to save. Every half-crown that she dropped into the box under Nathan's bed—and he was bed-ridden now—eased a little the pain of the lesson that years of poverty, pinching, scraping and working had taught her. Nothing mattered, since Annie's death, but to be safe from want. The joy of living had been taken away when Annie went, and Polly knew that with Uncle Robert's proferred help Richard would soon no longer need her care. Bob would be working in a short time now and, with his keen eye for business and natural instinct for trade, inherited from Polly, it was certain he would get on in the world.

What remained for Polly to do was to get them all beyond the reach of bad times.

If Annie had lived, the ardour Polly showed in the building up of her business would have been coloured by the thought of this child, her little fingers soon to be taught to wear a thimble, soon to know the feel of silk under the swiftly flying needle while she learned, also, the smells of straw and imitation flowers, and the joy of creating beauty from wisps of lace and gauze and shimmering ribbon.

The boys would go from home—already Richard was almost gone—but Annie would have grown to girlhood and womanhood beside Polly until the wider sphere of married life should have taken her from her mother's side, but never from her heart. The boys would soon be able to do without their mother, but a daughter—a daughter . . . !

Polly could never think of Annie without the hot tears starting and the pain at her heart throbbing. The sight of a little girl, or even the sound of baby voices, would set the tears swimming into her eyes, and all her life long she judged time's distance by the age Annie would have been had she lived. Sorrow's calendar is the saddest time-table in the universe, and is written in every language for every man to read.

Being known in Moonta as a woman who had lived intimately with sickness and death, Polly was often called upon for advice or consolation and, by reason of her having borne four children and buried two, she was, by some curious reckoning, given credit for familiarity with all manner of illnesses of which, actually, she knew nothing. Oftentimes she would be called from her work by a frantic message to come to a sick bedside, and she grew accustomed to the sudden flash of a lantern shining in at her bedroom window, and was ready, on these occasions, to go out into the night and help some other woman in trouble just as others had helped her in her own. So willing and eager was she to do what she could that, from these days onward, "Go for Mrs Thomas!" came to be a cry for help that went out from many homes in Moonta; and Polly's stout little figure was often first to cross a troubled threshold, even before doctor or minister had been called.

When Richard was seventeen it became apparent that Uncle Robert Menadue's offer could be denied no longer. As Uncle Robert had written:

There can be no good done by allowing Richard to remain in the colony when, for some time, you have been settled in your mind that it is best for his future that he should be sent to us. I should prefer to have him before his eighteenth birthday, and would have made him welcome before this, sister, had not the loss of your beloved daughter so altered your decision—and most naturally—of a further separation from one of your children. I was indeed gratified to read, in your last letter, of the upward trend of your fortunes. Keep a brave heart, my dear sister, and do not hesitate to enlighten me of any change in your affairs. The draft I shall send regularly to compensate you for the loss of Richard's earnings, on which I know you in part rely, is sent in love and brotherly commiseration. I am far from being a rich man, but what I can do for you, my dear Mary Elizabeth, I do willingly, and what I shall do for your son, if he will allow me—and I most certainly see no reason why he should not—I do as gladly.

The enclosed draft is for his passage money, the amount of which I have already ascertained, and the residue is for the expenses of the journey. Be not neglectful in advising me of his plans, proposed vessel and date of sailing and, from the moment of his setting out from Australia, everything will be dependent on himself. A chance I can give him, but what he will make of it is entirely a matter for his own capabilities and conscience.

I, as you know, with little schooling in my youth, have fitted myself, by conscientiousness, application and a desire to learn, for the position I now hold. Everything I possess has been obtained by my own unaided efforts, and I now feel it my duty to smooth the path for at least one of my own kin, for I have found the climbing upward in this world to be very, very hard, and I lost something on the way, Mary Elizabeth, which I fain would have now—my trust in my fellow man. Perhaps God will see fit to restore my faith through your son.

"Well," said Polly to Nathan, when this letter had been read by him to the assembled family, "Robert 'ave said the last word, I'm thinkin', an' now 'tis up to us." She turned a grim face on her boys as they sat by Nathan's bed. "Now thees can see what money'll do! But I don't think 'ardly on Robert for what 'e be goin' to do for Rich. I be a grateful woman, but 'e'll 'ave to wait a bit longer yet— just long enough for me to be a grateful mother. 'Tis not an aisy matter to give up a son to the minute, an' I won't be bustled."

Coming home on a roundabout route from his work at the printing office, Richard saw Annabelle Mack for the first time. It is probable he had seen her many times before, since she had lived all her life at Moonta, but it was not until this evening in November, 1882, that Richard saw her with seeing eyes.

She was walking just ahead of him along Caroline Street— a thin, long-legged girl of sixteen in a sprigged, pink muslin dress with a rose-coloured sash. The sash first caught Richard's eyes. "That's pretty," he thought to himself.

Annabelle, a few yards ahead of him, was swinging in her hand a canvas bag filled with paper parcels. As she walked she lifted her patent-leather, low-heeled shoes just high enough for Richard, his visual sense already stimulated by the rose-pink sash, to be capable of taking in the fact that the soles of the shoes were scarcely scratched with wear. He could see the shiny unworn patch between heel and sole and, with a curious satisfaction, registered the thought, "New shoes!" This constituted Richard's first interest in the tender sex.

Before Annabelle reached the corner where she would turn left and Richard right, two little girls of seven and nine, who had been playing hopscotch on the road, picked up their tiles, put them into a pocket of their white pinnies, faced each other grinning broadly, then, placing the palms of their hands together, began to clap and chant:

> "Annie Mack, dressed in black,
> Silver buttons down her back.
> She likes coffee, she likes tea,
> She likes sitting on a Chinaman's knee.
>
> "My mother said, I never should
> Play with the pixies in the wood.
> If I did, she would say,
> Naughty girl to disobey.
> Disobey one, disobey two,
> Disobey all the water's blue."

Even Richard, who never noticed girls at all—much less scraggy-haired *little* girls in white pinnies—thought their singsong chant particularly high and piercing. The song he recognized: an old folk-song with which most Cornish children at home, in the colonies or in "furrin parts" were familiar. The song was habitually accompanied by a rhythmic clapping of hands and, hearing these little girls singing it in their shrill voices, Richard for the first time disliked it.

As the girl in the pink muslin dress drew abreast of the two children they raised their voices even louder and, walking beside her for a few steps, continued clapping and singing,

> "My young man's gone to France,
> To teach the ladies how to dance,
> First on heel, then on toe,
> That's the way the ladies go."

There was a note of triumph in their voices that made Richard realize that they were singing for the purpose of annoying the girl in front, and the little wretches were succeeding.

As he came to the corner around which the girl had turned a moment ago he stopped dead, for he had almost trodden on a large potato that was in the centre of the footpath. Several more lay about and, just around the corner, was the girl in the pink dress, picking them up and stuffing them back into the canvas bag. Richard was on his knees before he had time to think, and was picking up potatoes too, and handing them to the girl.

"They dropped out of the bag," she said in a funny little voice.

"Did they?" said Richard politely, passing over a dirt-encrusted potato.

"Yes," she said shakily, and Richard looked up under her hat into eyes which he thought were like blue forget-me-nots drowning in tears.

He had enough of Polly in him to account for his going straight to the point. "What are you crying for?"

The girl gulped, then took out her pocket handkerchief from the front of her sash, blew her nose and stood up. Richard, with the last potato in his hand, stood up too, and was surprised to see that they were equal in height— she as tall as he.

"Those children, they tease me. They always do."

"What did they say?" asked Richard, trying to catch another glimpse of the forget-me-nots.

"Didn't you hear them?" she answered. "I thought they were yelling loud enough for all Moonta to hear."

"Singing Annie Mack?"

She winced. "Yes."

"Well, I shouldn't take any notice of that. We all used to sing it at school. It's as old as the hills."

"Oh I know that, but—well, don't you know that my name's Annabelle Mack, and all the children call me Annie—Annie Mack?"

"Oh," said Richard, taken aback. After a moment he added heartily. "Well, I shouldn't take any notice, really I shouldn't. If you just ignore them they'll soon shut up."

"I've tried that. I've tried it a dozen times, but it doesn't act, and now I can't help wanting to run when they start up singing, but until to-day I never have."

They stood in silence, not knowing what else to say, so Richard had to begin thinking of raising his hat and going on his way.

"Don't pay any attention to them if they sing it next time. That's my advice," he said at last, wishing fervently he could think of something more to say on a less delicate subject.

"Well, I will try again," said Annabelle, giving Richard a sight of her face bright with smiles. "I won't run next time. I promise. But," and she was very serious, "if two little boys kept calling after you in the street like this: 'Rich Thomas! Which Thomas? Rich Thomas!' you know you wouldn't like it, don't you?"

Richard, his face a bright red, raised his hat with great deliberation. "No, I shouldn't," he said. "Good-bye." And he turned about in the direction of home, his mind reeling at her audacity.

Crossing over the street and chancing to look down it, he saw one of the little girls standing in the middle of the road, and he had an uneasy feeling that she was retreating from a position that had given a good view of himself and Annabelle Mack in the dust of the footpath scrambling for potatoes. He was sure of it as her voice, soft, but sufficiently strong, called tauntingly to him from a safe distance, "I know yer gir-l. I know yer gir-l."

Richard kicked savagely at a stone, and thought bitterly about all women and young ones in particular.

At tea he was singularly unaffected by the sight of the stuffed shoulder of mutton that Polly was carefully carving, and left a good portion of his meal untouched.

"What 'ee da want," said Polly, eyeing his plate, "be a good dose o' brimstone an' treacle. Must be summat wrong with a boy's insides that can't fancy stuffed meat an' cabbage."

In Richard's head thoughts were whirling round: She knew my name! She's got the bluest eyes I've ever seen! And the embarrassing recollection of her boldness in making that rhyme about himself—"Rich Thomas! Which Thomas? Rich Thomas!"—made him redden to the ears.

Polly laid down her fork—she was left-handed, and held her fork in the right hand. "Are 'ee sickenin' for summat, Rich? Thee be as red as a turkey-cock. What's come over 'ee?"

Rich grunted, "Nothing's the matter with me," and made a feint of attacking his milk pudding with gusto.

Polly was not satisfied. "Thee's 'ad evrathin' but 'oopin'-cough. Don't tell me 'ee be gettin' that now, at this time o' day?"

"There's nothing wrong with me," said Richard, trying to show more enthusiasm in his dinner.

"Did I ever tell 'ee what me boy Allen what died said once, Becky?" said Polly, turning to Rebecca Trelawny, the young freckle-faced girl who helped Polly in the millinery shop for five shilling a week and her meals, and who was now seated at the table with the family.

"Thee's told me a lot," Becky answered, swallowing the pudding she had in her mouth with a visible effort, "but I can't lay mind to what 'ee mean this time, Miz Thomas, ma'am."

"Well, 'earken," said Polly, leaning back in her chair. " 'Twas like this 'ere. Allen 'ad a terrible cold in the 'ead—snufflin' and sneezin' all the time 'e were—so I kept un in bed close on two days, an' then let 'im up an' told un to stay in by fireside whilst I were out the back doin' the washin'. 'Alf-way through mornin' I thought to meself, ' 'E's awful quiet in there. What's 'e up to?' An' I goes to the back door an' looks in. No Allen there, so I walks round to front, an' there 'e be swingin' on gate talkin' to two little uns of Miz Trevaskis's. ' 'Ere Allen,' I calls out, 'come inside. Thees'll be givin' a cold to they Trevaskises.' An' what do 'ee think 'e up an' said?"

"I dunno, I'm sure, Miz Thomas," said Becky, reaching for another slice of bread. Polly, with a set face, passed her the bread on the point of the bread-knife and, after having watched her spread a layer of melon jam over it, resumed the narrative.

"Well," said Polly, smiling at the memory of Allen on the sapling gate, " 'e up an' said, 'It be all right, mother,' says 'e, 'they won't catch me cold. They both got the 'oopin'-cough their own selves.' "

"Then what 'appened, ma'am?" said Becky, whose attention had been divided.

"What 'appened?" said Polly, annoyed. "Nothin' 'appened but that Allen got the 'oopin'-cough too, an' gave un to the lot of us. We was all 'oopin' for months. That were a purty miserable three months we 'ad the 'ole pack of us. But Rich 'ere, 'e never give as much as an 'oop. It just passed 'im by."

After Becky had washed the dishes and gone to her home at Moonta Mines, Polly said to Richard, as she quite often did, "That there girl'll eat us out of 'ouse an' 'ome afore she've done. I never seed a body take in sich a quantity o' food in all me born days. She'll keep us poor."

Richard did not reply. A most uncomfortable idea was forming in his mind: Did Annabelle Mack drop those potatoes on purpose?

On Sunday evening, in church, Richard saw Annabelle again. She was in the choir, on the soprano side, and with a shock he remembered having seen such a girl there in the singing-seats many times before. Could it possibly be that he had seen Annabelle and had not been interested enough to remember her? He doubted it, but the disturbing thought that this was not the first time she had sat in the choir made him wriggle in his seat. What had been the matter with him all these months—years, perhaps, he thought incredulously—that he should have overlooked a girl like Annabelle Mack.

All through the service his eyes were gliding away from the preacher's face and coming to rest on Annabelle. He decided that he was very much in favour of straw hats with poppy wreaths about them, but wished that some of them had been turned up in front instead of at the back, for, he decided, the shadows over people's faces made it hard to find out where people were really looking. During the anthem he had an admirable opportunity to see Annabelle. He could not quite distinguish her voice, but was certain that the highest, sweetest notes were hers.

"My golly," he said confidentially to himself, "she can sing all right."

He even cast a kindly eye on her father—a grey-haired fierce-faced, middle-aged man who taught music for a living and was reputed to be a secret drinker, but who was an inoffensive and respected citizen on Sundays and an acquisition to the church orchestra on anniversary days. Richard, looking benevolently towards him, wished fervently he could find an adequate excuse for wanting to learn the piccolo or the bass-viol in his spare time. "I might be quite good at something like that," he thought.

Sitting next to Mr Mack was Walter his son, and Richard determined to revive an acquaintanceship there.

After church, Richard and Tom Francis, Skinny Soper and Martin Killigrew always walked together about the streets or took a stroll up the road towards Moonta Mines, but on this Sunday night Richard kept the boys standing in front of the church for a longer time than usual—just time enough, in fact, to see Annabelle, her arm linked in that of Hester Bodmin, leave the church ahead of them.

When Annabelle had gone Richard, who now had no excuse for remaining, said, "Come on, chaps, let's go for a walk." And they followed a hundred yards behind the girls. His voice was the loudest as they talked, and secretly he had a great contempt for himself, but that made him no quieter, and not until Annabelle turned round to see who was following her and Hester did he feel panic and veer the other boys in the opposite direction. He had little to say on the rest of the walk, and could not believe that it was by his own doing that they should at last find themselves passing the house where Annabelle lived.

It was a calm night with a clear sky, and the Southern Cross shone brightly in the multitude of stars. The gentle breeze that ruffled the boys' hair brought a fragrance of green things from the Mack front garden, an odour of balm and rosemary and scented verbena.

From the parlour window, which was open and uncurtained, came the sound of music, and the boys, looking over the front fence, could see into the room. Mr Mack, his broad back towards them, was at the harmonium, and Walter, fiddle to chin, was playing an obligato to the hymn tune "Trentham". Several people stood singing in a group about the harmonium, peering over Mr Mack's shoulder at the words and the music. Annabelle was not to be seen, and after a while Richard consented to move along.

"That Wallie Mack's a big goat," said Martin Killigrew hoarsely, "always squiggling away on his squeaky little fiddle. He'd give a body a bellyache."

"Oh, he's not so bad," said Richard, magnanimously, then, with a sudden qualm that Annabelle's name might be mentioned next, smartly changed the subject. But, stretching out his hand as they passed the end of the Mack fence, he pulled carelessly at the soft grey leaves of a wormwood bush that grew there, and throughout the rest of the walk home its bitter scent enveloped him, and was not quite gone from his fingers when he got into bed.

A week later he spoke to her. It was at the young peoples' social—a boisterous event that took place in the church lecture-room—and in the noisy whirl of Push the Business On, which is the nearest a Methodist must approach to dancing, he held her hands for a short twenty seconds. She smiled. He said "Hullo," and she passed on to her next partner.

At supper-time she came at last to him with a little basket of sandwiches. He took one, then said with a great show of ease and good humour, "Well, did you try what I told you to?"

She reddened. "I did," she said, "but it didn't work."

He felt a clumsy fool. What an ass he was to have said anything about that unfortunate incident! He was seized with a strong desire to speak to her again. He could not apologize, but at least he could be pleasant.

His chance came. Jolly Miller was announced as the final game, and Richard crossed the floor, feeling as if every eye were upon him, and asked Annabelle to be his partner.

While waiting for the music to begin and perspiring freely with the effort to seem at ease, Richard, with relief, heard her speak first.

"Have you any more ideas for me to try? I'll do anything to stop being teased," she said.

Richard became terribly earnest. "It's not right," he said. "Somebody ought to whip those kids and teach them some manners. You ought to ask your father to do something."

"Oh, father would be no use," said Annabelle very decidedly.

"Listen," Rich volunteered, "you should try this. Next time they start up, you join in and ask to play too. That'll stop them, and after a while it won't even seem funny to them."

"What won't seem funny to them?" asked Annabelle, opening her eyes wide. "Me?"

"No, the game."

" 'Annie Mack' you mean?"

Richard nodded. He could not speak. "My golly," he thought, "what an *awful* name!"

For a fortnight after this Richard carefully avoided any place where Annabelle might be. Then one Saturday night, returning from doing some shopping for Polly, he overtook her quite by accident as she too was coming home, and he had to speak.

"Hullo, Annabelle," he said, remembering immediately after that he should have said "Miss Mack".

"Hullo, Rich," she said easily, without the slightest hesitation. It almost seemed as if she had been rehearsing it but a few moments before.

They fell into step together.

"Everything's all right now," Annabelle said brightly. "I've been wanting to see you for over a week to tell you that the children don't tease me any more. I stopped and played 'Annie Mack' fourteen times the first week, and I didn't mind one bit. I liked it. And when the children saw I liked it they lost interest. So I've told them that any time they want me I'll play with them, but I'd rather not play

'Annie Mack'. They want me to teach them 'Harvey Darvey'. That's an old, old game my grandma used to play in Redruth when she was a little girl."

"It's a funny thing," Richard put in awkwardly, wrinkling his brows and quoting Nathan, "but the best way to master anything you're afraid of is to run to meet it."

Annabelle thought Richard's philosophy the outcome of his occupation, and she said, "You work at the printing office, don't you?"

"Sometimes," Rich answered.

"Sometimes? Why, what else do you do?"

"Sometimes I loaf."

As Rich had hoped, this proved very amusing repartee. Annabelle's laugh was the prettiest that Richard had ever heard, and throughout the walk home he made a fool of himself—or so he convinced himself as he lay awake in bed an hour or two later—just for a repetition of that sweet pleasure.

He walked with her to her gate, opened it, shut it behind her, said good night and went swiftly home, whistling "The Pretty Mocking Bird" loud and clear.

He entered the kitchen door and Polly, looking up from her hat-trimming, said, "Well, what 'ee got there?"

Richard's heart contracted. He had Annabelle's grocery parcel in his arms as well as his own.

He dropped his parcel on the table and went out again without a word, not knowing in the least how he would manage to get Annabelle's parcel back to her. First he thought of whistling at her back fence, then, remembering that Annabelle had a dog, he thought it highly probable that the dog would be all he might get for his whistling. To drop the parcel into the front garden was not to be considered either, because of the same animal. To hang about the house until Walter or Annabelle appeared was also impossible: Richard could not imagine himself pressing a bundle of groceries on Walter without the necessary explanations. One cannot simply say "Here's your week's groceries," and run. No, Richard reluctantly came to the conclusion that he must go boldly to the Mack front door and brave it out.

" 'Run to meet what you're afraid of.' Well, I'll try it

out just this once and see if it works for me." And he set off at a jog-trot for the Macks' house.

At the corner of their fence something dark waited in the shadow of the wormwood bush, and it was Annabelle.

"Rich," she called softly, "here I am."

Relief surged over him as he pushed the parcel into her arms, and at that moment the last tip of a cloud passed from before the moon's face, and silver light flooded the little street and the cluster of low white houses and the untidy fences and the wormwood bush, the boy, the girl, and her dog. They stood so a minute's space, caught in the web of the moon's magic, then Richard moved his hands from the crackly newspaper and the spell was broken.

"I'm sorry I forgot it, Annabelle," he said and, as his fingers left the parcel, he felt, for one tiny instant, the gentle caress of the little frill of pleated lace that Annabelle wore at her breast.

Richard walked back with his hands in his pockets and his head in the clouds. He did not whistle. He could not, for his throat was dry and tight and he was happier than he thought it possible for mortal man to be.

This friendship between Annabelle and Richard progressed through weeks of casual meetings—casual in that the two of them had not planned to meet, although Richard's "Are you going to be at the church meeting?" or some such remark was understood to constitute an offer to see Annabelle home—until, by January, they were appearing openly together, although still very shy about letting any one know they felt a proprietary interest in each other. Richard shunned the company of his boy friends, at this time, rather than submit to their jests and banterings. Tom Francis alone was encouraged, and that for the express purpose of finding somebody to take Hester Bodmin off Annabelle's hands.

"You know Hester Bodmin?" Rich said to Tom after running in circles about the subject for some time.

"The one that goes about with Annabelle?" answered Tom, showing a slight interest.

"Yes, the fair-haired girl."

"A bit too fat," opinioned Tom,

"Oh, she's all right," enthused Richard. "Anyway, she's gone on you, Tom."

Tom gave a guffaw. "Tell that to black Susie," he said derisively.

"Well, Annabelle says she is. That's all I know."

"Aw, go 'n' bury yourself. I don't hardly know the girl," Tom protested, not wholly displeased.

Having let this announcement of Hester's fancy sink into the roomy cavities of Tom's mind, Richard was not surprised that Tom should show a strong preference for his company on Sunday evening after church, ignoring the repeated calls of Skinny Soper and Martin Killigrew to "Come on", and, whether from curiosity, friendly helpfulness or sudden attraction, being quite ready to be persuaded by Richard to walk home with Hester.

Tom, if reminded of this incident a score of years later, might possibly have smiled broadly and said, "Yes, that was the night I first walked home with Hetty. Two children and a double chin have changed her looks, but I still think it was a lucky night for me. She's been a tiptop wife and can toss together a good breakfast quicker than any woman I know, and y'can judge 'em by that! Got a mind of her own, though, and knows what she wants. But I like 'em that way—always did. You ask her!"

Over Richard's and Annabelle's walking out there hung a shadow in the prospect of their separation, for it was understood that he should go to England before his eighteenth birthday.

"So you see, Annabelle," said Richard, on one of their "casual" meetings, "I'm to go to my uncle in London very soon now. Mother's put it off a long time, but it's decided that I have to go. It's a chance I can't afford to miss, but I don't want to go—much. Bob's still at the model school. He's only eleven and won't be working for years. And besides, it means leaving everybody."

"Yes, I s'pose you'll have to go," said Annabelle. Then she added seriously, "I wish I could go to London, but I know I never shall. I'd like to be sent abroad to learn singing. Father says I've a good voice and it could be trained, but I shall never leave Moonta, I know. I'll be here until I die."

Richard, surprised at her earnestness, said, "Listen, Annabelle. Wouldn't it be funny if you ever did get to London and became a famous singer and I wrote you up for the London *Times*? It could happen, you know, because I may get a job on a paper over there. Uncle's going to put me into a publishing house, but I want to do something else on my own. I'm going to try a hand at everything."

"You'll get on in the world all right, Rich, but I'll never do anything—never, never! Just stay here in Moonta, and go to church, and be on a stall at the fair, and sing at the socials, and teach music with father and Wallie, and by and by get married like everybody else. Nothing will ever happen to me!"

Richard was silent, and they walked on for some distance without a word. His arm was about her waist, and quite suddenly he felt lonely and miserable and London seemed a long way off and infinitely unreal. Something came into his throat and he felt he would choke.

At last he spoke. "I'll come back," he said.

Annabelle turned a little in the circle of his arm, and they stood facing each other. Tears were on her cheeks, and they glistened in the moonlight. Rich kissed her clumsily and she turned away her head.

"Don't cry," he said in a low voice.

She broke away from him and replied uncertainly, "I'm not crying," and brushed away her tears with the palm of her hand.

They walked back towards Annabelle's home, taking a short cut through the cow paddock that led to her back gate and, as they stood there in the moonlight, the noises of the hot still night came to their ears like sounds from far away. A group of miners back in the town, setting out from the hotel, were singing in harmony a belated Christmas carol; a dog in the next street howled to the moon; magpies, surprised at the moon's brightness, warbled drowsily in the scrub, and a child's voice, crying from some hot stuffy bedroom, pierced the summer night. The sound of a squeaky pump as somebody pumped cool water from an underground tank, the muted tone of voices from a neighbour's back yard, expressed each in its own way the discomfort of a January night.

Rover, Annabelle's dog, squeezing himself through a gap in the back fence, brought a round stone and laid it carefully at Richard's feet, looking up at him with head cocked on one side and eyes alert. Richard took no notice. His lips were on Annabelle's, and all other senses but the sense of touch—the touch of Annabelle's mouth that he had so lately learned to kiss—were dead.

Rover raised a paw and, scraping it across Richard's boot, uttered a sharp bark. Richard's and Annabelle's lips parted and Richard, hardly moving his eyes from Annabelle's face, stooped, felt for and found the stone and hurled it out across the paddock. Rover was off like the wind, a dark shape racing over the dry stubble of the paddock. He snuffled about for a while, smelt out the stone and bounded back with it to Richard, laying it at his feet as before.

"Annabelle," Richard was saying, "I'm sorry I made you miserable out there to-night."

"You didn't make me miserable, Rich. It's just me. I'm always wanting something I can't have. It's not just discontent. I don't know what to call it."

"What can't you have?" asked Rich, after a pause.

Rover jumped up, here, and wiped his dirty paws on Richard's navy serge trousers from knee to ankle. Richard disregarded him.

"What is it you want, Annabelle, that makes you cry because you can't get it?"

Annabelle's answer, if she had one, was lost in a series of staccato yaps from Rover, followed by another scratching bout across Richard's boot.

"Here, you," said Richard, bending down. "Chase this!" And he flung the stone with all his force into the clump of mallee at the end of the paddock. "You'll be a long time finding that!"

"Isn't he a nuisance!" complained Annabelle, then wished she hadn't.

Richard returned to the subject. "What made you cry?" he persisted.

His reason for pursuing this conversation was the wild

hope that he might wring from Annabelle the answer that she would miss him. Nothing would give him greater satisfaction than to know that Annabelle would hate to have him go. At least it would be something to find that somebody besides himself could be miserable for that reason!

"Don't pester me, Rich. Don't ask me any more," she pleaded. "Please don't, Rich."

Richard felt the pressure of the hard lump in his throat, and when he spoke his voice astounded himself, for it trembled. "Annabelle," he said, "is it—is it because——"

He could not finish. Rover, triumphant, had dashed upon him, bent on placing the stone in Richard's hand. Richard stepped back a pace, and the dog bounded up leaving a trail of saliva across Richard's Sunday waistcoat.

"Get down, you pest!" cried Richard, pushing the big dog back with both hands.

Rover, delighted, dropped the stone and jumped up again, thinking this a new version of the game. Richard, his back tensed against the gate-post, met the dog's next advances with outstretched arms and, with all his strength, pushed outwards against the leaping body and threw the dog backwards on to the dusty ground. Rover rose, intensely annoyed, shook the dust from his fur and looked menacingly at Richard. Then from his throat came a low, rumbling growl.

"Come in, Rover," said Annabelle, hurriedly opening the gate. "Come inside at once."

Rover remained motionless, and the hair on his throat stiffened into a ruff.

"Come on now, Rover," commanded Annabelle, and Richard, taking out his pocket handkerchief, began to wipe away the stains from his waistcoat.

At the first movement of Richard's hand Rover burst into a loud, continuous barking. The sounds echoed and re-echoed in the night, and awakened other sounds. To Richard it seemed as if all the dogs in Moonta took up Rover's savage cries.

Annabelle dashed from the gateway and grasped the barking dog by the collar. Rover strained towards Richard, eyes blazing in the moonlight, and above the noise Annabelle made herself heard.

"Go home, Rich. Please go home at once. Father will come out in a minute. Do go. I can't hold Rover if you stay any longer."

Richard wormed his way across the space left between the fence and the dog. It would be untruthful to say he was not frightened. He was, horribly, and as much at the thought of Mr Mack as at the sight and sound of Rover.

Suddenly the back door of Annabelle's house was flung open and her father, silhouetted against the lamplight, sent a shrill whistle across the yard. Rover's barks died away to a low growl.

"What in God's name's that bloody row about?" roared Mr Mack in a drunken voice. "Come here, Rover! I'll skin the hide off yer if you don't lay low." He paused, then shouted, "Annabelle!"

Annabelle straightened, but did not reply.

"Annabelle!"

"Yes, father," said Annabelle, faintly.

"Come inside or I'll take the hide off you too. If you can't be brought home by the front gate you'd better not be brought home at all. I want nobody bringing my girl home who doesn't know his manners. Come inside, Annabelle, and I'll give y'a clip over the ear for hanging about the back streets."

Richard's brain refused to function until he was almost at his own gate. Then, "Oh, my holy smoke," he said fervently to himself, "you'll never catch me making a fool of myself like that again! That's the finish for me!" And for several nights he did not fall asleep without the voice of Annabelle's father cutting across his dreams, and even in his sleep he blushed and sweated.

CHAPTER XVI

Richard left for England in May 1883, by the steamship *William Tell*. The last familiar sight that he saw as the ship left the wharf was the figure of his mother's old friend Mrs Lillywhite, holding on to her hat with both hands as the chilly west wind swirled her skirts about in a great flurry of bombasine, while she kept up a rhythmic nodding of her head as betokening affectionate good-bye.

Polly, unable to leave Nathan, now a complete invalid, had written to ask this favour of her friend, and stood now, in the person of her substitute, sending a motherly farewell to her son across the widening space of water.

When Mrs Lillywhite's black dress had merged into the blur of the vanishing wharf Richard turned away and, thrusting his hands deep into the pockets of his new black greatcoat, faced about and went below to unpack his shiny valise. It was not until much later, when the cabin light was at last extinguished and the good-nights of his cabin-mates had been spoken, that he turned his face to the unfamiliar hardness of his pillow and cried for his mother.

Richard's second letter from London, July 1883:

The Towers,
Massington Road,
Fulham.

My dear mother and father,

How are you? What a long, long time it seems since I last saw you both, and how I wish I could be at home and hear your voices and see the old house and the shop and know that you were both well! I am not lonely. Don't think that, mother. But I miss the freedom and the associations of home.

I am beginning to feel a little less strange here now, and everything is being done by Uncle Robert to make me feel at ease. He is very kind, and I have already written to you about my first impressions on meeting him at the docks, and what a shock I received at seeing him so old in face and small in stature. I had never imagined him old and fat, but always tall and commanding. He was very abrupt at first, but was so anxious to hear all I had to say about you and my life in Australia that interest took the place of self-consciousness, and we are getting on well together.

Mother, you will want to know about Uncle Robert's house, won't you? Well, it is very plain and is three stories high and, I suppose, very imposing; but it is too severe for my liking—in appearance, I mean—and I miss the verandas that I always thought so necessary in a big residence. Inside, the house is furnished with a bewildering amount of heavy furniture, pictures, knick-knacks and velvet plush draping. The drawing-room fairly takes my breath away, and I feel awkward and clumsy in it and fear I shall break something or knock over a screen—there are two handsome Chinese ones in the room—or crash into a cabinet before I have been here very long.

I am writing in my own bedroom, which Aunt Caroline has arranged with writing-table and book-shelves for my private use.

Aunt (have I told you?) is tall and thin and very dignified, and rustles a good deal when she walks. You, mother, would appreciate her silk gown and gold watch-chain and lockets, but I can't describe them, although I must try if I am ever to make a success with my pen, for one must learn to dress people on paper since it is there that ninety per cent of authors fail, I am told.

Uncle seems pleased with what education and knowledge I seem to have and pays a tribute to Mr Martin who, as you know, taught me a great deal more in those night classes at Moonta than he was ever paid to teach. Please tell Mr Martin how pleased my uncle is with my progress.

I have a tutor who comes daily and gives me a vast amount of work to do and has begun to teach me French. Fancy, mother, my learning languages! And he was surprised that I should know enough to be, in his own words, "singularly well-informed for my age and showing definite literary talent". He does not despair of my mathematics, and complimented me on my geography. He does not realize that in my trip to London I traversed half the globe and took voluminous notes on the journey, nor does he know that I have listened to father reading Uncle Peter's wonderful letters from China every month for as long as I can remember.

My cousin Euphemia is fifteen, and tall like Aunt Caroline, but I see little of her as she attends a young ladies' seminary near by and already can speak French fluently, which is galling. She is apt to be contemptuous of me, but that is understandable.

Otherwise I have been made to feel at home, and know I am expected to study hard and be as pleasant as possible.

Did you know that Uncle Robert's business is that of a wine merchant? We seem never to have known what he did for a living, and it was rather a shock for me to discover that it was in wine and spirits that he traded.

Already I have visited the British Museum and have spent many hours there among the books. Uncle has given me glimpses of London in small doses. He says that is the only way to get my perspective, and I realize he is right, for each time we drive out—and uncle has a fine carriage with a pair of greys—I find myself becoming more accustomed to London's vastness and noise.

Through my tutor I have learned that my speech is not all that could be desired. I am careless, my uncle told him, and slur my words together, and do not speak English as I write it. That is perfectly true, for my pen can write what my tongue could never say. So I am having lessons in diction which, as father will tell you, mother, is just the art of speech, and there are as many styles in speech as there are in millinery, and the rules are somewhat similar—flowers *or* plumes, as you often say, but never flowers *and* plumes. By the way, I can now say "rum" when I mean "room", and I know the kitchen as the "scullery", say "happile" when I mean "happily" and "dute" when I mean "duty". But my hardest battle has been with the "ow" sound, and I have seen Aunt Caroline wince when I have said "now". She says it "nohw", and it seems I must too.

Uncle Robert drove me along Fleet Street on Tuesday afternoon to see the building in which, with his influence, I may find work one day. It is a narrow, winding street and follows the course of the Fleet Stream, long since disappeared and forgotten or turned into a covered sewer running into the Thames. Fleet Street Prison, built in the twelfth century, several times rebuilt and now demolished, once stood near by, and it is from such beginnings and in such surroundings that Fleet Street has developed. It is and, some say, always will be the hub of the newspaper world. Careers are made in that narrow street, and mine may be one of them.

I have tried in this letter to give father some idea of the style of writing I wish to adopt—a smooth, flowing form that my tutor advises me is most important. If there is a superfluity of adjectives you must excuse them, as time and study will cure me of showiness.

That last paragraph was for father, as I know he greatly wishes to know what chance there is for me to be a success. The next paragraph is for you, mother.

My clothes were as good as anybody's on the ship and, as you wished, I have bought new drawers and two night-shirts in London. Uncle was dissatisfied with the cut of my coat—and well he might be, for it was, of course, my first suit not made by you, mother, and I always knew that travelling tailor who made it was no good. I now have a fine serge suit made by uncle's own tailor, lined with satin, with a watch pocket and other pockets galore, and uncle has presented me with a new razor. I do *not* wear the red flannel binder, mother, as I do not feel any discomfort from the change of climate and the days are still warm and summery.

Tell Bob I shall write to him by this same mail and will continue to write to you both once a month as I promised.

Good-bye, dear mother and father. You both know how much I love you and how much I miss you.

Write to me often.

Ever your loving son,

RICH

RICHARD MILTON THOMAS

P.S. I am considering growing a moustache when I am able, but think I had better consult Uncle Robert first.

P.P.S. I have a silk hat, but am afraid to wear it!

Nathan read this letter to Polly as she sat by his bed with a quilt about her knees, running a ruching for a white silk wedding-bonnet. Every emotion she had registered as the letter proceeded had shown itself on her face, but her needle continued to fly in and out of the silk, and she paused only to tighten a drawstring now and then. When Nathan had finished she laid the bonnet on her lap and, taking off her spectacles—she wore silver-rimmed ones now, which left a tiny green line on the bridge of her nose—looked across at him with shining eyes.

"Dear lad," she said. " 'E've been missin' of us cruel, but 'e be settlin' down now, poor lamb." She screwed up her mouth. "So Robert be in the wine an' liquor trade? Never said a word to we about un all these year. 'E must 'ave 'ad a good idea what thee'd 'ave said about un if thee's knawed sooner. Thee's allus been so set agin liquor, Nat. Never 'ad no time for anabody what drunk it neither, did 'ee, dear?"

"Well, mother, 'tis summat us Methodists set our 'earts agin, an' that's all there is to it. I've knawed many a good man as never tasted a drop an' I've knawed many a good man oo 'ave—too many, Pol. An' I allus say this 'ere, I never met man yet oo weren't better without un! That's what I maintain."

"Well, if things da fall out that our Rich da learn to liquor up I'll never forgive Robert till me dyin' day. I'd a sight rather see me boy dead nor drunken."

"Steady, Pol. Don't 'ee get worked up 'bout what'll never 'appen. Rich 'ave an 'ead on 'is shoulders, an' brother Robert too, I fancy. It says naught in this letter 'bout thy brother drinkin' the liquor 'e sells, an' barrin' knawin' 'ow the money's made I don't mind guessin' that's all Rich ever da knaw o' the 'ole business."

"Fancy our Rich with a silk hat," marvelled Polly, switching off on another track, "an' talkin' 'bout growin' a beard on 'is face!" Her lips quivered. "Lawks, Nat, I've a grawed man for a son, no mistake."

" 'E've gone in the right spirit," mused Nathan. " 'E've an open mind an' don't resent correction. If 'e be willin' to learn 'e'll get on all right, an' good luck to un. I be proud o' me boy, ain't 'ee, mother?"

"Wait till 'e've done summat. Praise where praise be

due, Nat, but up to now Rich 'ave done naught but talk. I'll say me say when I lay me eye to summat in black an' white—printer's ink an' paper."

Nathan's proudest moment came a few years later when, upon opening a copy of the London weekly magazine the *Reflector* sent to him by Richard, he saw on the third page, heavily scored in blue pencil, a short story entitled "Blawed Up", and under the title three initials, R.M.T.

"Come 'ere, mother," called Nathan in the loudest tones of excitement. "Come 'ere, quick!"

Polly, in the shop, hearing his cries, picked up her black silk skirt—she had a black silk for afternoons now—and flew to his bedroom.

"Lan' sakes," she panted with relief as she saw his eager face, "I thought 'ee must be dead an' gone. Don't 'ee ever do that agin, Nat, unless 'ee be powerful bad. I bain't so spry as I used to be, not by a purty lot."

He waved the paper at her. " 'Earken," he said triumphantly, "Rich 'ave done it! See 'ere, 'e've 'ad a story published at last in a London paper. Sit down mother, an' let's read un."

It was a story that Polly and Nathan had heard when they first came to Moonta—the story of Johnnie Phillips who, it was claimed, always said he had been "blawed to pieces fower times".

The story goes that Johnnie had, on the occasion of his third mine explosion in the Tregambeth mine in Cornwall, declared that he was tired of being "blawed to pieces" in the old country and would try his luck at Moonta, in the new. He must have possessed a fatal attraction for misfortune for, while stoking up the boilers beside one of the engine-houses at Moonta Mines, a boiler burst and buried Johnnie beneath a pile of wood, iron and masonwork, stunning him, tearing his scalp, crushing a hand and rendering him unconscious. His peculiar imperviousness to explosions caused him to be left with breath in his body and the luck to be still alive. He crawled from the masonry during the evening of the day following the accident, unaided and unnoticed, horribly confused, a mass of bruises and with blood caked to his torn clothes.

It would seem incredible that a man could be left buried under fallen stonework for a day and a half with no attempt made to search for him, but truth is always stranger than fiction, and this really happened to Johnnie Phillips. It was nobody's fault and the mistake—and there was one— was made by the fact that after the explosion, when the miners had rushed to the spot and had begun to tear away the stonework, word was passed around that Johnnie Phillips the boiler man had been alone there stoking the furnace, the engine driver having left the engine-house a few minutes previously.

A frenzied five-minute search revealed at last the broken, blood-stained wreck of what once had been a man. The head and face and part of the chest had been battered beyond recognition, most of the clothes had been torn from the scalded body, and in one hand was still clasped a crib-bag inside of which were the crushed remnants of a pasty, a salt-shaker and some saffron buns.

The body was identified as Johnnie's who, it was decided, had died while in the act of opening his crib-bag to eat his Saturday dinner, which he always ate at the mines to ensure an early Saturday afternoon dash to the Miners' Arms Hotel in Moonta. Mary Rose Phillips, Johnnie's wife, and Samson Phillips his brother both established his identity, and Mary Rose wept unrestrainedly at sight of the blue salt-shaker and the crushed food that she had cooked the night before for Johnnie's lunch.

Nobody knew what Johnnie himself could have told them had he not been lying unconscious and deathly quiet under the heap of stones, that a stranger, drenched with rain, had walked unseen into the engine-house and had asked Johnnie's permission to stay inside until his clothes dried.

"Stay, an' welcome," Johnnie had said good-naturedly, "an' if thee's got naught under thy weskit, sitty down an' 'ave a bite o' me pasty. Me crib-bag's over yonder in the corner. Go to!" And no sooner had the stranger picked up Johnnie's crib-bag than the world dissolved away for both of them in a cataclysm of terrific noise, stones and steam.

Johnnie, by some miraculous intervention of the gods who care for careless men, was not scalded and, having been hurled back against the stone wall of the engine-house, fell to the ground while an iron stanchion, catching above his head, spared his skull and made a barricade for him, hemming him in and forming a foot or two of freedom from the stones that piled up in a heap above him.

Johnnie gave a groan or two when partly recovering consciousness, and lay still for a long time, unable to move for the dreadful pain in his head. Then, his brain clearing, he crawled out at last from under the stones and stood swaying in the cold night air.

It was Sunday night, and the faint sound of hymn-singing from the Moonta Mines Wesleyan Chapel was borne to his puzzled ears on the icy wind. He shook his head several times and, drawing his ragged shirt about him, stumbled off in the direction of the sound, his bemused condition and what he had suffered accounting for his muttering, "I be dead, dead as mutton."

Before reaching the chapel he had to pass the gate of his own cottage, and something familiar in the way the pepper-tree hung its leaves over the fence or something in the sight of the crooked gate he had always been promising to mend or of the broken pane of glass in the front window—each or all of these struck some faint chord of memory, and Johnnie Phillips, with rolling gait and reeling head, walked up to his own front door and banged on it with a shaking fist.

The door was opened by his wife, wearing a black dress and holding aloft a lighted lamp. She peered out into the windy darkness, then, as the flickering light fell on the figure before her, she gave one look at him and shut the door very quickly, chained it inside and proceeded to send terrified screams through the house. Following the sound of many alarmed voices, silence descended, and Johnnie could hear women talking excitedly in the bedroom.

"Come out o' that," he called faintly, "an' let me in."

No answer came, and he leaned against the door and began to cry weakly, "Let me in, somebody."

Suddenly the chain was taken from the hook, and Samson Phillips thrust his head out from a crack in the door. Johnnie's face rolled towards him, and Samson felt the touch of Johnnie's whiskers and smelled the smell of earth and blood. He shut the door as quickly as Mary Rose had done.

"My Gawd!" he said in a loud voice. " 'Tis Johnnie come back from the dead!"

A woman's shriek answered him, and Johnnie heard his cousin Martha begin to recite the Lord's Prayer.

"Yes, I be dead all right," he said, sinking to his knees before the door.

Nothing stirred within the house and, growing colder and feeling much worse, he groaned several times in a fearful manner.

From inside the house Samson's voice rang out. "Oo ever be playin' that joke on me an' me brother Johnnie's missus an' 'is mother-in-law an' all of us, get theirselves out o' it or I'll go for parson an' Cap'n Skinner this minute."

Johnnie answered with a burst of groaning.

"Oo be there?" called Samson as loudly, but not as confidently as before.

"Johnnie Phillips I be. 'Ee knaw me, Samson. Johnnie!"

The sound of a woman's noisy weeping came to Johnnie's buzzing ears, and he called waveringly, "Mary Rose, Mary Rose!"

The crying ceased, and a woman's voice asked in a frightened whisper, "Oo be 'ee?"

Johnnie, not hearing, kept calling, "Mary Rose, Mary Rose, 'tis Johnnie come 'ome."

Gaining momentary courage, the woman shrilled out from behind the closed door, "Whatever 'ee be, ghost or man or God knaws what, I'll 'ave 'ee knaw me Johnnie was blawed to pieces yesterday an' we buried 'im out to the cemetery this afternoon. Now go 'way an' leave me in peace." And the crying burst out afresh.

Suddenly, the film that had been across Johnnie's brain cleared, and he listened there outside his own front door to the sound of his wife's weeping. He struggled to his feet and, swaying with his hand on the latch, must have thought it was Saturday night, and that he had returned from the hotel at Moonta in his usual Saturday-night condition, for drawing himself up to his full height and battering with his hand on the door, he opened his mouth and cursed his wife roundly and well.

"Open this door, 'ee ————," he roared, "or I'll smash ev'ry ———— bone in thy ———— body. Let me in, I tell 'ee!" And his voice died away in mumbling obscenities.

Inside the house, Mary Rose Phillips brushed aside her brother-in-law and, loosening the chain, flung the door wide.

"Well, why coulden 'ee say afore it were 'ee?" was all she said, and held out her hands to Johnnie.

That is the story that Richard wrote in the *Reflector*, but he added a postscript:

This tale has always been told in my family as a true story and is believed as such in my village, but whether or not it really happened should not matter, for it very easily could have happened—although it probably did not!

Nathan read this last paragraph aloud several times, wrinkling his forehead over it, then looked at Polly. "From what I make out," he said, "there never were no Johnnie Phillips 'ere in Moonta, nor no explosion neither. Dang me if I aven been made a fool of all these year, an' it da take Rich to tell me so!" He smiled. " 'E didden call the place 'Moonta' though, did 'e, Pol?"

"Nobody'd knaw where 'twas back 'ome," said Polly.

"Well, I woulden 'ave thought Rich coulda made a story out o' Johnnie Phillips," marvelled Nathan.

"Well, I only 'opes as 'e got paid for un," said Polly matter-of-factly.

When Richard was twenty-one he joined the publishing house of Laurence and Lee, and became one of the company of young authors who contributed stories to the magazines *Youth* and *Boys' Weekly*.

All these young writers, including one well-known author who was neither young nor lacking a reading public for the travel-books he had already written, wrote collectively under the nom de plume of "Harvey Adam", the christian names of Mr Laurence and Mr Lee respectively. Every week with clockwork regularity a long story by Harvey Adam appeared in the *Boys' Weekly*, and on alternate Wednesdays *Youth* appeared with a collection of articles and tales by the same prolific writer. Nobody was ever

known to have been curious about the extraordinary pro-
ductiveness of Harvey Adam, and if they even pondered
over his identity it was never voiced, and the scheme
admirably suited the firm of Laurence and Lee who sold
thousands of magazines weekly, and the boys who bought
them had no other interest but the stories. Neither had
the collaborative authors any cause for complaint, since
they were obtaining employment, experience, a certain
liberty of style and the opportunity to do free-lancing in
their spare time.

Randolph Hawker wrote the cricketing stories, and
Bertram Oxford, a giant of a young man with red whiskers,
wrote the love scenes and tender passages in the ladies'
supplement to *Youth*. He had had previous experience on
Bow Bells and was considered an indispensable addition to
the staff. The well-known author of the travel-books set
the stage for stories of adventure, and Herbert George
Fowler, fresh from Winchester, gave the true atmosphere
to the public-school tales.

To Richard was given the task of writing sea stories and
the "Peeps at Foreign Lands" series that ran for nine con-
secutive issues. His one sea trip and the fact that he now
could speak French were more accountable for his appointment on the staff than his literary ability or his Uncle
Robert's influence with Mr Lee. The last writer of sea
stories for the *Boys' Weekly* had died of congestion of the
lungs a few days before Richard applied for a position
with Laurence and Lee.

The amount of knowledge Richard packed into his head
concerning vessels that sailed or steamed into the Thames,
during the years that followed his appointment with the
publishing house, would have astounded a British admiral.
He read every book he could lay his hands on that mentioned life at sea and the management of ships, and took
to haunting the East India docks and picking up acquaint-
anceships with dusky sailors with gold rings in their ears
and silk shawls and ivory fans in their sea-chests.

In between writing his share of the Harvey Adam tales
for *Youth* and the *Boys' Weekly*, Richard sent short stories
to every magazine in London reputed to pay its con-
tributors, and was as proud as Nathan when he saw

"Blawed Up" in print, the first story for which he had been given credit, if only in as far as it bore his own initials.

The illustrations in these papers for which Richard and his colleagues wrote their composite thirty-thousand-word stories each week were made by a system of etching, consisting of a photograph taken of an artist's drawing being placed above a plate of gelatine chemically sensitized. The parts of the gelatine exposed to the light became hard and the remainder was brushed away with warm water, and from this an electrotype could be made direct. Already Laurence and Lee were considering the use of acid baths for etching, and a new system then being used in current publications of photographing on zinc.

The day of wood-engraving, like that of the hand press and of the plaster of Paris for stereotyping, was gone for ever, and Richard wondered with a rueful smile how long it would be before the little printing office in Moonta's Ellen Street would resound as did the printing rooms below him here in Fleet Street, which rattled and shook with the crashing, whirring, rhythmic motion of a four-feeder Hoe press and Prestonian machine capable of producing and folding ten thousand copies in a single hour.

Letters from the editor of the Moonta paper came to him regularly. In one of them he was informed, to his amazement, that the *Advertiser*, an Adelaide daily, had both of these machines; but at Moonta everything was as he had left it. Richard remembered his late employer with affection, and knew that to some extent all he might become would be due to this man's advice.

"If you want to make a success of literary work," Mr Richards had said, "and by that I mean literary composition of any kind, you must not be too proud to carry your little notebooks with you wherever you go. Make notes of everything that interests you or you think may interest others. From now on, everything that comes to you is grist for your mill. Remember that!

"Every emotion you have ever shown has left a mark on your brain. Train yourself to bring these experiences to the surface. Use them, work on them, regardless of what memories you may awaken, and you will be able to write something that every man can understand. What you have experienced in your short life is kin to what every one else has suffered, known or will know in their lives.

"You were reared in a simple home. Set your characters in a similar atmosphere, such as you can appreciate and depict faithfully, until further experiences give you wider scope. Have you known death? I know you have—a brother and a sister. Draw upon those. It may cost you many a heart-pang, but remember, if you want to be read you must write life's language.

"Nothing is too great or too small to be overlooked. Make a note of it! The late Mr Dickens made voluminous notes, and how could he have written as he did without them? Human memory is too fickle. Write it down!

"Every person you have intimately known—mother, father, sweetheart, any one—all will have to serve your purpose. Don't strive for sensationalism. Simply be human. Write about what you know, and the rest, Richard, will be added unto you.

"Life is opening out before you, and whatever you experience, wherever you go, whomever you meet, all, all are to be the grist for your mill."

When Richard was twenty-three he took a busman's holiday and wrote a collection of short stories for children: incidents from his own boyhood linked to people of his acquaintance and imagination and set in two imaginary towns in South Australia and Victoria. He introduced Australian birds and animals and, after much seeking in the British Museum, learned the habits of the bandicoot, the platypus, the wombat, the emu and the native bear, and allied them to the other Australian animals he had known in his youth. Marsupial birth he did not mention, for where authorities disagreed he was not courageous enough to uphold any theory.

Seventeen stories he wrote, and took them after much rewriting to Mr Lee. Mr Lee was sceptical, said there never was and never would be any market for Australian books, but agreed to publish them at Richard's expense.

This little collection, by the generosity of Uncle Robert, saw the light of day on 9 October 1889, was received

dubiously by Uncle Robert, shamefacedly by Richard himself, rapturously by Nathan and Polly two months later,
and would have died a lonely death on the street book-
stands had not a county school, receiving it in a case of
geography textbooks, where its Australian title had caused
it to be mistakenly included, decided to use it as an aid to
the teaching of Australian natural history and as a gesture
of confidence in the British as a colonizing people. Later,
a young ladies' school at Chester included it in their
syllabus as being instructive though not intensive, and a
famous boys' school in the West Riding used it as an *hors
d'œuvre* for the more solid meat of the *History of the
British Empire.*

It appeared in a cheap edition for the use of schools, and
royalties for this, Richard's first-born, pursued him through
the course of his life into the four corners of the world.
"My first and only success!" he was often to call it.

CHAPTER XVII

POLLY was glad when Bob went to work at Soper's hardware store when he was thirteen years of age. She felt that, given a proper outlet for his activity, his restlessness would now be curbed. The chance to be busy and earning money appealed hugely to Bob, and he was as pleased as Polly when he began to work at Soper's.

Polly declared privately to Nathan that Bob had given her more anxiety than all her other children put together.

"Why, I don't believe young Allen, oo were born to be a roamer an' a wild un, coulda give me more trouble than Bob. 'E've a passion for bein' a nuisance, an' no mistake." There was a note of motherly pride in Polly's voice as well as of irritation.

In the chronicle of Bob's misdemeanours there were several that stood out prominently, and one was that occasion, soon after their arrival at Moonta, when he had fallen into the pickling tub at the butcher's shop. He had emerged odorous and greasy and walked slowly home to his mother and, after loitering about by the back door, at last summoned up courage to go into the kitchen, standing there in his stiff clothes from which little trickles of brine ran down and formed a miniature salt lake on the floor. Polly said he smelt like a polecat and boxed his ears, scolding all the while about the state of his pants and tunic, while he had the good sense to say nothing, and considered himself lucky only to be sent to bed without his tea.

On one occasion, at Moonta Mines, he fell into a costeen-pit twenty feet deep, and was dragged up in a very bruised and frightened condition by two stalwart miners who had been summoned to the scene by Bob's friends. The miners considered taking Bob home to his father to be thrashed,

but, on hearing that he was crippled Nathan Thomas's
son, they let him go with a caution that if they caught
him there again he would be taken to the mine captain,
who was no man to be trifled with or to brook any
trespassing or monkey-tricks on the mines.

It was during the afternoon of the school picnic that,
while tunnelling into a sandhill at Moonta Bay, the sides
of the tunnel collapsed on Bob, leaving his wriggling toes
to mark the spot where the rest of him might be found.
He was frenziedly dug out by Mr Jenkins the teacher, and
pulled into the bright sunlight half dead—almost choked
with sand. It took quite a long time for the effects of this
escapade in the sandhills to wear off, for he had been
thoroughly scared, and suffered nightmares for many weeks
after. Polly heard of the incident quite by accident for,
coming as it did so soon after Annie's death, it had been
kept from her, but when she did hear of it she led Bob out
to the shed and gave him the " 'idin' of 'is young life".
Then later, as he lay sobbing on his bed, she knelt down
beside him and cried as if her heart would break. To Bob,
all tears at this time were connected with grief for Annie,
and for the first time he realized how near to dying he
had been so, lifting up his head, he cried harder than ever.

In the early days of their life at Moonta the Spotted Boy
and the model of the Strasbourg Clock had visited the town
and had been on show in the old Institute Hall. Bob had
not seen the Spotted Boy, but had been allowed to view
the Strasbourg Clock and was impressed by the moving
figures of the disciples and the mellow note of the clock's
gong. However, the Spotted Boy, whom he did not see,
interested him more. He listened avidly to descriptions of
the curiously blotched condition of the boy's skin, and one
Saturday morning Bob dotted his own body with thick
brown paint and sawdust, and charged his friends an
empty bottle to come to see him in the shed in a nude
and bespeckled condition. The paint had refused to budge
from his skin when the performance was over and the six
empty bottles were stowed away under a sack in the corner
of the shed. Water and sand would not move it without
removing the skin, so at last Polly was sent for by one of
Bob's onlookers.

"Bob wants you out in the shed," he said to Polly, backing out of the kitchen and scuttling for home.

Polly clung weakly to the shed door when she saw Bob's spotted face and, when he meekly pulled up his flannel shirt and showed her the raw places where he had unsuccessfully tried to scrape off the paint and sawdust, she descended on him and, catching him by an ear, marched him in to Nathan and later into a scalding bath with half a pound of soft soap with which to lather himself.

"I'll lather un," Polly had said, wrenching his arms this way and that the better to look for more spots, "an' it won't be wi' soft soap, neither. I'll tell 'ee this much, me lad, thees'll be a spotted boy for many a day yet. These 'ere spots'll only come off by wearin' off."

It was on the great occasion in 1881 when the Duke of Clarence and his brother Prince George, who was later to succeed to the throne of England, were on a state visit to South Australia and had come to Yorke's Peninsula to inspect the copper mines that Bob brought public disgrace upon the Thomas family.

The two princes, who had arrived at Moonta amid tumultuous cheers and flag-waving, were driven in state to look over the mines. The driver of the conveyance was James Henry Brown, hero of a dash from Moonta to Adelaide in the early days. Crowds had assembled at Moonta Mines to give the princes a loyal welcome, but as the trap rolled along cheers gave way to grins and chuckles for, whillying behind, sometimes sitting on a projecting spring and sometimes holding to the trap and running behind it, was Bob Thomas.

Mr Brown guessed what was amiss before they had proceeded very far and, bending slightly to the right, with one deft swish of his long-lashed whip he cut Bob across his two bare legs, making a small red weal on the skin and causing Bob to yell, lose his balance and fall on to the dust of the road. Polly was spared the necessity for whipping Bob since his Sunday-school teacher, who had seen the whole incident, took him behind a screen of wattle saplings and stung him good and hard with a leafy switch for showing disrespect to the good Queen's grandsons.

On the night of 9 January 1880, Thompson's Great
Confederate Diorama was shown in the Moonta Institute,
and at three o'clock on Saturday the 10th Bob, with as
many school children as the hall would hold, was crammed
up in expectant darkness awaiting the commencement of
the special matinee. Nothing that ever happened to Bob in
later years gave him as great a thrill as did Thompson's
diorama of the American civil war.

The paintings ranged from scenes in the cotton fields
with moonlight effects on the great Mississippi River to
the Battle of Bull Run, and began with the massacre at
Harper's Ferry. Painted in transparent colours on some thin
fabric, often with one scene superimposed upon another
or painted on the two faces of the fabric, these pictures
were subjected to lights of varying intensity coming from
different angles and transmitted through the picture itself,
one scene changing to another according to the lights used.
Quick altering of the lighting arrangements created a
variety of effects, and coloured lighting was especially
effective for battle scenes, moonlight and fire studies.

It would be safe to say that nothing quite so wonderful
and mystifying as Thompson's diorama had as yet been
experienced by those children at Moonta.

Some of the battle pictures in panoramic style were
painted on a long roll of thin canvas and wound between
two upright spindles, each picture being as wide as the
distance between the spindles and all following each other
in sequence. A strong light with coloured glass for various
effects was placed behind the canvas, bringing out the
detail in each picture. The battle pictures were wound
across quickly, accompanied by a running fire of talk from
the showman. Each separate picture showed trees, cannon
and horses, but each differed in action from the preceding
one of the sequence. In the battle of Bull Run the gun was
in action, the gunner's hand raised, and the Union troops
visible through the trees. The rapid talk of the military-
looking showman drowned the grating of the spindles. The
picture changed, the red lights glowed, and—hey presto!—
the gun was discharging in fire and smoke, the gunner's
hand was lowered and the Union lines were in disorder,
with the whole scene bathed in a gory glow. The school

children sat as if glued to their chairs, tense with excitement. The picture changed, accompanied by furious winding and more impassioned oratory, and next the gun was shown upturned, a total wreck, blue moonlight streaming over the gunner stretched out in an attitude of dying despair, legs flung wide and eyes on heaven.

For years these pictures of the Confederate aspect of the civil war were talked of in Moonta, and it was a long time before the marvel of them faded away from Moonta memories.

It took three years for the seed sown that afternoon to spring to life and blossom in Bob's mind, and when he was twelve years of age he constructed a model of the picture screen from many six-inch rolls of ribbon paper. He made spindles of wire, fixed a bent wire handle to each spindle and wound the ribbon paper from one to the other. With ink and pencil he divided the paper into sections corresponding in width to the distance between the spindles, and on these sections, with coloured paints, made a series of pictures copied from books or illustrating a story. He had been gifted with artistic ability and, by holding brush or pencil between his thumb and second finger, could draw recognizable and creditable sketches of any incident that came to his mind.

When several rolls of ribbon paper had been divided into sections and each section filled with a coloured drawing, Bob mounted the whole apparatus in a big cardboard box retrieved, as the ribbon paper had been, from behind Polly's counter, and set a small lamp at the back. The light from the lamp shone through the ribbon paper, bringing out the colour in the paintings and giving a bold outline to the black and white drawings.

Bob's fame as a showman spread like wildfire among the boys at Moonta and Moonta Mines. His idea was copied, though never with great success, by many of them, for Bob's originality, drawing ability and dry sense of humour, and the volubility of his descriptions as he explained the scenes while turning the spindle made several youthful *entrepreneurs* green with envy. Bob charged one penny admission to the show, which was held in the back shed with the audience seated on planks set on barrels, and he showed enough business intelligence to ensure a continued repetition of his successes by adding a new roll of scenes once a week.

The Thomas back yard overflowed with boys of all ages from eight in the morning until six at night on every Saturday for three months, when, growing tired of it despite the number of pence he had made from it, Bob sold his invention to Edgar Killigrew for three shillings and six-pence and, with this sum as a nucleus, began a back-yard industry of moulding and modelling in plaster of Paris mixed with vinegar and liquid gum.

He progressed through plaster of Paris to one-stringed fiddles made from a cigar box and a broom handle, from which instrument he could draw a series of powerful and nerve-tearing sounds; and next he became a trainer of billy-goats in carts for a grand race along the Moonta Bay Road, when, owing to a blunder on the part of his own billy-goat, Bob's cart was upset, rendering himself uncon-scious for two days and spoiling his chances in the race.

When he was fourteen he contracted typhoid fever, and when convalescent was sent to Mrs Lillywhite in Adelaide for a holiday. While there he renewed his youthful friend-ship with Bunty and, after seeing him at work behind the counter of a large Rundle Street drapery store, Bob vowed he would never rest until he too was in Adelaide, working and making money.

He had been almost twelve years of age when Richard left for England, and the parting from this brother whom he loved with all the ardour of his young heart had been a bitter blow to him. Since Nathan's talk to them of brotherly love and duty, Richard had encouraged instead of snubbing his younger brother and had listened to his enthusiastic talk without seeming to lose interest or being annoyed. The forbearance he showed towards his brother was repaid a thousandfold by the hundred and one prac-tical ways through which Bob expressed his worshipping admiration for Richard. To outward eyes Richard was as short with Bob as he had always been, but at night, when on the borderline of sleep, drowsy wisps of talk were exchanged across the bedroom. Bob looked forward to this brief ten minutes with his brother in the dark, and even

Richard from the attitude of his almost six years' seniority was able, in the stillness and under the cloak of darkness, to forget the embarrassing burden of kinship with this eager, restless boy and to talk to him as one human being to another.

Bob fretted in the months after Richard's departure, and shed tears at night under cover of the bed-clothes, but when letters from Richard came to him, addressed to Master Robert M. Thomas, the keen edge of his unhappiness blunted, and he began once more to take an interest in his food and to whistle about the house.

"Praise be," said Polly to Nathan one night, gently massaging his stiff knees, "Bob 'ave got a bit o' sense in 'is noddle at last. 'E've just begun to learn that tidden no good grievin' in this world over what be gone. It don't do to set one's 'eart too much on anathin', nor to love any one too strong."

"Still bitter, Pol?" asked Nathan, understanding Polly's meaning and thinking of his dead children.

"Still bitter, Nat," Polly replied, pausing in her rubbing, "an' will be till I die. Nothin' can't never make me see what good were done to give two little childern life an' take it 'way afore they'd lived at all."

" 'Tis not in years a life be lived, me dear," said Nathan, striving to find a grain of comfort to offer Polly.

"Well, what in?" Polly answered, pulling the bed-clothes over Nathan. "In laughin' an' cryin' or eatin' an' dyin'? Be that all to make a life, Nat? 'Tis all me two little uns that be under sod did knaw o' life." Here she screwed up her face, and hot tears ran down the wrinkles on her cheeks. "Once," she said in a strangled whisper, "once I thrashed our Allen—raised great welts on 'im with a stick. 'Twas that time 'e ran away to Wallaroo. Many an' many a time I've thought o' that. 'Im with so short a time to live, to be thrashed an' walloped for takin' 'is bit o' pleasure in 'is own way. I never said 'arsh word to our Annie, but I were 'ard with Allen, an' I think sadly o' that now, I can tell 'ee."

"Don't grieve, Pol," Nathan said, shaken. "Don't question. Just be resigned, me dear. 'Tis easier in long run."

"Resigned!" she answered sharply, raising her tear-wet

face. "Thee should talk o' resigned! Thy patience da rile me, Nat, an' I could scream at 'ee sometimes, for thee da take thy own troubles too calm for me t' understand. What sort o' life do 'ee lead 'ere, chained to bed like a log?"

"Don't! Don't! Don't!" cried Nathan in an anguished voice, turning his face to the wall. "Cruel words, Polly. They strike deeper nor thees'll ever knaw. What do I knaw of life? Only this 'ere, that there be a purpose be'ind it all—Allen, Annie, an' even Richard's goin' 'way. We be all wove together in a pattern, an' ev'ry one of us, livin' or dead, be wove into the stuff o' some other body's life. 'Ear this," he said, turning his face to her. "Parson read me this, an' 'tis the answer I've looked for long an' 'ard. 'Tis a quotation, an' I set meself to learn un off. 'The 'ole earth is the tomb of 'eroes. Their story, is not graven only in the stone over their clay, but abides everywhere with visible symbol, wove into the stuff o' other men's lives.' Annie and Allen be wove into the stuff of our lives, for they 'ad the grace to be young an' brave an' full o' fun in a world that's old wi' cares. Me time'll come, Pol—soon, I sometimes think—an' all'll be over for me, but even though I've been lyin' ere like a log, as 'ee say, me dear, I be in the pattern too, for wi' God's 'elp I've shouldered me broken life with a brave 'eart, an' that be all the 'ero-work I were left to do."

Polly was on her knees beside the bed, her wide eyes strained on Nathan's brightened face. "An' me?" she cried earnestly, "what o' me, Nat? I've bore me share with an 'ard 'eart an' a bitter tongue. There be no place for me in the pattern, I knaw that."

"Polly, me dear," answered he, smoothing her whitening hair, "in the stuff that's bein' wove be a thread o' pure gold, bright, strong, 'ard an' glowin', an' that gold thread, me dear, be Polly Thomas!"

Bob, in the passage where he had been standing lonely and miserable in his white night-shirt, pressed both hands to the peeling plaster of the walls, listened till his father's voice was silent, then slipped back to his bedroom and lay awake a long time, enduring that peculiar unhappiness which is a part of growing up and which is far more real than any sadness that comes with the wisdom of years.

When he reached the age of eighteen he succeeded in realizing his ambition of going to Adelaide and seeking employment there.

"What's to become of me?" he argued on one occasion, before Polly had reluctantly given her consent. "I can't stay here all my life, weighing out nails and tacks and all that sort of thing. That'll get me nowhere, mother. Now, if I went to Adelaide I could get something to do like Bunty Lillywhite. He gets two pounds a week now, and all I get is a measly fifteen shillings."

"Two pounds a week," rejoined Polly severely, "be the most thy father earned in a week all 'is days."

"Well, that won't suit me. I'm going to get on in the world," Bob replied, with no intention of hurting Nathan's feelings. "I want to do something with my life, and earn decent pay for it."

"Well, 'tis certain sure 'ee won't get no better pay to Soper's," said Polly truthfully. "I knaw thee can't stay there for ever, but what's there for 'ee to do. Would'st like to be carpenter or summat like that? 'Tis not too late in the day to be 'prenticed."

"Aw, mother, steady on! I don't want to learn a trade. I want to make some money. You never heard of a carpenter getting rich, did you?"

"Well, thy cousin Peter 'ad a well-lined purse, I knaw that."

"Well, I bet somebody left him the money."

"'E be right there, Pol," struck in Nathan. "Peter's father what married me sister Jenny were a journeyman tailor, an' 'e afterwards 'ad a shop in 'Igh 'Olburn. When 'e died, Peter got 'is money. Bob be right there, mother."

"Well," said Polly, "argue it out atween thyselves, an' let me knaw when thee's finished an' I'll 'ave the last word."

She had the last word three weeks later, and in the meantime Bob had written secretly to Mrs Lillywhite asking if, in the event of his coming to Adelaide, he might stay with them and, receiving a kindly letter in reply with fond remembrances to Polly and the assurance of a bed and a home for as long as he cared to stay, Bob set about collecting references from the minister, his Sunday-school teacher and Mr Soper himself. He pledged Mr Soper to say nothing to Polly until all was arranged, and promised to find a suitable boy to take his place at a lower wage before he left for Adelaide.

Faced with the sheaf of references and Mrs Lillywhite's letter, Polly was forced to admit that there might be chances for Bob in Adelaide that Moonta did not offer. "Thee be one too smart for me, Bob," she said, not unkindly.

She was at this time receiving two pounds a month from Richard and, with what she earned at her trade, felt she could manage to keep herself and Nathan; so at last, in November 1889, she agreed to let Bob try his fortune in Adelaide.

The day after his arrival in Adelaide, Bob put on his Sunday suit and began his conquest of the city. He walked the length of Hindley and Rundle Streets to get his bearings, then went systematically to work, inquiring at every shop of size whether they needed an assistant. He had come to Adelaide at the right time, shop assistants being needed for the approaching Christmas season. Several shops had vacancies, but Bob felt sure they would be only temporary ones and that after the Christmas shopping rush he would be once more searching for work. Finally, he arrived at a mercer's shop in Rundle Street, and asked to see the manager. The manager, whom he found he had addressed, was standing in his shirt-sleeves behind the counter sorting out ties for a special window display.

"What work can you do?" he asked Bob, upon hearing his application.

"I can turn my hand to anything," answered Bob, in much the same words that Polly had used on a similar occasion.

"Well," said Mr South, glancing at Bob's references, "these say a good deal about your cheerfulness and activity, but what about your selling powers. I want more than good humour and energy from an assistant. I want cash sales."

Bob looked about him at the ill-assorted neckwear on the counter. "If I could sell a dozen ties in a day, would that be any good?" he said at a venture. "I could guarantee to sell that many the first day I was here, if I got the job."

"The profit on them wouldn't pay your salary for one day. And anyway, how would you go about it?"

"I don't know," said Bob, unabashed, "but I s'pose if you let me start on Monday I'd put in all day Sunday trying to persuade my friends to come to your shop next day and buy a tie from me. I don't know how else I'd sell that many."

Mr South smiled. "Let me tell you something, young man, that will help you all your shop life. Never expect a friend to buy anything from you in business. Of the dozens of friends you may have, perhaps one will be glad to do you a good turn, but the rest. . . . He clicked his fingers. "No! It's not from friends the business comes, my lad, but from strangers. Strangers every time."

"Well, I've learned something to-day," said Bob.

A middle-aged man walked into the shop, and Bob moved a little to one side while Mr South attended to the customer.

"A tie?" said Mr South. "Black or coloured, sir?"

The buyer was uncertain. He went through Mr South's meagre stock and seemed disinclined to decide on any of them. Bob, who had been casually observant, here stretched out an arm and lifted a striped tie from the counter.

"Pretty," he said to himself, holding it at arm's length. "Very."

Mr South stared at him. The customer gave him a glance, and then resumed his survey of the neckwear.

"Give me half a dozen—all striped," Bob said negligently to Mr South. "I can wait until this gentleman has been attended to." And he strolled to the end of the shop and back again. "Stripes are all the go," he said conversationally to the astounded Mr South. "You see them on all the best people."

The customer hesitated a moment, then said in a low voice to Mr South, "I'll take two."

"Plain or striped?" queried Mr South.

"Er—striped," said the middle-aged man.

Bob, his back to the counter, watched the customer's hand hovering over a purple striped tie, and he said in a bored voice to the shop at large, "It's strange how popular blue is this season. Particularly becoming colour, I always think."

The customer's hand ceased to hesitate. He picked up two ties, one dark and one pale blue striped, and handed them to Mr South, paid for them, received his parcel and, with a brief look at Bob's back, left the shop.

"There!" said Bob, turning round suddenly as soon as the customer had disappeared. "I sold eight ties for you in one pop. I've only four more to make the dozen."

"Eight?" said the astounded Mr South. "You really intend to take six yourself?"

"I'd take the whole twelve to get the job, but I've only got twenty-two and ninepence to last me until I find something to do, so you'll have to take the difference out of my wages."

"Do you still want to work here?" queried Mr South.

"I do, sir," said Bob respectfully and eagerly. "Have I got a chance?"

"I think you have, young man. That fellow who just went out has been in here three times for ties, if I remember rightly, and I've never been able to get him to buy as much as a stud."

"Next time he comes," said Bob grinning, "I'll send him out with a Homburg hat. See if I don't!"

Mr South laughed, then recollected himself. "Steady, young man, no levity! Play-time's over, and you've got a position here in my shop. Go into the back room there and take off your coat, then help me to dress this window."

Bob put his hand into his pocket.

"I'll pay for my ties now," he said, drawing out some money.

"What," said his new employer, "you mean to say you genuinely want half a dozen ties?"

"Perhaps I don't *want* the whole half-dozen, but I said I'd buy them and I'll stick to it." Bob fingered the narrow, frayed black tie he was wearing. "I can't wear this and ask people to buy new ties. That's why I had to keep my back turned just now."

Mr South spread the striped ties out in a line. "Take your pick," he said, "and have one for threepence less than the price ticket shows."

Bob chose one swiftly, and knotted it in his hands to see how well it would tie when around the neck. "Blue stripes are all the go. *Are* they, sir?"

"Well, that's something it'll be your business to find out from now on. South's my name, Thomas," he added. "Get busy. You work here now, you know."

Bob learned before the day was out that his wages were to be one pound a week, and he wrote a short, happy letter to Polly that night telling her all that had happened to him.

CHAPTER XVIII

POLLY was very lonely after Bob left home, and found to her surprise that she had quite a lot more to do in the house than she had bargained for. There was no one to cut the wood, to pump the water, to clean her shoes, to milk the goat, to deliver the millinery or to make up the accounts.

"I never made 'alf enough fuss of our Bob whilst 'e were to 'ome," she owned to Nathan. "I were too busy meself to give thought to 'ow much the lad 'elped me. I think I'll be missin' 'im more than I did Rich, do 'ee knaw that?"

"That be because 'e took on all Rich's jobs when Rich went away," said Nathan. "Bob were more use than us ever gave un credit for."

" 'Ow I'll ever make up they accounts beats me," Polly moaned. "Bob 'ave done them ever since 'e were ten year old. Dost mind the time 'e wrote one addressed to Miz Hoppy-Dick Trevivers? I just caught un in time. I'd 'a' lost a purty good customer if I adden laid eye to it."

"Yes, I mind the time, an' I mind that 'ee made un rewrite it to Miz Richard Trevivers, an' nobody knawed oo 'twas!"

"Well, that's what da come of 'avin' an 'usband with one leg shorter than t'other," Polly rejoined.

"I wonder what they da call me?" said Nathan. " 'Crippled Nat Thomas', I dare say." And Polly remained silent, knowing it to be the truth.

For a year after Bob's departure all went well with the millinery business, but in March 1890 a number of miners at Wallaroo Mines created a disturbance and demanded the eight-hour working day now prevailing through the colony, and it seemed as if the trouble might extend to the Moonta miners, and consequently the women's purse-strings were tightened and new bonnets became a luxury.

During the latter part of the previous year the Wallaroo and Moonta mining companies had amalgamated and the resulting merger was now known as the Wallaroo and Moonta Mining and Smelting Company, Limited, and one board of directors governed both mines with Captain H. R. Hancock as general manager.

At the first meeting of the new company the question of working hours arose, for the problem was now acute at Wallaroo Mines in view of eighteen men being out of employment owing to the stop-work attitude of engine- and boiler-men at Harvey's shaft. The men affirmed that sixteen hours in two eight-hour shifts was sufficient for the mine engines to be worked, and that the water in the mine could be kept down in those hours and that the engines need not be worked, as they were, continuously.

It was the first official act of the new company to recognize an eight-hour day for both Wallaroo and Moonta Mines, and the trouble at Harvey's shaft, Wallaroo Mines, was satisfactorily ended.

Three years before the amalgamation, copper being at the low figure of £40 a ton, a ten-per-cent wage cut had been imposed on the Moonta miners. A short while later copper had risen to £100 a ton and dividends had been paid to the shareholders, but the cut had not been restored to the men. The Amalgamated Miners' Association deposed that the miners should be paid the old rate, but the directors continually affirmed that the price of copper did not warrant the rise in wages. The price fell, and in 1890 was £49 10s. a ton, but the men, who declared that the mines were paying well, were becoming impatient.

The main reason for their dissatisfaction was the galling knowledge that at the time of the amalgamation the Wallaroo miners, having refused to submit to a wage cut in 1889, were now receiving a higher rate of pay than the men at the Moonta Mines. Consequently, when the eight-hour working day came into force at both mines, the new company decided upon a uniformity of wages; but all aged and injured miners working on the Moonta Mines were summarily dismissed.

This state of affairs lasted for some months, and the Broken Hill and shipping strikes that occurred in the latter part of 1890 had the effect of bringing the Moonta miners' troubles to the surface, and the fact that the Wallaroo smelters were threatened with a shortage of coal and consequent stoppage of work did not ease matters.

Broken Hill resumed work, and the shipping strike came to an end without serious results, but the unrest at Moonta continued for twelve months until, on 28 September 1891, the Moonta miners struck work and, except for the pumping engines which had then to be attended by officers of the company, all work at the mines ceased.

The claims set before the directors by the Amalgamated Miners' Association were fair and simple. The association asked for all able-bodied men to be paid at the rate of five shillings and sixpence per day until copper should reach £65 a ton, and then for a ten-per-cent rise to be given. Also it asked that miners be given a private setting or contract at the rate of two guineas per week.

The strike continued over Christmas into the New Year, and then the ex-president of the Moonta branch of the Amalgamated Miners' Association, Mr John Verran, together with Mr Hooper, Mr Polmear and several associates, journeyed to Adelaide to place the miners' case before the board of directors and, although given a sympathetic hearing, had to return to Moonta with the decision of the board unchanged.

By February 1892 the miners' resistance was worn out, and mass meetings were held by them asking for their old places at the mines and accepting the wage cut. By this time anything was better than unemployment.

The directors announced their decision of pay for surface hands to be fixed at five shillings a day and miners' wages to be not less than £2 per week. Contracts were posted at the new conditions, and a large number of tenders were sent in by the miners who, tired of indolence, meagre strike pay and the imminence of poverty, were clamouring to work again at almost any rate of pay.

So the strike ended after one hundred and twenty-six days of futile fighting on the part of the miners and steely obstinacy on the part of the board of directors. Work began at the mines immediately, but it was some time before all the miners were absorbed.

When the miners went on strike Polly Thomas went on strike too, but, while there was work for the miners if they would do it, there was none for Polly, since the miners' wives had no money to spend on hats and very little to spend on anything else. The savings-bank book, which Polly kept in the wooden box since Richard had insisted that she transfer her money to the bank, was brought forth, and she and Nathan spent a good deal of their time wondering how long the strike would last and how long the money in the savings bank would keep them.

Nathan's friends, with plenty of time on their hands during the months of stop-work, visited him often, never a day passing without one of them dropping in to discuss the strike and to argue about their rights and wrongs.

Polly had moved all the furniture except the big bed from Nathan's room, and she used the room that had been the boys' as her dressing-room. In Nathan's room she placed the best carpet—the rag rugs had worn out years before—three cedar chairs from the kitchen, a gypsy table, and a rocking-chair for herself. An oil stove burned there on wintry days, and altogether the room was pleasant and cosy for Nathan and his friends. On Nathan's bedside table Polly would place a "vawse" of flowers brought to her by a friendly customer or gathered from her own little garden strip at the back of the house. In the autumn she placed there an old cloam bowl she had brought from Cornwall, and in it she planted two daffodil bulbs for Nathan to watch as they sprang to life and flowered.

Polly would often stay in her little showroom with the door leading into the passage ajar and, sitting there knitting socks for her boys, would cock an ear to all that went on in the bed-sitting-room. Many subjects besides the strike were debated, and the field of discussion seemed limitless.

Once a knock came at the kitchen door and a voice called into the house: "Anybody to 'ome?"

"Come right in, Mr Trebellin'. I knaw thy voice," called Polly from the showroom. "Nat's to 'ome as usual. Go on in, do. Mr Poldoon an' 'Enery Trefusis be there too. Walk right in."

Polly could hear the other men greeting Joe Trebelling.

"Well, Joe, 'ow're 'ee doin'?" called out Henry Trefusis in his deep-chested voice.

"Doin'? Doin' nothin'! That's the trouble," was the reply.

"Any more news as 'ee come by?"

"Silas Boner did tell me there were a rumour that it'd be over in two-three weeks. Johnnie Verran be gone t'Adelaide to see directors, 'an', says 'e, ' 'twon't be long now!' "

"That's Sily Boner for 'ee!" said Timmy Poldoon. " 'E don't knaw big A from a duck's track. But what 'e says 'bout Johnnie Verran be true 'nough. Us 'ave got faith in our Johnnie, but they directors be an 'ard lot. 'Ard as stone."

"Well I wish I 'ad a few of un under me 'ammer this minute!" said Joe truculently.

"Thee ud give un a smack!" said Nathan laughing.

"I'd smash un to flinders," Joe replied. "I would so."

" 'Tis a big problem," said Nathan.

"Talkin' o' problems," spoke up Henry, taking a long pull at his pipe, "did'st 'ear 'Enery George down Institute 'All year afore last speakin' on the problem o' the civilized world? *That* be a problem, right 'nough!" And there ensued a lively discussion on Mr Henry George, the American orator and world-reformer who had visited Moonta in 1890.

"Well," struck in Timmy Poldoon, "I never went to 'ear 'Enery George, but I mind goin' to 'ear the Moonta Fisks an' the Quintrell family singin' an' playin' in the institute. My! That were grand. Never 'eared anathin' to touch un."

"Do 'ee call to mind they 'ad a man there oo could whistle like a pair o' parrots?" asked Joe Trebelling.

"Do I?" Timmy enthused. "That there chap were as purty a little whistler as ever cocked lip! I clapped un so 'ard the missus said I'd skin me 'ands."

There was a pause, then Nathan asked, "What dost think o' this new free eddication? Some say as it be free for rich an' poor childern alike."

"Iss," responded Henry. "But there be a catch to un. The childern 'ave to stay to school till they be thirteen! Now, I paid me sixpence a week for each o' me five boys till they was nine year old, an' ev'ry man jack o' them was workin' by the time they was ten—four on the picky-tables an' one up township. Now, by this 'ere new-fangled free eddication, I'd 'ave to up an' keep un to school four more year each. Free schoolin' I knaw 'twould be, but what 'bout all they years o' work they'd be missin'? Let's see, five fours be twenty. Je-ru-salem! Twenty year wasted atween the lot of un! Tidden possible. Five fours—twenty year! Why, be rights I should be grandaddy by that time!"

"Steady there," interrupted Nathan. "Twenty year atween the lot, an' not strung out in a long line, neither."

"Well, leastways, twenty year worth o' wages," said Henry decisively. "An' 'ee can string *they* out in a long line!"

In the winter of 1893 Nathan caught a severe cold. "Influenza" the doctor named it, but Polly as usual had her own ideas on the subject and called it "a cruel bad cold in 'is 'ead an' a terrible cough on 'is chest". He was ill for a week before Polly realized that he was in a serious condition and, hastily summoning the doctor, heard—and this time believed—his verdict of "Pneumonia!"

From this time the symptoms developed rapidly, and Polly was forced to believe at last that Bob must be sent for and that there was little hope of Nathan's recovery. The condition of his heart and the strain that the illness brought to bear upon it, coupled with his weakened condition through years of invalidism, would make him an easy victim to the disease.

Polly, with anguished heart, saw clearly that Death must soon claim her husband, and she bent over the bed listening to his short, rapid breathing and the feverish murmurings of his voice. Her eyes, sharpened with the knowledge of sad experience, saw Death's handprint in the greyness of his face and the thin, pinched outline of his nose. She slipped a hand beneath his damp head and smoothed back his thick grey hair. He knew her, but looked dumbly up at her, or mouthed strange sounds that she knew were meant for love-words. After a while he sank into an uneasy sleep, but she still sat by him, reluctant to leave him for a moment of the time that still remained.

Bob arrived late on Tuesday afternoon, but by this time Nathan was in a coma, and the house was filled with the noisy rise and fall of his breathing. Nathan lived without moving or speaking for two days longer, and no sound disturbed the sick-room except the whispers of the two about his bed or the tiptoe goings to and fro of Grace Treneer in the kitchen—no sound but the dreadful noise of his breathing which fell away to silence then began once more, died away then came again, rasping upwards then quietening, on and on.

On Thursday evening, just before midnight, he opened his eyes wide and looked with an unseeing stare at Polly and Bob. They rushed to his side, each holding one of his damp, listless hands, and Nathan died with no sign other than a brief, sharp struggle and a rattling breath that, ceasing, left him calm and lifeless on the bed.

"Nat! Nat!" called Polly wildly, and the silence answered her.

The grey, homespun thread of Nathan Thomas's life was broken, but it remained in the pattern of the lives around him as a row of weaving without flaw.

Polly bore Nathan's death with greater calm than that with which she had borne the death of her two children, for she had had more than a week in which to prepare herself for his leaving her and, after an hour's tearful prayer beside his bed, had strength of mind and body to see about the funeral arrangements herself and to word the announcements which, according to custom, would be displayed in the shop windows of Moonta and Kadina.

There was one ray of comfort for her in the unreality of the first few days after his burial.

"Me Nat 'ad a fine funeral," she said proudly to Mrs Ben Wilson, who had come from Wallaroo Mines to be near her. "There was fifty-one traps countin' they ones that was to the Kadina cemetery when we got there. Me Nat were well thought on."

Bob was completely broken up, and it eased Polly's heart to comfort him. He urged his mother to come back with him to Adelaide, but Polly was firm and said she had no intention of leaving Moonta.

"No," she said firmly, " 'ere I be an' 'ere I stay. Things won't be so diff'ent. Tissen as if I'd 'ad an able-bodied man to do for all these years. Cussen 'ee see, Bob, that I allus knawed 'twould come some time an' 'avin' father sick in bed so long smoothed the way. Many a time us've talked this 'ere over, Bob, an' thy father were o' the same mind as meself. I must just carry on till I feel ready to shut up shop, an' when that time da come I'll be thinkin' o' comin' to thee in Adelaide. The day that father died began when Annie left us an' when 'e took to bed for good an' all. Both of us knawed it, Bob, an' spoke of un often, quite natural-like. Thy father 'ad a word o' comfort for evrathin' that comed or were to come."

"I never knew a man like him," sobbed Bob.

"No, nor never will this side of 'eaven's gates!" said Polly, leaning her head on the table and giving way at last to tears.

Polly was fifty-five at this time, stout, grey-haired and lined of face, but with a flush of youthful redness still in her cheeks like the bloom on a wrinkled apple. Her body was as straight as it had ever been, and her eyes behind the spectacles as keen and kindly. There was not a soul in Moonta but knew and respected Mrs Polly Thomas—now Mrs Crippled Nat Thomas no longer—and, after Nathan's death released her from the cares of the sick-room, she began at fifty-five to live the life of a free woman.

Six months after her widowhood began she was taking an active part once more in the life of the Wesleyan Church and, with only herself to care for, was able to afford Grace Treneer's help in the millinery shop.

Polly dismantled the cedar bed and, not being disposed to sell it—for it had become part of her life—stored it under a sheet against the wall in the boys' bedroom which was now her own, and made of the other room a parlour. To this room came members of the Dorcas Society and the Foreign Mission supporters, for Polly was an enthusiastic worker for each of these branches of church work, and was respected and looked up to by all its members.

Nobody at the church knew why Polly showed no interest in the Women's Christian Temperance movement, and

Polly kept her own counsel, owning to herself that her attitude had everything to do with a sense of gratitude to her brother Robert, though acknowledging in her heart a secret yearning to wear the white bow on her breast that the temperance workers wore on theirs.

"But," she said, "if Robert da sell the stuff to 'ome an' 'is money be 'elpin' to keep me an' mine, then I'll up an' do me duty as I see un, an' that be to sit quiet an' be thankful."

She was glad at Christmas-time of that same year that she had been loyal to her sense of duty to Robert, for she received a letter from Richard then, informing her that her brother had died of an apoplectic stroke. It had been brought about by the complete destruction of his warehouse by fire, which not only destroyed his business but also rendered his wife and child penniless. Uncle Robert's faith in himself and lack of faith in any other man had made the omission of an insurance policy his own and his family's ruin.

Polly was stricken at this news of further disaster, and felt that her few remaining ties with the old country were being broken one by one.

A letter from Richard following the one announcing her brother's death came a month later and brought her the news that Richard had married his cousin Euphemia, whose mother had gone to live with a relative at Bayswater, and that Richard and his bride were already on their way to America.

This letter pleased and cheered Polly greatly. "Me Richard 'ave done the right thing," she said to herself. "Robert'd like to knaw that, for 'e cast 'is bread 'pon the waters an' it 'as come back to feed 'is cheeld. Robert got a son of 'is own at last, an' I wish 'e 'ad lived to see this day." But she little realized that if he had, Richard might never have found courage to ask his lovely cousin Euphemia to marry him, and Euphemia herself might never have found in her cousin a lover and a husband.

Polly at this time took a keen interest in politics, and the subject of women's suffrage was as heatedly discussed in her little back parlour as the shape of sulus for the heathen, and she exercised female franchise with the other women of South Australia for the first time in 1896, and put a bold cross on the ballot sheet beside her favoured candidate's name.

"Johnnie Verran knawed what 'e were talkin' 'bout," she said, "when 'e once said us Cornishwomen'd allus vote right."

In the first year of the new century the names of Lord Roberts and General Kitchener were on everybody's lips, and many new-born babies in Moonta were proudly christened "Robert Kitchener". These two soldiers were organizing new campaigns in South Africa against the Boers, whom open battle could not defeat though military strategy might. Soon the whole world was ringing with the joyful news of the raising of the siege of Ladysmith and Mafeking.

To Polly Thomas, in Moonta, the uprising of the murderous Boxers in China in 1900 had a personal interest. Nathan's cousin, Peter Tilbrook, was a missionary in Peking, and had been stationed in China for almost thirty years. In September of 1900 Polly received tidings in a letter from Richard that news had reached him from England of the murder, by the Boxers, of Peter, his missionary wife and their child at Peking eight weeks before Richard's letter had been written.

Polly felt that the last thread binding her to the old days was now severed, and for the first time she became conscious of her utter loneliness and apartness from her kindred. She experienced a great longing to be near her own and, being now sixty-two, felt the premonitory pangs of old age—not by any bodily signs, but by an intense yearning to be near her own flesh and blood. She was a grandmother now, to Richard's twin sons in America and to a baby girl of Bob's in Adelaide.

Bob had been married a year previously to Margaret Mortone, whom he had met at the Methodist Church in Franklin Street, and with his wife and month-old baby was living in a rented house in Lower North Adelaide. Polly seemed drawn to them by ties stronger than the ties that bound her to the home in Moonta, so she wrote to

Bob and told him she would come to him in Adelaide, saying:

I be the last one left. I be the last one of the old family alive. Mrs Ben Wilson passed away last Thursday, an that da show me I be gettin on ta be an ol woman too, an ad best shut up shop like I told thy father, an go down to Adelaide an finish me days in peace.

It was Christmas-time before she had sold up her little stock and had packed her household goods and was ready to go to Bob, and the sharp pain she felt at breaking up her home was assuaged by the feeling that life, perhaps, was not yet over for her: that there would still be adventures for her in a new setting. She had not the smallest intention of making a permanent home with her son, saying to herself, "Young folks be best left to theirselves. An' anaways, I've me own life to live an' I idden done for yet—not by a long chalk."

It was the night before Christmas Eve and Polly was to leave Moonta next day so, donning her best black dress and a smart little silk hat that she had made to look her best for the journey, she locked her shop door behind her and went out to walk the Moonta streets for the last time.

Green boughs were tied to the veranda-posts of the shops in George Street, and people were about looking into the brightly lit windows and listening to the Salvation Army band playing Christmas carols outside the institute. It seemed a fitting time to be saying farewell to Moonta, when the streets were bright and the music of Christmas carols was in the air.

Some of the carols that were being played and sung had been written by Cornishmen in Moonta. Fine tunes they were, and gave scope to all four parts of harmony. A drag, whereon was seated the choir from the Wesleyan Church, stood at one corner, and the occupants sang unaccompanied all the old tunes with which Polly was familiar as well as some of the newer carols that already were making themselves dear to the hymn-loving Methodists.

A young woman on the drag stood up at the close of one of the carols, and Polly recognized her. It was Annabelle Mack, and she sang the hymn that Polly remembered, with a catch in her throat, as being the one Allen had sung at the Bible Christian Anniversary at Wallaroo Mines so many years ago.

> Hark! Hark, my soul! Angelic songs are swelling
> O'er earth's green fields and ocean's wave-beat shore:
> How sweet the truth those blessed strains are telling
> Of that new life when sin shall be no more!
> Angels of Jesus, Angels of light,
> Singing to welcome the pilgrims of the night!

The other members of the choir hummed an obligato, but Annabelle's voice rose clear and sweet above the harmony.

Polly knew the words of the hymn, for it was a custom, brought from the old country and still used in Methodist churches, for the minister to read the words of each verse of a hymn at the close of the singing of the previous verse. This had been necessary in Cornwall in the old days owing to the fact that so few of the congregation could read. In this way the words became familiar to everybody, and even the young children could sing half a dozen verses of a hymn without once missing a word.

> Angels, sing on, your faithful watches keeping;
> Sing us sweet fragments of the songs above.
> Till morning's joy shall end the night of weeping
> And life's long shadows break in cloudless love.
> Angels of Jesus, Angels of light,
> Singing to welcome the pilgrims of the night.

Annabelle's lovely voice died away, and a solemn hush fell on the listening people. Scarcely a heart but was moved by the young woman's pure, well-trained voice, scarcely a soul but felt the beauty of the well-known words, and more than one ear caught in Annabelle's voice the echo of the angels' song.

"Ah," said Polly to a friend who stood beside her, "that be a message to carry 'way with me this night. Only once 'ave I ever 'eared that song sung sweeter."

"That's Annabelle Mack, come down from Adelaide to spend Christmas with her people," the friend replied. "Some say her voice is very well thought of in the city. I've heard tell that she's to go to London next year."

"Well, wherever she da go," said Polly, "she'll never sing better than she did to-night."

Polly felt a touch on her arm, and turned about to find Annabelle standing behind her.

"May I speak to you, Mrs Thomas?" asked Annabelle.

"You may, me dear," said Polly kindly.

"Don't you remember me, Mrs Thomas?"

"I didn't at first, but I knaw 'ee now, Annabelle Mack. Thee 'ave altered."

"I've grown up, I suppose," said Annabelle, smiling down at Polly. "You know I've been studying singing in Melbourne, don't you, Mrs Thomas?"

"Can't say as I da mind ever 'avin' 'eared so," answered Polly, "but I da knaw a power o' trainin' went to make that voice o' yourn. I never 'eared a woman sing so sweet."

"Thank you, Mrs Thomas. I tried to do my best, but really there was little scope for fine singing in that hymn. You should hear me in something colourful. I'm leaving for London in March, you know, and hope to sing in opera there. My teachers tell me there is a future for me."

"London? My, that's flyin' 'igh, idden it?"

"Not so high as I want to fly," said Annabelle loudly. "There's Paris and Berlin and New York after that."

"New York! America, idden it?" questioned Polly, her eye brightening. "Me eldest boy be over there. 'E've got a wife, an' twin boys too, goin' on for four year old. An' me youngest boy Bob, 'e be settled down in Adelaide with a wife of 'is own an' a new babby."

"Is Richard happy?" Annabelle asked, after a pause.

"'Appy? Well, if 'e idden 'e oughta be! 'Is wife were brought up to be a lady, an' were me own brother Robert's only dotter."

"When you write to Rich will you give him a message for me?"

"Certainly, me dear. I write to Rich reg'lar. What be the message?"

"Just this, that you saw me to-night and heard me sing, and that I am going to London as I always hoped I should."

"Be that all?" asked Polly.

"Just one thing more," said Annabelle, smiling. "Please say that if I ever get to New York I shall commission him to do my press notices and write me up as the Moonta nightingale. I'll insist on that."

Polly watched Annabelle go back to the drag. "Thee may sing like a angel, miss," she mused, "but there be a bit o' devil in 'ee, sure 'nough. Success 'ave made 'ee saucy. Write that to me Rich? Not me!"

CHAPTER XIX

Bob's house was a little square box of a place with four rooms, and a wide shady veranda stretching across the two front rooms and painted an indeterminate shade of green. The house faced south, and in wooden tubs on the veranda Bob's wife Margaret, who had the traditional "green hand", had planted fuchsias, ferns, gay painted-lady geraniums and large-flowered pink hydrangeas. A young Virginia creeper was beginning its tortuous journey over the stone walls, and one end of the veranda was shaded by a hawthorn-tree planted years ago by a previous tenant, a Sussex man.

In the space before the house Bob had tried his hand at gardening, and had made a splendid job of it. A curved path, cobbled with stones, led from the green front gate to the veranda steps, and on both sides of the path rosemary hedges, trimmed to a scant six inches in height, marked the outline of the flower-beds. Poppies rioted there, and tall snapdragons and sunflowers and love-in-a-mist.

The most noticeable feature was the dove-cote set in the exact centre of the right-hand garden bed, mounted on an untrimmed length of gum sapling. The cote was made from a small round keg and thatched with straw. In the front face of the bird-house Bob had cut little square windows, with quaint shutters flung wide, and a taller opening that suggested a door. He had painted the keg white, but the shutters and the perches which jutted from the base were coloured a bright grass green.

Polly's eyes alighted first on the dove-cote as she and Bob stood at the green front gate where they were pausing a moment before entering. Polly had arrived in Adelaide that day, and this was her introduction to her son's home.

Bob's face was beaming as he saw the light of approval

in his mother's eyes, and he had the air of a showman about to exhibit his bag of tricks.

"Like it, mother?" he asked, watching Polly as she viewed the dove-cote.

"Like it? I should say I do," answered Polly, whose motto had always been "Praise where praise be due". " 'Ast any birds in un?"

"No," replied Bob. This was a sore point, and trust his mother to find it out! "Meg and I tried to get a pair of fantail pigeons to stay, but they flew off, and we won't try another pair until spring."

"Thees be best off without un," said Polly practically. "They'd make a mess o' the roof in no time."

"Look," said Bob, directing Polly's attention to the front gate. "Watch this." He pressed a round wooden knob let into the gate-post, and Polly heard the latch click on the other side, and the gate swung open. "There," said Bob, reaching over and shutting the gate. "You try it, mother."

Polly pressed the wooden knob with her forefinger, and once more the gate swung ajar.

"Not bad, is it?" Bob said, with almost boyish enthusiasm. "It's an idea of my own. I'll show you how it works one day."

Polly walked slowly along the garden path and drank in the heavy perfume of the sun-drenched flowers.

"It be as purty as a picsher, an' no mistake, Bob," she said.

"It took a lot of water," Bob answered matter-of-factly, looking at the bright colours and stooping to pull up a seeding thistle from between the cobble-stones. He looked up. "Here's Meg," he said. "Meg," he called to his wife, "here's mother."

Meg Thomas, Bob's age, regular-featured and kindly-faced, came down the veranda steps carrying her young baby, and the two women met in the pathway. They kissed.

"Come inside, mother," said Meg, taking Polly's elbow in the warm palm of her hand. "I've a cup of tea ready. All's on the table."

It was with difficulty that Polly mounted the three wooden steps to the veranda and stood at last among the fresh greenness of the geraniums and ferns. As she listened to the kindly words of her daughter-in-law's greeting a strange trembling seized her knees, and a feeling she had never known took possession of her, and she fumbled uncertainly with the edge of the black lace trimming on the bodice of her frock.

Bob held back the cheese-cloth curtain that hung across the front door to keep the flies out. "Come in, mother," he said, reaching out a hand to guide her over the step.

The first thing of which Polly was conscious in the passageway of Bob's house was the pleasant coolness after the outside heat. She blinked, owing to the sudden change from the sunlight, and allowed herself to be led into the room that was to be hers. There was a small strip of carpet on the scrubbed board floor, a low stretcher bed covered with a snowy counterpane, a high-backed chair, and a ewer and basin on an iron stand.

"This is just until your things arrive, mother," said Meg. "Do you mind it being so bare?"

"Bare?" began Polly, finding her voice at last. "Bare it may be, but I could eat me dinner off the floor, me dear. 'Tis as clean as a pin." She looked about. "But, thee 'ave give me a room to the front. Why for?"

"It's so cool here," Margaret answered, "and the window opens on to the veranda. It's a pleasant room in the summer."

"This be the best room in the 'ouse, I be thinkin', an' 'twas thy room an' Bob's," Polly said, peering through the cheese-cloth window screen at the crazy-quilt effect of the garden. "Own up, me dear."

"It was ours," said Meg, without any hesitation, "but we'll be just as comfortable at the back, and you're very welcome to this one. Perhaps you won't mind if the baby sleeps here too, on hot nights?"

Polly set down her string bag and black morocco purse. "Give me the babby," she said, holding out her arms for the child.

Meg handed it over, turning up the little face for the grandmother to see. Polly blinked hard behind her spectacles, and the baby's face swam before her as in a mist. She bent and kissed the yellow down on the little creature's head, and handed her back to Meg.

"I be a proud woman this day," was all she said.

"She's four months old to-morrow," said Meg, while Polly removed her silk hat and black gossamer. "Now that you are here we shall have her christened at the church. Bob badly wanted you to be here for that. You know she's to be called Margaret Mary Elizabeth, don't you, mother?"

Polly smiled, and went over to Meg and the baby. "Then we be both proud women, Meg, me dear—terrible proud." She looked quizzically at her daughter-in-law. "Thee's got a look about 'ee like me little dotter Annie what died. 'Tis in thy eyes. Smilin' eyes, they be." Polly tilted her head on one side, examining Meg as would an inquisitive bird. "Thee be purtier than when Bob brought 'ee up to Moonta to show me last year. Bein' a married woman suits 'ee like it do the rest of us." Then she added feelingly, "Thee've made Bob 'appy. 'E be a lucky lad, an' me too!"

She said this ungrudgingly, and if Nathan could have heard her he of all people would have known the struggle it must have cost Polly to acknowledge her family's indebtedness to anybody else, and he would have understood that it was Polly's declaration of love for Meg.

Polly dropped the bomb-shell—her decision to seek a home of her own—while the three of them were seated at table that night eating corned beef and lettuce salad.

"What?" said Bob. "You've only just got here, and talking of going off already! Meg and I thought you had come to us for good. Talk sense, mother. You couldn't manage on your own without the shop. I'll still do my part, mother, and be proud to do it; but you can't live and pay rent on what Rich and I manage to give you. Wait a few days. Meg will make you feel at home and, if you still wish to, we'll talk this over again at the week-end. I have a say too, you know, mother."

Polly was amazed at Bob's masterliness. Never since Peter Tilbrook, in the early days of their coming to Adelaide, had reprimanded her, with a look, for her vanity had anybody save Nathan stood out against her. She had been so accustomed to doing everything without consulting any one that it came as a queer surprise to find her younger son offering her advice and expecting her to take it. She smiled to herself, and owned that there was more go in

Bob than she had expected. "Nevertheless," she said to herself, "I'll say me say in two-three days, an' then go look for an 'ouse."

On the morning of Christmas Day Bob took Polly to the large shed at the back of his house.

"Now, mother," he said, as they approached the door, "this is something I haven't told you about."

"Well, for a shed 'tis purty big," said Polly looking at the long iron building.

"That's the point," Bob replied. "It isn't a shed, mother. It's a manufacturing plant!"

"Manu—— what?" ejaculated Polly. "It da look like plain shed to me."

Bob unlocked the door, and that in itself amazed Polly, coming as she did from a town where locks, though installed, were never used. She walked ahead of him into the building. The iron walls and roof were painted white. That was the first thing Polly noticed, and the second was the smell—and not a nice smell at that. She sniffed.

"What can I smell?" she asked.

"Rabbit skins," said Bob.

"Lan' sakes, rabbit skins! What do 'ee want wi' they there."

Bob faced her squarely. "Mother," he said, "I haven't told you, but I'm not at South's any longer. Seven months ago I left there and began in business on my own account."

"Not—not rabbits!" said Polly wildly, genuinely upset.

Bob took a deep breath. "Rabbit skins are something to do with it, mother. You see, I'm in partnership with a man called Cherringford, and we make felt hats."

"Felt hats? What from?" questioned Polly.

"Rabbit skins," answered Bob.

Polly took a moment to realize what he had been saying, then she cried out in panic, "Thee must be mad, Bob. Why, thee was gettin' two pound ten to South's, wassen 'ee?"

"Three pounds, mother, when I left. Mr South had raised my salary when I married Meg."

"An'," said Polly, incredulously, "thee da chuck up a good-payin' job like that there to go an' make felt 'ats out o' stinkin' rabbit skins. Bob, thee's daft. I be 'shamed of 'ee!"

"Not so daft as you may think, mother. My partner is a man who knows the trade from A to Z. He worked in a factory in Munton, near Manchester, for twenty years, and was sent to Australia for his health's sake. He's consumptive, but he can work as hard and as long as I can, and he's teaching me all he knows. Mother, there's money in hats—felt hats. You see, there's a chance of a fortune if I can work up the business."

"'Ats!" said Polly disgustedly. "Don't talk to me about 'ats. I knaw all there be to knaw 'bout un outside an' in, but I never 'eared tell o' felt 'ats made o' rabbit skins afore this. I never did."

"Well, what did you think they were made from?"

Polly was nonplussed. "Never gave un a thought," she owned up at last.

"Well I did, mother," said Bob, warming to his subject. "Look here, mother. What sort of hats do men wear?"

"Straw boaters," said Polly at once, "from what I seed o' men in Adelaide, yesterday. The women wear un too, I see. Some do down to Moonta, an' I 'ate the sight o' the things. Give me an 'at that da take time an' trouble to make. There be no profit in women's straw boaters for me. They be the ruin o' milliners."

"What do men wear at Moonta?" Bob asked. "Straw deckers?"

"The young lads do," said Polly, "but all the rest da wear 'ard-'itters."

"There!" said Bob, vastly pleased. "And they are made of felt!"

"Thee don't say!"

"I do that. And what's more, I can make them here in my shed."

"Show!" commanded Polly, alive at last.

"Well, come on," said Bob, his heart pumping, for he had banked on his mother's approval. She was a business woman to her finger-tips.

He showed her the benches where the fur was combed from the rabbit skins then teased, and he lifted the top of a huge box-like apparatus, and Polly saw the loose fur lying there in a pile ready to be agitated by a blower which, as Bob explained, kept it in motion, causing particles of matted fur and seeds to fall to the bottom of the box.

"See, mother," said Bob, "a belt carries the loose, clean fur from that compartment to this one, and here the fur is further agitated and comes into contact with the dampened perforated metal cones on this revolving disk. The fur adheres to the tall cones layer by layer, and at certain intervals we spray the 'bat', as it is called, with boiling water, and then more fur is allowed to settle in layers on the cone."

Polly nodded. "I understand," she said.

"Well," continued Bob, "we take the loose shapeless-looking bat from the cone and swathe in it damp cloths, put it with several more and place them between the rollers above this vat which, when the process is in oper-ation, is filled with steaming water. The rollers are called 'settlers', mother, and roll the fur more closely together, making it cohere—stick together—and the steam serves to shrink it."

"Sounds clear 'nough," commented Polly.

Bob laughed. "We can hardly see across the shed for steam when the settlers are going." He walked towards another vat in the corner. "This bath is to shrink them once more, mother, and in the hot water we place a mixture of acid and a secret ingredient of my partner's who, by the way, is a clever man." He paused then, and pointed to a large tub in one corner. "That's the dyeing vat," he explained.

Polly crossed to it and looked in. "Black!" she said.

"The hats are black," said Bob. "Next," he continued, eager to resume the narrative, "the bat is dipped in the shrinking vat again, then is placed on this revolving cone, with another steam-heated cone on top of it, and pressed into a rough shape. Even then it hardly resembles a hat."

He pointed this way and that, and Polly followed him about, fingering and inspecting everything as Bob explained it to her.

"This bath," he went on, "is the dipping-bath where the bats are stiffened with a varnish of shellac and borax. And," he smiled at Polly, "you'll recognize this kind of wooden hat-shape, mother. Well, here we steam the bat to any head size. And this," he finished proudly, pointing, "this is the blocking machine."

Polly was interested now and in a familiar province. "I blocks all me 'ats by 'and," she said, "wi' wet cloths an' 'ot irons."

"Well, this is something new, mother. We've only installed this recently, and it cost a good bit of money, and we're lucky to have it. You see, on this metal die the bat has its first good shaping, and we do the edges later with a hand iron."

"Well, I be glad to see machines can't do evrathin'," said Polly. "Some o' the old ways be still 'ard to beat."

"Yes, but machines will do everything in a little while, mother. This plant will change a dozen times in the next twenty years, and the machines will be better every time." He drew a deep breath, and walked towards a narrow table under a high window. "Last of all, mother, the finishing-table. Here the brims are turned and cut, and after a final shaping the hat—for it has changed its name now—is polished with fine sand-paper. That's the lot, mother. That's a rough outline of the way in which Mr Cherringford and I make men's felt hats."

"What's that there sewin'-machine for?" asked Polly, pointing to one mounted on a dais at the far end of the shed.

"That's for binding the edges. The linings we stick in by hand. Then we band them."

Bob let down the flap of a wide cupboard, and Polly saw there two rows of black hard-hitter hats.

"Good law!" Polly exclaimed. "They da look like 'ats!"

Bob selected one, glanced at the size and tried it on.

Polly walked round him. "They be real 'ats," she said at last.

It was enough for Bob, and he was now assured of his mother's interest. They sat on the dais with their backs to the sewing-machine, and Bob talked to Polly for an hour of the lucky chance that had brought the consumptive Mr Cherringford to Mr South's shop in Rundle Street, and of Mr South's refusing to have anything to do with the scheme and Bob's following the man out and obtaining his address. He told, too, of Meg's father's generosity in lending them one hundred pounds with which to begin the venture, of its undoubted success and the evident future of the little hat-manufacturing plant.

"There's money in it, mother—real money," he convinced Polly. "I'm actually making a little, and I've great hopes of making a good deal more. You see, there is going to be a gradual change in men's headgear. Soon they won't trouble to wear straw hats in summer and hard felt hats in winter. Already there is talk of a soft felt hat that I think men in Australia will wear universally, all the year round. We can make them: the shape's all that counts, and we can block any shape we want. Straw hats will die right out, because men want something that will last and not smash up or blow off, something comfortable and long-wearing—and the answer is felt hats! . . . I'm right, mother. You see if I'm not."

Polly got to her feet. "Well, Bob," she said, simply, "us 'ave lived by 'ats all our lives, so can't do no 'arm to go on livin' by un. I got faith in 'ee, me son, sure 'nough."

Bob stood up too now, his face alight. "Mother, I knew you'd understand," he said, gritting his teeth in the old manner of his boyhood when excited or deeply moved. "I'll be a rich man yet, and the hats'll do the trick."

Polly had a quiet talk with Meg after the Christmas dinner, which had consisted of boiled mutton and greens and sweet mince pies for dessert. They were washing up the dishes, and Bob was sitting on the veranda beside the baby who was awake but quiet in its crib.

"Well," said Meg to Polly, "what do you think of Bob's new business, mother?"

Polly, still not quite accustomed to the pleasant sensation of having Meg call her "mother", waited a moment before replying. " 'E seems to think it'll pay all right," she said, wiping a plate very carefully and placing it on the pile beside her. "An' I be of a mind to say it may too. What dost 'ee think of un, me dear?"

Meg laughed softly, wiping the suds from her hands. "If Bob thinks it's all right, I do too," she said. "But he's more keen to know what you think of it, mother. He values your opinion more than any one else's, I think."

"That be 'cause 'ats be me trade," said Polly.

"I think he's satisfied," continued Meg, "now that you've seen the plant and know what he's doing. It worried him a little at first to know if he were doing the right thing, but lately he's been easier in his mind."

"That be 'cause things be workin' out better," said Polly. " 'Ow dost manage 'bout the money part, Meg?"

"Well, mother, as long as I get a pound or so for rent and housekeeping I don't mind a scrap. Bob knows what he's about, and it doesn't cost much for us to live. I'm careful, mother. You'll find that out. We live sparingly, and I grow our own vegetables and keep half a dozen fowls, and we don't spend anything for luxuries. I can make a shilling go as far as most people and more than some, but I never scrimp or stint—just go carefully."

"Well, if Bob da watch what da go into the purse an' thee da keep an eye on what da come out, I'll say there ull be a bit left down bottom of un for a rainy day, me dear, an' that be all to it. As they da say back 'ome, ' 'Tis not the money that da go through thy 'ands, but what sticks to thy fingers, that counts.' "

"Bob's a saver," Meg praised.

" 'E musta been," said Polly. " 'Ow ever 'e got this 'ere furniture 'bout 'im beats me. 'E've sent me five shillin' of 'is week's wages since 'e started earnin'."

"It's all second-hand, mother," said Meg. "Bob picked it up at auction marts, and we painted it afresh ourselves."

" 'Tis a credit, an' no mistake," said Polly. "An' I 'ave a feelin' 'ere," she touched the bosom of her frock, "that thees won't allus 'ave deal chairs, me dear. Bob 'ave got is 'ead screwed on the right way an' da knaw a good thing when 'e da see un, in more ways nor one." And Meg construed that rightly to mean praise for herself, and gave Polly a kiss for it, to Polly's secret satisfaction.

By March of 1901 Polly was settled in a small cottage in Archer Street, North Adelaide, a short walk across the Park Lands from Meg and Bob. Bob printed a card and placed it in her parlour window—"Ladies' hats cleaned, trimmed.

Ladies' smart hats made to order on the premises"—for Polly was determined to work if she could find work to do.

She dug and planted a little front garden, sowing it with seeds she had always wanted to grow and had never had time to plant in Moonta, since the ground of her miniature back yard there had had to be trenched before plots could be made. She emulated Meg and filled the front veranda of her one-eyed little cottage with green and flowering things, and longed for the time when her garden would be bright with balsams, cherry-pie, lavender and candytuft.

She also made the big boxes in which Bob packed his hats for sale to the warehouses in Adelaide, pleased that she too had a hand in the business of Thomas and Cherringford, Hatters. She cut the boxes from great sheets of cardboard, oval in shape and a yard in depth, and covered them on completion with shiny white paper, making them so expertly and quickly that Bob was moved to declare that he did not know which was the better job, the box or the hats inside it.

This was Polly's life for five years. Then, Bob's business expanding and new premises being urgently necessary, the shed was dismantled and the contents were moved to a commodious iron building in Wright Street, Adelaide, where Bob and his partner installed a new plant and engaged more hands. The unbelievable was coming true and Bob was getting on in the world, but he and his wife and their three children—they had three girls, one an infant in arms, now—stayed on in their house in Lower North Adelaide.

When Bob moved into his new factory he gave the contract for the hat-boxes to a firm of cardboard-box makers, and Polly, left thus with more time on her hands, once again began to think about living the life of a lady. She unpinned the notice from the parlour lace curtains, and made a bonfire of her hat-shapes in the back yard.

"I be finished wi' makin' 'ats for other people, thank God. An' nobody but me an' 'Im knaws 'ow glad I be." She was now receiving enough from her sons to keep her happily comfortable, and at last turned her mind to enjoying her old age.

She had kept a scrapbook through the years of all

Richard's literary publications, for he had sent cuttings of his compositions to her regularly, as they appeared in the American papers; but she had been receiving few of late, for Richard was now a partner in the publishing and book-binding firm of the Walton Press in Philadelphia, and was more interested in what went on to a book than into it.

Polly was proud of her boys, and longed for the day when Richard would come back to Australia. The yearning she felt towards Richard was akin to the hopeless longing she felt to see Allen, Annie and Nathan once more, for to her it seemed as if Richard had gone as far away as the limits of another world.

The photo of the group of Richard, Euphemia and the boys, taken especially for his mother years ago, held pride of place on her mantelshelf, and she often peered at them all through her near-sighted eyes, tracing in Richard's broad forehead a likeness to Nathan's wide brow and seeing her own smile in his eyes. Euphemia she passed over as being too elegant and therefore too much like her mother Caroline, whom Polly had never seen but towards whom she had always felt an unaccountable dislike. The two boys, Roderick and Theodore, she loved intensely, and almost forgave Euphemia her elegance because of her astounding liberality in having supplied Richard with two such fine sons at a birth.

The Great War of 1914-18 made little difference to Bob's hat-manufacturing business, for his prophecy of the soft-felt hat as the universal headwear for Australian men had been realized years before, and consequently this was to his advantage. Except for the fact that the places left in the factory by young men, when these enlisted for active service, had to be filled by older men for the dyeing and vat work and by young girls at the finishing-tables, there was no difference in the output of felt hats. When it became evident that fewer men's hats could reasonably be expected to sell, the firm turned its attention to making felt hats for women, and also accepted a government contract for the Australian soldiers' felt hats, and the dye in the big vats was changed to khaki and the factory continued to prosper.

Thomas and Cherringford opened a city distributing centre and wholesale showroom to the trade in Hindley Street, and Bob went there himself every day in a grey tailored suit, and left the smelly, steaming factory in charge of a capable foreman. In 1915 he bought out his partner, Edmund Cherringford, and saw him off at the Outer Harbour on a trip to Switzerland and a sanatorium there.

The greatest evidence of Thomas prosperity was the moving of Bob and his family to a many-gabled residence in Brougham Place, North Adelaide: that exclusive, elevated street overlooking a fine public garden and with a panoramic view of all Adelaide and the hills beyond. Bob did not forget his mother in this era of prosperity, and bought for her the little house in Archer Street from which she would be moved neither by argument nor persuasion, for Polly at seventy-seven had as strong a will and as steady a purpose as she had had at twenty-seven.

Although Bob was eligible for active service with the Australian forces abroad he was not accepted, the loss of his trigger-finger proving the bar to his enlistment.

Polly consoled him with the practical advice that, "Never thee mind, Bob, me son. Somebody 'ave got to stay to 'ome an' make money, an' it might as well be thee."

Young Margaret, finishing off an education which, in her later school-days, had included everything in the curriculum of the fashionable school she attended, was happiest when visiting her grandmother at the house in Archer Street, now so near to her own beautiful home. Her sisters, Eleanor and Penelope, called by the family "El" and "Pen", had been eager to accompany her to Polly's in the days of their living in Lower North Adelaide; but the change in their surroundings and the increasing pleasure of living in a new home with a fully-equipped doll's house and sand-pile, and a chestnut pony named "Dandy" to be ridden in the early mornings and on Saturday afternoons dimmed their memory of the quiet pleasures of their grandmother's little house in Archer Street.

But with Margaret it was different. The old woman and the young spent their happiest hours together there, unearthing the faded glories of Polly's clothes-chest, unwrapping the wax doll, and once more going over the story of little Annie who went away. The hours of Polly's life that might have been lonely were filled with joy in this pretty grand-daughter who was content to spare a little of her time for an old woman who had nothing to give her in return but a host of stories, a quaint philosophy of life and the advice that it was a good thing for any young woman to know how to use a needle. The story of the little shop at Moonta was the most fascinating tale of all, and how was Polly to know that twenty years later this grand-daughter was to own the most exclusive hat shop in London with an old-fashioned, hand-painted sign—"The Bonnet Shop"—above its patrician glass door and with the smartest women in London for its clientele, among them a foreign princess who was to wed a British prince.

In 1921 Bob, being now in his fiftieth year and having amassed what he owned to be a "fair thing", retired from business and planned to take his wife and three daughters for a trip to England. Polly, who longed to go but knew her strength forbade it, farewelled them with a heavy heart, wondering how she, at eighty-three, would be able to fill in a year until they returned.

Bob had installed a young woman, Hilda Humphrey, a semi-trained nurse, to housekeep for and tend to Polly, and left his mother in her charge with many misgivings. His wife Meg was most anxious to make the trip and, the girls being of an age when travel was considered a desirable adjunct to an already liberal education, he resigned himself to leaving Polly, and turned his face towards the long-delayed fulfilment of his heart's desire: a trip to the old country.

Bob and his family had been away from Australia but two months when Polly received a letter from Richard bearing the astounding news that he, Euphemia and one of their sons were coming to Australia, Richard having obtained the managership of Lee, Crompton and Sons, Publishing and Printing House, in George Street, Sydney.

For the first time in Polly's life she did not know what to do. Holding the open letter in her hand, she walked to and fro from room to room in trembling uncertainty. Had Bob and Meg been at home she would have tied on her black silk hat and, grasping her silver-topped ebony cane, would have walked to Brougham Place and electrified the family with the news; but there was no one to tell now. Polly's mind was in a tumult with the knowledge that she alone must undertake the joyous though bewildering pleasure of welcoming Richard, and for half an hour after the reading of the letter she could do no more than walk about the house and garden with limbs that shook. After a while, however, she regained her strength and went in to Miss Humphrey with a firm step.

"Us'll 'ave to look lively, miss," Polly said. "The 'ole 'ouse 'ave got to be turned out from front bedroom to back, an' I'll get a man in to paint the roof an' all the woodwork, outside an' in. This place 'ave got to shine like a new threepenny bit afore me Rich da set eye 'pon it."

"Don't you think you'd better write and consult Mr Robert about it, my dear?" asked Miss Humphrey, an anxious tone in her voice. "Do you think it wise to have the painting done before he returns?"

"Fiddlesticks!" said Polly with asperity. "I don't 'ave to write to me Bob 'bout ev'ry breath I da draw. If I da want 'ouse painted, 'ouse'll be painted, an' that's all to it."

The house was painted and the garden ready and waiting for Richard two weeks before he arrived in Sydney, and he stayed there a week before journeying to Adelaide.

He was accompanied by his wife and son, Theodore. Roderick had married his fiancée, a young nurse, on the eve of his parents' departure for Australia and, although a qualified medical practitioner, was completing a special course at a Philadelphian Medical College, wishing later to specialize in laryngology and otology, which Richard was to describe to Polly as being merely the treatment of the diseases of the throat, larynx and ear. He was very surprised, later, when Polly expressed her satisfaction at Roderick's decision to stay in America and applauded his good sense.

"No good," she told Richard at that time, "were ever done by uprootin' a man afore 'e've finished what 'e've set 'is mind on. Change o' scene da most times mean a change o' plan. Besides, 'twill do un good to be left by 'isself. A wife'll be a drivin' power to un, an' 'e'll find 'is feet quickest when there be fewest of 'is own about to watch 'is step. 'Tis a good thing for a man to make 'is own way up in the world."

The last few weeks of waiting for Richard's arrival in Adelaide had been hard for Polly to bear, and equally trying for poor harassed Miss Humphrey, who took Polly for long walks about North Adelaide by way of diverting the old woman's mind from the subject of the impending reunion with her son.

On one of these walks they were passing Polly's church, the Archer Street Methodist, when Polly stopped stock still, listening to children's voices proceeding from the hall at the rear of the church.

"What's that?" asked Polly, turning her head in the direction of the voices.

"It's children playing," Miss Humphrey told her patiently.

"I knaw that," Polly answered sharply, "but what they doin' there? Tissen Sunday-school day."

"There's a Montessori Kindergarten there now. It has been open since Easter," said Miss Humphrey, who had gleaned the information herself a few days previously.

Polly walked in the direction of the sound, and peered in through the wooden bars of the picket gate. She saw in the yard numbers of poorly-clad young children whose ages ranged from two to six years and who were being taught by the free, self-development methods of the Montessori sytem of child education.

"I be goin' in to watch," Polly announced suddenly. And, in spite of all that Miss Humphrey could do, Polly walked boldly in and addressed one of the young teachers, asking if they might stay and see the children. Visitors were welcome, she discovered, so Polly went into the building and, the children being now assembled, she and Miss Humphrey sat in chairs placed along one side of the room and watched the little ones at their work.

Polly was amazed to see the tiny children dusting chairs, arranging flowers, grading multi-shaded colours that were part of the Montessori material, unrolling grass mats, choosing work from the big cupboard in the room, showing no interest in the visitors, but concentrating on those exercises which trained both mind and hand and were all part of this modern educational system. With motherly appreciation Polly saw a little child in a check apron undress a doll, bath it, clothe it in a clean dress, put it in a cradle and then sit rocking it with her foot in much the same way as Polly had done with her own children so many years before. This, of all the things Polly saw that morning, most touched her heart.

She came to the kindergarten several times during the time that remained before Richard's arrival, and on one occasion brought with her a parcel wrapped carefully in white linen. She gave the parcel to the directress, saying, "I brought this for the childern, me dear. I 'ad a little girl o' me own once, an' this were 'ers. I want 'ee to let these little uns 'ave it."

The parcel was the wax bride doll in its yellowing finery, with eyes still bright and still opening and closing when the doll was moved. The faded gold hair, puffed about the temples in two little mounds, was arranged in the style that Queen Victoria had worn as a young woman. The directress thanked her and, after Polly had gone, showed it to one of her assistants.

"Whatever are we to *do* with this?" she said. "I can't let the children play with it. It can't be undressed; its body is made of sawdust, so it can't be bathed, and it will melt in the sun if the children take it outside. What on earth shall I do with it?"

The young assistant, who had seen the look in Polly's eyes when she had handed it over, quietly answered, "Give it to me. I'll put it in the cupboard in the other room, and when Christmas comes I'll make a crown for its head and it can go on the top of the tree. It will look like a fairy up there, and it would please the old lady to know we'd found such a good use for her little girl's doll."

"That's a splendid idea," said the directress briskly, returning to her table and drawing out the notebook in which she recorded her assistants' merits and demerits; and beside the word "Originality" she wrote "Very good indeed".

The day of Richard's arrival dawned cold and clear, and Polly was awake and dressed an hour before her usual time and, by dint of bullying Miss Humphrey, was on the Adelaide platform awaiting the Melbourne express a full half-hour before it was due to arrive.

When the train, with a roar of steam and a grinding of brakes, at last stopped at the platform, Polly's heart was bounding so in her breast that she felt she might faint before she set eyes on her son.

"Steady, my dear," Miss Humphrey consoled, feeling Polly's hand trembling on her arm. "Be calm, now."

Polly had no breath for a rejoinder even if she had heard Miss Humphrey, which she did not, for her whole attention was on the moving crowd about her, searching each face for a memory of her son whom she had not seen for almost forty years.

Richard, with Euphemia and Theodore beside him, stepped from the train almost in front of Polly, but she was so intent on peering over the heads of those about her towards the carriages that extended farther along the platform that she did not see the grey-haired man with the neatly-clipped, short vandyke beard who stood watching her from the doorway of the carriage he had just left.

Richard knew his mother immediately. The years that had whitened his hair appeared to have dealt kindly with Polly. The spectacles were unfamiliar and she seemed to have grown shorter, but the straight, stout, black-clad little figure remained the same. Sorrow, time and loneliness had set a stamp upon her features, but he knew the tender mouth, the firm chin and the smooth soft skin that he had kept seeing in his dreams for so many years. He knew his mother.

"That's mother," Richard said softly to his wife and son. "Wait here a moment. I'd like to meet her by myself." And he walked towards Polly and stood a few feet from her.

Miss Humphrey sensed who he was, and put out a hand to touch Polly's arm, meaning to draw her attention towards him, but he shook his head at her and, walking forward a step or two, took off his hat.

Polly, noticing this gesture in her survey of all about her, glanced at him, then over and beyond him. He stood still, looking at her, and she, ever seeking, found her eyes drawn again to his. She looked away, then sharply back again. He smiled at her—the grey-haired man smiled at her! Her lips turned upwards in polite response, then the lower lip sagged a little and her eyes opened wide. Her breath stopped and her heart turned over in her breast.

The grey-haired man came closer, put out a hand and touched her. "Mother!" he said.

Polly threw back her head at that, and a light leapt into her eyes like an uprising flame. She flung wide her short, trembling arms, and her face shone like the morning. The years dropped from her and, like a mantle, fell too from the man before her.

She spoke, and in her voice was a triumphant sound, as of one who has found what she never thought to find again. "My boy!" she said, smiling up into his face. "My boy!"

CHAPTER XX

RICHARD, Euphemia and Theodore stayed for a fortnight in Adelaide at an hotel on North Terrace and, from his window in the early mornings, Richard would look out over the bulk of Parliament House and beyond the tree-bordered Torrens Lake and the tall spires of St Peter's Cathedral towards North Adelaide. He picked out the pointed roof of the Archer Street church and knew that in its shadow his mother would be living for the last few years that remained to her.

Richard's disappointment at not seeing his brother Bob and Bob's wife and children helped more than anything to make him realize the loneliness that Polly must have endured since Nathan's death and since her sons left her and, not for the first time, he felt in his heart that restless, irritable sensation of mind and body that men who have driven themselves too hard in life and taken too few rests by the wayside feel when, at almost sixty, they are continuing to do the work they did at thirty.

"God," he said to himself, "if I could only have done with business and throw everything up and settle down to enjoy a few years of peace! I haven't the same kick I had in me a few years back."

He breathed in deeply of the chill morning air, and Euphemia's voice called to him from the bed.

"Will it be a pleasant day, Richard?" she asked, yawning behind her white hand and smoothing her soft grey, marcelled hair from her eyes and tucking it under her lace boudoir-cap.

"Cold," he answered shortly, turning from the window.

Euphemia looked at him quizzically. "Not moody again, are you, Richard?"

"Moody?" said Richard, in an aggrieved voice. "What do you mean 'moody', Phemie?" Then he sighed and, without awaiting her answer, continued: "It's not moodiness, my dear, but plain tiredness. Standing there this morning, I discovered a painful truth. I'm not as young as I used to be—which in itself is a confession that to-day, at least, I'm feeling my age."

Euphemia made a wry face. "Oh Richard, please don't! Remember I'm over fifty too, and grey as a badger. We woke up too early this morning, that's the trouble. We'll feel better as the day advances. I think it's the climate, or the lack of steam heating, or too much meat in our diet that's making us both so miserable here. We haven't adjusted ourselves to these conditions yet. That may be the trouble. We want to develop an easy optimism, I'm told, and a total disregard of good manners in order to feel at home in Australia."

Richard was indignant. "Phemie, that will do! I'll not have you running down this country. I'll admit I've been out of it too long and find it hard to readjust myself to everything." He paused. "But anyway, an easy optimism is a jolly good thing to have. I've always had a nervous pessimism in regard to my life and work. I would be a happier man now, Euphemia, if I'd been a little less conscious of my duty to make a success of myself. I've always driven myself with the goad of conscience and the wish to be a credit to the faith—your father's and mine—in me. That has hung over me ever since I left Australia, and I often wonder if I shouldn't have done better for myself and my mother if I'd stayed here and cultivated that easy optimism you despise, my dear, and kept my execrable manners."

Euphemia smiled quite pleasantly. "Now, Richard dear, calm down. I meant no harm, and we're not going to quarrel at our age. We have a reputation for marital felicity to maintain, haven't we? Don't let's be silly," she added, sitting up and throwing back the bed-clothes preparatory to getting out of bed. "Besides," she continued, "haven't you thought that if you'd never left Australia, if father hadn't given you your 'chance' as you so often call it, and if you hadn't come to England, then you wouldn't have met me—and where, oh where, would be Theodore and Roderick? Surely they're tangible proof that you were meant to come to England. Explain that, Richard! It will take all your logic and your wisdom and your wit."

Richard flung up his hands. "There is no explanation, my dear, except the word 'chance' that you object to, but this time its meaning is coincidence." He ruffled his hair with a heavy hand and smiled.

"Richard, don't be exasperating! I haven't the least idea what you mean, but I'm sure by the look in your eye that you're being wittily cruel," Euphemia said severely, putting her feet with great deliberation into her satin mules.

Richard found a great many features in Adelaide that Philadelphia possessed. Each city has been laid out with mathematical precision and is in the form of a parallelogram. The streets of both cities run east and west and north and south, and at the points of intersection of the main thoroughfares the same system of open spaces planted with trees and shrubs exists.

Sitting beside Polly on a circular seat placed around the bole of a spreading Moreton Bay fig-tree in Victoria Square, Richard told his mother of the fine Washington and Franklin Squares in Philadelphia and of the great Franklin fountain there.

"That's what Adelaide needs here," he said to Polly, nodding towards the four areas of tree-surrounded lawns that comprised Victoria Square. "It would give an impression of coolness, and the trees would form a splendid background for the spray of water."

He told her, too, of the public buildings in Philadelphia in many of which was incorporated snowy white marble hewn from the adjacent quarries of Chester and Montgomery, and Polly listened to him describe the Custom House built on the pattern of the Parthenon at Athens with a Doric portico of eight marble columns, and the Girard, Pennsylvanian and North American Banks, all faced with white marble, magnificently glistening.

"Do you know, mother," he said, as they turned to look down the imposing length of King William Street which extends through Adelaide from North to South Terraces, "I think that in time Adelaide will be a younger sister to Philadelphia. This fine King William Street compares favourably with our Market Street, and this square here, if those iron railings were removed and these great Morton Bay figs cut down, the turf renewed and the square planted with more ornamental trees and banks of flowers—why, this would be a beauty spot!"

" 'Tis purty enough as 'tis," said Polly.

"Ah yes, mother, but a city doesn't want prettiness, it wants beauty. There's a difference. Adelaide has done well, but she wants to go much farther to earn a reputation for beauty. Adelaide wants professional men on her city council—men of vision and experience, who can imagine this a great and beautiful city and have sense enough to turn their visions into reality. The bar that holds these men back from municipal positions is the fact that, with all their ability and skill, they could only suggest a scheme and could have no hand in putting it into practice themselves. An architect on a city council would never be free from the public opinion that he was 'getting something out of it'. I realize that a scheme to admit practising professional men to civic positions and to allow them to tender for work done would never be condoned, because of the fear of graft and the fact that some men would take advantage of their position to further their own private interests; but I see no reason why a committee of architects, business men and qualified landscape gardeners couldn't form, in every city, a Committee of Civic Beautification. What if they did earn a good fee for their work? It would result in the making of a city-beautiful, and men deserve to be paid well for that. What do you say, mother?"

"I up'olds evrathin' 'ee da say, me son. But go on, do. I dearly loves to 'ear the sound o' thy voice."

"Take North Terrace," continued Richard, warming to his subject. "That's got the makings of the loveliest boulevard in the Southern hemisphere. Very few cities have a finer row of public buildings than those extending from Government House to East Terrace. They'd make a dignified background for an ambitious scheme of trees and turf and flowers. The time is not far distant, mother, when every city in the Commonwealth will envy Adelaide her North Terrace."

"Well," said Polly, "give us time, me son. Us can't do

evrathin' to once. Us'll 'ave un yet, Rich—marble banks, fountains galore an' streets full o' trees—but give us time!"

Rich laughed. "I won't expect too many marble buildings, mother. There's not enough of the stuff available, and what there is of it has never been fully exploited. I hear South Australia has a quantity of fine marble at Macclesfield and Angaston. Perhaps that will be put to good architectural use in time." He became very serious. "And I don't see why there shouldn't be granite buildings, mother. South Australia has enough granite on her southern coasts to reface every bank in Australia—and jolly lovely they'd look, too!"

"Well," said Polly contentedly, "thees 'ad better write to the newspapers 'bout un, Rich."

Polly was a little in awe of her grandson at first, and Theodore, frankly bored with Adelaide and his father's reminiscences, improved the shining hour by giving his grandmother extravagant details about the life he and his family had led in Philadelphia. He had a wealth of stories and funny incidents which, in lieu of a better audience, he told to Polly. After a few days of accustoming herself to his quick, nasal speech she ventured to imitate him, laughing with him then at her very good attempt. Theodore, assured of a good reception, imitated her in turn, and a mutual interest sprang up between them, and Theodore owned to himself that there was "life in the old girl yet". He developed quite an affection for his grandmother, admired her wit, her straight body and active mind, and saw some of his own characteristics in her. She had been a worker, and so was he. She made hats, but he, Theodore Menadue Thomas, would build houses, churches—cathedrals maybe. He was to be an architect and, on completing his war-interrupted studies and attaining his associateship, would practise his profession in Sydney. Already he saw sky-scrapers rearing their heads above glorious Sydney harbour—sky-scrapers that he would build!

Richard, Euphemia and Theodore returned to Sydney, and there Bob met them some months later on his return from England and America, and the two families—with the exception of Polly in Adelaide, Margaret in London where

she had remained to study dress designing, and Roderick—
met, inspected and approved of each other.

Two years later Richard came to Adelaide to spend
Christmas there, and when about to return he said to
Polly, "Mother, I've an idea. I've wanted to do this thing
for years, but it hasn't been convenient when I've been in
Adelaide. Listen, will you come back with me to the
peninsula when I'm in South Australia again? You and
Bob and I will go back for a day or two and see the old
cottage at Wallaroo Mines and the shop at Moonta, and
revive old memories. The mines are all closed now, mother,
but there'll still be plenty for us to see. Will you come?"

"I'll come like a shot," said Polly. " 'Tis summat I've
allus yearned to do—to go back. But Rich, me son, thees'll
'ave to 'urry. I be an old woman, me dear, an' me time
be almost come."

Richard was not in Adelaide again until September of
the year 1927, and Polly at that time was eighty-nine years
of age.

She was still active, and worked about in her little garden
weeding, planting and cultivating her flower patch, and
went for a long walk with Miss Humphrey each afternoon.

"Do you think mother is fit to go?" Richard asked Miss
Humphrey when the trip to the peninsula was discussed.
"She's almost ninety, and it will be a long journey for an
old woman."

"Well, Mr Thomas," said Miss Humphrey, sighing, "I'm
sure I don't know what I shall do with her if she doesn't
go. She's set her heart on this trip, and Mr Robert has
asked Dr Buller what he thinks about it and he is of the
opinion that if she wants to go it will probably be a good
thing for her. She's grown a little feebler these last few
years, but she's still strong—much stronger than you'd
guess. I really think, Mr Thomas, that she'd break her
heart if you didn't take her. . . . There's so little left for
her to enjoy," she added kindly.

So the day came when Polly, Bob and Richard, in Bob's
modern and comfortable motor-car, set out for Yorke's
Peninsula. They took with them Bob's chauffeur Millington
and Miss Humphrey.

The weather was mild as they drove along, and Polly sniffed the sweet spring air appreciatively.

" 'Twill be wattle-time," she said excitedly. "Us'll go out in the scrub, won't us, Rich?" she asked.

"I guess so," said Richard promptly, for he too felt the exhilarating essence of the spring and was as glad as his mother to find himself going back at last to the scenes of his boyhood.

"Funny thing we've never thought to go back before," mused Bob. "We could have made the trip a dozen times in the last twenty years since mother came to Adelaide. Don't know why we didn't."

"Thees 'ave 'ad no time, Bob," put in Polly. "An' besides, us never woulda gone now if Rich adden been so set on un. No matter 'ow much our thoughts da go back, us never do up an' go ourselves till somebody da make first move, though I weren't allus like that, I can tell 'ee."

Bob had arranged the trip so that Polly would not be too tired to appreciate her surroundings and it was decided that, by leaving in the late afternoon, the night could be spent at Port Wakefield and the following day be devoted to completing the journey to the peninsula and taking a trip from Kadina to Wallaroo Mines and Moonta.

Miss Humphrey was sensible of the responsibility they all took in bringing an old woman on such a journey.

Between Adelaide and Port Wakefield Polly made Millington stop the car several times while she related incidents of the coach journeys she had made along this road in the early days: " 'Ere 'twas we stopped for change of 'orses." Or, "See there? I went past when that there Institute 'All was bein' built. There was two black gins 'elpin' carry the stones." Or, "Wait a minute. See this 'ere 'ouse? I mind the coach stoppin' 'ere to set down a one-legged man with an 'arp on 'is back. Many's the time I wondered what 'e were doin' an' where 'e were goin'."

Polly's memory was as tenacious as ever, but as the journey progressed, Bob and Richard could not help noticing that the incidents Polly related to them were trifles that had impressed her at the time of their happening, and that the farther they receded from Adelaide the greater became her fund of simple reminiscences concerning the friends of their boyhood. Names that they both had forgotten for forty years were once more in their ears, and the nearer they came to Yorke's Peninsula the clearer did their vision of the old days become, until the present withdrew into the background and it seemed to all three of them that they were returning to the most real part of their lives.

By the time Port Wakefield was reached Polly was tired and silent, and Miss Humphrey helped her from the car. They all spent the night at an hotel there, Bob and Richard being quite content on this occasion to conform with their mother's pace. Only Millington was irked by his having to make the car crawl over a trip that could easily have been completed in two and a half hours, and did a little private cursing on the subject, so fortunately his opinion was not required.

Next morning they were on the latter half of the journey by ten o'clock, Polly, fresh after her sleep, feeling eager to be on her way. She remembered the hummocks, and related the incident of the red-hot axle and the can of cream. At the summit they stopped and looked back over the beautiful view across Port Wakefield and the blue shallows of the head of St Vincent Gulf, then once more turned the nose of the car along the straight white road that wound over the flat land towards their destination.

The way was still bordered with mallee and tea-tree, and the golden wattle and white paper daisies bloomed beside the road. Beyond stretched fertile paddocks of green wheat, oats and barley, with here and there a comfortable farmhouse red-roofed and backed with sheds, haystacks and a little strip of orchard and encircled with the acres of waving green. Wide paddocks lay fallow to the sun, with fat draught mares browsing on the last year's stubble, and long-legged foals that shied away, tossing their heels ridiculously and galloping after their mothers when Millington sounded the horn. For miles and miles the waving wheat paddocks extended, broken only by the strips of fallow and the acre that surrounded each homestead.

"What a harvest there will be here this year!" said Bob. "In a couple of months the crops will be as high as the fences. One would never guess this limestony country could be made to bear crops like this year after year."

"Nothing grew here but mallee in the old days," said Rich.

"Mallee land is wheat land," Bob replied. "It took the farmers a long time to find that out, but they realized it in the end and," he waved his hand toward the spread of green acres, "this is the result."

They were in Kadina before midday, and lunched at the Exchange Hotel. Then, after Polly had had a short rest, they entered the car again and began their pilgrimage to the scenes of their own life in the peninsula towns.

"Where first, mother?" asked Bob.

"To father an' the childern," said Polly steadily.

The car took them to the Kadina cemetery and stopped at the tall wrought-iron gates set in the long stone wall.

They found the grave of Nathan, Allen and Annie in the shade of a cypress-tree. The marble cross that Bob had had erected many years before was white and clean, and they all read the black-lettered names soberly.

Polly shed not a tear, for tears come less frequently to old eyes than many suppose. She loosened Miss Humphrey's clasp of her arm and sat slowly down on the raised marbled surface of the grave, and her black skirts flowed out on to the wild grass. She did not pray, but Bob, whose ears were keener than Richard's, heard her saying softly to herself, "Where be the rosemary? Where be me little Allen's rosemary gone to?"

She stretched out her hand and plucked two or three plants of shivery grass that had pushed their way up through the cement and the marble chips, then she patted down the dusty earth she had pulled up with their roots and smoothed back the white chips.

"I wonder what she is thinking of?" Richard asked himself. "She hardly seems moved at all. Poor mother, she's lived over her sorrow so often that now she is old it has lost its importance. Time heals all wounds."

Polly must have sensed his thoughts, for she put a hand on his knee and Richard, bending down, helped her to rise.

" 'Tis all so long ago," she said, pitifully.

They boarded the car and Millington, at Bob's direction, began the journey back to Kadina and thence to Wallaroo Mines.

"Mother," said Bob, as they drove silently along Graves Street, "you'll remember what I told you about Wallaroo Mines, won't you? You'll remember that mining operations have ceased there these four years and the machinery is dismantled and many of the cottages are already demolished? It won't look anything like it did when Rich and I were children. He and I are prepared to be disillusioned, mother, and I want you to remember that everything has its day and that the day for Wallaroo Mines is over. . . . But it was a good day while it lasted."

Millington turned to the left over the railway line, and they entered a wide tree-shaded street, Lipson Avenue.

"Wait," said Polly, alert at once. "Thee's taken wrong turnin'. This be township crossin', though they fine 'ouses 'ere be new since my time."

Back they went, and continued parallel with the railway line. Then, as they neared the mines crossing, Bob called out excitedly, "Well, here's our crossing, mother."

Polly covered her face with her black-gloved hands. "Go up to the gate an' stop, then I'll look," she said in a muffled voice.

"Ah," thought Rich, "this moves her! Home!" He glanced down at Polly's bent head, and something in his throat swelled and he looked away hurriedly.

Polly sat hunched up with her hands to her eyes. She felt the bump, bump of the tyres as they passed over the metalled strip between the railway lines, and she knew then they were in sight of the little white cottage, their first and only real home.

Bob leaned forward and the car slowed and stopped, but Polly waited.

"Shall I take un down now?" she asked.

There was a pause, then Rich put his hand on his mother's knee. "Take down your hands, mother," he said, "but there's nothing to see. My dear, the house is gone and there's nothing left but a pile of stones."

Never as long as he lived would Richard forget the look

on his old mother's face when she saw the spot where the cottage had been.

Except for the heaps of white stones and the scarred wreck of an old pepper-tree there was no sign that a house had once stood on that deserted spot.

"Where be Trevennick's 'ouse gone to?" Polly asked later, standing in the waste patch that had once been her little front garden. "Where be Trevaskis's and Johnny Poldoon's?"

Her sons could do nothing but shake their heads and point to other heaps of stones near by. "Gone!" said Bob, tersely.

"Farther along," said Rich, "the houses are still standing. They told me at the hotel that many of the occupants who have work in the township will stay on here, but that gradually, as the miners leave, the houses will be pulled down and the stones used for building purposes elsewhere. There were some comfortable houses on the mines built after our time here, you know. Let's take the car up to Office Shaft, Bob. I'd like to see the fitting-sheds if they're still there, and the stables. But I suppose they were pulled down before anything else."

"Let me bide 'ere," said Polly, sitting down slowly on the heap of stones. " 'Tis nice 'ere in the sun. Miss'll stay by me. Besides, I've seen enough, more'n enough!"

Miss Humphrey adjusted Polly's black silk umbrella, and stood beside her after the big car had gone away silently towards the old mine buildings.

"Just as well mother didn't come," said Rich, as he and Bob looked at the ruin of the mine offices: the great stone buildings with iron roofs missing, and the vacant, windowless wrecks open to the sun. The stables where the mine horses had been kept was a gaunt deserted pile of masonry. The tall, stone engine-houses still stood beside the shafts, but the engines and the boilers were gone, and two men were at work on Office Shaft dismantling the last of the gear. No sound other than the muffled noise of the wreckers at work disturbed the stillness of the spring afternoon, and to Bob and Richard the silence was uncanny.

"Remember the noise hereabouts in the old days, Rich?" asked Bob.

"Yes," Rich replied, "and I've heard folks who lived close

to the shafts say they got so used to the consant noise day and night that if they went away for a holiday they couldn't sleep, and if the skips here stopped at night they'd wake up."

Back by the stones, Polly was impatiently answering Miss Humphrey's questions.

"What's that hill over there called?" asked Miss Humphrey, pointing to a tall hill-like formation in the near distance.

"'Ill?" said Polly sharply, adjusting her spectacles. "That's no 'ill, that be a dump—rubbish from the mines."

"Tell me, Mrs Thomas," persisted Miss Humphrey, "were you really happy in this flat, arid spot?"

"Flat this spot may be an' arid too, for ought I da knaw o' the word, but mark this, me girl, I were 'appy 'ere, make no mistake. This little 'eap o' stones were the only 'ouse me an' me man ever bought an' paid for. 'Twas the only spot we was ever in we could call our own. I bore three childern 'ere an' buried one, an' more o' me life than I can call to mind now were lived be'ind they chimney stones. 'Appy? Yes, me dear. I can say I were 'appy, true 'nough."

Polly must have dozed there in the sun, or Miss Humphrey, seeing her sitting so still, must have thought she dozed, for when she saw the car returning she shook Polly gently by the arm, and the old woman opened her eyes and raised her head.

"Come along, dear," said Miss Humphrey, shutting the umbrella and placing her hand beneath Polly's arm. "Up-a-daisy."

Polly shook off the nurse's hand and rose unaided to her feet, standing there shakily until Richard came forward to help her to the car. Suddenly Polly stopped, and pointed to something shining among the stones.

"What is it?" asked Richard. "Have you lost something?"

Polly peered closer and, as Richard bent to pick up the shining object, she said firmly, "No, found summat." And Richard, straightening up, handed his mother the base of a small, triangular-shaped blue glass bottle.

"Look here, Bob," he called to his brother. "You mightn't remember this, but I do. It was stuck in the ground to outline the garden beds. Remember it?" He turned to Polly. "You do, mother."

"Well," said Bob, "I don't."

Polly reached out her hand for the piece of glass bottle. "Now I be sure they stones was our 'ouse," she said, smiling. "I didden quite believe it inside me till I saw that there." And she dropped it into the black silk bag that hung by a cord to her wrist.

They continued their drive along the back road to Moonta—not a bush track now, but a wide metalled road—and turned off at Cross Roads, and went into Moonta Mines by the way they had come in the wagonette so many years ago.

Now Polly saw the deserted mines where once had been activity and prosperity, saw the empty forsaken cottages and the roofless mine offices. But she seemed only half awake, and even the sight of the little shop, now plate-glassed in front with a green-tiled base to the window, could not rouse her beyond a wordless appraisement.

"I think we should be getting back to the hotel now," Miss Humphrey said quietly to Richard who, looking at his mother's tired face, agreed with her.

The car sped into Wallaroo with its deserted though not yet dismantled Smelting Works, and Rich pointed out to Polly the three jetties, and the enormous stacks of wheat beside the biggest jetty waiting to be shipped away. Here at least was definite proof that Yorke Peninsula was now a wheat-growing centre, and the Smelting Works' smoke-less chimneys were the monuments of a dead industry.

Next day, back in Adelaide again, Richard farewelled his mother as she lay in bed in her quiet little house.

"Good-bye, mother dear," he said, kissing her forehead.

"Good-bye, me son, an' God bless 'ee," she answered, running her old hand through his grey hair.

It was a few moments before he spoke again. "It wasn't a success, that going back, was it, mother?" he said, apologetically. "I might have known. One can't go back in life. It doesn't do to try."

"No," Polly answered, "there be no good done by goin' over agin what be past an' gone. Places like people da grow old, an' 'tis best to remember both when they was young."

And Richard had just arrived in Melbourne on his way to Sydney when the telegram reached him saying that his mother was dead.

The two brothers sat for a long while in the parlour of their dead mother's house. Meg and her daughters had left some hours ago, and Miss Humphrey had brought in tea and sandwiches to the two men as they sat over the gas fire talking about the old days when they had been young together.

"Well," said Bob, setting down his empty cup, "let's open mother's box. Miss Humphrey said mother kept her will there and her bank-book and that she always impressed it on her that we should open it together. I've never seen the will, but I always knew mother had made one."

The box had stood for years beside Polly's bed and was now on the gypsy table in the parlour, so Bob, rising and getting the box, sat down again with it on his knees. Miss Humphrey had placed the key in the lock as Polly had so often told her to do in this circumstance, and Bob turned it carefully and lifted the lid.

The box was of inlaid walnut, made as a jewel-box and given to Polly by Meg for some Christmas long past. Inside, neatly folded, was Polly's last will and testament, on a sixpenny will-form. Inserted between the folds was a bank-book. Bob placed both of these aside and, lifting the padded velvet tray, looked in at Polly's jewels.

They consisted of a man's silver watch and chain, and a gold brooch in the form of a sword with the word "Mizpah" on the hilt. Richard recognized this as being one that his mother had worn in their childhood, it being a parting gift from her brother Robert in England on the occasion of her departure for Australia. Beside the brooch was a tissue-paper packet, and this contained four curls of fine hair, two fair, one brown and one bright chestnut. In another packet was a small, red, buttoned boot, and at the bottom of the box, scattered on the blue velvet lining, were dried shrivelled leaves from a withered twig of rosemary; and the last jewel of all was the piece of blue glass bottle.

Neither of the men spoke and Bob slowly put the contents of the box into the lower compartment again and fitted back the velvet tray. He closed the lid quietly, then handed the will and the bank-book to Richard.

"You read it, Rich," he said huskily. "You're the elder."

There was no sound in the room except the crackling of the thick paper as Richard unfolded Polly's last request. He read it through to himself, then, with a brief look at Bob, reread it aloud.

This is the last Will and Testament of me:

MARY ELIZABETH THOMAS.

Everything I have I leave to my dear grandchildren in the hope that they may never have to leave home, but if they feel to go that they take their share of this and be beholden to nobody.

(Signed) MARY ELIZABETH THOMAS.

Witnesses.

WILLIAM NOBLE GRAY.

EMMALINA GRAY.

"Poor mother," said Bob at last, "she had little enough to leave them."

Richard opened the bank-book, glanced at it and handed it to Bob.

"Good Lord!" exclaimed Bob, raising his eyebrows. "Four hundred and thirty-five pounds!"

"How did she manage to do it?" Richard mused, closing the book. "She had no income."

Bob took the bank-book and looked down the list of amounts paid in and the dates beside them. "They go back to 1900," he said. "That's when mother came to Adelaide. This thirty-two pounds must have been for the sale of her stock at Moonta, and the hundred and two pounds brought forward must represent what she saved in the last years of her living at Moonta. The rest she saved in the next twenty-seven years. How did she do it!"

"Ah," said Rich meditatively, "we'll never know that, but the repeated not-available-till-cheque-collected stamps seem to hint that part of it at least consists of birthday and Christmas cheques that you and I sent her. She couldn't have used a penny of them, and the rest she must have saved from the money we jointly allowed her or from what she herself earned with hat-making since she came to Adelaide. Brave mother!" he added, genuinely moved.

"She must have saved it for the children all these years, from the time when there were only your two boys and my Margaret," said Bob.

"Who wrote the will?" Richard asked, glancing at the well-written document. "William Gray, I suppose. This signature and the writing are the same. There were Grays living next to us in Moonta. He was a clerk on the mines. They must be the people who helped mother make it out."

"She worded it herself," said Bob.

"Trust mother for that," Rich replied, smiling.

"Let's see, what does it say again?" said Bob, " '. . . to my dear grandchildren in the hope that they may never leave home. . . .'" He looked at Rich. "What did she mean by that? Do you think it comes from her own experience—that she was sorry about ever coming to Australia herself?"

Richard shook his head. "No, Bob. She always said she 'felt to come'. She uses that word here, too—'but if they feel to go'. That seems to imply a special right to go from home if the urge arises." He rubbed the edge of the bankbook with his lean finger. "There's a deeper meaning in it, Bob," he said. "I've an idea mother knew all along that I should never have been persuaded to leave home, and I think she wanted our children to stay in their own environment. Mother understood, Bob. She knew all the time that I'd never be the success I hoped to be."

"No," said Bob. "I think it broke her heart when you left home. That's her meaning."

"Perhaps," Rich answered, nodding.

" '. . . but if they feel to go'," Bob continued, " 'that they take their share of this and be beholden to nobody.' "

"Ah!" said Richard. "That's mother, through and through—'and be beholden to nobody'! She always wanted independence, but, except for those few years at Wallaroo Mines, she never had it. Beholden to Uncle Peter for a nominated passage to Australia; beholden to Uncle Robert for money she allowed to be stolen from her; beholden to the warehouse for her start in business; beholden to you and me, Bob, all the rest of her days because she had the misfortune to have a crippled miner for a husband." He stood up suddenly. " 'Beholden'! I know what she means, all right. I've been hag-ridden by it ever since I left Australia, and little by little it crushed the something I had in me—talent. . . . Now I know for sure what's kept me back all these years. I was too careful—too careful of myself and my duty to Uncle Robert to take a chance with life. You were always free, Bob. You had the pluck and the talent for trade, and nothing to hold you back."

"No," said Bob, thoughtfully. "I had a lucky escape, that was all. I had my start when Meg's father lent me a hundred pounds, and the thought of that money worried me night and day for a year, but old Mr Mortone died then and left all he had to Meg, his only child. He hadn't much to leave, heaven knows, and in time I repaid the hundred pounds to Meg, and she put it back in the business. That was my escape—but I had a taste of being 'beholden'!"

There was silence for a while, then Richard spoke. "What comfort there must have been for mother, all these years, saving her money bit by bit for our children to share! The possibility that they might not need it didn't worry her a jot. Mother could never forget those times in her own life when a little money would have meant independence for us all. . . . Let me see, when she made that will there were three grandchildren, and they'd each have had forty-four pounds of the money she had at that time. That forty-four pounds, in mother's day, would have kept a grown man a year or paid for his apprenticeship to a trade, given a girl a dowry or set her up in a shop and kept her for six months. Bob, old man, there is the experience of mother's whole lifetime in those words of hers—'that they may never have to leave home, but if they feel to go that they take their share of this and be beholden to nobody'."

"Mother's plea for freedom," said Bob.

Placing the bank-book and the will-form in the velvet-lined jewel box and turning the key slowly in the lock, "Mother's whole story," Richard answered gently.